# NO ONE
# WILL
# SAVE US

Teresa,
Thank you for
entering the
Goodreads
Giveaway. Enjoy!

## JULIE L. BROWN

ATR

No One Will Save Us © 2024 by Julie L. Brown

Printed in the United States of America.

For information, address JAB Press, P.O. Box 9462, Seattle, WA 98109.

Cover Design by Damonza

Library of Congress Control Number: 2024909474

ISBN 978-1-7354750-3-5 (paperback)
ISBN 978-1-7354750-4-2 (Kindle)
ISBN 978-1-7354750-5-9 (EPUB)

First Edition: June 2024

# BY J. L. BROWN

**Books**

*The Divide*

*Rule of Law*

*Don't Speak*

**Short Story**

*Few Are Chosen*

# BY J. L. BROWN

**Books**

*The Divide*

*Rule of Law*

*Don't Speak*


**Short Story**

*Few Are Chosen*

To Audi

*The function of freedom is to free someone else.*

—TONI MORRISON

*The master's tools will never dismantle the master's house.*

—AUDRE LORDE

*No one is coming to save Black women.*
*We have to save ourselves and each other.*

—AUDI L. BROWN

# Chapter One

# Loyalty...

*Kana, 1609*

GRAY MONKEYS SCREECHED in the forest as I ran over dirt, branches, and small rocks on the wide path carved out with machetes by my ancestors. I loved feeling the earth beneath my feet. The rough terrain didn't bother me. My mother had once remarked that I could walk over fire with my bare, calloused feet, though she'd warned me not to try.

I liked these times alone. In the obieze, someone always hovered nearby. An attendant bathed me. Another watched me eat. Still another lingered in the hallway, ready to relay to my mother that she had observed me running indoors. I'd sneak out of the compound to escape the fanti. Although I was sure my mother knew of my escapades, she never prevented me from leaving.

A square-tailed bird with purple and blue feathers glided above me; I didn't see the low-hanging branch.

"Aba!"

I stopped, touching the new scratch on my cheek. Blood, sweat, and rain covered my fingers. Although I was only ten dry seasons old, my mother had warned me that because of who I was, I must protect my face. She would scold me when I returned home. Worse, if she had heard me curse. I wiped the blood off with my brown tunic and resumed running, pretending the enemy was chasing me.

A tree trunk lay across the path. I scrambled across it and leaped over a red anthill. The warriors said these insects could mobilize like an army and not only sting, but kill you.

The leaves of the mahogany trees, the tops of which soared higher than the obieze, formed a canopy. My tunic clung to me from the sweltering air. I didn't understand why an attendant bathed me daily when I'd be drenched as soon as I left the compound. The rainy season kept few of us indoors.

I drew my daga from its leather sheath at my waist. The five-fingerbreadth double-edged iron blade was a present from my mother; she had given it to me when I reached the age of six. It had been her first weapon, too. I squeezed the lion carved into the wooden grip. I recalled my mother's words: see your target, account for your speed and distance, and throw your daga where the target will be, not where it is.

I flung it at a tree, aiming for a spot where the bark was a different shade, and missed my mark. I swiped my brown hair out of my eyes, along with the rivulets of sweat and rain from my brow.

The fresh scent of damp moss filled my lungs. A gentle patter of droplets hit the thick green foliage. I stepped up to the tree, pulled my daga out, and threw it at the next tree, grinning when it thunked into the bark. I left the path, hopped over a shrub, and pulled the knife out.

A girl's head popped out from behind the trunk. "Stop! You're hurting it!"

"Aba!" I jumped back, dropping the daga.

I picked it up and pointed it at her.

The girl stepped over the tree's gnarled roots. She was slender and around my age. Her damp hair, braided into many rows, flowed halfway down her back. She wore a purple silk pano, a long rectangular cloth that wrapped snugly around her torso but flowed freely about her legs.

She laughed. "Did I scare you?"

No one had ever laughed at me. "No."

"You almost hit me. Thank goddesses you can't throw!"

My face grew hot. "I wouldn't have hit you unless I wanted to. It's not my fault you were hiding. What were you doing? Spying on me?"

"Spying? I was studying."

"Studying what?"

The girl glanced upward and placed her palms on the bark above a winding vine. "This mountain fig. It's beautiful, don't you think?"

She spoke Kanaian, but since residents of our region were multilingual, that didn't tell me where she lived.

"I suppose." To impress her, I added, "Our healer uses its bark to mend certain ailments."

"Trees speak to us." The girl's voice was reverential, as if she were praying to Bele Alua, the Tree Goddess. "They've lived for hundreds of seasons and tell stories of what they have witnessed."

This girl was no threat to me. I lowered my daga. "I don't hear anything."

"Then you're not listening." She pointed. "Look at the leaves. See how they sway? They're speaking."

The leaves *were* moving. I waved my hand. "That's only the wind. Why do you think about such things?"

"Why aren't you thinking about them?"

"I have more important concerns."

She twisted a braid. "Like practicing throwing your daga?"

A round-eyed galago rooted around in search of insects underneath the thick vegetation lining the path. I squeezed the daga's handle and opened my mouth to tell her I practiced every day, but I hesitated. I *should* be a better thrower. "I'm a warrior."

"Your army won't win many wars if they throw like you." The girl's hands went to her hips. "And you shouldn't hurt the trees. Can't you aim your daga at something else?"

The insolence! I gritted my teeth. "You should be more careful with your words. What's your name?"

She relaxed her arms. "Efe."

"F-A?" I repeated.

"What's yours?" she asked sincerely.

"You don't know?"

She shook her head.

I lifted my chin. "I'm Princess Chibuike of the Queendom of Kana, the land of the women warriors. But everyone calls me Chi...except for my mother."

The girl's expression didn't change. "Let's agree on something, Che-boo-kay. I'll be more careful of what I say as soon as you're more careful of where you aim."

She took off on the southeastern path.

"Wait!" I called after her. "I said 'wait!'"

Efe did not stop. She wasn't fast. Her gait was graceless. She could never be a warrior.

I headed north in the direction of home, concentrating

extra hard on my daga-throwing. I needed to get better, so no one would question my abilities again.

A tree branch snapped. Efe had returned and was following me. This time, I would scare her.

I crouched behind a dense bush and gripped my daga. I scanned the woods and drew in a sharp breath.

A man stood ten paces away, facing the other direction.

His clothing was strange. The tan bottoms enclosed each leg separately; the top was an orange garment that covered his arms and torso. On his head was a covering in the shape of a triangle surrounded by a circular brim. Hands in front of him, legs set wide apart, he sent a stream of dark yellow liquid across the air in an arc; it spattered the leaves and sticks and moss on the ground.

I clapped a hand over my mouth. I'd never seen a man make water, not even my father.

The man fiddled with his private part. When he finished, he turned in a slow circle. I ducked behind the bush before peering out again with one eye, holding my breath. His light eyes swept the area, unhurried, until it lingered on the spot above where I squatted.

Finally, he ambled away, heading in the same direction as Efe. I stayed still until his foot coverings no longer disturbed the leaves.

I stood, exhaling. My shaking hand still clutched the knife. My heart was beating as fast as a cheetah on the trail of an antelope.

I wasn't fearful because he was a man. In the Kanaian market, larger men than him shook when my gaze fell upon them.

It was his face that had unsettled me.

It was pale.

⤳

From the forest, I raced past the outlying farms, slowing when I reached the outer edge of town, where the slippery grass transitioned to wet earth. I squeezed the mud between my toes.

The main thoroughfare was like an obstacle course on the obieze training ground. I dashed through small pools of water reflecting the blue-black clouds. Thatched-roofed mud homes lined both sides of the street. Outdoors, residents tended their private gardens. Clothing, left out overnight, lay damp on lines of twine.

I weaved through the women and men who balanced jugs of river water or baskets of produce on their heads, and the mothers with babies wrapped in cloth sacks against their chests. They waved and called out to me: "Good evening, Adaeze!" I waved back, but did not slow.

Younger children tried to keep pace with me, giggling and squealing, "Princess Chibuike! Princess Chibuike!" But I was too fast for them.

Wet and dirty residents, trudging home from a day of mining gold in the rivers and basins, offered weary greetings. Along with the fertile land, gold was the reason our ancestors had settled here over twenty generations ago. Now the queendom comprised the town and ten villages, stretching from the mountains in the northwest to the sandstone of the northeast to the forest in the south.

At the town center, I entered the market. Merchants hawked their wares, their tables laden with delights. A buyer and seller haggled over the price of shea nuts. A few farmers sat behind their tables without speaking; the quality of their goods sold themselves. Men sang. A boy of ten somersaulted backward. The old seer sat in her usual chair. I never asked her to examine the lines on my palm, since my future was certain.

I dodged two squawking chickens and a guinea fowl, also available for sale or barter. On the iroko wood tables, round plates held cowrie shell jewelry and kapok clothing. I ran my hand over a weighty cloth embroidered with gorillas and zebras that reminded me of the tapestries in the Obieze Gallery.

Bypassing the okra and beans, I stopped at a table with udalas, ichekus, and agbalumos piled high in baskets. My mouth watered. I reached for an agbalumo but stopped. I'd brought no cowrie shells with me.

An old man, missing all but his three bottom teeth, sat on a wooden box. He gestured with his hand. "Take one, Adaeze."

A princess did not have to pay.

I bit into the fruit, savoring the sweet pulpy flavor, the juice running down my chin.

Someone touched my arm. I jumped. By the intensity with which he was examining the wares on his table, it seemed the old man hadn't noticed my fright. I gripped my daga's pommel as I glared at the boy standing next to me. He was a couple of seasons older than I. His chest was bare, and he wore a palm wrap around his waist that ended at his knees. Unlike my father, whose scent was flowery, he stank like a goat.

"Why did you touch me? What's your name?"

His dark eyes lingered on my fruit. "What does that taste like?"

"An agbalumo. What do you think?"

He glanced at the ground. "I wouldn't know."

I frowned. "You've never eaten one?"

Raindrops sprinkled from his face as he shook his head. His hairline started high on his forehead, and his ears stuck out.

"I am the youngest of six. Some days, I'm lucky to eat. But when I'm the town's blacksmith, I'll eat what I want. Azeze."

"What?"

"That's my name."

The white and scarlet flag atop the obieze was drenched in rain.

"I must go." I handed him my half-eaten fruit, turned, and ran.

Leaving the market behind, I scampered over a wooden bridge that spanned the muddy ditch, abutting the seven-spear-length-high walls with the row of rampant lions etched into their red clay.

Two fanti, in the scarlet tunic of the queen's bodyguards, stood sentry on either side of the entrance.

The women bowed. "Welcome home, Adaeze."

They pushed open the heavy iron gate. I raced by them with a wave and entered the compound.

⊷

I ran past a small, walled courtyard and into the Grand Square, where my mother held festivals and state functions. The area was muddy and vacant.

On the training ground, a group of women, their brown tunics stuck to their bodies from the rain and sweat, stood at attention, listening to a woman a few seasons older than them. The officer, dressed in a sleeveless white tunic, was tall and had big thighs. Her arms were chiseled like one of the Obieze Gallery's statues. I halted and glanced at my slender arms. The other women were also muscular, their expressions stoic. They focused on the officer's words, the rain bouncing off their bald heads.

At their leader's command, the women let out an ear-splitting "Ike!"—the war cry, then scaled the three-spear-length-high training wall with a rope and dropped to the ground on the opposite side. It was harder to do than it looked. I had tried it once—when no one was around—and fallen back after one step.

The warriors crawled through the mud, armed with knives, swords, spears, and axes. The warrior at the head of the line trilled the drongo call. When each warrior reached the edge of the Grand Square, she rose and rushed past me, without a glance, in the direction of the compound's main entrance.

Even with the weapons' extra weight, they were fast. I stepped to follow them, but dropped my head and sighed. My mother would be worried and send a fanti to search for me. If she did that, it would be many moons until she'd allow me to leave the compound again. As the warriors said, it was better to live to fight another day.

I mimicked the bird sound as I ran to the obieze.

The obieze's walls were made of the same red earth as the surrounding compound walls. A fanti stood next to the immense walnut doors at the entrance. Since it was not dark, the palm oil candles within the sconces on either side were unlit.

"My mother?" I asked.

"She's in the Council Room."

The fanti pulled on the brass handle with two hands, and I slipped by her before the door slid all the way open.

I yelled "thank you!" over my shoulder.

"You're welcome, Adaeze," she called after me.

White clay coated the interior walls, although in some places the red clay bled through. I hurried across the Great Hall to a room in the north wing, where my mother preferred to accept visitors.

I hesitated at the Council Room door and peeked inside. A mahogany table commanded the room, with four matching chairs on each long side and one at the end. A warrior had once said that mahogany was the wood of the wealthy. At the head of the table in the grandest chair, made of gold, sat my mother, Queen Adebola. The yellow robe she wore blinded like a midday sun during the dry season. She was talking to a woman of about thirty-two dry seasons who wore a white tunic.

Although I was disappointed to find my mother occupied, warmth filled my chest at the sight of her oval face, her long hair wrapped in a yellow gele. Beneath arched eyebrows, her light brown, almond-shaped eyes turned toward me. "Yes, my nwa?"

"Sorry, Nne, I didn't mean to interrupt. I can come back."

"No, you will stay." She nodded at the woman. "We're finished."

"I haven't completed my report. It's important."

"So is my daughter. That will be all."

General Udo, the defense minister, hesitated. A white cloth encased the shoulder of her missing arm. She grabbed the wooden cane with the lion couchant handle leaning against her chair and bowed to the queen.

"When you're ready to resume our discussion, I'll be in my work chamber."

She turned her broad back to my mother and hobbled across the room. She glared at me with dark, deep-set eyes underneath bushy eyebrows. A shiver slithered down my arm. The general passed me and left the room, her cane thumping on the clay floor with every other step.

"Come sit," my mother said.

As I walked, I slid my forefinger along the table's smooth surface, then hopped onto the chair next to my mother. My legs dangled.

My mother scanned my soiled tunic and lifted my chin. "The scratches on your face. And an attendant will need to scrub this juice off!" She licked her thumb and rubbed it against my chin. I squirmed. She withdrew her hand, lifted my mud-spattered leg, and examined the bottom of my foot. "You're supposed to wipe your feet before entering the obieze."

I grinned. "I was in a hurry."

Her eyes brightened, as though she were silently laughing.

"You're always in a hurry." She lowered my leg. "If you don't slow down, you'll miss many things in this life."

"But I needed to tell you what I saw today."

"And you don't listen."

I composed my face into a grown-up expression. "I'll listen from now on."

"Do not add lying to your list of transgressions. Tell me what you observed."

"A man. In the forest."

My mother's smile vanished. "Did he hurt you?"

"No. He was making water."

"I'm sorry you witnessed that. Did you see his...um..."

"That's not what I wanted to tell you."

She exhaled. "Praise goddesses!"

"He looked different. He was pale. Like elephant tusks. He had light eyes. And he wore funny clothes."

Adebola fiddled with her gold necklace. "I see."

"He didn't belong there."

She looked at me with a concerned expression. "You're home safe now."

"But that's not all."

I relayed how I met the strange girl in the forest and the boy at the market. "Why don't we grow more food to feed those who are hungry?" My mother was staring at the wall. "Nne, are you listening to me?"

"I am, my nwa." She leaned forward and clasped my hands. "Find the healer so she can apply salve to your cuts."

"Do I have to?"

"Yes. And wipe that scowl from your face. To lead the queendom, you must control your emotions."

I took my hands out of hers, jumped from the chair, and flung my arms around her taut neck, not having to wait long for the return embrace. I could have remained there forever, inhaling her lavender scent. She stroked my damp hair and lifted me onto her lap. "My, you're getting heavy."

"I'm too heavy for you to carry."

My mother touched my nose. "*That* you will never be." She kissed my cheek and set me on the floor. "Go on."

When I reached the door, she said "Chibuike?"

I turned. "Yes, Nne?"

"Before you go to the healer, stop by General Udo's work chamber and tell her to return. We have another matter to discuss."

# Chapter Two

# ...to the queen

FIVE FULL MOONS later, I floated on the River Ome, which snaked through the land from north to south. It was wide, but shallow in some places. Although I was an excellent swimmer, my mother had warned that the current could drag me under, and I would never resurface.

Women and men fished on the grassy riverbanks. Not for sport, but for food or trade. My attendant waited for me on the shore. I had left my daga in care of the woman in the scarlet tunic standing next to her. On orders from the queen, a fanti now accompanied me whenever I explored. I suspected it was because of the pale man I'd seen in the forest.

I couldn't evade my minders' scrutiny.

I inhaled the fresh scent of the grayish blue water.

A child's pudgy arms flailed nearby. I breathed deeply. My attendant yelled, "Adaeze!" before I dove below the surface.

A girl was sinking. I swam to her and grasped her hand. I tugged on it, but she didn't budge. I embraced her from behind and kicked. As we ascended through the blackness, breath beckoned, though I dared not breathe.

A ray of light filtered through the surface. We burst through it, gasping for air. Treading water, I held the girl's arm with one hand and swiped the wet hair out of my eyes with the other. The girl's mouth opened, her neck jerked backward, and she vomited.

I recoiled and released her. "Your filth touched me!"

I washed it off. The girl slipped lower into the water. I grabbed her.

She wiped her mouth. "Sor—" And threw up again.

I leaned away but held onto her. "Come. Let's get you to shore before you foul the entire river."

When we were five paces from the riverbank, my attendant and the fanti splashed through the hyacinth and water lilies toward us. Their eyes were wide. If something were to happen to me while in their care, my mother would be unforgiving. After ensuring them I was all right, the attendant put her arm around the girl and assisted her to shore. The fanti reached out to me.

I stumbled past her. "I can make it on my own."

The girl and I collapsed onto our backs on the grass, panting. The two women retreated to a respectful distance. I spread my arms like the statue of Age-Fon in the temple and stared up at the wispy clouds. An eagle soared overhead.

"Now, what will I do?" the girl asked.

She had soft brown eyes and appeared to be my age.

"What do you mean?"

"I live on the opposite side of the river."

"Ha! Aren't you an ungrateful one? Why were you out there, anyway?"

"I was fishing."

"Where's your stick and string?"

She looked away. "I must have dropped it."

"In the *middle* of the river?"

"I…lost my footing, and the current took me."

Sitting up, I rested my arms on top of my knees. "Can't you swim?"

"No."

"What's your name?"

"Fatimata."

"Where are you from?"

"Banaan."

"But your people are fisherfolk!"

Fatimata pursed her lips. "The fish swim. My people catch the fish."

"Seems dangerous for a fishergirl to be unable to swim."

"I'm not a fishergirl." She coughed. River water dribbled down her round cheeks and onto her neck. "You know much."

I grinned. "One day, I'll be queen. I need to know everything." I stood. "I must go before my mother worries. Can you make it back across?"

She hesitated. "Yes."

I pointed. "The river is shallowest there. You should be fine. Good luck."

I held out my hand. My mother's bodyguard stepped forward and placed my daga in it.

∽

A full moon later, the sweet chorus of birdsong outside awakened me. I stared at the clay strokes on the bedchamber ceiling.

The clicking sound that had inhabited my dream faded. Dust particles seeped from beneath the shutters and danced in the sunlight onto the floor. The palm oil candles in the brass holders were still burning; Ola, my attendant, kept them lit throughout the night to prevent me from awaking in darkness.

In a scarlet linen nightshirt that reached the top of my calves, I left my chamber and padded barefoot down the hall to the private dining room, the clay floor warm from the heat outside. When I entered, an attendant pulled a chair away from the oval walnut table.

I climbed onto it. "My mother?"

She pushed in the chair. "The queen has eaten, Adaeze, and is being bathed."

In looking forward to tomorrow, I'd forgotten today's importance: the arrival of the rulers from Banaan and Asanti, the villages to the south.

I did not bother to ask the attendant where my father was. He wasn't an early riser, and, like a lion, spent most of his day at rest.

After a hurried meal of yam porridge and custard apples, I returned to my bedchamber, where, in front of my made bed, there was a brass basin filled with water heated from the hearth. After Ola closed the door, I pulled the nightshirt over my head, dropped it on the floor, and climbed onto the wooden step. I lowered myself in. Ola knelt next to the tub and dipped a cloth saturated with karite soap into the water.

"Try to be still, Adaeze."

"I can't help my excitement."

"I'll be quick."

She rubbed the cloth against my skin, the soap seeping

into a slit on my arm from daga throwing in the forest the previous sunrise. The wound blazed with pain.

"Aba!"

The attendant snatched the cloth away. "My apologies, Adaeze. I didn't mean to cause you harm."

Blood tinged the soap bubbles on my arm red.

"I won't tell my mother if you don't tell her I cursed."

My mother believed cursing was unbecoming of royalty. She would be disappointed if she knew how often I did so.

Ola lowered her head, hiding a smile. "I heard nothing, Adaeze."

"Good. Please continue."

Although it stung every time the soap penetrated a wound, I bit my lip and made no sound. I didn't want to risk another scolding should Ola inform my mother that I was in pain. Besides, I was a warrior. Even in a washbasin, I must endure suffering with courage.

Two attendants bathed my mother. A male attendant, whom my mother called Eunuch, bathed my father. Since women were proficient at all things, I asked her once why a woman didn't attend to him. My mother said, "When you get married, you'll understand." When I replied I'd never marry, she smiled.

Later that morning, I stood in front of the obieze's entrance dressed in a palm-bark tunic. I refused to wear a pano like the rest of the girls and women, preferring clothing that allowed freedom of movement in case I needed to run.

My mother stood next to me wearing a blue silk robe, her long hair tucked into a gele. Cochineal reddened her lips. Her favorite earrings sparkled in the sunlight. Each gold earring was divided into four quadrants, inside of which were a lion, the obieze, a likeness of my mother, and one of me.

On my mother's opposite side stood my father, King Kwasi, in a matching blue agbada. His face was long, his hair cropped short. He leaned forward and winked at me. I winked back, returning my attention to the gate.

While the rest of Kana's dignitaries stood behind us, the staff and the army formed two lines that stretched from the Thema Obieze's entrance through the Grand Square and past a courtyard to either side of the compound's main gate.

In the distance, the iron gates eased open to a contingent of twenty people. A woman in an orange shawl over a matching pano led them. She reached my mother, her retinue halting behind her.

A Kanaian attendant stepped forward. "Queen Adebola, may I present Yaa, the ruler of the village of Banaan."

"Welcome to the Queendom of Kana," my mother said.

The three leaders were introduced every year. My mother told me these traditions were important. I vowed to skip the formalities and begin with the feast when I became queen.

Yaa held her hands in front of her considerable bosom. "Thank you for receiving us."

Her hair was short and curly. Atop her head rested a headdress made of twigs fastened with fish glue.

"I trust your journey went well," said Adebola.

"Fortunately, it's not a long walk." Yaa gestured at two male attendants holding a hammock. Sweat poured down their faces. "It helps they carried me most of the way."

"Come, let's wait for the others inside."

Earlier, my mother had told me that the ruler of Asanti was always late.

Yaa peered down at me, a smile forming on her smooth, round face. "Hello. I owe you my gratitude."

"Why?"

She stepped aside. Behind her was a familiar, plump girl.

My mother looked from me to the girl and back to Yaa. "What's this regarding?"

"When the moon was last full, your daughter saved Fatimata from drowning. If not for her courage, my eldest daughter's spirit would lie beneath the riverbed. Praise Oshun!"

Banaans believed in the river deity, who was also the goddess of fertility, femininity, beauty, divinity, and love.

My mother beamed. "Ah! Chibuike mentioned this incident to me many times."

Yaa's smile reached her eyes. "She'll make a fine warrior-queen someday."

My chest expanded at her praise. Fatimata gave me a slow, bashful grin.

⌒

The guards opened the grand doors. My mother steered the Banaan ruler in the Council Room's direction; Fatimata and I followed. The girl craned her neck to take in the lofty ceilings of the Great Hall. The attendants brought up the rear.

General Udo headed to her customary seat at the table.

"Udo," said my mother, "this meeting is only for rulers."

I held my breath. The general's step faltered, and she pressed the cane into the floor to stop her momentum. "As you desire, but I believe I could be useful to your discussions."

"We'll manage."

The general left the room. I released my breath.

Everyone else remained in the Great Hall, including Kwasi. My mother told me this was where the queendom's work was accomplished. My father would not remain there for long, instead retreating unnoticed upstairs to the private residence, where he could gaze out the window and study the birds. He bored quickly of political conversations.

My mother instructed me to stand behind her. This was my first time attending the queen's meeting. Yaa sat to my mother's left. Two attendants stood against the wall, and Fatimata alongside them. The open windows did little to cool the room.

"Salamatu," my mother said, "water please."

The attendant's elongated face was expressionless as she turned to a large iroko bowl on the service table. Her tight braids ended at the base of her neck. I didn't know where Salamatu was from, but my mother had told me she was born with one leg shorter than the other. She filled two cups and placed them in front of each ruler.

A fanti opened the door and stepped inside. "Your Amara? I present Dayo, the ruler of the village of Asanti."

Dayo's copper accessories tinkled as she breezed past the guard. "Good afternoon, everyone!" She stopped and raised her arms. "I've arrived!"

The petite leader was striking in her purple pano. Her braids were piled high above her wide forehead.

A girl entered the room. She was the same height as the diminutive queen. She giggled at my expression. Her hair was still braided into many rows, as it had been when I met her six full moons ago.

"As we agreed," said Dayo, "I've brought my eldest daughter, Efe."

Efe hadn't told me she came from a ruling family.

She bowed to the queen. My mother turned to me with a look that said *where are your manners?* Her glare could halt stampeding rhinoceroses.

I tore my gaze from my mother's. "Welcome to Kana."

"You may stand with Fatimata, Efe." My mother gestured at a chair. "Dayo." After Dayo sat, the queen declared, "We're here today to acknowledge our mutual respect and to discuss our present interests and those that will benefit posterity."

That's why the two girls were here. They, too, would rule someday.

Salamatu placed a cup of water in front of Dayo and retreated. I licked my lips. I knew better than to ask the attendant for a drink.

Dayo's copper bracelets chimed as she peered into the cup. "No palm wine?"

"First, we talk," Queen Adebola said. "Then we feast."

Dayo raised her cup. "To quick discussions." She sipped and set it down.

"Let's discuss your annual tribute."

"I'm afraid the season wasn't productive."

Efe's brow furrowed.

"I've been informed differently," said Adebola.

Dayo fiddled with her enormous earrings. "I may have understated our productivity. We can contribute exquisite pottery pieces."

The queen turned to Yaa. "And you?"

"Our fish and livestock are a small price to pay for your protection. The sheep and pigs have multiplied."

"Like you?" Dayo laughed. "It's nice to see you without a child in your belly for once."

Yaa pursed her generous lips.

"Perhaps it's not her love for children that keeps her belly full," my mother said, a smile in her voice.

Dayo laughed again. "She should produce palm-oil-filled sponges, instead of raising animals."

My mother's shoulders shook as she laughed. Yaa's face remained stern until she broke into a smile, then joined in the laughter. I looked from one woman to another as I followed their conversation. I didn't understand what was so funny.

When the laughter faded, Dayo looked at my mother. "I saw many elephants on your land. Ivory makes for fine jewelry."

"We have no interest in harming those beautiful creatures."

Dayo's full lips were painted the color of blood. She smiled as if she knew a secret. "The ivory would be worth plenty."

"And I'm sure you heard me the first time."

I gasped. Everyone's attention was fixed on the three women sitting at the table. My mother's tone was the same one she used with me whenever she paid an unexpected visit to my bedchamber to find my clothes strewn across the floor.

A true ruler need not yell.

Dayo shifted in her chair. "It was only an inquiry."

"We have another important matter to discuss. Chibuike, take the girls outside and frolic."

I scowled. "Frolic? I want to stay and listen. How else will I learn how to rule?"

She ignored me. My shoulders slumped.

At the door, I waved to the girls to join me. "Come."

Fatimata walked over to me. Efe, still looking at my mother, hesitated, then followed.

☙

I led the girls to a small courtyard I liked to come to for target practice.

In deference to the queen's meeting, the compound was quiet. The obieze staff—fanti, messengers, attendants, cooks, servants—stayed inside the building in case the queen needed them. The warriors had remained indoors, too, since the region's three most powerful leaders were in the same location.

I pulled on the metal latch to open the wooden door and allowed the girls to enter before closing it. The courtyard walls were high. A vine spiraled downward from the top of a wall, an iron bench beneath it; we sat. I swung my legs back and forth. Fatimata played with the hem of her pano. Efe remained still. Although the sun was no longer straight above, the air shimmered in the heat rising from the clay.

Fatimata asked what we wanted to do.

"Throw dagas?" I responded. "I can find extra ones if you didn't bring yours."

Unlike me, neither girl wore one at the waist.

"I don't own a daga," said Fatimata. "I wouldn't want to hurt anyone."

My legs ceased moving. "What!"

"I don't believe in fighting," Efe said.

"What!" I repeated.

"You shouldn't either. I've seen you throw, Chibuike, remember?"

"I have improved in that area."

Efe glanced over at the palm tree. "Anyway, I prefer games of the mind."

A drongo flapped its wings above us and settled on a frond.

"You want to race?" Fatimata asked me.

"You?" I asked.

"Why not?"

"I'm not racing." Efe strolled over to the tree and plopped down onto the dirt underneath it, crossed her legs, and stared at its branches.

I shook my head. "There she goes again." To Fatimata, I said, "You asked for it."

We left the courtyard. I scanned the grounds. Sixty paces away, I spotted a shed where the attendants kept maintenance tools. I pointed. "First one to touch it wins. Ready? Proceed!"

I took off without waiting for a reply. I didn't consider it cheating. My obieze, my rules. As I ran, I grinned at my impending triumph but felt bad for Fatimata.

I heard footfalls behind me. With thirty paces to go, Fatimata ran abreast of me. With twenty left, she pulled ahead a few steps. When she reached the shed, she slapped it with her palms. Several moments later, I joined her, bent over and huffing.

Fatimata grinned. "Sometimes I get off to a slow start."

"I'd like to see you throw a daga," I muttered.

# Chapter Three

# ...with absolute obedience

WHEN WE THREE girls returned to the obieze, a fanti steered us to a place I rarely visited.

Weighty cloths adorned the walls of the Obieze Gallery. On stone pedestals rested intricate black sculptures—animals, my ancestors, or exalted warriors—created by Kanaian craftspeople. Efe, Fatimata, and I joined our mothers in the rectangular room. As we examined each item, my mother told its story in a hushed voice. They moved to the next sculpture: an elephant, its front leg raised.

I remained behind to stare up at a tapestry, my mother's words lingering in my mind. Woven into it was the likeness of a woman dressed in an army officer's white tunic. Sunlight beamed onto her bald head. She clutched the wooden shaft of a spear, its tip pointed at me. The other hand held a calla lily.

Muscles rippled her thighs. I'd have wagered she'd never lost a race. Could I live up to my grandmother's legacy? Her light brown eyes were fixed on an unknown opponent. I set my jaw, imitating her expression, and reached out to the cloth.

She died before I was born.

"Chibuike," my mother said, "don't touch."

I lowered my arm.

Adebola liked to say, "Not all women are destined to birth humans. Some are destined to birth empires." My nne nne, Queen Thema, had accomplished both.

"Come, everyone." My mother's voice filled the room. "Let us feast."

Dayo clapped. "Finally!"

In the Dining Hall, the kitchen staff had laid out brass plates, bowls, and cups. The queen and the other leaders sat at the table on the dais, joined by us girls and my father. Dignitaries from the three states mingled at long wooden tables below.

Like the standing torches that illuminated the Kanaian streets at night, palm-oil wicks burned on each table and in copper wall sconces. Fanti stood with their backs to the walls at a distance of ten paces, except at the three doors, where a guard was stationed on each side.

Most of the women guests were attired in colorful panos. The few men present wore beige and brown tunics. Servants shuttled into the room from the adjacent kitchen carrying plates of delicacies like pork and honey, along with guinea hens, cassava dumplings, maize, plantains, and fried yam cakes. The rumblings in my stomach grew louder as the mixed aromas wafted up to my nose. Fatimata, who'd been slouching next to me, sat up.

"Let us lift our hands," my mother said.

I'd never been so happy to pray.

The queen intoned, "We give gratitude to our ancestors and goddesses for the food we're about to receive. May it nourish our bodies and give us strength. Àse."

Everyone said "Àse" except Yaa and Fatimata, who said "Praise Oshun."

During the meal, Adebola, Yaa, and Dayo talked and laughed. Servants topped off their chalices with palm wine. My mother was never this expressive with my father, who ate his meal at the end of the table in silence. Fatimata, Efe, and I talked. It was fun having girls my age here. I wondered whether I'd have to wait a year until they returned. Efe didn't eat her pork or hen.

Afterward, everyone moved across the hall to the Audience Court—the largest room in the obieze—which housed my mother's throne. Every candle on the tables and walls was lit, making it the brightest room in the queendom. The chairs and benches that obieze staff and town residents normally sat in to observe deliberations of state affairs or petitions to the queen were pushed against the wall to accommodate the dancing. The wine and conversation flowed late into the night.

I heard of the affair from my mother the next day. To keep pace with Fatimata, I had gorged on two plates of all the delicious foods and fallen asleep at the banquet table. My mother had momentarily excused herself and carried me to my bedchamber.

꙳

The next afternoon, under a fiery sky, dust swirled from the ground as seven barefoot women warriors in brown battle tunics with matching headbands danced, clubs and sabers in hand, to a rhythm generated by a trio of warriors. One clapped her hands. Another slapped her thighs. And the third played a hollowed-out tree trunk covered with goatskin. The dancers jumped and stomped, their hips gyrating. I moved to the beat in my chair. My mother later told me she'd feared I'd fall off. On some days, she joined the warriors—she was an excellent dancer—but not today.

No one in the queendom worked on Queen's Day. Adebola invited notable Kanaian residents and their families to the compound. The women wore green, blue, and yellow panos made more vivid by the sunlight. They waved square white cloths at the dancers. The market traders and craftswomen displayed cowrie shells on their wrists and ankles and in their elaborate headpieces. Girls and boys younger than I tried to touch the dancers, although it was forbidden. I gripped the smooth arms of my chair, wanting to get closer to the warriors, too; but, unwilling to risk my mother's wrath, I didn't.

The ruling families sat on the platform erected on one side of the Grand Square. Dignitaries of the three rulers sat behind us.

An attendant rang a brass bell, and the queen clapped her hands twice. The dancers ceased their movements and ran back to the obieze, where they would hurry to the barracks on the lowest floor to change.

Sitting beside my mother, I listened as the ministers discussed the dancers' skills in excited whispers. In a green silk pano, Commerce Minister Mojisola, whom everyone called Sola, silently sized up Dayo's bright red outfit. Sola favored bright-colored silk fabrics received in trade from the Portuguese. My mother sat on her golden outdoor throne, most of which was concealed by her long scarlet robes. Her hands graced the arm supports, the gold rings on her fingers matching her sparkling earrings.

In a scarlet agbada, the king sat on her opposite side. He rested his hand on top of hers. After a moment, she withdrew her hand and pointed out someone in the crowd to the other rulers. My father returned his hand to the arm of his chair. I pretended not to notice.

My father liked to tease me. That morning, in the front room of the private residence, he'd told me that when I fell asleep at the feast, I snored like a lion. Horrified, I'd responded, "Really?"

A dimple had creased his chin. "No, Little One."

I'd thrown my arms around his waist, turning to rest my cheek against his soft belly. I'd closed my eyes, finding comfort in his strength—which differed from my mother's—as he returned my hug.

An attendant brought each ruler a chalice of palm wine, bringing me back to the present. She fanned them as they drank, the large glossy palm frond making a loud swooshing sound.

"Nne, my feet hurt." I extended my legs. "Can I take these off?"

My mother glanced down at the sandals she'd forced me to wear for this special occasion.

"No."

"Why?"

"Because I said so."

"That's not a reason."

"I'm the queen. I don't need a reason."

"But how can I sneak up on people?"

"You won't be sneaking up on anyone today."

A drum boomed. I stood first, but everyone on the platform joined me and clapped as a warrior marched toward us carrying the Kanaian flag: a scarlet lion on a white silk background. Two warriors followed, holding a banner with the same markings.

Next came the musicians. A woman beat the drum. Another played a trumpet made from the tusk of a fallen elephant. Behind them, four warriors bore long wooden clubs. They threw them in the air, spun around in a circle, and caught them, still in step. The warriors turned and clashed their club with the club of the warrior beside her. They stared straight ahead and repeated the movements. One woman spun twice in the time it took the others to turn once.

Next came the officers, wearing white calico tunics embroidered in scarlet. The rest of the company followed, marching eight across. Most of them were tall, at least two spear lengths. They ranged in age from sixteen to thirty-five, although a warrior couldn't be inducted into the army until she turned eighteen. The youngest warriors held bows. The arrows' tips would have been poisoned if this had been a procession into battle.

In six more years, I would be holding a bow.

My mother glanced down at me and smiled. "Your time will come, my nwa."

All of them paraded past the platform, in step with the women in their row.

"Loyalty to the queen, with absolute obedience…"

As they sang the warrior song, I sang along with them. I knew every word.

When each row drew abreast of the queen, the women

turned their heads to her and raised an arm, forefinger extended. Queen Adebola saluted them back.

"They're the finest warriors in the land," Yaa remarked.

"They'll need to be," said Dayo.

My mother looked sharply at her. The Asanti ruler glanced at me and spoke no further.

After passing the viewing stand and the conical tents in which nobles, obieze residents, and guests would later enjoy food, drink, and dance, the warriors marched out the main gate. Outside the compound, town dwellers lined the streets for a glimpse of the Kanaian army.

When the last warrior passed by, I hopped out of my chair and jumped off the platform onto the sunbaked clay. I kicked off my sandals and ran after the warriors.

"Chibuike!" my mother called. "Where are you going?"

I yelled over my shoulder, "With them!"

# Chapter Four

# We are proud...

*Kana, 1615*

"GET UP...*PRINCESS*," CAME General Udo's voice from above me.

Face down on the ground, I lifted my head. It was difficult to distinguish the mud splatter from the skin of my arms and the short sleeves of my brown tunic.

We had been crawling on the forest floor—over dirt, rocks, sticks, roots, animal droppings—for more spear lengths than I could count. We must have been going in circles; I didn't recall the Kanaian Forest being this vast.

Prior to this training exercise, the recruits had been provided limited rations of beans and ugu. Since then, Udo had made us fast to prepare our bodies for long battles without food. Our stomachs howled, and we snapped at each other for no reason. We hadn't drunk anything since sunrise. My parched mouth made swallowing difficult. And what I wouldn't have given for a bowl of hot yam porridge!

We hadn't bathed either, and I smelled foul.

"I said, 'Get up!'" the general repeated.

Overhead, an indigo bird sang. The daga at my waist and the musket on my back remained sheathed.

As was my destiny, I'd joined the army when I reached sixteen dry seasons. That day, my mother presented me with a two-handbreadths daga the blacksmith had made especially for me. I carried it everywhere. I would have slept with it, but couldn't risk accidentally cutting myself. Instead, I kept it within reach on a stand by my bed.

During that first month, we recruits—although technically, as the princess, I wasn't recruited—learned how to throw spears and knives and shoot arrows, before graduating to muskets. We also trained in wrestling, foot racing, and jumping.

"Goddess Gbadu! You're hopeless!" Udo barked at me and waved her arm impatiently. "How will you ever lead?"

She turned her back and limped away. The audacity! I hoped her cane would get stuck in the mud and she'd fall.

"Better than you," I mumbled.

My palms sank deeper into the squishy mud, and the earth seemed ready to swallow my entire body. Arms trembling, I pushed myself up.

While the general yelled at another recruit, an officer stepped over to me and grabbed my arm. Her barely marred white tunic fit her as if it were painted on. A sword was sheathed on each hip.

"I don't need your assistance," I said.

Her greenish-gray eyes were the only light in the jungle, which was as dark as the inside of the Obieze Temple...and my current plight.

"Yes, you do."

She hauled me up and hurried back to where she'd been standing.

Udo turned around, her eyes widening when she saw me upright.

I raised my chin. She would not defeat me.

The general recovered. "Glad you could join us, Princess." To the rest of the recruits, she commanded, "Rise!" Everyone struggled to their feet. "Return to the compound!"

Too exhausted to cheer, we didn't move until the officers shouted at us to do so. We jogged at a much slower pace than the one at which we had left the compound nine sunrises before. As we ran, the officer who assisted me fell in beside me.

"Thank you for helping me," I said.

"I wasn't helping you. If you hadn't risen, we'd have to spend another moon out here. I need to sleep." A cocky smile. "The hyenas are driving me mad."

She looked identical to another officer.

"My sister is Major Kunto," she said, as if hearing my thoughts. "I'm Major Kayin. The better-looking one."

As I was about to tell her I would remember this kindness, she ran ahead to urge on the recruits in front of me.

༗

## Kana, 1619

"I've selected a man for you to marry."

I stood behind my mother as she worked at her ebony desk. At twenty dry seasons, I was learning how to run the queendom and sometimes offered her my counsel. Although our relationship had evolved, she was quick to remind me she was the parent whenever I lost sight of this. In my scarlet-edged white military tunic, I glanced at the three white stripes painted around my bicep, the sinewy muscle at rest.

I stopped smiling. "What did you say, Nne?"

"You heard me. I know you have dreamed of being a warrior since you were a girl, but it's time you prepare yourself to be queen. You'll need an exceptional king, and I've found him. His name is Okeke."

"I have no wish to marry. I'm called to lead, not love. Besides, I don't know him."

Without turning, she said, "I served with his mother. And wipe that scowl from your face."

I obeyed and let out an involuntary giggle. Standing next to me was Mukambu, the healer. She had a trim physique, tightly curled hair, and a cleft in her chin. She'd replaced her nne nne, who died of natural causes two dry seasons ago. She wasn't much older than I, but she displayed a bearing far beyond her age. Mukambu smelled like the herbs she used in her practice.

The open shutters bordering the tall windows allowed late-morning sunlight to fill the spacious room and reveal tiny lines on my mother's neck—lines that had not been there ten dry seasons ago. My mother was still a considerable presence, but now, when we faced each other, I had to lower my sight to look into her eyes.

"Have I told you how I met your father?" she asked.

"Many times, Nne."

She laughed. "You know how we Kanaians love to tell stories."

My parents had not met at a festival, gazed across the Grand Square, and fallen in love. They'd met on their wedding day. My father was the son of a former warrior who paired with another former warrior's son after she completed her military service. The children from these unions became warriors, if they were girls, or warriors' husbands, if they were boys.

"And I wish the same for you," my mother finished.

The physician remained expressionless. Mukambu was used to listening to our personal exchanges. We stood behind the queen for hours, in case she needed our assistance.

"What if I don't want that, Nne?"

I hadn't changed my mind regarding marriage since childhood, especially if it meant enduring a loveless relationship like my parents'. If one must spend one's life with another person, shouldn't there be more to it than procreation?

Raised voices came from the hallway outside the queen's work chamber. I gripped the lion-engraved brass handle of my daga, which was sheathed in the bronze scabbard at my waist.

I positioned myself between the desk and the door.

"Let me in," a woman said. "I must speak to her."

"Who is it?" I called to the fanti.

"Let go of me!" The voice, louder, sounded familiar, but I couldn't place it.

The guard opened the door but blocked the intruder from entering the room. "Lieutenant Colonel Chi, she says she needs to speak to the queen. I told her Her Amara was occupied."

I stepped closer and took the daga out of the scabbard. "Let me see her."

The fanti came in, grasping the woman's arm.

I lowered my weapon. "It's you!"

The intruder's braids were longer than they were the last time I'd seen her. Sweat ran down her pained, slender face.

"I see you're still holding that weapon, Chibuike. You look...different."

I refrained from rubbing my bald head as I sheathed my daga. "I could say the same."

Unlike me, her body curved at the breasts and hips. A blue pano clung to her, damp from the heat and sweat. She was a younger, taller version of her mother, Dayo.

Efe and I hadn't seen each other in many seasons. She and Fatimata had joined their mothers on Queen's Day a few more times after the first one we'd all participated in, but they had stopped coming. Our mothers believed we'd have plenty of time to spend together when we assumed our leadership positions.

Efe tried to extricate herself from the fanti's grip.

"Release her," said my mother from behind me.

The guard obeyed and exited.

Efe kneaded her arm.

"Are you all right?" I asked. "What are you doing here?"

"Chibuike," my mother chided, "you still haven't learned your manners. Salamatu, please pour some water for our guest and bring her something to eat. Efe, come sit."

I perched on the corner of the desk so that I could observe her and my mother's expressions as they spoke. The attendant placed a cup in Efe's trembling hand and left the room. Efe sipped the water and placed the cup on the desk.

"What brings you to Kana?" Queen Adebola asked.

"My mother sent me to bring urgent information to you."

"Where's Dayo?"

"Back in Asanti."

"How is she?"

Efe rubbed her arms as if hugging herself. "Somewhat shaken, Your Amara."

My swinging foot stilled.

"I see you are, as well," my mother said. "Tell me what happened."

A tear escaped and ran down Efe's cheek. "The Banaans have disappeared."

A vivid memory came to me of Fatimata's shy grin on that Queen's Day ten dry seasons ago. *Fatimata!*

*"What?"* I asked, my voice raising in pitch.

My mother blanched. "How do you know this?"

"A Banaan escaped. She'd been hunting hare and returned home to find everyone gone. Or...dead. She arrived in our village, screaming."

My mind raced. How could an entire population disappear?

Salamatu returned, followed by a servant carrying a wooden plate of grapes, sliced oranges, and bananas. She set it on the desk. Efe glanced at the food and thanked the server, who bowed and retreated. Salamatu resumed her place next to the service table.

"Did Dayo confirm this report?" my mother asked.

Efe did not eat. "No. She told me to come to you first."

"Why is that?"

"You have the army."

"Wise. Anything else?" Efe shook her head. "Thank you for this information. Someone will show you to a bedchamber where you may rest until the evening meal and your appetite comes back. You may go home in the morning."

"I couldn't impose. Besides, my mother's expecting me."

"We'll send someone to reassure her of your whereabouts."

Efe bowed her head. "I'm grateful for your hospitality."

She glanced at me, then followed Salamatu out of the room.

Worry lines creased my mother's forehead.

"What do you think happened, Nne?"

My mother scanned the scroll on her desk. Ignoring my question, she said, "Summon the Great Council."

∽

"What's happened?" asked General Udo.

She and two women sat with Queen Adebola around the table in the Council Room. A summoning of the council was rare, since they dispensed with queendom business during their regular meeting every four sunrises.

My mother sat at the head of the table, facing the entrance. I stood in my customary position behind her. My mother relayed to the council what Efe had told us.

"My husband's people are from Banaan!" said Commerce Minister Sola. Her thin face grew pensive. "Could they have gone willingly?"

"Were they sold?" Udo asked. "Maybe they were indebted. Or criminals."

Sola lifted her pointed chin toward Udo. "My husband's people are not criminals."

The general and Sola rarely agreed. Adebola always found the truth somewhere in the middle of their arguments. Although Udo was my commanding officer, I tried to stay objective, as my mother had taught me.

"An entire village?" asked Ndidi, the minister of foreign affairs and, at sixty, the oldest council member. We Kanaians respected our elders, since they were the closest in age to our ancestors. Her short hair was coiled and gray, and her half-lidded eyes missed nothing. "Efe said *everyone* disappeared. They wouldn't all sell themselves to repay their debts. And they can't all be criminals."

Sola looked at Udo. "Hmph."

Udo's thick eyebrows knotted together. "Gangs?"

Groups of men and women from poor villages traveled through the woods, capturing individuals unaware and selling them into slavery to city-states. Slavery had been outlawed in Kana for generations.

"What if their gods took them?" asked Sola, her voice shrill.

"We're not certain anyone has taken them," said Ndidi.

Since Ndidi imparted something of import when she spoke, everyone listened to her. She had also been my teacher. It was difficult for me to look at her without fondness. My mother told me a leader doesn't have all the answers and seeks advice from those she trusts. Ndidi was that person for her. And for me.

"How do we know the girl is telling the truth?" asked Udo.

"I know Efe's character," replied Queen Adebola. "And her mother's. Besides, I saw fear in her eyes. They spoke the truth. Nevertheless, after this meeting is over, I shall dispatch Chibuike and a team of warriors to confirm the young woman's account."

I started at the mention of my name.

"Shouldn't I decide who to send on this mission?" asked the general.

Udo should have known better than to question my mother's decision.

I wanted to lead and find out what happened to Fatimata. "I can do it."

"And you will," Adebola said. To Udo, she said, "Until we determine what has become of the Banaans, we must increase our defenses and patrols."

The general hesitated, then nodded. "I'll take care of it after this meeting."

"Will those precautions be enough?" asked Sola.

The queen gazed out a window. Warriors grunted and shouted commands as they practiced military maneuvers on the training ground. Obieze residents chatted in passing outside, their words indiscernible.

My mother faced the council members. "Let's wait to see what the situation demands before we undertake additional measures."

"I agree," said Ndidi. "I recommend caution until we understand what—or whom—we're dealing with. Although I have my suspicions."

"As do I." My mother stood, signaling the meeting's conclusion. "Thank you all for your wise counsel." She turned to me. "Go to Banaan. And be careful."

I saluted her. "I will."

# Chapter Five

# ...brave

I STRODE OUT of the Council Room, across the Great Hall, and up the staircase two steps at a time to my bedchamber. I grabbed my musket and removed the cloth encasing the weapon. Although my daga was my primary weapon, I was unsure of what I would face and wanted to be prepared. I slung the leather strap over my shoulder, the gun flat against my back between my shoulder blades.

On top of the dresser was a large wooden box divided into sections, in which most women would store their cowrie shells and jewelry. From it, I scooped gunpowder to fill a black pouch, then tied it next to the scabbard at my waist.

At the wardrobe, I donned my brass breastplate and copper headgear.

After closing the wardrobe doors, a strong premonition came over me. I returned to the dresser and removed an empty leather satchel. I patted the scabbard to ensure my daga was secure and left the room.

On the first floor, I went to the Dining Hall, where the warriors were now consuming their midday meal. The noise level was high; the women talked as much as they ate. From the entrance, I scanned the faces at the front of the room, where the officers sat, until my gaze fell on the twins, Kayin and Kunto. When they outranked me, they used to jest with me, each pretending to be the other. After serving with them for four dry seasons, I could tell them apart with ease. And now I outranked them.

As I walked toward them, my mouth watered from the aroma of quail and yam porridge.

Kayin watched me approach. Kunto and the others, engrossed in conversation, hadn't noticed me yet.

Kayin looked me up and down with her hazel eyes. "Going somewhere?"

The rest of the warriors at the table ceased their conversations.

"*We're* going on a mission. You and Kunto. Make haste to the barracks to arm yourselves." I pointed at two officers. "You, too."

Kayin glanced down at the bronze swords on her hips. She could brandish them simultaneously, her hands of equal dexterity. "I'm already armed."

"You'll need muskets. And protective gear. Meet me in front of the obieze."

Kunto chewed a kola nut and swallowed. "Where are we going, Lieutenant Colonel?"

Unlike most warriors who shaved their heads bald, Kunto had a two-fingerbreadth strip of hair starting at the edge of her forehead and ending at the base of her crown. Although both the twins' faces were square, Kunto had a softer jaw line. She was also the humbler of the two. Kayin's face was imprinted with a permanent smirk.

"You'll find out," I replied. "And if you keep chewing those nuts, you will never sleep."

Kunto popped another nut into her mouth. "I'll sleep when I join my ancestors."

"Which will happen soon, if you die of exhaustion. Or choke speaking with your mouth full."

I turned to leave.

"Can I go?"

At the end of the table—apart from the others—sat a lieutenant. A scar ran from her temple to her jaw, marring her otherwise unblemished complexion. No one asked her how she'd received the scar, and she was unforthcoming with the information.

"Yes, Itoro," I said. "Why not?"

The warriors joined me outside. Kunto and Itoro were still wearing the same tunics under their breastplates, but Kayin had changed into a fresh one. The twins wore shells around their necks, while Itoro wore stones. The other two warriors sported beads. I preferred a simple gold necklace. Stones, shells, and beads made noise. I never wanted the enemy to know I was coming.

After glancing at Itoro and wondering why I'd included her in this expedition, Kayin asked me where we were going.

"Banaan."

"Is this related to the woman who arrived earlier? I was on the training ground when I saw her enter the obieze."

I nodded.

As we exited the compound's main gate, a man, whose ears stuck out, stopped walking to avoid crossing my path. He gripped the wooden handle of a hammer that rested on his shoulder.

He bowed. "Adaeze." His body was taut, like a string that could snap at the slightest touch. "My name is Azeze. I'm the blacksmith's apprentice."

Since the blacksmith made the warriors' weapons, he held a prestigious position in the queendom. His apprentice's gaze lingered on my face a moment longer than permitted, as if we were familiar. Laws forbid a common man from staring at a warrior or a woman of the ruling family. I was both.

"You should avert your eyes."

"My apologies." He gestured at my daga. "Might I inquire into the sharpness of your weapon?"

I unsheathed it and held it out.

He scanned it with a practiced gaze. "I could sharpen it for you."

"It'll do."

"As you desire."

"But…thank you, anyway." To the warriors, I said, "Let's go."

We took off running.

Cumulus clouds dotted the cerulean sky. With the sun straight above, moisture soon formed on our foreheads underneath our helmets. Sweat dripped into our eyes by the time we entered the canopied Kanaian Forest. We ran barefoot on the dirt path, the tall mahogany trees and thick bushes forming a wall on each side. The scent of moss and wood embraced me. Birds chirped. Monkeys chattered. This was my second home.

After two thousand spear lengths, we exited the forest at its southern end and spotted a pride of lions at rest in the tall grass. Like Kanaian warriors, they did not bother anyone who did not bother them, although it was best to be cautious around both.

In the River Ome, ducks and geese swam out of the way as we waded through the shallow part of the warm water. A white hawk with black-tipped wings shrilled overhead.

On the east bank, pirogues sat idle. Usually, the grassy riverbanks teemed with Banaan fisherwomen and men, who bartered and sold their catches to nearby villages.

We climbed a hill and stopped near a ukwa tree on the periphery of Fatimata's village, the sun at our backs. The weather was cooler in the hills of Banaan than in the flatlands of Kana. We'd spoken little on the journey. The banter we engaged in before mock battles was absent.

Outside the village, I loaded gunpowder into my musket. The warriors did the same. I was in a hurry to find Fatimata but didn't want to make a mistake. The fresh air was accompanied by complete silence. A foreboding spread through my veins.

I pointed to a nearby hut made from reeds, brought my finger to my lips, and raised the gun, peering through its sight as I took furtive steps toward the house, the warriors behind me. I signaled for them to wait outside. Using the muzzle, I eased the grass door open.

It was an empty single-room dwelling. I lowered my weapon.

While the warriors stood guard, I inspected the hut. It was strange to be in someone else's home. I'd never been in one except my own. On the low table, bowls and spoons were set out for a meal. Ants crawled over cornstarch paste in a bowl.

I walked back outside and shook my head at the others. We made our way to the next hut, passing a few clucking chickens. There was no one inside the single room, but something vile had happened here. A bitten-into baobab lay by an overturned table. Near a wall, a bed pallet was broken into pieces. Smashed bowls on the table. My heart hammered in my chest, and I clenched the musket tighter, my palms moist. Hearing that the Banaans had disappeared and seeing it for myself were two different things. None of our training exercises had prepared me for this. I was once afraid of my childhood nightmares. Those fears paled compared to this.

The third home was like the second. Fish and ukwa seeds mixed among the shards of shattered plates on the dirt floor. The room smelled of the interrupted meal and of body odor.

"Are you all right?" Kayin whispered when I came outside. "You look like you've seen a spirit."

I nodded, unable to speak. The warriors shared concerned looks.

The front room of the obieze's private residence was often vacant, while my mother worked. But it never felt empty; I knew she would return.

"Where is everyone?" asked Kunto.

"I don't know," I replied. "Let's keep looking."

The silence of the village unnerved me. Fishing sticks littered the street. I stepped around a container used to carry water from the river. Its contents had seeped into the grass.

At the next house, a dead man lay in the yard, clenching a comb. Closer to the village center, more dead people lay outside their homes, with combs, sticks, hoes, or knives clutched in their hands or on the grass beside them. The stench of blood, entrails, and death enswathed the air. My stomach roiled, and bile rose in my throat. The rest of the warriors seemed to be in the same condition.

In front of a hut, I squatted next to the body of a man lying on his back, the handle of a knife protruding from his exposed abdomen. His intestines and dried blood spattered his skin and the surrounding earth. The angle of the knife's entry was odd.

Kayin stood beside me. "The Banaans put up a fight."

I squinted up at her. "It looks like—"

She crouched next to me. "He killed himself."

"Yes."

"What is worth more than life?"

My mouth parted. "Freedom."

We resumed walking.

My gait slowed the closer we came to Yaa's home on the eastern side of the village, dreading what I would find inside. The door was open. I hesitated, swallowed, and entered.

It was a large hut. No one gathered around the modest fire pit. On the table, bowls still contained the remnants of white-pepper soup.

A pallet was separated from nine others. As the eldest of ten children, this must have been Fatimata's. Clay sculptures lay cracked on the floor. I hadn't known of her interest in art. Propped up on her bed was a doll, made from a twig with goat fur glued to the top for hair and millet grains for eyes. A leg was missing. What did this doll mean to her? She was long past the age of playing with one. I picked it up, placed it in the satchel at my waist, and walked over to the opposite side of the hut and the sizable bed Yaa shared with her husband. The thin covering was askew, half of it on the floor.

On a teak chair, I spotted Yaa's headdress, made of twigs

bound by fish glue. I picked it up. The longer I held the rough twigs, the more Yaa's strength and energy flowed through me. Yaa wouldn't have left it behind. I vowed to find her and return it. I placed it in my satchel next to the doll.

Back outside, Kayin flexed her jaw, her face stoic. Itoro's eyes bulged, unblinking. Sweat beaded above the two other warriors' lips, despite the coolness of the air.

Kunto's body was rigid. "What do you think happened?"

"I'm not sure," I said.

We scoured the area for Fatimata, surviving Banaans, or attackers and found no sign of them. Where was she?

Itoro then stood guard as the rest of us dug a huge hole in the grass with shovels we'd taken from several huts, straining our muscles and wiping sweat from our eyes, the mood somber. I attacked the soft earth with my shovel, an outlet for my rage and revulsion and—if I were honest with myself—fear.

Under the setting sun, we gathered the dead of Banaan and buried them in a mass grave near a samba tree outside the village. As was tradition, we retrieved a personal item from the hut nearest to where we'd found each body and placed it on top of the grave. We were unsure the items we selected belonged to the victims, but it was the best we could do.

When we finished, we holstered our weapons and trekked back to Kana.

Darkness had fallen by the time we arrived at the obieze. I parted with the warriors on the first floor. While they headed down to the barracks, I hastened upstairs, knowing my mother wouldn't retire until I returned from my mission. Her work chamber was dark, except for the wick burning in its holder on her desk.

Besides Salamatu, Adebola was alone, writing on a

goatskin document. She looked up when I entered the room. Her writing instrument stilled, and she set it on the desk.

She knew by my expression what had happened without my having to speak.

## Chapter Six

# ...and fierce

FASTER THAN A fire during a harmattan, word of the vanished Banaans spread throughout the Queendom of Kana. From the barracks to the market to meal tables, residents talked of little else. When we were alone in the officers' room or outside taking a break from training, Kayin, Kunto, Itoro, and I, haunted, discussed what we had witnessed. But in front of others, we put on brave faces and remained silent.

The army increased its vigilance. General Udo deployed reinforcements, adding warriors who normally didn't patrol the premises to the rotation schedule and sending younger warriors on reconnaissance missions to other villages to see if there had been more disappearances.

But after three full moons with no further incidents, life in Kana returned to normal. Soon thereafter, some residents believed this confirmed the gods had punished the Banaans—despite their people's good-natured disposition—for past misdeeds. A rumor also circulated that they had left of their own accord in search of a warmer home, farther south.

One day, I was overseeing the warriors practicing weapon drills on the training ground. My attention was on Nsia, a wiry young woman I'd recruited from Doba, a village south of Kana from which General Udo also hailed. Doba rarely produced girls qualified to join the Kanaian army.

Nsia was an exception.

My primary responsibility was to discover new warriors for the army. Once a year, I traveled throughout the queendom to meet girls who'd turned sixteen since the last enlistment. Scrutinizing their muscle tone, and whether they projected confidence or avoided my gaze, I asked them questions for insight into which were intelligent, learned, or savvy enough to one day become officers.

Nsia was bald like most of us, except for a single lock of hair above her forehead, dyed a deep reddish-blue from an indigo plant. On the training ground, she was sword fighting four opponents as if she were only battling one.

"It's too easy," said Itoro.

"No," I said. "She makes it look easy."

As an older officer barked instructions for the next drill, Efe marched out the obieze's doors, heading in our direction.

Kayin groaned. "What does she want?"

After I'd spoken to my mother upon returning from Banaan, I went to Efe's bedchamber. I showed her Yaa's head-dress, and she cradled it in her hands. "The limbs come from the iroko tree. Banaans believe it possesses extraordinary powers."

That those powers had deserted Yaa, I did not say.

After the Banaans' disappearance, Efe visited me often.

She would send word, and I would dispatch several warriors to Asanti to escort her to Kana. It was as if she feared I'd also disappear.

Efe stood next to me. "I want to learn to fight."

Kayin guffawed.

"You believe in reason," I said. "To fight with ideals and words, not weapons."

"I can believe in one thing and prepare for another."

I held her gaze for a moment, then walked over to a pile of dagas laying on the ground and picked one up. "Come."

Kayin's gaze tickled the back of my neck as I led Efe past the Grand Square to a smaller courtyard. Inside, the closed door muffled the sounds of the compound. I strode to the only tree in the yard.

Gouges marred the trunk from my past daga-throwing sessions. Efe rushed past me and placed her palm on a spot absent of bark. "Poor tree. I wonder what happened to it."

"I did."

Her expression was stony. "You sound proud." She turned back to examine the palm tree, rubbing the spot. "You're hurting its soul. I'm surprised it continues to grow."

Before she continued her lecture, I said, "Let's begin."

She put her hands on her hips. "I want to learn to throw a daga without harming the trees."

I exhaled. At the door, I ordered a warrior over and told her what I wanted. She left and returned with a rectangular piece of wood from the maintenance shed.

The warrior leaned it against the tree and retreated from the courtyard.

"Satisfied?" I asked Efe.

"It'll do."

I handed her the knife. She clasped it in her fist, as if to pound a table with it.

"No, not that way. Hold it like this." I repositioned the daga in her hands, stepped to the wood, and patted its center. "Aim here."

Efe raised her arm.

"Wait!" I jumped backward. "Let me get out of the way."

She lowered her arm and giggled. "I've never seen you hop, Princess Chibuike. You don't trust me?"

"Not yet." I moved several paces away. "I think I'm safe here. Focus on your target and throw."

Efe reared back and threw the daga. It sailed through the air and clattered on the sunbaked clay near the iron bench. I passed a hand over my face. "How could you miss from three paces?"

"I did it on purpose."

I tried not to smile. "I think not."

Efe didn't move. I pointed at the dagger. "Well, retrieve it. It won't come back to you on its own."

She reclaimed the knife and returned to the same spot.

I moved behind her, our heads touching. Her braids smelled like sweet berries. Reaching down, I encircled her hand and lifted it until the blade was next to her ear.

"See the target?" I whispered. She nodded. "Your weapon will find it. Take a breath and hold it." Efe complied. "Let it out." I stepped back. "Throw."

This time, she hit the wood. But barely.

"Try again," I said.

After six more failed attempts to get closer to the mark, I took the daga from her. "Watch me."

First, I went through the motions slowly, then I showed

her the movements at normal speed. The third time, I threw the daga with my arm covering my eyes. All three times, I struck the same spot.

She clapped. "How you flaunt your skills!"

I didn't bother to hide my smirk as I handed the knife to her and turned toward the courtyard door.

"Where are you going?" she called after me.

I kept walking. After twenty paces, I yelled, "Lower yourself!"

I grabbed my favorite daga from the scabbard at my waist, spun it on the back of my fist, turned, and threw the knife all in one motion. I loved that feeling: when it was hard to discern where my hand ended and the daga began. Efe crouched, her braids swinging as she watched the knife fly, spinning, over her head. After it thudded into the wood, she stared at me, her eyes wide. I was grateful she'd listened to me for once; how could I have explained killing her to my mother?

I raised my chin. "Go look."

Efe approached the board. The daga was stuck in the exact spot it had hit thrice before.

She turned to me, her eyes alight. "Teach me how to do that!"

⌁

Kayin, Kunto, Itoro, and I were practicing military maneuvers on the southern end of the Kanaian Forest by the River Ome.

Kayin lowered her musket. "I've had enough. Let's return to the compound."

"I'm hungry," said Kunto.

"You're always hungry."

"Warriors have to eat. We need our strength."

Across the grayish-blue water, the opposite riverbank was devoid of people. The bright sun was sinking through wisps of clouds toward the distant line where the sky graced the earth. We'd trained for most of the afternoon.

"Let's go to Asanti," I said.

"Why?" asked Kayin. "To see Efe?"

"Since we're close."

But it was more than that. Something was *propelling* me to check on her. My mother had told me that when I received a nudge, I should listen.

"But it's time for the evening meal."

"That's what I said," added Kunto.

I holstered my weapon. "I need to do this."

"I'll come with you, Lieutenant Colonel Chi," said Itoro.

I secured my musket and ran across the grassy riverbank to the water. Lieutenant Itoro fell in step beside me. Brine hardened her sharp fingernails: one of her weapons.

The twins' footfalls came from behind me. They followed me because I was their leader, and because they wouldn't want to incur my mother's wrath for allowing the princess-warrior to travel alone, no matter how good a fighter I was.

We waded through the river. When we emerged, instead of going east to Banaan, we headed west. After crossing the plain, we reached the edge of the Asanti plateau. I stopped and cocked my head. The warriors stopped, too.

"Listen," I said.

"I don't hear anything," said Kunto.

"Exactly."

I ran to the village. Kayin, Kunto, and Itoro caught up to me.

We passed a man's body lying in the dirt. Aba! A woman's body sprawled in a hut's doorway. A large cassava root that children should have been kicking sat immobile next to her.

At one house, three bodies were piled like logs. Flies buzzed around the blood-congealed circles of musket ball-entry wounds. The stench in the air was similar to the one we'd confronted in Banaan.

Unlike Kana, where streets were parallel and perpendicular, Asanti was designed in circles. Round thatched huts sat on circular streets.

I passed homes and bodies and picked up the pace. My destination was the largest house at the village's center.

In front of it, the grass showed impressions of different foot sizes, and not the design of the sandals Efe's family wore. I scanned the village, listening for any sound or movement. Nothing. Even the animals hadn't been left behind. A scream welled inside me. *Efe! Please, goddesses, don't let her be dead!* I motioned for the officers to stand guard and rushed into the hut through the open door, my daga ready.

A tipped-over spinning wheel. Fabric strewn over the earthen floor. Near the meal table, damaged chairs lay on their sides. Shelves built into the walls held unbroken masks with faces of elephants, monkeys, and zebras. Near what must have been Efe's bed were lines of leaves and rocks.

In one corner of the room, a person lay on a bed, as if she were sleeping. Given the condition of the house, she couldn't be. The weight of a stone lodged in my stomach. I trudged over to her as if I were walking through starch paste.

I swept away the delicate curtain that separated this area from the rest of the home and stepped closer. I drew in a ragged breath, closed my eyes, and prayed in silence to the goddesses for Dayo. And Efe.

When I opened them, the ruler of Asanti—a woman full of life—was staring sightlessly at the ceiling. A handbreadth-large wound gaped between her breasts.

I returned my daga to its scabbard.

From outside, a scream sounded far away.

There was movement at the hut's entrance.

"Get out of my way!" came Efe's voice. "Why are you blocking the door to my home?"

A surge of relief flowed through me.

Efe brushed past Itoro and stared at her mother's body. She ran to the bed, wailing like a trapped animal.

Kayin joined me at the side of the bed. We waited until Efe's wails became sobs; her sobs became sniffles; and her sniffles diminished into silence.

"Who killed my mother?" she screamed. "Where are my people?"

I knelt beside her and held her.

She shook as she cried. At last, she asked, "What shall I do?"

"You will grieve her, and when it's time, you'll pick up your mother's mantle and prevail."

"How will I?"

"You must find a way. You're the ruler of Asanti."

"I never wanted that."

"It doesn't matter what we want. It's our destiny."

She whipped her head toward me. "Ruler of whom? Everyone's gone!"

"This is your ala. Your land. And they're still your people. No matter where they are." I paused. "Where were you?"

She turned back to her mother. "In the forest. To the west. Observing the moss. I should have been here."

*Then you would also be missing or dead.*

Kunto stepped forward. "Lieutenant Colonel Chi, we must go after who did this. They could still be close by."

"I don't think so," I said.

"Why?"

I pointed to the blood on Dayo's chest. It was dry.

Kunto flexed her jaw like Kayin. "We should at least try."

"There are four of us," Chi said. "We don't know how many we'd be up against."

"I'm willing to take that chance."

"I am not. We'll wait to fight another day."

I lifted Dayo's hand. Blood and dead skin encrusted her fingernails. I lowered it gently to the bed covering. "She resisted."

I'd overstepped. But Efe nodded.

Encouraged, I continued: "But this isn't where the struggle took place. She wouldn't be lying here at peace. Someone must have moved her."

"Maybe it was my father."

"Maybe. Where's her shroud?"

Efe pointed to a chest. I opened it and gathered the soft sheer material in my arms and returned to her.

"Say goodbye."

A fresh gush of tears fell from Efe's eyes. She threw herself on Dayo's body again, sobbing. "Goodbye, Nne." She lifted her head, gazed at her mother's face—as if memorizing every feature—and kissed the middle of her forehead.

After Efe closed her mother's eyes, I helped her to her feet. I motioned for Kayin to come hold her. Kayin hesitated, then stiffly put an arm around Efe.

I set aside the sharp pangs of grief in my stomach and pasted a stoic expression on my face as I wrapped the older woman in the shroud with care, in a manner fit for a queen. My movements were efficient, the result of much practice during mock battles.

"I wish I could do more. She deserves more. But we need to take our leave. Darkness will descend soon." Efe did not move. "Gather your things. You're coming with us."

Kayin grimaced.

"What of my mother?" asked Efe. "Everyone else in the village?"

"Dayo will receive a proper burial. As will your people."

On the way out of the house, I spotted something caught in a splinter on the table. It was a swath of coarse beige fabric. As I rubbed it between my fingers, a tingle crept up my arm.

The Asantis didn't wear clothing made of this material. They preferred bark or kente cloth. The ruling family wore silk.

But I'd seen this type of cloth before.

A memory I'd suppressed for over ten dry seasons came rushing back to me like the current of the River Ome, as if the pale man in the forest was suddenly in the room with me. I shuddered. Kayin was guiding Efe outside. I folded the fabric and slipped it into the pouch at my waist, my hand shaking.

# Chapter Seven

# When we fight...

UNDER A PURPLE, pink, and orange sky, we ran from Asanti. After we left Efe's house, she fainted. I ran, carrying her over my shoulder. We needed to hurry. The moon would soon be overhead, and the forest was full of danger—from those who belonged there, and those who didn't. I sent Itoro ahead to deliver a message asking Queen Adebola to summon the Great Council prior to our return, but she was not to share with them what we'd observed. She didn't want to leave me, but I told her it was an order.

Loud voices met us as we entered the obieze. I rushed to the Council Room but hesitated at its entrance. Efe was with me. Kayin and Kunto had gone to the barracks.

Udo and Sola stood across the table, shouting at each other, the general towering over the petite commerce minister. Foreign Minister Ndidi, seated, watched them with pursed lips.

When the fanti announced our arrival, my mother clapped her hands to silence them.

"Oh, my goddesses!" Sola exclaimed.

Dried blood caked Efe's face, hair, chest, and arms. Blood covered me from carrying her.

"Chibuike," my mother said, "tell us what you discovered."

I'm not sure if anyone else noticed the tremor in her voice.

I saluted the queen. The way she held her head, fragile though strong, made me want to protect her from the news I was about to impart. Nevertheless, I described what we'd found in Asanti.

"Dayo!" my mother cried.

I reached into the pouch for the beige fabric and walked around the table to give it to her, willing my hand not to shake. "I found this."

My mother examined the cloth.

"Remember the pale man in the forest all those years ago?" I asked.

"How could I forget?"

"It's from a shirt that belongs to him, or someone like him."

"Where did you find it?"

"In Dayo's home."

My mother dropped the cloth on the table and went to Efe, still lurking near the door.

Efe raised her hand. "Please don't come closer, Queen Adebola. I'm covered in my mother's blood."

"What greater honor is there?" The queen enveloped her in an embrace. "Dayo did not die in vain. I promise." My mother released her and grasped her shoulders. "You need to wipe your tears. It's time to lead."

My head bowed. I flicked a tear from my cheek with my finger. I could not cry in front of the general. The ministers. My queen. Anyone.

My mother gestured to a chair as she returned to her seat. "Efe, please join us."

The council members stole glances at one another. Efe looked to me for permission that wasn't mine to give. I wrestled with the fact that she would sit at the Kanaian council table before I did as I moved to my customary place behind the queen's chair.

"What should be our course of action?" asked Adebola.

"Those villagers aren't warriors like us," Udo said. "With the queen's foresight ten dry seasons ago, we taught everyone in the queendom how to use household items to defend themselves."

"The Banaans tried that," I said in a low voice the general couldn't hear.

"We will pursue the perpetrators with the full force of the military," Udo continued. "Overpower and torture them until they divulge where they've taken the Asantis and the Banaans."

"People lie under torture," said Ndidi. "Instead, we can send out a select group of warriors to assess the situation and report back before we decide."

Efe had a glazed look on her face.

Udo rubbed the cloth on her shoulder where her arm should have been. "But they might be outnumbered."

"We should leave." Sola's voice shook. "Ndidi has said this land is vast. We can settle someplace else where we'll be left alone."

"We will not abandon our homeland," said Queen Adebola. "Our families have been here for—"

"No, Nne." I pressed my lips together.

Everyone looked at me, then shifted their gaze to the queen. No one interrupted my mother.

She turned to me. Her eyes narrowed to slits, the same expression I faced when I was a child and arrived back at the obieze after dark. My mother never struck me. Her punishment was to stare at me. Every child in the queendom was familiar with that look from their mother.

"Since bravery flows in your veins, what are you proposing, my nwa?"

"This isn't about taking land and wealth."

"It's the people," said Ndidi.

I nodded. "Since they're not killing all of them, they must be enslaving them. Whoever kidnapped the Banaans and the Asantis will come for us. When they do, we will allow them to capture us."

The general leaned forward in her chair and stared at me as if my wits had departed. "Why would we do *that*, Princess?"

"To find out where they've taken the villagers."

"That's ludicrous! Are you a coward?"

"No," Efe said. "Chibuike is being astute."

Sola gasped. Everyone's heads—including the attendants standing near the service table—swiveled to Efe. I read their expressions like an unfurled scroll. Challenging Udo was unwise, especially in the presence of others. The outcome had not been favorable to former warriors who had done so.

"And she's one of the bravest people I know," Efe continued, unaware of the consternation she was causing.

Udo's deep-set eyes narrowed, which brought back a vague recollection.

My commanding officer shot out of her chair, its legs scraping against the sunbaked-clay floor. She reached for the sword at her hip.

"Take your seat, Udo," said the queen. "There will be no

bloodshed in this chamber. And you'll certainly not slay a leader friendly to our interests."

"We have the best warriors in the world." The general lowered herself to her chair. "We should hunt the hunters. Besides,"—she glanced at me—"they'll know you're warriors by looking at you, and kill you instead of capturing you."

"We'll disguise ourselves," I said.

"As what?"

Good question.

"We started trading with the Portuguese ten dry seasons ago," Ndidi said.

Every year, Ndidi led a contingent of Kanaian brokers to the coast to trade gold, pepper, and palm oil with the foreigners for silk, sugar, spices, and muskets.

"What of it?" asked Sola.

"It's no coincidence people are disappearing."

"It can't be the Portuguese. They wouldn't antagonize us. Our relationship is mutually prosperous." Sola glanced down at her new silk pano. "Imagine the impact on market revenue if what you're saying proved true!"

Udo shook her head. "How can you be counting cowrie shells at a time like this?"

Sola straightened in her seat. "It's my responsibility."

"Among us, I've had the most interaction with the Portuguese," Ndidi said. "I wouldn't be surprised if they had their own agenda. Let Chi speak."

Sola's thin face quivered. Udo stared at me. My mother's face was inscrutable. Efe gave me a half smile of encouragement.

"I believe we should let the Portuguese take us to the Asantis and the Banaans so we can free them and bring them back home." I turned to General Udo. "Who's the coward now?"

ᡧ

"On the shelves in my work chamber, you'll find texts that might interest you," Queen Adebola told Efe the following morning after breakfast. "You have free rein of the obieze and grounds. Please make yourself at home. Chibuike, come with me."

My heart quickened. When I was young, I loved going on adventures with my mother. Whether it was watching the warriors execute their drills, visiting the market surrounded by a bevy of fanti, or—on the best days—heading to a smaller courtyard, the two of us, to practice throwing dagas. I hadn't inherited my skill from my father.

As we walked down the hallway toward the staircase, I asked, "Where are we going?"

"To the temple."

"Oh."

"You need to learn to hide your emotions better."

"So you keep telling me."

Outside, my mother waved off the attendants carrying the hammock used to transport her over long distances. Instead, we strolled through the Grand Square. Butterflies flitted among the bougainvillea and canna lilies in the Obieze Garden. Two attendants walked in front of the queen. One held an umbrella to shade her from the sweltering morning sun. The other rang a bell to ensure everyone stayed out of her way. As Adebola passed, people stopped whatever they were doing, knelt, brushed a finger against the red dust, and slid it across their foreheads.

The Obieze Temple was a medium-sized building with a thatched roof, made of the same mud clay as the rest of the compound's buildings. Like many homes in Kana, it didn't have a door. Although the army doubled as a police force, drawing weapons on our own residents was rare. Another reason my Nne Nne Thema had had the temple built without a door was to encourage obieze residents to commune with our goddesses, day or night. On both sides of the entrance were two shutterless windows.

My mother and I climbed the step and entered the building. It was empty and smelled of incense.

"Why doesn't the priestess light candles in here?"

"Are you still afraid of the dark?"

I snickered. "Of course not."

We continued walking, passing rows of wooden benches.

"The darkness has its secrets, but it also brings stillness. You can pray to the goddesses without distraction. And it's a metaphor for life."

"In what way?"

"Darkness will come—it always does—but so does light. The light inside you will protect you. You'd know this if you visited here more often."

"I visit." In the blackness, she could not search my face for the untruth.

"When was the last time?"

"When we thanked the goddesses for the productive harvest."

"The harvest season will begin soon."

"I can't help it that the seasons pass faster than a panther."

"That's not all you cannot help, my nwa."

My cheeks warmed. "I'll do better."

"An exceptional warrior not only fights with valor but also prays to our ancestors and goddesses for strength and guidance. Lean on them. Listen and they will lead you."

Like they led me to Asanti. "What if I can't hear them?"

"Listen to your belly."

"My belly?"

"It's how they guide you."

At the altar, we knelt in front of the three largest sculptures in the building: the Goddess Nana Buluku, the creator of all things, with her determined gaze and raised arm; Gbadu, the Goddess of Destiny; and Age-Fon, the Hunter Goddess, with coiled hair, a broad nose, and muscular arms, holding a daga and a spear. When I looked at Age-Fon, I saw myself.

"What's more important, destiny or the goddesses' will?" I asked.

"They are the same. Close your eyes. Let's pray," my mother said.

"Oh mighty goddesses,

The line between life and death is blurred.

We ask our ancestors for strength and well-being,

To guide us and guard us,

To protect our queendom forever,

And my nwa from what's to come.

Àse."

"Àse," I said, opening my eyes.

Adebola was gazing at Nana Buluku. I did, too, the silence in the room complete. My body relaxed. My mind was serene.

My mother smiled at me. "You feel it, too. That feeling is peace. It's what happens when you call on your ancestors. You must know them, or you will be lost."

"What about strength?"

"You can be strong and at peace at the same time." She paused. "The winds have changed. You'll be going on a journey, and we won't see each other for a while."

Tears threatened to fall. "I'm not sure I can leave you, Nne."

"After you saw the pale man, I called General Udo back into my office. She dispatched reconnaissance warriors, and we learned the Portuguese were trading with Bamidele. At first, it was goods. Like our relationship with the Portuguese. I've suspected over the last two seasons he's been exchanging his residents for guns. And kidnapping others from nearby villages for the same purpose. With these guns, he is a threat to Kana, our people, and our way of life."

King Bamidele ruled Aon, a city-state southwest of the queendom, near the coast. He'd ascended to the throne after his older brother died—it was rumored—from poisoning. The Aons hailed Bamidele as the "greatest of all men." My mother remarked that didn't make him great, only the best of half the population.

"This is the real reason I wanted to bring you here. Away from the prying eyes and loose lips of the servants, attendants, and even the ministers. I also didn't wish to scare them. When you showed me that cloth yesterday, I realized the day had come. My heart aches for Dayo and Yaa and Fatimata. We're up against a formidable opponent." She cupped my face in her soft hands. "It won't do for you to stay and rule over a land with no people, like Efe. Or to allow the pale men to take the strongest among us. This is more important than you, me, our family, or our dynasty. We must think of posterity." She released me. "You have a calling. A greater purpose. You've been chosen to lead."

"Me?" My voice was loud in this reverent space. "How do you know?"

My mother looked back up at Nana Buluku. "She told me."

⤚

The next day, the ministers sat at the table in the Council Room, with Efe sitting opposite Adebola. The queen cleared the room of attendants except for Salamatu, the one she trusted most.

"We'll move forward with Chibuike's proposal," announced my mother. "And she will lead the mission."

I tried not to smile.

"Princess Chi?" Udo asked. "Surely other officers are more...suited for this purpose. Kayin. Even Kunto has more experience."

"Are you saying my nwa is unqualified?"

My heart jumped at my mother coming to my defense. The angrier she became, the more polite her speech.

Udo also knew this. She bowed her head. "Forgive me. I might have misspoken."

Grabbing her cane, Udo walked around the table and stood before me. I tensed. The general's eyes were dark as she placed a heavy hand on the shoulder of my officer's tunic.

"Adebola has faith in you. I have faith in you. Most important, the warriors have faith in you. You're a fine choice." She patted my shoulder. A dismissal more than reassurance.

"Thank you, General," I said to her back as she returned to her chair.

"Where should the kidnapping occur?" Queen Adebola continued.

"The forest," I blurted, "during training."

Udo countered with restraint. "They'd know you're warriors."

I lowered my head so my commanding officer couldn't see my flushed face.

"By the River Ome?" suggested Sola.

"We'd be exposed," said Udo.

"The coast?" offered Ndidi. "If it's the Portuguese, that's where they'll return."

"We don't know that area and will not have time to assess it."

A pause enveloped the room.

"The market?" asked my mother. "The warriors can dress like villagers and blend in with them."

"And the men traders? We won't have time to train them. I'm not sure what good that would do, anyway."

"The kidnappers will take them, thinking they're stronger and more worthy," Ndidi said.

"But wouldn't the villagers be at risk, Queen Adebola?" Efe asked.

"They can take care of themselves," my mother replied.

Efe's face tightened at the implication that the Banaans and the Asantis could not.

Ndidi tapped her finger on the table. "You're suggesting our warriors should hide in the open."

"Does anyone have a better suggestion?" The ministers seldom did when she posed this question. "May I see a show of hands? All in favor of our plan?" Ndidi and Sola's hands shot up. Udo raised hers slowly. "Opposed?"

"Everyone has voted, Your Amara," said Sola.

"Efe hasn't."

What was this? The queen never considered a noncouncil member's wishes, including mine. The members were equally surprised, as evidenced by the displeasure on their faces.

"'For,'" said Efe, "with reservations."

"Noted. My vote makes five. General Udo, prepare the

obieze." My mother glanced at me. "Chibuike, communicate our plan to the warriors."

"But that's my responsibility," argued Udo.

Adebola stood. "But I have spoken."

A vein pulsed in Udo's neck, but she didn't respond.

I saluted the queen and turned to leave, grateful to begin the mission and escape from the tension in the room.

"Wait!" Efe said. "I'm going with you."

"It's not safe."

"I've already lost everything."

"I've lost Fatimata. I don't want to lose you, too."

"I still want to go."

I ached with pity for her. I couldn't envision living in a world without a mother. "Very well."

On the obieze's lowest floor, we passed the tomb enshrining my ancestors and the barracks comprising five enormous rooms with sleeping mats lined up in rows of twenty. I summoned the nine officers to a small room we used for planning and explained the mission. Some of them met my words with quiet acceptance. Others were hesitant to leave Kana, the only home they'd ever known. Kayin's gaze never left my face, but she remained silent throughout the discussion. Itoro's opposition was uncharacteristic. After I convinced her we wouldn't be captives for long, she concurred.

A consensus reached, we pulled the map scrolls off a shelf and went to work.

# Chapter Eight

# ...we do not fear

"AZEZE, THE BLACKSMITH'S apprentice."

A warrior stood in the doorway to the planning room outside the barracks where Kayin and I had been poring over maps. Kayin left to check on the warriors' training.

"Send him in."

Azeze stepped into the room, bringing with him the acrid smell of smoke and sweat. He had the nose of a male sculpture. Or at least what I imagined a male sculpture to look like, since I'd never seen one. The muscles on his bare chest lay at rest. It was unheard of for anyone outside the Kanaian army to be invited to the obieze's bottom floor, but time was dear and we needed to prepare. And what I had to tell him required secrecy.

"You're wondering why I summoned you."

"It crossed my mind."

"We won't let what happened to the Banaans and the Asantis happen to us."

"I wouldn't think so."

"We require more weapons."

"What do you need?"

I told him.

"But that's not all you require."

"How do you know?"

"You would have sent a messenger to the blacksmith at the workshop."

Strong and smart. I'd made the right choice. "We're going on a mission. And you are coming with us."

"Me?"

"We're in need of your services."

I swore him to secrecy on the queen's life and told him our plan to get kidnapped. His eyes kept widening; I thought they would slide out of their sockets.

"Why didn't you ask the blacksmith?"

"We need him to remain in Kana. Aren't you up to the task?"

This was a rhetorical question. After I'd encountered Azeze on the way to Banaan, my attendant had delivered my daga to him to be sharpened. When it was returned, the tip could have drawn blood merely touching skin.

He crossed his arms over his chest. "Are you going on this mission?"

"I am."

"Then I'll go. I wouldn't want you to go alone."

I wasn't sure why he said that, since I would be with the rest of the warriors, but it made me smile just the same. "Thank you, Azeze. That will be all."

❧

We warriors sat around a fire built earlier by recruits. It wasn't for warmth, since the night still carried heat from the day. Wood smoke and popping sounds provided a backdrop for what would happen next.

The three-quarter moon poured a shaft of light upon us. Several warriors passed long wooden pipes packed with tobacco. Most of them were drinking rum. Though I didn't enjoy the taste of libations, I sipped a millet beer.

Efe wasn't present. When I had left her, she was in the front room of the private residence, reading texts she'd borrowed from my mother's work chamber.

Beside me, Itoro clutched a goblet. Lying on the sunbaked clay next to her was a blade attached to a long wooden handle. I'd picked it up once, needing to use two hands. When she held it, she used one, carrying it over her shoulder like an umbrella.

Itoro hummed for a moment, parted her thick lips, and sang, "Loyalty to the queen—"

The rest of us joined in:
"with absolute obedience
We are proud, brave, and fierce
When we fight, we do not fear
We refuse to surrender
and will never retreat
We will never leave a sister warrior behind
Each one is precious
We, the elite warriors of Kana, are invincible
and will eliminate the enemy without and within
Until we prevail or die
Arise, warriors of Kana!
Because valor is our virtue

Live to fight another day
And as long as we live
Kana will stand
We would gladly die for Queen Adebola
The queen of queens
And, if we shall perish,
Let the queen dance and sing our names
forevermore."

When the last refrain drifted away, tears stung my eyes. I've listened to the warrior song a thousand times. It must be the wind. Or Itoro's sweet voice. Or the premonition that the number of nights we'd be together were few. To most warriors, separated from their families at an early age, the Kanaian army was their family. My landswomen's faces shone from the fire's heat. Kayin raised her goblet to me.

Aba! She was the last person I wished to see me cry.

She whispered into the ear of the warrior sitting next to her. Abeni giggled, her cheeks round like small oranges.

"May I join you?"

My commanding officer stood behind me. Sounds from the fire and the singing had obscured her approach. This proved I could never be comfortable amid my tribe. We scrambled to our feet, snapped out our arms, and pointed one finger at her.

I gestured at a spot. "Yes, General."

Udo signaled for us to lower our arms and resume our positions. The women shuffled apart to make room for her in the circle. She shifted the machete sheathed in crimson velvet on her hip. Itoro hurried to a large bucket and returned with a goblet of rum. She handed it to the general, bowed, and returned to her place next to me.

"I'm glad you're all gathered in unity. It's important we

remain as one." Udo sipped her drink and peered into her cup. "Hmm. That's good." She looked up. "Earlier generations of warriors assembled on this sacred ground, where their ancestors shared wisdom. Would you like to hear a story?"

"Yes, General," we answered in unison.

Storytelling was part of our culture and our military. We preferred oral tales over written ones; an adversary could use the written word against you.

"I come from Doba," Udo began. "When I marked five dry seasons, an old woman in the village invited me and other girls into her home. She selected me, because times were hard for my family. My nne died birthing me, and my nna wasn't strong enough to raise three young daughters without her.

"The old woman didn't teach us how to read texts or write letters, or about philosophy or mathematics, but about life. Over time, she taught us many lessons. But the one that meant the most to me was to fight for what is rightfully mine.

"One sunrise, a Kanaian officer arrived. We huddled around her in the village center, and she described what our lives would be like if she selected us for the army. I loved the way she carried herself. I wanted to be her. She put us through many exercises. Afterward, she chose an older girl and told everyone else she would return every dry season, though since our village was small, a girl wouldn't be selected every time. When I turned sixteen, I was ready. I'd trained for *eleven* dry seasons." She scanned our faces. "Alas, I wasn't chosen."

The warriors, mesmerized by the tale, cast looks of disbelief. Pretending to drink my beer, I hid my surprise behind my goblet. I'd never heard this story of Udo's rejection by a predecessor of the job I held.

"As you can imagine, I was devastated. I couldn't stay

home. My nna was struggling to provide for me and my sisters."

"What did you do?" asked Kunto.

An older warrior clicked her tongue at her.

Udo raised her hand. "It's all right. I kept training harder, Kunto. Until my time came."

"How long did that take, General?" Kayin asked.

The older warrior *tsked* again. I cut a glance at her. Reprimanding them was fruitless. The twins did everything together.

"It was a strange thing," Udo said. "Not long after the recruiter left, a hunter from our village found the selected girl's body in the jungle, her neck twisted. Everyone agreed it was unlucky for her to have tripped over a tree root before her departure."

"That is…unlucky," remarked Kayin.

"Quite. Nevertheless, her misfortune was my gain. Four sunrises later, the officer sent for me to take her place."

I masked my revulsion. Did my mother know this story?

"Do you know the moral of this tale?" Udo asked.

Most warriors answered affirmatively.

"That's why you're the best army in the world." The general held out her goblet and waited for us to raise ours. "Take back what is rightfully mine."

"Take back what is rightfully mine," we repeated.

A shiver stole across my outstretched arm.

Udo drank and set her cup on the ground. She unwrapped the cloth covering her shoulder. The bone ended in a scarred nub. "*This* is what bravery looks like."

I tried not to flinch.

The general had never brought attention to her

impairment. She'd lost her arm in a battle a generation ago. If the older warriors were to be believed, a man from the Zatopa Province chopped it off with a sword. Udo had glanced at the blood gushing from her shoulder and roared. With her remaining arm, she'd seized his weapon and beheaded him with a single stroke. She'd picked the victim's head up off the ground and quaffed his blood.

She rewrapped her shoulder and pushed herself up. "And with that, I bid you all goodnight."

We stood and saluted. "Goodnight, General."

After she departed, warriors excused themselves to retire to the barracks. The caked mud underneath me was colder. The fire blazed while others struck up conversations, mostly concerning men. Warriors took a vow of celibacy, although some of them did not adhere to it. I had long since come to understand the joke among the rulers about the palm oil-filled sponges, used for fear of becoming with child. If that were to happen, they would be forced out of the army in disgrace, bringing shame upon their families.

A sweet, earthly aroma wafted off the walnut logs. A mist of dust rose as Kayin plopped down next to me. Abeni drifted alone to the obieze.

"You're not going with her?" I asked.

I suspected she lay with this woman in the barracks at night, as a few warriors did, in search of intimacy. Kayin and Abeni had been inseparable for a few full moons.

She followed my gaze. "I'll see her later."

I was unwilling to discuss the topic further.

"I've had enough rum." She turned her goblet upside down, shook out the remaining dregs, and refilled it with beer from a calabash. Kayin suspended the calabash over my cup, resting on my knee. I nodded. She poured and set the container on the ground. A snake was carved into the iron grips of her swords.

"Some story," she said. "Do you think the general killed that girl?"

"I have no doubt."

"Me neither."

We gazed into the dying fire and sipped our beer, its grainy flavor improving with the second cup.

After a while, Kayin said, "Our residents are here. Safe. Why save outlanders?"

This was what she had wanted to ask me when I told the officers about the mission, but she'd refrained from questioning me in front of them.

Our lives would be easier if I did what she suggested. But the easy way had never suited me.

I finished my beer. "We'd become involved in these affairs eventually, whether we wanted to or not."

# Chapter Nine

# We refuse to surrender...

WHEN I ROSE the next morning, my bed was still in shadows. My habit was to wake up to the chorus of birdsong outside my window as sunlight crept into my bedchamber. I required little sleep—a trait I inherited from my mother. "I cannot rule while I'm sleeping," she'd say.

I did not wait for an attendant. I filled the basin with a few handbreadths of water, not bothering to warm it in the hearth first, and bathed myself. I rubbed the cloth filled with karite soap against my skin, breathing in the fruity aroma.

At the mahogany wardrobe, I grazed the smooth fabric of my white calico tunic with my fingertips before donning the coarse brown one I wore when I cleaned my musket.

From the dresser, I lifted my beloved daga with both hands and eyed the lion engraved on the brass handle. A heaviness spread through my limbs. My daga couldn't go where I was going. This fight would be with my hands and wits.

I laid it gently on the hippopotamus tusk stand. It was

like parting with a dear friend, although I had no experience of what that felt like.

I slung the strap of the leather satchel containing Yaa's headdress and Fatimata's doll over my shoulder. The satchel rested against my hip. I prayed no one would take it from me.

The obieze was quiet. My sandals flapped against the clay floor as I made my way to breakfast. I passed four empty bed-chambers. My mother had been with child many times, but none of my sisters had lived beyond her first breath. Had their deaths caused the silence between my parents? I'd never asked.

Attired in a purple pano, my mother sat at the table. She dabbed her lips with a small, white cloth, although the food on her plate was untouched.

I kissed her cheek.

She searched my face. Hers looked gaunt. I imagined what she'd look like as an elder.

"By the way you're dressed, I surmise the hour is upon us."

I sat. "I believe so. The scouts reported the pale men are south of Doba."

"A moon away. Are you prepared?"

A lump formed in my throat. I was saved from answering because Efe entered the room.

"Good morning, Queen Adebola," Efe said. "Chibuike."

"Now that you're both here," my mother said, "I'll pray again." We closed our eyes. "To our ancestors and goddesses, we are grateful for the food we're about to receive and the strength for what's to come. Àse."

"Àse," Efe and I responded.

My mouth watered as the aroma of yam porridge drifted up from my bowl, awakening my appetite.

Not much conversation took place during the meal.

Spoons scraped against bowls. My mother barely lifted her utensil.

What was there to say? How many times could one say *I love you?* I kept looking at my queen—her oval face, arched eyebrows, almond-shaped eyes, her regal bearing, her graceful hands—inscribing every feature into my memory. My heart hurt.

These thoughts had to stop, or I would never leave her.

A servant removed my empty bowl. I caressed the lions incised into the chair's armrests as I waited for Efe to finish eating. When she set down her spoon, I said, "We must go."

"I need to retrieve something from my room."

She could bring nothing with her. She was giving me time alone with my mother.

Efe kissed Adebola on the cheek and hugged her. "Thank you for everything."

"You're quite welcome. Be safe."

Efe hurried out of the room.

My mother's arms parted, ready to envelop me. I went to her. "I love you, Nne."

"I love you, Chibuike." She held me tight. "My nwa."

I leaned back to look at her. Her penetrating gaze conveyed her love and strength.

"I'm no longer a child."

"No matter your age, you'll still be my nwa."

"I'll make you proud."

"You always have."

I hugged her once more. "Until I see you."

"Goddess Gbadu willing. You have nothing to fear. She will protect you."

I kissed the middle of her forehead.

Although what we planned to do was right, it did not lessen the pain of not knowing whether I would ever see my mother again.

⌘

Compound residents crisscrossed the grounds on the queen's business. On any other day, I would have been one of them, leading an officers' meeting in the barracks, heading to the training ground for morning exercises, or leaving for another village in search of new recruits.

A red finch chirped as Efe and I passed a small courtyard. At the main entrance, the two fanti, each armed with a sword, stood at attention on either side of the gate. They scrutinized the drab brown tunic I wore instead of my officer's one. They saluted. "Lieutenant Colonel Chi!"

I saluted and kept going. I forced myself not to look back at the obieze—my home—or up at a window in the private residence to check whether my mother was watching me. I wouldn't have been able to see her from this distance. She was supposed to be hiding in the tombs, protected by fanti and the remaining Kanaian warriors—an adequate number to defend our queen and country.

My father would join her after he rose. I couldn't afford to think of him, either.

We walked past the row of rampant lions etched into the red clay wall and crossed the wooden bridge that spanned the moat. The sweet sounds and smells of a Kanaian morning greeted us. Traders—unfamiliar young men, not the usual market vendors—hawked fresh fruits, smoked meats, rice, and yams. Chickens, turkeys, and a goat roamed. The aroma of spices and herbs hovered in the air.

But no one was dancing. Or gossiping. Children were absent, as well as their laughter.

Kunto, Kayin, Itoro, and scores of warriors blended in with the townspeople and villagers, although they were handbreadths taller than them. My eyes widened at the sight of Mukambu, the healer, listening to a man holding a live, plump chicken for sale. Standing next to them was the priestess' daughter, Yetunde.

As I made my way over to order them to return to the obieze, I spotted a table piled high with baobabs, womanned by a young girl. Her mother stood behind her, coaching her in the art of negotiation, reminding me of the many seasons I had stood behind the queen, learning how to govern. I veered toward them. The girl straightened when she recognized me, but recovered and drew my attention to the fruit.

"You're not supposed to be here," I told her mother.

The woman's eyebrows drew together. "I'm here every sunrise, Adaeze."

"You should have received word to stay home."

The woman scanned the rest of the vendors. "Why?"

Despite the market noise, there was a shift in the air south of us. Kayin's hand rested on a tapestry she would never purchase. She nodded. She'd heard it, too.

A warrior scout dressed as a farmer brushed by me and said under her breath, "They're here."

I turned to the trader. "Where do you live?" She pointed north. "Take your daughter and go." She glanced at the table, the fruit representing a season of work. "Leave it. Run now!"

She stared into my eyes, grabbed her daughter's hand, and ran.

The vendors and buyers ceased haggling.

Silence.

It seemed infinite, but only lasted a few moments. Pounding footsteps headed our way, sounds different from the ones made by sandals or bare feet on our dirt streets.

Pale men entered the market from the south and west, their muskets swinging. Although the warriors and selected villagers had been instructed to appear scared, some were not acting, and a few villagers fled.

The Portuguese chased the runners. Two men stepped up to me and Efe. My breath caught as I stared into the barrel of a musket, but instead of my daga, my hand brushed the satchel. Efe gulped. The men wore dirty white, billowing shirts and tan trousers tucked into dusty knee-high black leather foot coverings. One man's eyes were the same color as one of my mother's panos. The same color as the pale man's eyes I'd seen in the forest.

Blue Eyes shouted at us in Portuguese to move to the center of the street. Although Ndidi had taught me the language when I was a child, I pretended not to understand.

Blue Eyes motioned with his musket. Efe and I shuffled to the place he indicated. The second man circled behind us. My nose wrinkled. He reeked of sweat and urine.

While Blue Eyes kept his gun trained on us, the second man's weapon hit the ground. It took all of my control not to back-kick him. He clamped the shackles around my wrists, the sound like the closing of an iron gate.

I was no longer free.

He shackled Efe and crouched to chain us together at the ankles.

"I'm scared, Chibuike," Efe whispered.

Doubt shivered through me. But Queen Adebola, Udo, the warriors, and Kana were depending on me.

"I'm with you," I said.

The man picked up his gun and came around to stand in front of us. He smiled, his teeth brown and rotten. His breath smelled like lamb dung. He opened my satchel, reached in, and pulled out Yaa's headdress and Fatimata's doll. He held them up and asked Blue Eyes what he should do with them. Their conversation was rapid, and I couldn't make out every word, but understood the gist: they thought these precious items were sticks.

Blue Eyes looked at me. To prevent him from seeing the defiance on my face, I lowered my head, as I'd witnessed people in the village do when I passed them. He told Rotten Teeth to return the items to the satchel. Sticks never hurt anyone, he said.

I exhaled.

Rotten Teeth threw the satchel's strap around his neck. *"Eu estou mantendo isso."* I'm keeping it.

I jerked. Efe gripped my wrist, holding me back.

Blue Eyes shrugged and waved the musket again for us to join the women captives, who were standing in groups of two. Kayin was bound to Kunto, her expression unreadable. A few paces away, Itoro glared at a pale man as she tried to free her hands. I stared at her until she relaxed.

We wanted to be captured. Otherwise, the Portuguese would never have reached the queendom. They'd be dead.

Across the street, Kanaian men stood shackled together. Azeze, the blacksmith's apprentice, was the only one I recognized. He turned to us, his mouth parting. Although I had informed him of our intentions, it must have been a sight to see warriors in shackles.

There was a flash of a bright color. Wearing a red pano, Sola rushed into the market, her gaze darting from one pale man to another.

Her appearance was not part of the plan.

∽

"You're Portuguese!" Sola shouted in Kanaian, her eyes frantic. "We are your trading partners. Why are you shackling our residents?"

Blue Eyes stared at her blankly. He instructed his men to finish their work.

Sola's face transformed into an ugly mask. She was not used to being ignored. "Listen to me!"

*"Faz pouco barulho,"* he said. Be quiet.

When Sola did not comply, Blue Eyes repeated it. She didn't listen.

Rotten Teeth stomped over to her. *"Cale-te!"* Shut up.

She looked over at us, her gaze landing on me. *Don't give us away!*

She turned back to him and clutched his sleeve. "For the love of Goddess Nana Buluku, don't do this!"

He tried to shake her off.

"This can't be! This can't be!" she cried.

Though I had known Sola my entire life, I couldn't help her—in saving her, the rest of us would be lost. General Udo had selected our best, most experienced fighters for this mission, and now they were in chains.

Sola wouldn't release Rotten Teeth's arm. It was as though her fingers had transformed into claws.

He slapped her, but Sola held on. He punched her in the belly and when she doubled over, he struck her forehead with the butt of his musket. She yelped, her face contorting in pain. My gut clenched as if he'd hit me. A gash opened on her temple, and blood poured down her cheek.

She let out a bloodcurdling scream and continued screaming. He kept hitting her in the head until her eye swelled shut, her lip bled, and two teeth flew out. Mukambu's instinct would be to help the minister, but the healer stared at the ground. Efe stepped closer to me and touched my fingers with hers, her eyes blinking rapidly.

A loud report rang out. The screaming ceased. Captives shrieked. I flinched and clamped my mouth shut. Efe looked away.

Commerce Minister Sola lay on her back, legs splayed. Brain matter and blood smeared her pano.

Rotten Teeth had shot her in the mouth.

Bowing my head, I said a silent prayer to the goddesses for Sola's safe passage to our ancestors.

Rotten Teeth sneered at the body. *"Como a mulher em Asanti. Ela não iria calar."*

I stiffened.

"What did he say?" Efe whispered.

I hesitated. "'Like the woman in Asanti. She wouldn't shut up.'"

Dayo had been the only woman among the dead in her village. Efe tensed.

"No," I said under my breath. "Our time will come."

Her nostrils flared, and tears fell down her cheeks, but she remained, standing, next to me.

As if Sola had never appeared, the Portuguese shackled each pair of women to the pair in front and the pair behind them, and did the same with the men before forcing us into lines. I estimated there were ninety of us: fifty warriors, about forty men, Mukambu, and Yetunde.

Once we were all linked, Blue Eyes shouted, *"Vamos!"*

Clouds drifted across the pale blue sky. Above the Thema Obieze's red clay walls, the scarlet lion on the white silk flag flapped in the gentle eastward wind. A lump formed in my throat.

When I faced forward, I vowed not to look back.

I would return.

As we marched from the market, I refused to pause as I passed Sola's corpse.

My focus was on the living.

# Part II

## Chapter Ten

# ...and will never retreat

IN THE WOODS, I stepped on sticks, stones, and dirt. I had lost my sandals in the market, but despite my chained wrists and ankles, I felt at home. I'd run on these paths my entire life. Though I exuded calm, I was nervous. With each step, my uncertainty about the plan grew.

"Are you all right?" Kayin asked. I nodded, even though Sola's murder still upset me. "The commerce minister shouldn't have meddled in affairs that didn't concern her."

Kayin was wrong. The Portuguese should concern everyone. I couldn't fault Sola for doing what she believed was right, although her approach had cost her her life. I did not bother explaining this to Kayin, who would never understand. To her, everything was either scarlet or white. Right or wrong. With no shades of pink.

Ahead, a villager tumbled to the ground. The captives halted. We cast furtive glances at one another and at the pale men, wondering how they'd react.

The man chained to the fallen man hunched over him, the chain at his wrist preventing him from straightening. Rotten Teeth stomped over to them, yelling rapidly in Portuguese, spittle spraying from his foul mouth. I willed my landsman to stand. Rotten Teeth prodded him in the abdomen with the butt of his gun. The Kanaian man cried out and looked at me, his eyes beseeching. I worried he would give away my identity. I didn't recognize him. "You must rise!" I said.

The man attached to him helped him up. And the march resumed.

The trees' overhanging leaves and branches provided a welcome reprieve from the sun's heat. For once, the monkeys' and the hyenas' screeching comforted rather than irritated me.

We kept up a steady pace. The irons chafed my ankles. I wanted to stop and remove them, or at least scratch the irritated skin. The more my ankles itched, the more I yearned to scratch them. To take my mind off my discomfort, I visualized Rotten Teeth standing with his back against a tree while I threw my daga repeatedly into his chest.

I wrinkled my nose. He walked alongside us. He smelled worse than the rest of the pale men. Efe clenched her jaw.

Next to a shrub was a tall mound of dirt, such as the ones I used to jump over as a child. Scared off by the warriors' stories, I'd never touched one. Red ants ascended and descended their hill in a synchronized march.

I felt a tug on the wrist manacle. Efe's petite hands were balled into fists. Dread spread through me. She slammed her shoulder into Rotten Teeth, and he fell to the forest floor, releasing his weapon. I didn't dive for it, although my instinct howled at me to do so.

He screamed. Everyone stopped and stared at the large

ants parading over and inside his trousers. He shot up, still yelping, and threw off the satchel containing Yaa's headdress and Fatimata's doll to beat his private parts and buttocks. He slapped his arms and face as the insects traversed his eyes into his nose and mouth. His hips jerked back and forth.

No one—not even the pale men—attempted to help him.

Welts formed on his face and hairy arms. His slaps became taps, and his knees sank to the hard earth. He shouted. The Portuguese spoke in muted tones but remained where they stood.

No Kanaian divulged Mukambu was a doctor.

Rotten Teeth lay still. Their work complete, the surviving ants picked up their fallen brethren and marched back to their home.

One by one, the Kanaian warriors—including Kayin—looked over at Efe, a newfound respect reflected on their faces. Efe stared forward, as if she'd had no hand in what had occurred.

The pale men stood several paces from the corpse, glancing at it as they spoke, the captives forgotten. They must not have seen Efe push him. After a while, the men separated and gestured at us to reform our line and resume our journey. Unlike the ants or we Kanaians would do, they left Rotten Teeth behind.

As we passed the body, I scooped up the satchel and threw it around my neck. I whispered to Efe, "How did you know the ants would kill him?"

"You're not the only one who knows the forest."

❧

We waded through the River Ome, the water rising to our waists. On the savanna, the tall grass caressed our legs. An ostrich foraging for food near the undergrowth bolted away. A herd of giraffes devoured the leaves of an acacia tree, paying us no heed.

We arrived at a clearing before nightfall, and the Portuguese gestured for us to stop and sit. We warriors hesitated, then did so. The Portuguese butted the captives who didn't sit quickly enough in the stomach with their muskets, forcing them down. Their grunts and yelps were painful to my ears.

Azeze wouldn't stop staring at me. I pretended not to notice.

The captors handed out flimsy bowls with a modest serving of sorghum—a fraction of a warrior's daily diet—without utensils or anything to drink. I hadn't eaten with my fingers since I was an infant. On the journey here, many of us scooped up handfuls of fresh river water to quench our thirst. In the preceding days, at my direction, the warriors had eaten their fill and drunk as much water as they could absorb to ready themselves for this journey. We'd be fine for a few sunrises. The sweet, nutty grains would have been easier to chew with something to drink, though.

"Where are we?" whispered Kunto.

"We've traveled in a straight line!" I said.

Kayin shook her head. "Good thing I was born first, or we'd have never made it out of the womb."

"South of Banaan," Efe said.

"Thanks." Kunto stared at her bowl. "This will not fill me."

"It's all we have," I said. "Eat."

A pale man went behind a tree…to urinate, I presumed.

He did not return. Blue Eyes sent someone else to retrieve him. When he also failed to return, the remaining Portuguese gathered. They spoke in whispers, their eyes flicking toward the trees, thinking a leopard had taken the missing men. Blue Eyes didn't send anyone else to search for them.

Efe said, "I wonder what happened to them."

"It wasn't a leopard," I replied.

There had been no sounds of an altercation.

While we ate, the sun—a bright ball of orange—descended into the earth, the sky bleeding hues of orange and red like the canna lilies' flowers in the Obieze Garden. A sight I'd taken for granted.

After the meal, the captives, still chained together, lay on the soft grass. Although I preferred to sleep on my back, I lay on my side to listen for the vibrations that signaled the approach of dangerous animals. I had taken my comfortable bed in the obieze for granted, as well.

Our captors took turns sleeping, leaving an insufficient number of them to stand guard. We did not try to escape.

Despite the swoosh of the tall, swaying grass and the crickets' serenade, sleep didn't come easily that night.

⌇

From the grasslands, we trekked through a woodland much denser than the Kanaian Forest, crossed a freshwater swamp and more land, then forded a thigh-high saltwater marsh. Mosquitoes feasted on our skin. The Portuguese slapped their own faces and arms to bat them away. The insects stole our blood, also, but our shackled hands prevented us from disturbing their feast.

After four sunrises, I stepped upon tiny crystals that yielded to my feet; I had learned about these from Ndidi's stories. I scrunched them up between my toes and released them, the sand warming my feet as it coated my skin. A black and white feather lay nearby. Next to it was the hard covering of a sea animal. Although it was hotter here than in Kana, a cool breeze blew off the ocean. It smelled different from the River Ome. Like salt.

An enormous wave roared toward us. Ndidi had told me that the ocean possessed a strength a thousand times greater than the River Ome's, but these waves crashed with a power beyond what I'd envisioned from her tales. The wave diminished as it reached the shore, and then receded along with the crystals—as if the sea didn't wish to let them go—leaving the sand darker than it was where I was standing. Another white-capped swell formed before the last had fully retreated.

Efe bumped me with her shoulder. "Why did you stop?"

"It's beautiful," I said, my mouth dry.

We'd drunk nothing since we'd waded through the freshwater swamp.

Efe looked at the ocean. Sunlight picked up the red hues in her hair. "Sounds like something I would say." She inclined her head. "And did you see those palm trees?"

A pale man took a few steps our way, gun held over his shoulder. The trees' fronds made me think of an attendant fanning my mother while she strolled through the compound. I swallowed hard as Efe and I resumed walking. The man stopped and eyed our progress.

All the Kanaians survived the journey, except for the villager who had fallen on the first day, collapsed again the next, and never risen. He had been healthy when selected; perhaps his heart had given out from the ordeal. Some Kanaians had wept at his passing. The pale men had allowed us to cover the body with leaves and soft dirt, which would not have protected him from the animals…but we had no digging tool with which to bury him. Yetunde, the priestess' daughter, had said a few words. Though our mission was greater than one person, his loss was no less a loss. I hoped it would be our last.

We also lost two more Portuguese. Upon hearing noises in the woods, Blue Eyes had sent them to investigate. He wanted to capture more people to make up for the captive who died. But those men never returned, either.

A structure made of stone and wood loomed ahead. It was twice the size of the obieze. The building possessed several wings, many arched windows, and turrets. Ndidi referred to it as "the castle," where the Portuguese stored gold, ivory, cloth, and other items received in trade until shipping them to Portugal. She had told me that the six cannons jutting out of the walls were a recent addition. They didn't face inward toward the land to protect the castle from provincial attackers, but outward to the sea—to the competition. To safeguard the goods within from other European countries.

Closer to the building, the terrain changed from soft crystals to hard sand and dirt. I took in one more glimpse of the sea before the pale men led our caravan past a tall pole where the Portuguese flag snapped in the strong breeze.

The mammoth castle doors opened, and another group of Portuguese streamed outside, their muskets drawn. Efe squeezed my hand. I squeezed back before extricating mine. I might need it.

A gray-haired older man in beige leg coverings and a billowing white shirt surveyed us. To Blue Eyes, he said, "So many women."

"We grabbed plenty of men."

"Looks like you lost some of ours."

"Animals got them."

The Kanaian captives observed this exchange. I was the only one who understood Portuguese. I shifted my weight from one leg to the other. I didn't want to go through those doors.

"Our job is done," Blue Eyes continued. "They're yours. I need a bath and a drink." He scanned our faces until his gaze settled on Abeni. "And a woman."

His expression needed no translation. Kayin stepped forward, her progress halted by the chain connected to Kunto. Blue Eyes smirked at her and resumed walking. The men who accompanied him followed, blocking the ones from the castle from firing at us. The eyes of my landswomen and men flitted to the palm trees behind us. To escape. To freedom.

A whoosh came from overhead. A spear sliced through the air and landed in the middle of Blue Eyes's back. He grunted, toppled forward, and struck the hard sand face first. Kayin grinned.

A slew of spears hit Blue Eyes's men.

"Lower yourselves!" I ordered the captives as I yanked Efe to the ground.

Chains clanked as they complied.

The pale men in front of the castle raised their muskets.

"Don't hit the goods!" yelled the older man. "Don't hit the goods!"

He was referring to us.

I risked a glance over my shoulder. A row of women stood near the trees. I closed and opened my eyes. The warriors were still there, wearing the brown and white tunics of the Kanaian army. They ran in our direction, yelling the war cry, and carrying muskets, spears, and swords.

I yanked on the chain but couldn't free myself from Efe. The guards fired. Someone jumped over the captives on the ground. I glimpsed a single lock of indigo-dyed hair. Nsia.

She landed, put a hand on the earth, and spun forward in three full circles, slicing the necks of the gray-haired man and the two pale men on either side of him.

A warrior with a spear followed her, cutting down another man. The remaining Portuguese fired and our warriors fired their muskets in return. I shifted my body on top of Efe, my arms encircling her head. Dirt and sweat and sand matted her long, beautiful braids. She no longer smelled like berries.

A warrior took a musket ball in the stomach. She screamed and fell. I prayed for her and vowed revenge in her honor.

A man opened the castle door, peeked out at our army, and shut it, staying inside. One Portuguese guard tried to open the door from the outside, but it was locked. A few swore and ran for the side of the building. Two warriors fired their muskets, and the pale men dropped to the ground.

The stench of gunpowder, blood, and death permeated the air. In the stillness, the sound of footsteps on the hardened sand approached from behind me, the thump of a cane accompanying every second step.

I rolled off Efe. General Udo's pitted face hovered above me.

I pushed myself up into a seated position. "What are you doing here?"

"Your plan needed a modification."

I studied the doors I'd vowed not to enter. She was right,

but I would not admit that to her. I spit sand out of my mouth. "It was *our* plan. You didn't give it a chance."

She clasped my hand and hauled me to a standing position. The attached chains dragged Efe up, too.

Udo's breath tickled my ear. "Oh, I'd planned to, *Princess*."

"Why are you here, then?"

"Adebola didn't trust you to accomplish this mission on your own."

"I don't believe you."

"I'm your commanding officer. Why would I lie?" Udo snapped. "She sent us to follow you. 'Failure is not an option,' she said."

# Chapter Eleven

# We will never leave...

A WARRIOR WHO'D come with General Udo stepped over pale men's bodies until she reached Blue Eyes. She crouched next to his corpse and took out keys from the pouch in his leg coverings. She drifted from one captive to another, rising and lowering herself like a butterfly, and freed us from the chains. I'd been chained for four sunrises; it was enough. I'd never allow myself to be captured again.

Rubbing my raw wrists, I stared at the immense castle. "How will we take this building, General?"

She pointed at a warrior who had retrieved another set of keys from the deceased gray-haired man. "Through the front door."

Nsia strode over to me, her sword sheathed. "The queen told me to give you this."

She handed me my scabbard. Inside was my daga.

I gripped the familiar heft of the lion-engraved brass handle. I tapped my heart with my fist. "Thank you."

She nodded and walked away.

The recently arrived warriors handed out the rest of the weapons, helmets, and breastplates they'd brought with them on a cart.

The warriors gathered behind the one with the keys. After she'd inserted two different keys in the iron lock without success, the third one made a satisfying click. We rushed in, aiming our weapons high and low. The entrance was circular, with a stone floor and a high thatched roof supported by thick wooden beams.

A shot came from the hallway. The man who fired it ran before we returned fire.

"Go!" yelled Udo. Two warriors went after him. "But let him live!"

"Why?" I asked her.

"He'll tell others what happened here, and what will happen to them if they attempt to kidnap Kanaians in the future."

I signaled to the general where I was headed, taking with me a warrior armed with a musket and Kayin with one sword. I gripped my daga, and we descended the stone steps. No candles lit our way. The air was putrid. We arrived at an arched door with an unclasped lock. Shielding my body against the wall, I pushed the door open and peeked inside.

Massive rocks formed the walls. Light seeped through the vents near the ceiling. The heat was stifling. The stench of sweat, human waste, and fear lingered in the empty room. The thumping of my heart overpowered my queasiness. Overhead, a lone musket rested against the railing of a wooden balcony. I wasn't sure how they expected us all to fit into this room.

I returned to the main floor. A warrior standing in the

entranceway told me that aside from the deceased pale man who'd fired when we entered, the castle was empty. I asked where the general was. She pointed outside. I scanned the area. Warriors clustered together, talking and eating agbalumos and other fruits that Udo's party had brought in the cart. Kunto stood apart, juggling three musket balls. Efe sat under a palm tree, hugging her knees and talking to herself. I didn't see Udo. I walked to the side of the building. She stood alone by a palm tree facing the ocean. The setting sun reflected off the water.

A seagull mewed as it flew by. After the dungeon's odor, the breeze and scent of the sea were a balm on my body and mind. I walked across the hard-packed sand to the general.

"Why didn't she tell me the entire plan?" I asked.

"It's a wonder we all don't live here." She turned to me. "She believed the Portuguese wouldn't suspect they were being followed."

"That doesn't explain why she didn't tell me."

"You would have acted differently. She did not want to alert them."

My cheeks burned. "Do you trust me, General?"

Udo smiled. "I don't trust anyone. But your mother was always a good planner. I've learned much from her."

A reminder that prior to becoming queen, my mother was a Kanaian officer.

"And a good warrior," Udo continued, "and I expect nothing less from you." She pointed to the ocean. "Your transport awaits."

In the distance, a lone ship bobbed in the water.

❧

That evening, using the castle guards' plain soap, we washed ourselves in the ocean, but I yearned for a bath. To inhale the fruity aroma of karite soap and feel a soft cloth on my body.

The next sunrise, two row boats departed from the ship and headed toward the shore. When they reached it, four pale men disembarked, crossed the sand, and opened the thick wooden door to the castle's dungeon. They yelled in Portuguese for us to come out. Silence met their request.

"I'll get them," a man said and stepped inside. "What the…"

Expecting to see dirty, exhausted, chained people, he was looking into an empty room. The warriors streamed around both sides of the building, not giving the men a chance to raise their muskets. We cut them down with ease. Another four men remained in the boats, their hands raised, under the watchful eye of six Kanaian warriors.

Salty air rolled off the sea. I paused as the sun warmed my face, and the wind whispered in my ear. The ship was in the same place as it had been the previous evening.

Udo hobbled over to me. "This is where we part."

I burrowed my toes in the sand. "I'd like to bring Nsia with us."

Udo glanced over at Nsia, who was watching us—arms crossed over her chest, mouth puckered, her single lock of hair hanging down the center of her forehead. She stood too far away to hear that she was the subject of our discussion.

"I'm not sure she's ready. One day, she'll be one of our best."

"More reason for her to join us."

Udo hesitated. "Very well." She stepped back and saluted me. "Good luck, Lieutenant Colonel."

I saluted her in return.

The general climbed into a hammock carried by four warriors. Two others carried the deceased warrior, and the rest of them and the villagers, except for one, took off running for the palm trees toward Kana. Mukki, who managed a popular stall in the Kanaian market, wanted to remain with us because he thought he could be of use. A part of me wished I were going with the rest of them.

As I walked toward a canoe bobbing on the sea, the warm water reached my knees, my feet sinking into the yielding sand. I'd never been in a boat. Kanaians were land people. A Portuguese man in our canoe showed us how to use the oars. He was not being kind. The tip of Nsia's sword was a fingerbreadth from his neck, and Itoro sat growling nearby, the handle of her hatchet resting on her shoulder.

At first, our movements were awkward, especially Efe's. We rowed out of synchronization, slapping our oars against the water without rhythm, until we realized the canoe traveled faster and straighter when we paddled together.

Azeze was on the opposite side of the boat from me. As he rowed, his muscles flexed and relaxed. A stirring sneaked into my heart. He must have sensed me watching him, because he turned around. I studied the bald head of the warrior seated in front of me.

A gray fin attached to the largest fish I'd ever seen—two to three times the size of a woman—jutted out of the clear blue sea. Another fin surfaced. And another.

One of them broke through the water's surface and looked at me as if I were its next meal. It bumped the canoe with its conical snout, showing me its tough skin and rows of serrated teeth. I recoiled, my heart pounding. A Kanaian man screamed. Minister Ndidi had never told me about these monstrous fish! They were nothing like the friendly fish I'd swum with in the River Ome. I stopped rowing. I was not the only one. Everyone displayed the same expressions of horror, although Efe squinted, as if studying the animal.

The pale man rose and gesticulated to us to resume rowing, which we did at a frantic pace. Anything we confronted on the ship would be better than meeting one of these fish face-to-face.

As we came closer to the ship, I ignored the fish and shielded my eyes from the glare of the rising sun. The castle, sand, and palm trees were far away.

We were on our own.

※

At the pale man's direction, we maneuvered the rowboat beside the ship. I told him to act as if nothing were wrong, or he would join the menacing fish in the sea. He jerked at the sound of his language coming from my lips.

Waves slapped against the ship's hull. Round windows peeked above the waterline. I craned my neck. The ship was four times as long as a Banaan boat and at least eight times as high. Two Portuguese words I didn't recognize were painted in black near the bow.

Pale men looked down at us from the ship's railing. Their unshaven cheeks shone bright red; their hair was long and stringy.

A man's gaze met mine. Like the rest of them, he wore canvas breeches and a white linen shirt with a collar. The black hair on his chest showed above the low neckline. He pointed at me and elbowed the man next to him. They both laughed. What was so humorous?

I memorized their faces.

Thin blankets we'd brought from the castle hid our tunics. The warriors who'd accompanied Udo had brought fresh ones. Although I was nervous about leading my first battle, I didn't show it. I nodded imperceptibly to my sister warriors. The tip of a warrior's knife graced the belly of the pale man in the canoe to remind him not to shout out a warning.

I stood and threw off my blanket, and yelled, "Ike!" The war cry.

I grabbed the rope ladder attached to the ship and scaled it, as I'd done many times in mock battles on the obieze training ground. Itoro and Nsia were behind me. All my nervousness was gone. My sense of purpose returned, overshadowing the lingering doubt caused by my mother's lack of faith in me. I grasped the ship's rough wooden railing and catapulted myself over it, dropping onto the deck. Kayin and Kunto arrived on the opposite side.

Pigs and fowl roamed the planks. The crewmen were shorter than us. Most were around my age, although some were older, the youngest not yet a man. Armed with muskets, swords, or pistols, they stood motionless in surprise. Recovering, they shouted at each other to draw their weapons.

The man who had laughed at me earlier fumbled for the gun holstered against his hip. I seized my daga and stabbed him in the heart. He made a gurgling sound, blood escaping his lips, and when I retracted the knife, he collapsed onto the deck. My first kill.

Nsia spun in a half circle, her lock of hair flying and her sword's blade glinting in the sunlight as she slashed the throats of the two men close to her. They fell. Abeni twirled her spear three times and felled another man with it.

Kayin and the rest of the warriors approached the Portuguese from behind. Kayin glanced at me to see how we were faring. A few men turned to face them. A sailor grasped his cutlass, the lanyard on the handle secured around his wrist. He swung it at Kunto.

"That won't stop me." She raised her musket and fired, shooting him between the eyes, the gunshot booming in my ears. He dropped. What remained of his head thudded against the ship's wooden planks.

Kayin slashed a man with her sword, spun, and lunged at another coming up behind her. The sword's tip found its mark.

A sailor walked backward, turned—his cap falling off— and hurried toward a three-spear-length-high wall that divided the ship horizontally and stuck out two feet over the water on each side. He held a set of keys that, moments earlier, were jangling on a ring attached to a rope around his waist. Itoro rushed after him, dove, and shouldered him to the deck. She plunged her taloned nails into his cheeks. He howled and covered his face with his hands. She hacked at his chest with her hatchet. Blood spurted from the handbreadth wound.

The remaining crewmen dropped their weapons and raised their hands. A few warriors collected the weapons.

I allowed myself a tight smile. I'd won my first battle.

Kunto held up her musket and pointed it at the men.

Efe grabbed her arm. "Don't shoot them! We need them to show us how to steer the ship."

Although Efe had learned how to throw a daga, she'd stayed out of the fray.

"She's right." I sheathed my daga. To the men, I said, "Who's your leader?"

A pot-bellied man with ruddy cheeks, a beard, and shoulder-length hair stepped forward. He wore a broad-brimmed hat, a linen shirt and breeches, and foot coverings that rose to his ankles rather than the leather slip-on ones the crew wore.

He held my gaze. "*Capitão* Francisco de Silva."

"Princess Chibuike of the Queendom of Kana."

"*Princesa?*"

I nodded.

He shook his head and let out a stream of Portuguese. We'd heard similar curse words from the men who captured us in Kana.

"You don't look like pirates," he said.

"Pirates?"

"Thieves."

"We're not here to rob you. We're looking for someone who was captured."

He glanced at a square hole cut into the floor and covered by metal bars. Water sloshed against its curved lips. "When?"

"Twelve full moons ago. From Banaan."

He exhaled meat and mead. "That would have been my countrymen."

"Where would they have taken the Banaans?"

"To New Spain."

"We want to go there."

His mouth gaped. "You want to *stay* on the ship?"

"Yes."

"They won't be there."

"How do you know?"

"The English intercepted that ship."

"English." The word was unfamiliar on my tongue. "Where did they take them?"

"The Colony of Virginia."

"Where's that?"

"In English North America."

"Take us there."

He hesitated. "Will you pay?"

I glared at him. "Letting you live is payment."

After a long moment, he turned and shouted commands to the remaining crew.

They stood still. No one had ever looked at me with hatred. A sudden coldness spread throughout my body. I didn't understand why they hated me. They did not know me.

Nsia extended the tip of her sword to Silva's throat. *"Vamos!"* he exclaimed.

The sailors scattered, and the warriors followed them.

One sailor stayed behind. "I won't sail for them," he spat.

"You'll do as I say," I said.

Itoro took two steps and plunged her nails into the recalcitrant sailor's neck. Blood gushed from the five holes in his skin. She pushed him and he stumbled and fell, writhing on deck.

The captain removed his hat and ran a hand through his long hair before donning it again. Nsia kept her sword pointed at him as he stepped to the large wooden wheel and grasped two of the handles.

A loud sound rang out, like the pulling of a long chain.

"What's that?" I yelled.

Silva called over his shoulder. "The anchor. It keeps the ship stationary."

Sailors scampered up and down four joined rope ladders;

they reminded me of the red ants. They set the three large white canvases into position. The Portuguese flag waved in the gusty wind from the top of the highest pole. The ship was moving.

I went to the railing. Across the sea, the castle was a small dot. I couldn't see the trees.

Many of the Kanaians joined me. I was leaving my home. My land. I wanted to dive into the water and swim back to my homeland, despite the dangerous fish. I wiped the moisture from my eyes, not wanting to give the warriors any reason to doubt our course of action.

Kayin looked at me.

"Salt water," I said.

A few warriors' lips quivered. Itoro's eyes were round. We stared at our land until it was a speck, until we could no longer see it. Until we were surrounded by the blue of the ocean below and of the sky above.

Kunto approached me. "Lieutenant Colonel Chi? I must show you something."

# Chapter Twelve

# ...a sister warrior behind

KUNTO LED ME to the square hole in the floor Silva had glanced at earlier. Kayin and Itoro followed us. As we drew closer, an odor reminiscent of the stench in the castle's dungeon hit us.

The grate was open, the top of a metal ladder visible.

I crouched and peered inside, blinking to make sure my eyes weren't deceiving me. "My goddesses!"

Bodies. Many bodies. Naked and slick with sweat, legs and arms covered in sand. Chained at the wrists and ankles, the chest of one lay flat against the back of another. I heard a cough. Moaning. Whimpering. A child's crying. I fought the bile rising in my throat.

This could have been our fate.

Itoro joined us and cursed loudly at the sight.

My hands were shaking. I beat down the rage that was rising within me. I had to lead. "Itoro. Go down. One of the keys you found should free them." I pointed at Kayin and Kunto. "Go with her!"

They disappeared down the ladder.

Efe hastened over and looked down. "Are those my people? Fatimata's?"

"I don't know."

Azeze came and looked into the hold. He waved over Mukki, the other Kanaian man who remained.

I shimmied down the ladder rungs, which were slippery under my bare feet. The floor below was slick with sweat, urine, and excrement. I refrained from pinching my nose. The odor of human waste, mingling with that of suffering and despair, threatened to swallow me whole and empty my stomach of its contents; but now was not the time to be sick or weak.

Itoro found the correct key and freed a woman who had been crying plaintively.

"Where are you from?" I asked.

"Aon."

Azeze helped her to her feet, her legs wobbling, and guided her to the ladder. "Take your time," he said.

He held the woman's waist as she grabbed one rung with a shaky hand. After a few rungs, her steps became surer, and he let go. She climbed the rest of the way unassisted until she reached Mukki at the top and clasped onto his outstretched hand.

As Itoro freed each person, Azeze and I assisted them up the ladder. Did he mold steel as gently as he handled humans?

We rescued forty individuals from the hold. No one had died, praise goddesses.

Back on deck, I ordered several warriors to find the sailors' accommodations and retrieve their clothes.

"They need food," Efe said, her voice quiet.

Mukambu was bent over an Aon man, examining his wounds.

Captain Francisco de Silva's face paled further at our discovery.

There was a pounding in my ears as I stomped over to him.

He retreated and eyed the daga in the scabbard at my waist. "I—"

"You are a monster." I punched him in the nose.

He fell. The crew did not come to his aid. Because they didn't like or respect him, or because the warriors were pointing weapons at them, waiting for a signal from me.

"Lieutenant Colonel?"

I rubbed my fist, wondering whether I'd broken any bones. I turned. Itoro and Kunto were holding an overweight, yellow-haired man in food-stained clothing.

"We found him in the kitchen," Kunto said. "What should we do with him?"

Kayin and Efe joined us.

"Tie him up with that rope over there," I replied.

"But who will prepare our meals?"

"What if he puts something in our food?" countered Efe.

"Efe's right," I said. "We can't take the chance. We'll prepare our own meals."

Kayin looked at me askance. "When did you last prepare a meal?"

"The same time as you, I'd suspect. Tie him up."

Efe stared at the sailors' corpses strewn across the deck. "And them?"

Without a word, Itoro and Nsia lifted a body and swung him overboard. Azeze and Mukki grabbed another one. They dispatched four more bodies. The man Itoro had clawed was alive, his breath labored. Itoro wore a question on her face.

"Throw him over," I said. "But kill him first. We're not savages."

"Where was he running off to earlier?" asked Kunto.

She walked over to the prostrate figure and picked up the keys lying next to him.

"Don't get lost," Kayin said.

Kunto shot her a look, unlocked the door of the wall bisecting the ship, and passed through it. Itoro moved toward the dying man.

Kayin held up her hand. "I'll take care of this, Lieutenant."

"I can do it," Itoro said.

"You'll make a mess." Kayin rolled him over and dealt him a quick, efficient sword stroke to the stomach. Not a drop of blood soiled her tunic. After she removed the blade, Itoro threw him overboard.

At the railing, the wind whipped my tunic. The pale men's bodies bobbed on the waves. I squinted and spotted something cutting across the water in the ship's direction: a gray fin. The fish's snout rose out of the water and its mouth opened to display row upon row of jagged teeth. It bit off one man's arm and half his torso, thrashing its head from side to side. Other fins sped toward the site. Teeth tore into flesh—a leg devoured, a head snapped off—the sound of gnashing overtaking the noise produced on board.

"We hunted the hunters," I said.

"What?" asked Kayin.

I shook my head. "Something Udo said."

We did not turn away until there were no body parts left floating on the blood-darkened sea. I didn't feel empathy for the Portuguese. I suspected they and many sailors before them had meted out this same treatment to women and men and children from villages on our continent.

The door in the wall creaked open. Kunto stepped through it and walked over to us.

"Where have you been?" I asked.

"The gun room."

❦

The Aons and Kanaians ate an evening meal of salted meat with rice—what the crew would have eaten—prepared by Mukki. It didn't smell or taste as good as the food served in the obieze, but it was tolerable.

We Kanaian officers and Efe sat together, while the warriors ate in small groups. Unable to hear their conversations, I presumed they couldn't hear ours. Some warriors guarded the sailors bound near the high wall. The captain and the remaining crew received the former captives' food: a mash of beans, rice, and corn.

The sun was low in the sky.

"How's the hand?" asked Kayin.

"Mukambu said it's not broken." I flexed it. It still throbbed. "We must decide the fate of the sailors."

She yawned. "They planned to sell us into slavery. We should kill them."

"Few of us have been on a boat," said Efe, "much less a ship. We should learn how it operates."

I flicked off the sea salt that had settled on my arm. "We'll figure it out."

"How?"

I tapped my temple. "The same way one figures everything else out."

"The Aons must have some experience."

The Aons remained on one side of the ship. Clothed and fed, they had spoken little, still distressed by their ordeal.

A pale man looked over at us. Although he did not speak Kanaian, I said, "Let's cease discussing this for now."

When we finished eating, Efe and I walked over to the Aons. I told them we wanted to go to English North America. "Can any of you navigate this ship?"

None of them raised their hands or acknowledged my question.

"Your village abuts a river," Efe pressed. "Some of you must have sailing experience."

Silence.

At last, a stocky man, clad only in the trousers of a crewman, spoke up. "We want to return to Aon."

"That's not possible," I said.

"Don't you know who she is?" asked Efe.

He glanced at the rest of the Aons and eyed me. "We do not obey a woman's commands. Only our king's."

I recalled what my mother had told me concerning Aon's monarch: she suspected he'd been exchanging his residents for guns.

"King Bamidele is the reason you're here," I said. Their looks were blank. "Who do you think sold you?"

The Aons glanced at each other with confused expressions.

A woman hissed. "How do we know you're not like your general?"

*Udo?*

"We won't help you," the man said.

From behind me, Itoro grunted and stepped forward.

I touched her arm. "No, Itoro. We will not harm people like us. We'll find another way."

&

"Show us how to navigate the ship," I demanded.

Captain Silva had been at the helm, with the tip of Nsia's sword at his neck for motivation. But we needed to learn, in case something happened to him.

It was the day after we'd invaded the vessel, and I was standing beside the captain. The sun, unfiltered by clouds, beat down upon our heads and arms, while the wind sprinkled us with salt.

The ship's officers were grumpy. Silva had informed me they enjoyed a dram of whiskey prior to the start of their day; we forbade them this for fear they would become unruly. The warriors pointed weapons at them as they worked. We had slept on deck and taken turns guarding the crewmen throughout the night.

The captain showed me and Kayin how to steer, and Efe how to read the rudder that contained the sailing directions, tide tables, and maps. A compass in a wooden box indicated direction, with a fleur-de-lis showing which way was north. Efe appeared to possess an aptitude for languages; she nodded as he spoke to her in Portuguese, though many hand gestures were involved. She hadn't studied under Ndidi as I had, but it was just as well. I couldn't imagine Efe any smarter than she already was. I translated when I could.

Captain Silva explained to her how to anticipate storms and look out for pirate ships. Earlier, he'd taught us how to check the lines and hoist the sails. The letters on the side of the ship spelled its name, the *Isabella Maria.*

Efe pointed at an instrument. "What's that?"

"An astrolabe," the captain responded.

"What does it do?"

"It shows latitude." He moved his finger east to west and showed her how the pointer indicated our position by the degrees around the edge of the disk. "But not longitude." He gestured north to south. "That we guess."

"Guess? There must be a way to figure that out."

He furrowed his brow and looked at me.

"If anyone can," I said, "she can."

With one hand on the wheel, Kayin listened to this exchange. "We're learning his language. He should learn ours instead."

"It's better he doesn't. There might come a time when we don't want him to know what we're saying."

Kunto came up to us. "Excuse me, Lieutenant Colonel Chi. You wanted to inspect the gun room."

"Yes. Kayin, take over."

Her chest visibly expanded by a fingerbreadth as she looked out to the sea.

Kunto led me across the sun-warmed planks to the barricado, the wall that divided the ship. On previous voyages, it had been used to separate men and women captives. The netting surrounding the vessel prevented them from jumping overboard.

The room was below the stern and smelled of gunpowder. There were wooden shelves stacked with at least thirty muskets, fifteen swords, and twenty cutlasses. I picked up a cutlass with an iron hilt and guard. Its blade curved. But its edge was dull, and the weapon was heavy. Despite their subpar quality, it didn't hurt to have these extra weapons in case of an attack—though I wasn't worried about pirates. Or anyone else. We were the elite warriors of Kana.

Invincible.

※

As I returned to the deck, Efe yelled, "Chibuike!"

She stood still at the ship's wheel, staring at the compass.

I hurried over to her. "What's wrong?"

Efe looked up. "We're not going west."

I didn't need an instrument to show me that. The sun was approaching its apex on my right. Before Silva blinked, my daga graced his throat. A pinprick of blood formed and dribbled down his neck.

"Ouch!"

"Where are you taking us?" I asked.

The hatred we'd seen in his crew's eyes flashed in his. "To Portugal," he admitted. His breath reeked of rum. "Our country also needs slaves. Someone will pay."

Aba! This was my reward for trusting him.

Efe's eyes widened. "Why would you do this?"

"It's his nature," Kayin said.

"Itoro! Kunto!" I shouted. "Put him in the hold."

"No!" Silva shouted. "I'll steer us back on course. I promise."

Itoro and Kunto looked at me.

"Seize him," I commanded.

Each of them grabbed an arm and pulled his bulky frame toward the grate.

"We should kill him," Kayin said, "so he can't betray us again."

"I'll consider his fate later. Kayin, turn the ship so the sun is at our backs."

I walked over to the ship's crew, who had been observing our exchange with their captain. "Which one of you wants to eat proper food?"

All but the youngest sailor stared at me with scorn.

"I'll help you," he said.

The others cursed him vehemently.

I called over several warriors. "Take the rest of them to join their captain in the hold. Time spent down there might elicit their cooperation."

I scanned the boy's slight frame and hairless face. "What do you know about sailing?"

"My father was a captain. I'll be one, too, someday."

I studied his guileless expression, wondering if he would become a slave trader like Silva. But he wasn't like him yet. And we could prevent him from becoming so.

"Come with me."

## Chapter Thirteen

# Each one is precious...

MUKKI, WHO HAD cooked on the first night, continued to do so for the duration of the journey, though we didn't have enough food to sustain us until we reached our destination. The captain had planned on feeding only the edible food to the crew. There was, however, plenty of water, whiskey, and rum.

We collected buckets of seawater every four sunrises for bathing. Silva and the crew were still in the hold. We fed them twice a day and provided buckets into which they could urinate and defecate.

The Aons continued to chafe at my leadership. Azeze tried to convince them to listen to me. Although I appreciated his efforts, I didn't need the Aons' support. I just wanted them to stay out of my way. So far, my actions had been decisive, even when I was uncertain—the sign of a good leader. My mother and the general would be pleased.

We resumed training in the limited space, gathering on deck every morning for exercises. Azeze trained with us, bare-chested, looking like a god. But we couldn't train all day, so we danced, sang, played games, and told stories to pass the time. Efe sat alone, reading books she found in our cabin. She increased her proficiency in the Portuguese language.

One morning, as I finished donning my tunic, someone knocked on the door. Efe woke as I went to open it. It was Kayin. Her face was strained.

"What is it?" I asked.

She hesitated. "You're needed."

I frowned. Efe sprung from the bed and dressed. Kayin wasn't one to ask for help. We followed her to the main deck, where a few people gathered at a respectful distance around a figure lying on a hammock. It was Abeni.

"What's the matter?" I asked.

Abeni clutched her chest. "The pain."

Sweat dotted her forehead. She'd lost weight. There was a new sharpness to her cheeks.

"Rest. Someone can cover your duties.

"Shouldn't the healer examine her?" Kayin asked.

Whiffs of clouds floated across the sky.

"It's probably seasickness."

During the voyage's first few sunrises, many people had suffered from dizziness and roiled stomachs. They'd retched. Mukambu had deduced that the ship's motion caused this malady. After trying different cures, she discovered two things: when patients focused on the line where water met sky, and ate little, their symptoms abated or disappeared.

"But to ease your mind," I turned to Itoro, "summon Mukambu."

After a cursory examination, the healer told Abeni to rest and drink fresh water.

The next morning, Abeni was again too weak and feverish to rise from the hammock. Sweat plastered her short hair to her head. Her glazed eyes did not recognize me when I inquired about her condition. The stench of excrement and urine filled the air.

Bent over the sick warrior, the doctor pinched her own chin. "I wish I had mango bark to treat her fever."

Kayin touched Mukambu's arm. "Let's take her to my room, where you can examine her in private."

Abeni coughed. Spittle specked with blood escaped the side of her mouth and ran down her chin.

The physician shook her head. I'd seen that look before, when warriors carried ailing obieze residents into her evaluation room. None of them walked out.

"No," I said.

Kayin shot a look at me. "Why not?"

"Mukambu, continue to evaluate her here."

The healer wrapped her hands in cloth and touched Abeni's forehead and neck. She removed the cloths and lifted the patient's tunic to check her chest. After a moment, Mukambu smoothed the clothing back down and lowered her head. Her lips moved. She addressed me.

"I believe it's consumption."

"What's that?"

"A wasting disease that starts in the chest and consumes the entire body."

I waved at the ocean. "How was she afflicted out here?"

"Most likely from a sailor. A cough or a sneeze. I give her a few days. A week at the most."

Kayin's smile was cautious. "To heal?"

"To live."

A hyena-like sound escaped Kayin's lips. She dropped next to the sick woman. "Abeni."

Abeni's eyes were closed. Kayin reached for the young warrior's cheek.

"Don't touch her!" Mukambu said. She softened her voice. "You do not want to become ill."

For three days, Kayin did not eat and barely slept. She sat by Abeni, praying to our goddesses and pressing cold, wet cloths against her forehead and lips. Abeni's body continued to shrink.

I was at the ship's bow late one afternoon when Mukambu shook Kayin awake and said a few words to her. Kayin stood and looked at her friend, whose eyes were unblinking. White foam encircled Abeni's mouth. Kayin didn't lament. Instead, without looking at anyone, she strode to the wooden steps that led to the cabins below.

I was glad Abeni's suffering had ceased, although Kayin's was beginning.

Kunto, standing by me, took a step to follow her sister.

"Kunto, leave her be. Let her grieve alone first."

She looked over to where Kayin had disappeared, moved to starboard, and rested her forearms on the ship's railing. Itoro joined her. They stared out to sea in silence.

The rest of the Kanaians and Efe gathered in a half circle around Abeni.

Yetunde bowed her head. The rest of us did the same.

"Gbadu," she prayed, "Goddess of Destiny, take into your arms Abeni. She was one of us and one of yours. Please watch over her on her journey by way of the sea until she returns to the earth and joins our ancestors."

I nodded at two warriors. They wrapped Abeni's body in

her hammock, lifted her, and carried her to the ship's larboard side. Kunto didn't turn to watch. The women swung Abeni back, then threw her overboard. Her precious body landed with a splash, swaying on the water's surface. Shark fins emerged.

I turned and walked away, heading toward my cabin to avoid seeing or hearing their gnashing.

I was grateful Kayin wasn't on deck to witness it.

⁊

The sadness of Abeni's death lingered after seven sunrises. The warriors' usual banter was absent. The smiles were few. We tried to distract ourselves with training and navigation.

Over time, we acclimated to the ship's rocking, except for the night when the ocean raged, the wind moaned, and the rain pummeled our heads as the *Isabella Maria* listed to a horizontal position. We all clung to whatever stationary object we could find. Many of us disgorged our last meal. Or two.

One night, in the bed we shared in Silva's cabin, I conveyed to Efe my apprehension concerning the boy's help navigating. He had shown the warriors how to set the sails, and a Kanaian warrior remained at the wheel with him while he steered. The ship was on a westerly course, but I still didn't trust him.

Efe shared her theory that the waves moved in relation to the shape of the moon. Although I acted to the contrary, I loved listening to her thoughts and being privy to her intelligence, her fascination with nature.

"What does the moon have to do with my concern?" I asked.

"That Gleti will be our guide. She'll take us where we're meant to go."

"We might need more help than from the Moon Goddess, alone."

The cabin contained a narrow desk attached to the wall and floor, a built-in cabinet to store clothing, and a chamber pot. The musty straw mattress provided scant padding against the wooden bedstead. My daga rested within reach on the metal stand beside it. The flat down pillow offered no comfort. Fingers interlocked underneath my head, I stared up at the ceiling. "Do you know you talk in your sleep?"

Efe rolled over and looked at me. A cloth she'd found in the cabin wrapped her braids piled atop her head. "I do?"

"Even while sleeping, your mind doesn't rest."

"It's when my ideas come." We rocked in silence. "In Asanti, we'd be preparing for our annual craft festival now. Everyone in the queendom brought their handicrafts to the center of the village and displayed them."

"For sale?"

"No. My mother selected the best pieces and rewarded the winners with cowrie shells."

This was the first time she'd spoken of Dayo since the day we found her body. Efe didn't grieve in my presence. Late at night in the obieze, when I couldn't sleep, I would pace the hallways. There would be no light emanating from beneath her bedchamber door, the candle by which she read extinguished. With my ear against the smooth wood, I would listen to her cry. By morning, when we'd gather for breakfast in the private dining room, her tears would have dried. She'd never confided her woes to me, and I'd never mentioned the sounds I'd heard coming from her room.

My thoughts turned to home. To my father and his gentle smile. To how the Great Council was faring without Sola.

Who had replaced the commerce minister? And last, to my mother and whether she was thinking of me.

Efe's face was still wan. Unsure whether she would welcome my next question, I asked, "Do you miss her?"

"Every day. It's not the ruler I miss. She wished one of her sisters had been born first, so she could live without the eldest's responsibilities. She wanted to have fun. I was…ashamed of her flamboyance, her lack of care for the natural world. I regret that." Efe smiled faintly. "She didn't know where my reflective nature came from." She sobered. "It's her, the woman I long for. Her guidance. Her love. Sitting at her loom, surrounded by red and blue and yellow cloth, making our clothing."

"Your *mother* made your clothes?"

A faint smile. "She enjoyed it. As do I. The work is soothing." She glanced at my tunic. "Other colors exist."

"I don't always wear white."

"Chibuike, your brown tunic doesn't count."

The timbers in the cabin's ceiling creaked rhythmically. The sound reminded me of the noise Ndidi's knees made when she rose from a chair.

"I remember when I first mentioned you to my mother," Efe continued. "It was after I met you in the forest. She was weaving. I told her how strange you were." Efe smiled to soften her words. "Throwing that daga of yours and cursing when you missed your target. And your face looked like you had dove into a bush. I asked her why a girl would want to fight. You know what she said?" Tears clung to Efe's lashes.

I didn't *want* to fight. It was a necessity. I shook my head.

"She said 'Sometimes you have no choice. Women have to save themselves.' I asked why I wasn't taught to fight. Like the

Kanaians. And she replied we believe in diplomacy. Fighting with words, not swords. I said, 'Won't the swords always win?'"

Efe's nose was running, and her tears flowed freely.

I wish I could ease her pain. All I could do was protect her and find her people.

"What was her answer?" I asked.

"'Not if you find the right words.'"

◆

Under guard, I permitted Silva and the crew on deck during the day. Most days, Silva sat on the floor near the wheel, drunk, a tankard of rum resting on his sizable belly. I let him drink as much as he wanted to loosen his tongue. He provided guidance to whomever was steering. Efe or I translated.

One evening, I sat next to him, our backs against the side of the ship, Efe seated in front of us.

I held up a jug of grog. "This is not how you like your rum, but it will last longer."

The brown hat Silva wore was askew, and his linen shirt sported a considerable rum stain all the water in the ocean couldn't remove. He hesitated before holding out his tankard with a tanned, sun-wrinkled hand; after refilling it, I poured some of the liquid in a cup for myself and set the jug down on the wooden planks between us. Efe wasn't drinking.

I inhaled the ocean's briny scent. "When will we reach this Virginia colony?"

The sooner we arrived, the sooner we could return home.

He took a long pull of his drink.

"I can get Nsia," I added.

He must have had enough of Nsia's sword. "A few more weeks."

The boy had told us that what they called a *week* equated to seven rising suns.

We'd taken down the netting from the sides of the ship after our first day aboard, and, more recently, we'd loosened our supervision of Silva. We weren't concerned he'd jump. He liked his drink too much. I ordered that he was not to be killed if he troubled us; I still needed him. Although Efe might be right—that Goddess Gleti guided our path—he knew how to reach our specific destination.

"What would have happened when we arrived?" I asked Silva.

"In the New World?"

"It is newer than our world or yours?" Efe asked.

"Well...no...I imagine it's the same age. 'Undiscovered' might be a better way to describe it." Grog spilled over the lip of the tankard and onto his hand, and he licked it off. "They'd have baptized you."

I sipped my drink. The sweet watery taste was not to my liking. "What does that entail?"

"A ceremony. They would sprinkle water on your head, and you'd become a Christian."

"What is a Christian?"

"A person who practices our faith. You would have accepted our god. It's Portuguese law."

I didn't believe what I was hearing. "But why? We have our own goddesses."

Silva shrugged. "Ours is the one true God. The Creator."

"Says who?"

"Well...us."

Efe's brow furrowed. "And your god is a he?"

He scratched his beard. "Of course."

"But only a woman can give birth."

"But God created man first. It's in the Bible."

"What's that?"

"A book. Of stories."

"And who wrote this Bible?" Efe asked.

"Uh…men. Divined by god."

Efe twisted one of her braids. "That reasoning is… circular."

She could debate him all day. I needed to get us back on topic. "What happens after the ceremony?"

"You'd receive new names."

I shook my head at this lunacy. "First, you'd take away our goddesses, then our names? What is wrong with our given names?"

He belched. His breath was foul. "They're not Christian."

I patted my chest. "But they're ours."

"A servant owns nothing."

"Why would we want to be Christians," Efe said, "when they do such awful things?"

Silva opened and closed his mouth.

"What would happen next?" I asked.

"They'd hold an auction." He hesitated. "Sell each of you to the highest bidder."

My stomach heaved. While he drank, I allowed the boat's swaying and the crashing of the waves against the ship's hull to settle me.

"Where were you planning to take us?"

Silva stared into his tankard. "New Spain. Farther than where you want to go."

I gestured toward my landswomen and men on deck, who were talking in low voices or drinking, or both. Others were asleep on the wooden planks or in their hammocks. "What did you expect to receive in exchange for us?"

"Sugar, rum, molasses. The more servants I deliver, the more coin I earn."

Efe eyed him. "Call them what they are: slaves."

He shrugged. "That's what we call them."

"How can you transport human beings to be sold?"

"It's a job like any other."

Stars too numerous to count filled the black sky. The Moon Goddess was still leading us. "What happens when you don't deliver?" I asked.

Silva wiped the excess grog from his saturated mustache. "Not sure." He took another drink. "It won't be good."

"No."

"I have a question for you. What will happen to me? After we arrive."

"I don't know. That's partly up to you."

# Chapter Fourteen

# We, the elite...

I WAS RUNNING on the path that tunneled through the Kanaian Forest. Up ahead, a pale man urinated on the ground. He turned. It was Blue Eyes, but with Silva's face. He snarled, released his member, and reached for the musket strapped to his back. I clasped the handle of my daga. Not the one with the intricately carved lion, but the wooden one my mother had given me when I was a child.

Before I could hurl the knife at him, someone called my name. It was my mother, standing with my Nne Nne Thema, beckoning me to come closer. Why was my mother here? She rarely left the compound these days, but she was yelling.

Ala!

I opened my eyes. I was lying on my side in the bed in Silva's cabin, my legs drawn up, hand at my waist.

"Ala!" came a powerful voice from on deck. Kunto.

I reluctantly released the dream and threw off the threadbare blanket. Efe's side of the bed was empty. I picked up my tunic from the floor where I'd dropped it the previous night, donned it, and grabbed my daga off the nightstand. It was lying next to the chessboard Efe had found in a desk drawer. Silva had taught us how to play over the last fourteen sunrises.

I ran out into the hallway and climbed the stairs.

The crisp air on deck awakened me as I joined Kunto, Efe, and Silva at the ship's bow.

Silva pointed across the calm sea toward a green speck in the distance. The warriors crowded behind us. As the sun climbed above the horizon, a warrior navigated the *Isabella Maria* through the Chesapeake Bay until it met the slow-moving current of a river.

"What's this body of water called?" I asked.

"The James River," Silva replied.

Small boats were docked beneath a pier on which stood many pale men, their facial features indistinguishable from this distance. Behind them loomed high walls, reminiscent of those surrounding the obieze. Beyond, the land was vast, flat, and forested. As the ship approached the shore, the people on the dock waved and cheered. We didn't wave back. The Aons remained starboard, uninterested. Some lay on the deck, feigning sleep.

"We need to drop anchor," Silva said. "The ship's too big to go any closer. The boy can take care of it."

The rest of his crew was still in the hold.

The boy wove through the warriors to the barricado's door, which had remained open since the day Kunto unlocked it.

"Kunto! Itoro!" I said. "Go with him!"

The two officers followed. Although he had safely navigated us here, I still didn't trust the boy. Or Silva. They fooled me once. The anchor made a loud cranking sound as it descended into the water. The ship stopped moving.

I motioned at the land. "Where are we?"

"Fort Point Comfort," Silva responded.

If I wasn't mistaken, his breath didn't reek of rum.

Efe asked, "Is it a place of comfort?"

His look was puzzled.

"If it was," I said, "it won't be. It's been two full moons since we left."

Silva nodded. "Sixty days."

"How long would it have taken your experienced crew to arrive here?"

His weathered face reddened. "Sixty days."

"Hmph."

Several men on the pier jumped into a rowboat and headed for the *Isabella Maria*. What would General Udo do? To my knowledge, she'd never fought on water.

"Kayin!" I called.

She stepped forward. "Yes, Lieutenant Colonel."

I'd spoken little to Kayin since Abeni's death, except for the occasional command. Mukambu recommended she isolate from the rest of us to prevent further spread of the disease. After eight sunrises—the mourning period shortened from the customary moon cycle—she resumed her duties as an officer, overseeing the daily training regimen. But her heart wasn't it. She didn't join us for meals, preferring to eat alone in the cabin she shared with her sister. Kunto told me Kayin hardly ate. Her tight-fitting tunic hung loose on her muscular frame. Kunto said she didn't talk much either, not even to joke with her. I couldn't wait for a smirk to return to Kayin's handsome face.

"Make sure we're ready."

"We are. We'll need to find warmer clothes."

"It'll be our next order of business." I pointed in the direction of the oncoming boat. "After them."

Warriors retrieved additional muskets, swords, or cutlasses from the gun room. Kayin returned with a second sword. One of her swords from Kana rested in the bronze scabbard at her hip.

She slashed the air with the Portuguese one so swiftly the blade was imperceptible. "These aren't as good as ours."

"They'll do," I said.

She caught Nsia watching her. "There are more swords below."

Nsia flipped the lock of hair out of her eyes. "I only need one."

Kayin frowned and lowered her sword.

As the small boat drew closer, its occupants' features became clearer. These men were even paler than the Portuguese. Bushy beards covered their jaws and chins. Their smiles faded as they observed our defiant faces. And stances. A few of them cocked their heads.

They wore dark outer garments—I would learn later they were called doublets—and knee-length breeches. A man with long hair like sheep's wool yelled something, and the men ceased rowing. Gray Hair called up to Silva in a language that was not as melodic as Portuguese.

"What does he speak?" I asked.

"English," replied Silva.

Without taking my eyes off Gray Hair, I said to Silva, "Translate for us. And don't lie. I will know."

I'd become adept at detecting falsehoods after years of standing behind the queen in the Audience Court as she listened to villagers petitioning for forgiveness for their transgressions. Their eyes would shift. Other parts of the body lied, but the eyes spoke the truth.

"He asked, 'Why aren't they in chains? Where are your men?'" Silva said.

"Answer him."

Silva hesitated.

"What say you?" Gray Hair demanded. "Did they sever your tongue, man?"

Silva took a deep breath. "Some are...dead. The others are down below."

"Why, for Christ's sake?" Gray Hair asked.

"They've been...detained."

A reddish-haired man shook his fist. "We have to rescue them."

"And bid on our property," said another.

"Tell them to stay where they are," I told Silva. "Or there will be bloodshed."

Gray Hair yelled, "What is he saying to you?"

During the journey, the warriors' hair had grown out to at least four fingerbreadths. My brass breastplate covered my breasts. Gray Hair believed I was a he.

"I wouldn't come aboard if I were you," Silva called to him. "I've seen these women fight. You can't win."

Gray Hair barked. "Women! Ha! Why didn't you say so?" He looked at the rest of his men. "Take 'em!"

I murmured to Silva, "I tried to warn them. Itoro!"

She hurried to larboard and dropped the rope ladder into the river.

Gray Hair gestured at a man to scale it.

We flashed our weapons. The sound of steel zipping out of

scabbards simultaneously was a song I hadn't heard in so long. Midway up the ladder, the man hesitated.

"Go on!" commanded Gray Hair. "They're women!"

"You're making a mistake," Silva told him, dropping behind us. Smart man.

The other man reached the top of the ladder. Itoro thrust the hatchet into his chest and yanked it out in one efficient motion. He howled and fell backward into the river with a splash, barely missing the rowboat. The men in the boat stared at Gray Hair.

"Thomas, we're not armed!" insisted one. "We've come to collect servants, not engage in a fight. Let's go to the fort and retrieve our weapons."

"All right." Thomas looked up at me. "We'll be back."

As they rowed away, Efe asked, "What do we do now?"

I sheathed my daga. "We wait."

⸙

Light from the rising sun bathed the fort.

I was enjoying the morning's peace and solitude from the bow of the ship when a crowd of men assembled on the pier and along the shore of the James River.

Efe, Kayin, Kunto, and Itoro joined me, along with Silva. The warriors were behind us. Some unarmed Aons stood with them, intrigued by what had happened the previous day. After they had insulted me, I didn't trust them with weapons.

Last night, I'd asked Silva if a ball shot from the ship's cannon could reach the fort.

"No, but you wouldn't want to fire upon it, anyway. Unless you wish to declare war on England."

No, that was not what I wanted. My goal wasn't to take on a country, but to retrieve the Banaans and the Asantis and return home.

The men on the pier climbed into eight boats and rowed to the *Isabella Maria*.

All the warriors, including me, had slept on deck in case the Point Comfort men attacked us during the night. But they hadn't returned.

I puffed out my chest, squared my shoulders, and set my feet a little more than shoulder-width apart. No one spoke as the slow procession of rowboats headed our way. While I waited, I squeezed the lion on the handle of my daga, still in its scabbard.

Half of the boats veered left, the rest right. Thomas's boat stopped below us, his men armed with blunderbusses—short-barreled guns with flared muzzles. Silva whispered to me that these guns were ineffective at long distances. I wasn't sure why he was being helpful. I warily accepted his intelligence.

"We're coming aboard," Thomas said.

Silva translated.

Although they surrounded us, I was as calm as the river.

"You?" I raised an eyebrow. "Or your men?"

A few of his companions snickered.

"Silence!" Thomas bellowed. To me, "All of us."

"Very well."

"This is crazy!" he said to Silva. "Don't they know who we are?"

"They would ask you the same question," Silva replied.

At my signal, Azeze, carrying a spear, lowered the rope ladder starboard, while Itoro dropped one larboard. Several pale men clambered up the ladders onto the ship. Our swords and cutlasses zipped out of our scabbards. A man jumped on deck, pointing his gun at Nsia. "Drop your weapon!" he said.

They didn't want to kill or wound us. That would defeat their purpose. A dead slave was of no use to them.

Nsia drew her sword, spun as if she were in a military parade on the Grand Square, and sliced his neck. He choked out a cry and fell overboard. Two men attacked Kayin. She slashed their throats. They yelled for their god as they plummeted into the river. Efe thrust her daga around but didn't stab anyone. A pale man raised his musket and pointed it at Azeze. He used his spear to knock the gun from the man's hands and jabbed him between the ribs.

Azeze's form was poor.

He looked over at me. "I make weapons. I don't use them."

"Couldn't tell," I said.

We put down man after man. After the twelfth one fell into the river, Thomas yelled, "Retreat!"

This time, instead of watching them depart, I screamed the war cry. My blood pulsed through my body as I ran to the ladder and scrambled down it, several warriors following me.

The Englishmen in the boat stiffened.

"Retreat! Retreat!" yelled Thomas again.

"God help us!" beseeched one man.

Two men grabbed the oars. I dropped into the boat, daga raised, and stabbed them in rapid succession. I had warned the warriors not to use their guns, because I did not want a hole shot in the bottom of the boats. The men from the other boats didn't shoot at us for fear of killing their countrymen.

We dispatched everyone in the boat except for Thomas. I held my knife against the lump on his throat, which I learned later was called an Adam's apple. I yelled up to Silva in Portuguese. "Tell him to order the rest of the boats back to shore and abandon them or he dies."

Silva repeated my demand in English.

The rowboats turned toward the riverbank, save one, helmed by the man with the reddish hair. "They're not coming into the fort, except as servants! Thomas, this isn't about you. Our responsibility is to protect the fort."

Thomas stared at my daga, blinking rapidly. "Do as she says!"

"My duty is to king and country, not to you."

"Please!" He begged the red-haired man, but looked at me.

"This boat stays."

Mucus dripped out of Thomas's nose. "I tried."

Although my mind was resolute, I softened my gaze. "Sometimes, that's not good enough."

A slender hand grasped my arm. "Don't kill him!" Efe said. "He's surrendering."

I shrugged her off. "No, he is saving himself to fight another day."

Thomas's eyes were wide. I didn't want to kill him, but if I did not follow through on my promise, I would lose the respect of the warriors.

I sliced his throat. Blood gushed from the gap. Efe screamed. Thomas gurgled. Itoro growled and pushed him. He toppled backward into the James River. Her action was premature, since he wasn't dead. But he did not resurface.

I pointed at the remaining boat. "Go!"

Two warriors grabbed the wooden oars and rowed. The oars slapped against the water like a drumbeat. My heart pounded to the same rhythm. As we drew next to the vessel,

Itoro leaped into it, her hardened fingernails extended. The seated men gaped at her. I turned to Efe and yelled, "Stay here!"

She opened her mouth to protest.

"No argument," I said.

She exhaled and nodded.

The rest of us jumped into the boat. Before we could draw our weapons, a blast erupted. Everyone stopped moving. My heart felt as though it had stopped beating.

Itoro lay on the boat's floor, grabbing her arm, nostrils flaring as she panted. Blood poured from the gaping wound through her fingers. The man with red hair raised his blunderbuss and cocked back the lock, inserting another bullet.

He pointed the gun at me.

I held my breath, immobile. He grinned, his teeth black. "Ike!"

Our war cry pierced the silence as Kayin flew by me and dove at him. He fired as she slammed into him, both of them tumbling over the side of the boat and into the river.

I ran my hands over my body. No pain. No blood. Although I had been glued in place like the limbs of Yaa's headdress, the shot had missed me.

Kunto's shout of "Kayin!" brought me out of my trance. I scanned the water until I spotted ripples and dove, slicing through the shocking cold.

The river was clear. Kayin was wrestling with the red-haired man, but she was weakening. Though she was the better trained fighter, he weighed more. I swam up behind him and encircled his thick neck with my arm, my other hand clamping onto my wrist, and squeezed. He released her and clutched at my arm, trying to pry it away. He dug his fingers into my forearm. It hurt. But I held on to him with all my strength. It was him or me. He struggled. I squeezed harder.

Every instinct told me to breathe. But if I did, I would die.

I focused on calming myself.

He quit moving. I pushed him away and dove for Kayin's sinking body.

A school of fish dispersed as I swam by them. River water slipped into my mouth. When I reached Kayin, her eyes were closed, her chest still. I grabbed her underneath the arms and kicked, focusing on the light above me. I remembered rescuing Fatimata from drowning in the River Ome a lifetime ago.

As Kayin and I broke through the water's surface, powerful arms pulled her limp body out of the water. Hands yanked at me. They laid us in the boat's belly, the soles of my feet near the crown of her head.

Warriors gathered around me.

I gasped for air. "Don't...worry...about...me. Kayin..."

Kunto dropped next to her twin. "Breathe!"

I raised my head. Kayin didn't move.

"Do we have time to retrieve Mukambu?" asked Efe.

*No.*

The doctor was on the ship, in a cabin below deck. We couldn't take the chance of her being wounded or killed in battle.

"Breathe!" yelled Kunto again.

Kayin did not listen.

"No!" Kunto's jaw clenched, changing her once carefree appearance. She looked more like Kayin than herself. "Don't leave me! Don't leave me!" She pounded her sister's chest in concert. "Don't leave me!"

I shivered. A heaviness permeated my body, as if I were affixed to the bottom of the rowboat with cornstarch paste.

Efe grabbed Kunto's arm and tried to pull her away from Kayin. "She's gone, Kunto. She's gone."

Kunto wailed and fell on top of her sister.

Everyone quieted. Water lapped against the rowboat. A crow cawed in flight.

Our culture revered twins. They were gifts from the goddesses, the older twin the younger one's guardian spirit.

Kunto's guardian spirit had departed. She wept, her shoulders heaving. Itoro glared at the sky, the cords in her neck straining, and cursed at the goddesses. My chest heaved. I lowered my head until it rested at the bottom of the boat and covered my eyes with my arm to hide the tears.

There was a loud gasp, followed by the sound of gushing water. Kunto raised her head to peer at her twin.

Kayin coughed. And coughed again. I sat up.

Kunto gaped at the sight of her sister. "The goddesses! They brought her back to life!"

Kayin muttered something.

Kunto lowered her face to her sister's mouth. "What did you say?"

"Move off me. You're heavy."

# Chapter Fifteen

# ...warriors of Kana

FOR THE PAST two full moons, we'd subsisted on the crew's rations. Now the meat, rice, beans, and biscuits had run out. But if the boundlessness of the pale men's forest was any indication, a variety of food in ample supply awaited us on land.

Many of the warriors spent the rest of the afternoon on deck, rehashing that morning's battle. With no desire to talk to anyone, I retired to my room. Efe must have sensed that I preferred solitude, because she didn't join me. I last saw her talking with Azeze and Mukki about their lives back in Kana.

That afternoon, I sat at the desk in the cabin, writing. When I first appropriated this room, I'd found a goose-feather quill, a glass jar filled with ink, and blank parchment in a drawer. The ink emitted a strange, nutty smell. I'd always been more of a doer than an observer; by consequence, I'd never been much of a writer. I'd discovered, however, that I enjoyed recording my thoughts in the evening. One day I would show my mother these writings.

I wrote about the day's events and how close we came to losing Kayin.

Besides the creaking from the timber ceiling, the only sound in the room was the quill's scratching against the paper.

There was a tap on the door.

"Come in."

The door opened, and Mukambu leaned into the room. She glanced at the sheaf of papers on the desk. "Is it a good time?"

Motioning toward the cabin's other chair, I turned around and straddled the one I'd been sitting on, resting my forearms atop its back. "I'm glad you remained down here during the battle."

"I wouldn't have emerged until you were victorious."

"How would you know when that would be?"

"When the noise ceased."

Rain drummed against the sole window.

"How's Itoro?"

"It was a surface wound. In fact," Mukambu pointed over her shoulder, "she's back at her post, guarding your door."

Without a word spoken between us, Itoro had become my fanti. My protector.

I chuckled. "And Kayin?"

"Better. Her heartbeat is normal. The water she ingested expelled. I rubbed salve on her neck, so the bruises should fade where the man tried to choke her. She'll be fine."

"That is excellent news. If he hadn't almost killed her, her sister would have."

Mukambu's forehead wrinkled. "What do you mean?"

"Kunto was so distraught, she kept hitting Kayin in the chest." I demonstrated. "We believed Kayin had joined our ancestors. Her sister didn't stop hitting her until the goddesses intervened and saved her."

The doctor pinched her cleft chin. "Maybe it wasn't the goddesses."

"What are you saying?"

"Maybe Kayin died, and Kunto brought her back to life."

"*Kunto?*"

Mukambu stood.

"Where are you going?" I asked. *I didn't dismiss you.* I gestured for her to sit. "I've been wanting to ask you about that day in the market. You and Yetunde weren't supposed to be there."

"But we were. Queen Adebola commanded it."

"She did?"

"Yetunde was to provide you with spiritual guidance. The queen said you'd need me and forced me to renounce temporarily my sworn oath of fealty to her."

A lump formed in my throat. "But who is taking care of her?"

"She'd selected someone to replace me for the duration of our mission."

My mother, the planner.

"Though you're the finest physician in the land?"

She bowed her head briefly. "That's why no one else could accompany you but me." She paused. "You're the only child who lived. And the heir to the throne. I'm here to keep you safe. This is my service to her."

I smiled. "And she had spoken."

She grinned. "That, too."

After Mukambu left, my smile faded. An uncomfortable feeling enveloped me as I considered her words. My mother, the queen, believed our need for the best healer in Kana was greater than her own.

✍

With the moon at her peak, the warriors climbed into the boats we'd commandeered from the pale men. We left a few warriors on the ship to guard Silva and the prisoners and to keep a watchful eye on the Aons.

Warriors grabbed the oars.

"Wait!" Kayin stood at the ship's railing, her neck wrapped in cloth. "Lieutenant Colonel Chi, don't leave without me."

"You should rest, Major."

"I'll have plenty of time to rest later. I'm coming with you."

"What if that's an order?"

"I would ask you to reconsider."

Rising, I steadied myself and extended my arm. She came down the rope ladder and hopped into the swaying boat. She clasped my forearm, as I did hers. Long eyelashes framed her hazel eyes, and small brown spots sprinkled the bridge of her nose and cheeks.

"Thank you," I said.

"For what?"

"For saving my life."

"You would have done the same for me."

"Yes, I would have." I gestured at a bench. "Come. Take my seat."

Kunto wasn't the only one who had nursed Kayin while she convalesced. Efe had fussed over her as if they were related. Later, Kayin would tell me, "She took care of me. She holds

150

herself in such high esteem. I tried not to like her, but it's impossible."

We rowed to shore. The smell of fish and algae was pungent, the wind cool. Tiny bumps rose on my arms. I tried to rub them away, without success.

As the boat sliced through the swaying reeds near the riverbank, unfamiliar birds waded through the shallow water. Everything about them was long: their necks, legs, bills, and wings. A fish jumped out of the water and returned with a splash. The ebb and flow of the river left water lines at different levels of the wooden pillars supporting the pier.

We disembarked onto the soft brown soil of a foreign land. A wide dirt path lined with overgrown weeds and sweet-smelling wildflowers separated the fort from the river. I directed some warriors to circle the outside wooden wall. Kayin, Kunto, Efe, Itoro, and I, followed by a group of warriors, climbed a grassy hill and made our way to the large wooden door. I lurched as if I were still on the boat.

There were no symbols tooled into the wood like the lions in the walls surrounding the obieze compound. Above, four cannons jutted out from a curved section of the wall. It surprised me that no one stood guard.

Kayin stared at the imposing edifice. "How will we get in?"

"We can shove the door open with our shoulders," I said.

"Great idea," said Kunto.

Efe tilted her head, scrutinizing the door.

"Efe, we'll handle this," I said.

Kayin, Kunto, Itoro, and I crouched in front of the door. "Ready?" I asked.

Efe strolled past us and pushed it open.

The officers glanced at each other and straightened. Kayin shook her head.

Several buildings were visible in the moonlight. The largest structure had a thatched roof and was three spear lengths high in one part, six in the other, and constructed with two different kinds of wood as if at different times. No sound came from the dwellings. No candles were lit in the windows. The pale men seemed to be asleep.

A shot rang out.

A warrior screamed, grabbed her thigh, and fell. I spotted a musket protruding from a second-floor window before Itoro shielded me as we rushed from the fort. Kunto dragged the whimpering fighter with us. The light from the moon had also provided visibility for our adversaries.

While Kunto placed the wounded warrior in the boat, I pondered our next move.

But we needed food.

I heard a rustling of fabric behind us. I clutched the hilt of my daga. A woman wearing a white blouse and a plain beige wrap around her waist ran toward us. She hadn't come from the front of the fort; there must be another exit. Before she got close, the warriors brandished their weapons and pointed them at her. The woman halted and raised her hands.

She looked like us.

Her hair was parted down the middle, a braid surrounding her head. Her amber eyes, set in an angular face, shone in the moonlight. She looked over my face, my bare arms, and my hair, which I hadn't bothered to comb, much less cut. None of us had wished to shave our heads with the few straight-edged razors we'd found among the sailors' personal items.

"I am from Banaan." The woman's lilting voice carried me home.

My heartbeat accelerated. At last.

"They call me Joan."

I repeated the foreign word. "Joan."

The woman smiled at my expression. "A ridiculous name, isn't it? At least for me."

"I...don't think it suits you. What's your given name?"

"Kifunji," she replied, as if she hadn't said it in a long time. "I serve the general."

"Who?"

"General Thomas."

My mouth fell open. "Thomas was a general? But he let others fight his battles."

A sage smile graced the woman's face. "He calls it 'leading.' May I put my arms down?" I ordered the warriors to lower their weapons. "You said, 'was?'"

"He won't be coming home."

"His wife must have known. She loaded a horse cart with a few belongings and her children and fled."

"We need food and drink, Kifunji."

"How many of you are there?"

"Fifty-four." I remembered the Aons. "Ninety-four."

"In a few hours, many of the men will be asleep or drunk. There's another entrance." Kifunji pointed at the side of the wall. "I'll leave food for you." She gazed at us and broke out into a beatific smile. "It's nice to see our faces again."

❧

Kayin lay on my bed, her long legs crossed at the ankles. "Burn it to the ground."

"But there are innocent people inside," countered Efe, sitting on the edge of the bed, "like Kifunji."

We were back on the *Isabella Maria*. After waiting for a while—I'd neglected to ask Kifunji how long "a few hours" meant—and beginning to doubt she would keep her promise, the side gate had opened. We'd helped her haul out large bags of rice and beans and jugs of ale, loaded them onto the row-boats, and returned to the ship.

After everyone had eaten, the officers and Efe gathered in my cabin. The sweat from our excursions and the yeast from the ale we drank permeated the room, which was too small for the five of us. But I believed it best to meet in private so others could not listen to our deliberations. Itoro stood by the closed door.

"What if Fatimata's there? My family?" Efe asked. "We must talk to Kifunji again."

Kunto sat on the other side of the bed. She adjusted her cartridge belt. "Let's attack at the next new moon. Take them by surprise."

I hid my amazement at Kunto's strategic insight. I was sitting on top of the desk with my bare feet on the chair, holding a tankard. I took a sip of the fruity ale. *Not bad.* "I'm not sure we can surprise them now."

"Let's move the ship closer and fire the cannon," Kayin said.

Silva had told me that the English had crossed the ocean to claim this land and wouldn't forfeit it easily. "If our cannon balls can reach them, theirs can reach us. Efe's right. We should talk to Kifunji before we plan what to do next."

The next day, after the sun had descended, Kayin, Kunto, Efe, Itoro, and I returned to Point Comfort. We hid behind several trees near where we'd retrieved the food the night before, and we waited. Wisps of clouds floated beneath the moon and stars. At around the same time as the previous evening, Kifunji poked her head out the gate in the fort's side wall and scanned the area.

I made the sound of the drongo.

She closed the gate and crossed the grass. "I miss those birds. I thought you'd come back. Do you need more food?"

"Yes," I answered, "and your help."

"Is anyone here from Asanti?" Efe blurted.

"I'm the only one here in Point Comfort," Kifunji said. "They took everyone else to Jamestown."

I shook my head. "James River. Jamestown."

"They're named after their king."

"Where is this Jamestown?" I asked. She pointed northwest. "How far?"

"Forty miles."

"Miles?"

She shook her head. "Too complicated to explain."

"How many sunrises by foot?"

"Two. Three at most. You'll get there faster if you travel by horse. Or ship."

"We don't have any horses, much less know how to ride them. And I'm not sure I can convince my people to stay on that ship longer than necessary."

"You could steal the pale men's horses."

"We will walk."

"You still haven't told me your names or where you're from."

"I'm Princess Chibuike of the Queen—"

"Oh, my goddesses!" Kifunji dropped to her knees, dipped her finger in the brown soil, and drew it across her forehead. "Forgive me, your Adaeze. I did not recognize you. I meant no disrespect."

"Please rise. This is Efe, the ruler of Asanti. These are Majors Kayin and Kunto and Lieutenant Itoro of the Kanaian army."

Kifunji dusted off her skirt. "You traveled all this way to find us?" I nodded. She chewed her bottom lip. "What will become of me?"

"What do you mean?"

"The general is dead. After a time, one of the others will force me to serve him."

"But we're here. After we find those we've come for, we'll take you back to Banaan."

She pressed her palms to her cheeks. "Home?"

"Home." I grasped her shoulders and grinned. "You're free, Kifunji. You are free."

A small yelp escaped before she could cover her mouth with her hand. She shook her head slowly in disbelief and dropped to her knees. She kept repeating, "thank you."

I wasn't sure if she was addressing me or the goddesses.

# Chapter Sixteen

# ...are invincible

KIFUNJI BROUGHT US five woolen cassocks.

Efe donned the knee-length outer garment. "How did you get these?"

"I have my ways," Kifunji responded.

I liked her. She was resourceful. "We're grateful," I said.

A cloud descended around us, which Kifunji called "fog." It dampened our hair, skin, and clothing. Although the weather was already cool, she said that during the winter our teeth would chatter. If we didn't wear coverings outdoors, our hands could become affixed to metal objects. I wasn't looking forward to this predicament. This land experienced four seasons, not two. I wanted to be on our way back to Kana by the time the season changed.

Kifunji also provided a cart laden with food, including a few dead chickens.

"Won't you get in trouble for helping us?" Efe asked.

She waved away this concern. "I'll tell them I had no

choice, which is the truth. But they'll think it's because you forced me."

The men of Point Comfort didn't approach the *Isabella Maria* in their rowboats again. An unspoken truce.

The following night, Efe came to shore along with thirty Kanaian warriors. Francisco de Silva was with us. He would slow us down, being as unfit as he was, but he was a pale man and spoke English, so we could use him. The remaining warriors stayed behind to guard the ship and its prisoners. They would subsist on fish until we returned.

Kifunji waited on the pier, the water lapping against its pillars. She would join us.

The dirt road between Point Comfort and Jamestown sometimes ended and resumed a hundred paces later. Squirrels and rabbits darted in and out of our path. The trees stroked the sky; the diffused moonlight filtered through their shifting leaves. We walked slowly, afraid of turning an ankle or tripping on the uneven terrain. Insect songs crescendoed and cascaded through the night.

A noise came from the woods.

From behind me, Kayin asked in a low voice, "Why did you stop, Lieutenant Colonel?"

"I heard a noise."

"Rodents?"

"I'm not sure. Listen."

Everyone fell silent.

"I still hear nothing."

"It's like a whisper."

She smirked. "Are you sure the rum isn't dulling your senses?"

Earlier, Kifunji had brought rum in a half-empty cask

from Thomas's kitchen. She'd said the cask was full the day before we arrived in Point Comfort. Thomas must have been more concerned about us than he let on.

"I took a swallow." I resumed walking. "Perhaps two. But I heard what I heard."

We continued walking while the sun ascended from behind, and until it descended ahead of us. We halted next to the James River to rest for the evening.

Two warriors built a fire from the logs and fallen branches, their footsteps crunching on the dry grass. We cleared away pebbles and sticks and sat cross-legged on the soft earth, gathering around the fire for warmth. I relaxed, inhaling the smoke's pine scent and exhaling the uncertainty that lay ahead. Kunto juggled pine cones. Kifunji and a few warriors killed several wild turkeys, smoked them, and served the meat with porridge on trenchers that she'd brought.

When we finished eating the tasty meal, Itoro led us in singing the warrior song, her haunting voice accompanied by the insects' chorus. After the last refrain, Kunto told the tale of how Gbadu, the Goddess of Destiny, created the land on which the Queendom of Kana rests. It was a story passed down through generations of Kanaians. Everyone, except Efe and Kifunji, had listened to it many times, but its telling was never dull. Efe leaned forward, her chin resting on her clasped hands. I hadn't known Kunto was such a superb storyteller. I found comfort in listening to the song and the story with the other warriors.

We weren't home, but it was the next best thing.

But although the tale Kunto told was not scary, the back of my neck tingled.

Kayin sat beside me. "These mosquitoes are as bad as the

ones in Kana." She slapped her arm. The insect's whining ceased. "You keep looking at the trees. Are you hearing the whispering spirits again?"

I reached my palms out to the fire. "I am."

She chuckled. "What are they telling you?"

"That we're not alone."

"I feel it, too," Efe said.

✧

At dawn, we rose and shook the pine needles, dirt, and grass out of the blankets we'd brought from the ship.

Itoro scanned the area. "There it is!" She walked several paces from where she'd been sleeping and picked up her hatchet. "How did it get over here?"

She looked at the rest of us, and we shrugged.

"Maybe the whispering spirits moved it," Kayin said.

After we'd eaten, we cleaned the cooking pot, trenches, and utensils in the river, packed everything, and departed.

I ordered Itoro and Nsia to remain vigilant in case the pale men were following us. The day was fair. Sun dappled through the trees. Despite my concerns, travel the next day was uneventful.

Billowy clouds drifted across the sky as we splashed through shallow wetlands and into the woods outside Jamestown. Crows cawed above us, perched on the branches of red-leaved trees. I hoped their cries would not announce our arrival.

Leaving Kifunji, Silva, and the other Kanaians at the edge of the forest, Kayin, Kunto, Efe, Itoro, and I climbed a hill. At the top, we lay on our stomachs in the grass, surveying the town below. It was the same size as Kana proper.

People toiled on nearby farms. Farther away, others walked or rode horses along the town's dirt streets. Children played. Women and men entered and left one- and two-floor buildings, or stood in groups or pairs talking. The scene was not too different from what I would have observed in Kana, except that nearly everyone was pale-skinned, and nobody carried food baskets or water jugs on their heads. What a waste! The top of your head was like another pair of hands. I ignored the stab of pain in my gut, which I weathered whenever my thoughts drifted to my homeland.

"What's our plan?" Efe asked.

Kayin scowled and scratched the mosquito bites peppering her arms. "Simple. Find the kidnapped people, retrieve them, and leave."

"Burn it down," Kunto said, echoing what her twin had suggested regarding Point Comfort. "Then find the kidnapped people, retrieve them, and leave."

Kayin grinned. "That's my sister."

"We're not here to kill innocents," Efe said.

Kunto lowered her chin to her chest. "You're right."

"They have no problem killing ours," countered Kayin.

"They can't all be killers," said Efe.

"But the rest condone it."

"We should find their leader, Chibuike. Request food and shelter. And the release of our people. My family could be here."

Kayin turned to me. "I like our idea better. What say you, Lieutenant Colonel Chi?"

I'd been listening to them with part of my mind. I hadn't developed a plan for when we arrived, since I didn't know what we would face. I dismissed the idea of burning down the town. We did not want to kill the people we came to find. I also did not know the size of the pale men's army and couldn't risk losing any more warriors.

Maybe diplomacy could work. "We'll do this your way, Efe."

I returned to the rest of the group. Silva stood near a maple tree. He was sweating. He hadn't imbibed a libation in two moons.

"We need to talk to the person in charge," I said. "Take us to him."

"I don't know where he lives."

"He won't be hard to find. The town isn't that big. And do not try to escape."

"Wouldn't think of it." He ran his hand through his straggly hair, a handbreadth past his shoulders. "I want to live."

I waved Kayin and Efe over. "The four of us will go." To the warriors, I called, "Wait here. If you hear the war cry, come."

"I'm coming with you," Itoro said.

She would fight to her death to save me. "All right." I yelled over to Kunto, who was standing with some warriors. "You're in charge."

She grinned and saluted me.

Kayin glanced at her. "With respect, do you think that's wise?"

"With that question, you are disrespecting your sister's abilities or my decision. Which is it?"

Wisely, she didn't answer.

We climbed the hill again and walked down the opposite side through a field with rows of an unfamiliar brown vegetable, past a farmhouse, and entered Jamestown. On the dusty street, a yellow-haired woman held a young girl's hand. She stopped and stared at us, her mouth falling open. She pulled the girl close to her.

Efe, Kayin, and Itoro gaped. I was sure my expression mirrored theirs. We'd seen pale men, but none of us had seen a pale woman or child. The woman wore a red wool skirt and a beige bodice laced up with string and a white parlet that covered her shoulders and chest. A matching linen coif capped her hair. The girl was dressed the same in miniature.

"Silva," I said, "ask her where her leader lives."

He did. The woman turned and hurried away to the nearest house, tugging her daughter after her.

"That went well," said Kayin.

Moments later, a stocky man came out the door of the same timber-framed dwelling and huffed over to us. His face was splotched red, either from the cold or from drink. He wore a flat- brimmed cap, a doublet fastened with many buttons, and green wool breeches above black stockings that rose to his knees.

*It must take these pale people a long time to dress in the morning.*

He scanned our dirty tunics and wrinkled his nose as if we smelled—which we did, since we'd run out of the sailors' soap a full moon ago. Silva was also wearing the same clothes, the rum stain splayed across his shirt despite repeated washing in the river.

The pale man's eyes were slits. "My wife said you were looking for our leader."

"Tell us where he is," I said. Silva translated.

The man's hands resembled a bird's talons, ready to tear my limbs from my torso. "Why are you dressed that way? Who's your master?"

"Master?"

His gaze shifted to my hand on the pommel of my daga and back to me. "Who owns you?"

"No one. Where's your leader?"

He hesitated, then pointed down the street at a six-spear-length-high house with wooden shingles. "Our governor lives there, but he won't talk to you."

"'Governor.'" Efe's tone was contemplative. She would undoubtedly add English to her arsenal of languages in little time. It had taken me years to speak passable Portuguese under Ndidi's tutelage; Efe's proficiency equaled mine after two full moons.

"We'll take our chances," I said.

"'Tis none of my affair."

He spun and stomped to his home, slamming the door behind him.

A flock of geese honked overhead as they flew south. Unlike the house we'd just left behind, the governor's home had brick between its posts instead of clay. A woman answered our knock. She looked like us and was many dry seasons older than I. She stared at us, her gaze lingering on Itoro's scar, which was shaped like a meandering river.

"Yes?" the woman said at last.

"We're here to see the governor," Silva said.

"Who's calling?"

"He doesn't know me, but it's important."

"I'll fetch him." She shut the door.

"What's your name?" asked Efe. "Where are you from?"

The latch clicked.

After a lengthy wait, a heavyset man with swept-back brown hair opened the door. His forehead was broad, his nose pointed. He wore a long, frilly collared shirt of white linen tucked into red breeches that tapered at the knee and foot coverings made of leather, with a strap across the top. Wrapped around his leg was a small boy.

The man scanned our faces and looked at Silva. "I thought she was joking. Governor Sir George Yeardley, appointed by the Virginia Company of London. What business do you have with me?"

Silva translated the governor's words into Portuguese and removed his cap. "*Capitão* Francisco de Silva of the *Isabella Maria*, sailing under the flag of Portugal. This is Princess Chibuike."

Yeardley's brows drew together. "Why is she standing on my stoop?"

I was unused to the disrespect I'd endured from strangers since I left Kana. I didn't like it.

"She doesn't want any trouble. These women are searching for their friend who might be here in Jamestown."

"Are you serious?"

"Dead serious."

"How did they get here?"

"They seized my ship."

"I'll be damned!" Yeardley scratched his thick beard. "I need friends like that." His amusement dissipated. "If she's in Jamestown, she's a servant." He appraised us. "You look to be fine workers. We could use—"

The sound of unsheathed steel filled the air as the warriors—and Efe—pointed our weapons at him. The governor's eyes bulged, and he raised his hand. "Let's be calm!"

We lowered our weapons. Itoro was the last to do so.

The governor dropped his hand. "We traveled a long way to come to this country. Like you."

"Were you stolen, chained, beaten, and stuffed into a hold?" asked Efe.

"No."

"Then not like us."

"They're here to take their friend home," said Silva.

"She is home," Yeardley said.

"Back to Africa."

"They can visit with her, but she can't leave the family she serves."

"She serves no one," I said. "And we're not here only for her, but for all of our people."

Silva glanced at me and translated. Yeardley laughed. "We won't give them back. They work for us. We'll fight for them."

"Then it's a fight you shall get."

Governor Yeardley told us he would consider providing food and shelter, then shut the door in our faces. He didn't suggest when or how he'd supply these provisions, or where we could find our people.

We made camp in the woods behind the hill from where we'd first observed the town. The food we'd brought from Point Comfort would last a few sunrises; we retrieved fresh water from the river. I instructed everyone not to wander off, unsure of what dangers hid in this forest. Brown, yellow, and orange leaves swirled in the air and fell upon our heads and on the earth.

Throughout this time, I continued to feel watched, although I didn't share this with the warriors, or with Efe. They would think I was going mad. It was probably animals.

The news of our arrival spread quickly. Groups of Jamestown residents ventured to the nearest farm, craning their necks to glimpse us over the wooden fences. None of them came any closer.

That evening, we sat around a fire eating peppered corn. An insect flew by.

Itoro swore and swatted it away.

Kayin lowered her spoon. "What...*is*...that?"

I squinted. "It looks like a beetle."

"But its bottom is...green!"

Kunto shrilled, "And it's blinking!"

Warriors shrunk back. Some gasped.

"It's a spirit," Itoro said, a tremor in her voice.

Mukambu set her trencher on the ground. She cupped her hands, caught the bug, and stared at it. "I can use it to heal."

That night, I posted three warriors as guards while the rest of us slept. It was dark, though the trees had shed half their leaves. The squirrels and rabbits quit their fussing and settled down for the evening.

The sound of gunfire awakened me. My eyes shot open, and I sat up. Other warriors snapped awake. Only two warriors stood guard at the top of the hill. The third was lying on the grass, groaning.

I threw off my blanket, grabbed my daga, and crouched. A second gun blast felled another warrior on the hill. I yelled for the third to lower herself. But I was too late. They shot her as well.

Figures ran at us, moonlight revealing their pale, contorted faces. Many of the warriors took cover behind trees while others lay on their stomachs, muskets in position, and returned fire. Several men wailed, staggered, and fell, but one kept running. I stood, calculated where he would be, and threw.

The man yelped and tumbled face forward to the ground. The back of his breeches displayed a brown stain. Ignoring the stench, I knelt and grabbed his burly shoulder, rolled him over, and yanked my daga from the soft flesh between his ribs. I used the grass to rid my blade of his blood.

"Why did you attack us?" I asked.

He smiled with red-coated teeth, blood gushing down his chin. His breathing stopped.

I prepared to stand. Over my head, the whoosh of a knife sliced through the air. A man screamed, dropped his gun, and fell a few paces away from me.

I stared at his body, then turned to the person who'd saved my life.

Efe's smile lit up the night. "Like I said, 'I can believe in one thing and prepare for another.'"

I nodded my thanks and screamed to the warriors. "Ike!"

We charged, trying not to slip on the multitude of leaves underfoot. A man held up his musket with both arms to protect himself. Itoro snatched it, threw it on the ground, and clawed his face. She finished him by nearly chopping his head off with her hatchet. Nsia parried an opponent's weapon and thrust her sword into him. Turning to seek her next victim, she came face to face with two men, each holding a musket. From behind them, Kayin sliced the backs of their necks.

"Sometimes, only two swords will do." She smirked at Nsia and reentered the fray.

The men grunted and cursed as they fought. We had the advantage when fighting in proximity, rendering their guns useless. At one point, my back grazed Kayin's as we both fought off opponents—she with her swords, and I, my daga. Her power fed mine, and mine hers.

The smell of gunpowder hovered in the air. After a few more pale men fell, the rest retreated up the hill, still firing their muskets, except for one. Efe reared back to throw her daga at him, but her movement was slow. I shouted her name and raised my daga. But before I flung it at her oncoming attacker, an arrow pierced through the night into his arm and through his chest, its tip poking out the other arm. He screamed and dropped to the ground with his arms pinned to his body.

We hadn't brought our bows and arrows with us. I spun around and scanned the woods to see who'd released it.

There was no one there.

# Chapter Seventeen

# and will eliminate...

WE DIDN'T BUILD a fire, not out of fear of giving away our location—it was too late for that—but so that we weren't a lighted target. I posted several guards at the top of the hill to replace the fallen warriors, though I did not believe the pale men would return that night. Groups of warriors huddled together, talking. A few others kept to themselves, their backs against the trees. No one slept.

The officers sat on the hard ground around the remnants from an earlier fire.

Mukambu attended to the injured warriors. One had lost an eye and wore a cloth over the aperture. Another had been shot in the arm. She would live. The third suffered a stomach wound. Judging by the healer's impassivity, the outlook for that warrior was poor.

While our breathing returned to normal, I prayed for their recovery.

"Yeardley won't be providing food or shelter for us," Kayin said.

"No," I said.

Itoro coughed from the gunpowder smoke she'd inhaled. Kifunji brought her a cup of water.

As the officers relived the battle and analyzed every movement, I glanced at Efe, who was quiet. A wet leaf stuck out of her braid. I pulled it out and twirled it in my hand. I was thankful someone had prevented Efe from being killed. I didn't know how I would live with myself if something had happened to her.

"Are you all right?" I asked quietly.

She nodded.

"Thank you for saving my life," I said.

"You owe me nothing," Efe replied. "You're risking yours to save people you don't know. It's the least I can do. Besides, I've watched you throw that thing for years. When you were about to be killed, I just closed my eyes and threw."

I blinked, realizing how close I'd come to death. Again.

"Who shot that arrow?" Kunto asked. "The man fell like a tree." She brought her arms to her sides, pretended to scream, and fell sideways to the ground.

Kayin righted her sister. "It wasn't whispering spirits."

"It was someone who possessed great skill," I said. "Someone who has battled before."

"Maybe that person isn't watching us," Itoro said, "but watching over us."

The following day, we took turns lying on top of the hill, observing the town through our musket sights. In the fields below, a few men who looked like us planted the unfamiliar crop.

During our evening meal, Kayin and I sat on the grass

near the trees, apart from the rest of the warriors. The comforting aroma of beans and rice wafted up from my trencher.

"We shouldn't stay here," Kayin said. "The pale men will keep coming back until they capture or kill us all."

"This location isn't favorable to us." I ate a spoonful. It was delicious. Kifunji was an excellent cook. "Where should we go?"

Although they'd attacked from the hill the previous night, we received scant protection from the woods to the rear and on our flank. Swampland separated us from the James River to the south.

"Home. Back to Kana."

I lowered my spoon. "Don't you think I yearn for family and home?"

She looked at me aghast as I brushed a tear from my eye.

"I didn't mean to—"

"Are you atulu?"

She tensed. "Who are you calling sheep? I'm a lion, like you. Even more so."

"Why do you say that?"

"Nothing was given to me. Including rank. My mother was a yam trader in the market. She used to bring me and Kunto, hoping we'd take over her stall someday. Until we reached eight dry seasons and grew to a spear-and-a-half in height. Then there was only one path for us. Thank goddesses! Kunto would be happy as a trader, juggling yams all the time. I love yams, too, but I didn't want to spend the rest of my life with them. Our mother dreaded the day we left the hut for good and moved into the barracks."

We'd never discussed the twins' parents or upbringing; they'd only shared that their mother was a twin, as well as their grandmother. All the women in their family had the same hazel-colored eyes.

"And our mother served with yours, by the way."

"But the army takes care of former warriors for life!"

Kayin shrugged. "She wanted to work. And wanted us to work. Not to benefit from who we were rather than from what we did. Like you."

Heat rose to my face. "My circumstances benefited me"—I patted the sleeves of the doublet that covered the three stripes on my arm—"and, yes, I skipped you in rank, but I earned these."

She glanced at my hand and shook her head. "It's not the same."

"I—"

She was right. The circumstances of my birth favored me. If I hadn't been born into royalty, who knows where I would be? Ability and desire were not enough. I'd refused many strong and gifted girls from joining our ranks because there wasn't room in the army for all of them.

I spooned the remaining beans from my trencher into my mouth and swallowed. "You're right."

"I'm always right."

"Well..." We shared a smile. "We'll find a new location tomorrow."

"Should we return to the ship?" she asked.

"We need reinforcements. The warriors from the boat must come here."

Kayin flexed her jaw. "That wasn't what I meant."

"I know. But we're not finished here." I set down my trencher and called over two of our fastest fighters. "Go to the *Isabella Maria* and bring back help."

"How many?" asked one.

"All of them. Leave a few to guard the crewmen."

She looked at the warrior who had died from a stomach wound, wrapped in a blanket on the yellowed grass. The cold air had prevented her corpse from stinking. "And her?"

"We won't bury her in this land. We'll take her to the river so she can find her way home."

The two warriors saluted and took off running.

That night, we burrowed deeper into the woods to make camp. With the ground covered in dry leaves, the pale men couldn't ambush us. I ordered warriors to stand guard in shifts as a precaution.

The next morning, although the sun beamed down through the leafless branches, the air was chilly. We shared the cassocks Kifunji had brought, handing them over to another warrior once we'd warmed. Several warriors kept their blankets wrapped around them throughout the day.

A warrior posted on the eastern edge of the camp periodically whistled the drongo sound so the two warriors I'd sent to the *Isabella Maria* could find us. On the fourth day, they returned. Alone.

"Where's everyone else?" I asked. "I told you to bring back reinforcements."

Kayin crossed her arms over her chest. "I should have gone instead."

Despite the cold, the warriors' foreheads were slick with sweat. The one who'd spoken before they left pressed her lips together.

"Speak," I said.

"They cannot come."

My ears pounded. "It wasn't a choice. It was an order. Absolute obedience."

She hesitated. "They thought that after you knew why, you'd want them to stay at their post."

A leader doesn't have to raise her voice. "And the reason?"

"Another ship arrived. Filled with captives."

⋞

We left for Point Comfort the following morning.

Kayin wanted to stay and complete the mission first. I argued that if we waited, the captives would be sold before we arrived. Efe resisted at first, too, but she finally acquiesced. Although she desperately wanted to find her family, she didn't want anyone else to be sold into slavery. Kunto and Itoro agreed with my position.

The scent of pine trees filled my nostrils as I walked. A squirrel started to cross my path and changed her mind, scampering away under the thick bramble nearby. Blackbirds cawed as they headed south. Our bare feet crunched on the fallen leaves and pine needles. Silva trailed behind us, with warriors taking turns guarding him. We stopped for a nap, but ate while we walked. With haste, we made the journey in two sunrises. When the fort came into view, we picked up our pace.

We stopped at the edge of the woods. A larger ship stood anchored facing the *Isabella Maria*. The men of Point Comfort stood on the pier looking out over the water, their backs to us.

"What's happening?" Efe asked.

Kanaian warriors stood at the *Isabella Maria's* bow, their weapons drawn.

"It looks like we're not letting anyone off the other ship," I said.

"We should take the pale men," suggested Kayin. "They're distracted. Then take the fort."

"We've just arrived," said Efe. "Let's wait a sunrise to gather our strength."

"The longer we wait, the greater the chance we will lose captives."

"We'll rest when we join our ancestors," added Kunto.

"We're Kanaian warriors," I said. "Strong enough on our worst day. Ready yourselves. Dagas, swords, and spears only."

We unsheathed our weapons carefully, and the warriors looked at me.

Quietly, I said, "Ike."

We ran to the pier and came up behind the pale men facing the James River. One of them turned; Itoro sprung upon his back and clawed off most of his face. As he howled, Nsia twirled and slashed three men across the backs of their thighs with her sword. Their blood arced onto the pier.

A man turned to me, raising his blunderbuss. I aimed my daga at his heart and let it loose. The blade shot through the air and hit its target. He grunted, dropped the gun, and fell. I yanked out my daga and kicked his body into the river. Those men who did not fall into the water, we pushed.

The metallic stench of blood hung in the air. Dark stains saturated the pier's wooden planks.

"We need to hurry," I said. "Reinforcements from the fort may come soon."

We hopped into the rowboats, unmoored them, and paddled to the *Isabella Maria*'s larboard side.

I scurried up the rope ladder and onto the deck. The warrior I'd left in charge greeted me.

"Circumstances?" I asked.

"They pointed their weapons and cannon at us. We did the same to them. We've been locked in this position since." She glanced at the dock. "I see you took care of our flank."

"How are our warriors?"

"Hungry. We're tired of eating fish."

"After we take care of this, we'll add variety to your diet." The Aons stood starboard. "And them?"

"Restless."

I moved to the bow. The wind whistled in my ears. Silva, Efe, and Kayin joined me. "Who will speak for you?" I asked in Portuguese.

A compact man stepped forward, his dark eyes burning. "Me."

"What's your name?"

"I don't answer to you. You need to stand down. We've got business to conduct."

I pointed to the dead men floating in the shallow water near the dock. "Your customers are indisposed."

He waved. "There are others."

"Release the people you've taken captive."

"They're our property until we sell them."

"No person belongs to another." I turned my back to him and said to my warriors, "Let's pay him a visit. Efe and Silva stay here."

Under the cover of musket fire from the Kanaian warriors on the *Isabella Maria*, the rest of us took the rowboats to surround the other vessel. We scampered up the rope ladders and slashed our way through the crewmen.

We killed every one of them, including their rude captain.

The battle on the James River did not last long. Our adversaries wanted to sell the people they'd kidnapped and depart. We were hungry, tired, and determined women warriors from Kana. That was all the advantage we needed.

In the middle of the ship was a grate, similar to the one on the *Isabella Maria*. A chill swept through me, and my mouth dried as I approached it.

Kunto lifted the grate. The hold was roughly four spear lengths high. Inside, at least a hundred women, men, and children lay chest to back on wooden boards. The smell was overpowering—worse than when we had discovered the Aons, who'd been in the hold for four sunrises. These people had withstood the hold's conditions for two full moons. I swallowed hard and fought the surge of indignation that threatened to shatter the calm I evinced.

Some people appeared to be dead. Others averted their eyes. A few looked up at me, uninterested, until they noticed I wasn't a pale man. A young girl pointed me out to the woman lying beside her.

"I'm Princess Chibuike from the Queendom of Kana. You're safe now."

The people in the hold had been kidnapped from the Zatopa province. We released them from their shackles. They sat on the clean areas of the deck, avoiding the planks stained by the sailors' blood. The former crew had joined the pale men of Point Comfort in the James River, some still floating on its surface. The Kanaians and Aons from the *Isabella Maria* shared the fish they'd caught with the Zatopans and provided buckets of water for them to drink and bathe. Mukambu tended to their wounds.

After the following sunrise, Kayin, Kunto, Efe, Itoro, Kifunji, and I—accompanied by twenty warriors—filled the rowboats and headed to the fort.

We needed a place to stay on land.

Kunto pushed open the unlocked door while the rest of us pressed against the fort's outer walls, anticipating gunfire. None came. I pointed to several warriors to follow Kunto. They returned quickly. There was no one inside.

The remaining Point Comfort women and men had left during the night. I was glad we wouldn't be fighting today. We needed rest.

Kifunji gave us a tour of the fortress. First, she showed us Thomas's house. I inspected the study on the second floor. It smelled musty. A musket leaned against a wall in the corner. Had Thomas ever fired it? The fort also contained four smaller buildings with numerous cramped, dank rooms with rough pine floorboards, straw-stuffed canvas bags for beds, and small locked chests. The rooms were dark, with only rushlights for illumination.

"There's room here for everyone," Efe said.

She'd convinced me we needed to house the Zatopans and Aons until we were ready to depart for home. Unrest would ensue if they stayed on the ships.

"Yes," said Kifunji, "but…"

"What?" I asked.

A flock of sparrows headed southward.

"The men who lived here belonged to the English militia. You defeated them, but when word reaches him, he'll send more."

"'Him?'"

"James. The King."

I pursed my lips. "Hmph." I wished to meet this king they named everything after, but who ruled from so far away.

That morning, we retrieved everyone from both ships, leaving behind only the *Isabella Maria*'s prisoners and a few warriors to guard them, and settled them in rooms at the fort. My attention turned to feeding them. We located corn and beans in the buildings' storage rooms, along with the remaining food and ale in Thomas's pantry.

"I'll take you to where we keep the chickens," Kifunji said. "I hope someone's been feeding them in my absence."

She took us to a side yard. Behind a wire-enclosed pen, chickens strutted, stopped, and resumed strutting. Kifunji entered through a small wooden gate and ran after a shrieking fowl, her skirt billowing behind her. Cooing at the bird, she waited for it to slow, caught it, and broke its neck with a loud crack, her expression unchanging. She held it up, its blood spilling over her hand. "It's your turn."

"That doesn't look hard," I said.

"I've captured chickens before," said Itoro.

Kunto bounced on her toes. "Us, too."

Although I'd never caught a chicken in my life, I couldn't criticize General Thomas for not fighting alongside his men if I, myself, were unwilling to provide food for my own landswomen and men.

"I'll do it," I said.

After entering the pen, I hesitated. My eyes watered

from the overpowering odor of feces. Imitating Kifunji, I ran after the closest chicken. As I reached out, the clucking fowl zigged and zagged. The toe of the boot I'd appropriated from Thomas's house snagged on the heel of my other boot, and I fell, raising a cloud of dust.

"Aba!"

A giggle turned into a boisterous belly laugh. I rubbed my eyes to see who was so amused by my predicament, but I could have guessed: Kayin. She was bent over, holding her stomach. Efe laughed for the first time since her mother died. The others fought to contain their laughter. Kifunji concealed her smile with her hand.

Outside the pen, other warriors had joined in the laughter.

Sitting up, I wiped the dirt off my face and dusted off my tunic. "I wanted it to think I was clumsy."

"You succeeded, Lieutenant Colonel," Itoro said earnestly.

This made everyone laugh harder, including some of the Aons and Zatopans. I rested my arms on my bent legs. A sensation bubbled up from my stomach to my chest, tickling my throat until the laughter burst from me. I couldn't remember the last time I'd laughed this hard.

By this time, every chicken in the pen was screeching unbearably.

Itoro, Kayin, and Kunto caught ten chickens. Kayin killed them as if she did this daily.

That evening, we roasted the fowl over fires in the fort's clearing, and the people of Kana, Zatopa, and Aon—along with the ruler of Asanti—sat together on the ground eating the seasoned meat with corn, roasted eggs, beans, and bread. I sipped the ale. The warm drink smelled of barley.

At first, I had opposed Efe's suggestion that we have this

feast. I wanted to find Fatimata and return home. We now possessed two ships. We didn't have time for a long meal. But feasts, rituals, and celebrations were important to our culture. The people of the different provinces talked, laughed, and told stories. My belly was full.

It was a good day.

## Chapter Eighteen

# ...the enemy without...

THE FOLLOWING DAY, Efe, Silva, Azeze, and I set off for Jamestown with most of the Kanaian warriors. The air was no longer cool—it was frigid. We took the clothing that had been left behind by the women and men who had abandoned Point Comfort.

In the forest, I walked with my cassock unbuttoned so I could reach my daga. The fallen leaves were slick on the dirt path and gave off a fresh, moist scent. The skeletal trees provided an unimpeded view of the sky. Squirrels scampered over twigs and dirt before darting up tree trunks. I didn't see or hear any birds.

When we arrived on the outskirts of Jamestown two sunrises later, we remained in the woods and circled to the north of town. We slept on the hard ground, the added blankets we'd taken from Point Comfort affording little relief.

The next sunrise, I crested the hill with Kayin, Kunto,

Itoro, and Efe. A man, who wasn't pale, spread seeds in the nearest field. No one guarded him, but he didn't run away.

I pointed at Kunto. We had discussed our plan earlier. We needed help from within.

She released her musket and cartridge belt and sped toward the man. By the time he looked up, our strongest warrior was upon him. He dropped his bag of seeds. Kunto picked him up and carried him like a rug over her shoulder back to us.

She set him on the ground. The rest of the warriors, Azeze, and Silva stood apart, watching.

There was grass sticking out of the man's thick hair. His eyes grew large as he scanned our faces. He smelled of manure and hard work.

"Who are you?" he asked.

"I'm Princess Chibuike of the Queendom of Kana."

He scrunched up his face. "What…are you doing…here?"

"Looking for you. Where are you from?"

"Banaan."

Efe knelt next to him. "Is Fatimata, the ruler's daughter, here?"

"She's serving on a farm on the other side of town."

"Let's go get her!"

I held up my hand. "How many Banaans are here?" I asked him.

"Around twenty or thirty. The pale men took some upriver."

I'd worry about them later. "Come." I extended my hand to help him up. "Take us to Fatimata."

❧

The man's name was Akaba; the pale man who had purchased him called him John.

That afternoon, Akaba brought us to the woods on the opposite side of town. A lone woman knelt in the yellowed grass in front of a thatched farmhouse across the road. She wore a white shirt under a brown cassock and a beige skirt, and her hair was wrapped in a matching beige cloth. It was difficult to make out her features with the sunlight in my eyes.

I picked up a rock and threw it close enough to get her attention. The woman ceased tilling and looked in our direction.

I stepped out from behind the tree that concealed me. She rose and shook her head, the trowel tumbling out of her hand and onto the turned soil.

She walked toward me as if under a spell by the seer in the Kanaian market.

Then she ran. My heart soared when her familiar face came into focus.

"Chi!" she cried. "Chi!"

I raised a finger to my lips.

When she reached me, her gaze danced across my face. She placed her calloused hands upon my forehead, my cheeks, my lips, then grabbed my arms. "Praise Oshun! Are you a vision?"

Pressure was building behind my eyes. "No."

She smiled without revealing her teeth. "Is it really you?"

I returned the smile, my vision blurring. "It's me."

She touched my face again. "How did you get here?"

"It's a long story."

"How did you find me?"

"We wouldn't stop until we did."

Fatimata fell into my arms, shaking. I held her close, her scent of plain soap and earth. Against my neck, she whispered, "Again, you save me."

Fatimata's crying evolved into a loud, doleful sound. Her knees buckled, but I held her up. She wept for a long time, repeating her goddess's name. After she'd spent all her tears, she pulled away and studied me as if she still didn't believe I was real. I wiped a single eyelash from her cheek. She hugged me again.

After a moment, she let go. "Efe, you came."

Efe nodded repeatedly, smiling and crying at the same time. "Of course."

"What a beautiful woman you've become."

They embraced.

Efe held out her arm, and I slid between them. I could no longer hold back my tears. The three of us held each other and swayed.

After a while, I broke away. Kayin, Kunto, Itoro, and Akaba were fidgeting nearby, uncomfortable with the emotional reunion. I introduced them to Fatimata.

"Is there anyone here from Asanti?" Efe asked.

Fatimata's face grew solemn. "Your village, too?"

"They took everyone. Except...my mother."

Before Fatimata could ask about Dayo, I took her arm. "Come, Fatimata. It's time to find your people so we can take them home."

❧

"Tell us about your journey, Fatimata," said Efe.

"Fatimata." She paused. "It's been a long time since anyone has said my name."

Back at the camp, a group of us gathered around a fire. We sat on horsehair blankets. I'd posted guards to the north, south, east, and west. The pale men of Jamestown hadn't troubled us, though I was sure they knew we had returned. We snatched two more Banaan men from the fields. Although they were strangers, Fatimata hugged them.

I sipped water from a cup taken from Thomas's house. "What do they call you?"

"Anne."

Kayin spit out her drink. After a moment, everyone laughed, except for Fatimata. Kayin kept repeating—"Anne? Anne?"—which elicited further laughter.

A faint smile formed on Fatimata's face.

After the laughter dwindled, Efe asked, "What does it mean?"

"I don't think their names always have meaning," Fatimata replied. "Most of us were given the names Anne or Mary."

"Named after someone in England, I suppose," I said.

"They don't like our names," Kayin said.

"They change them to demean us," said Efe.

Fatimata spoke of her ordeal: the loud noises her family had heard outside their hut, the Portuguese tearing Banaans off the streets or from their homes and chaining them. Though frightened, she'd tried to comfort her crying siblings.

"Many of your landspeople killed themselves," I said.

"Chibuike!" Efe scolded me.

Fatimata's posture straightened in defiance. "They'd rather be dead and free."

Fatimata continued her story. On the ship, the Portuguese had whipped everyone, and raped Banaan women and girls. The food had been scarce. The Banaans had lain in the dark, fetid hold for most of the day, with only brief glimpses of the sea and sun during the hour the pale men allowed them on deck.

"I savored those moments," she said. "The sun's warmth on my face."

The sailors had forced the women to dance; women did not dance for men in our region. Banaan men had performed a different dance to the tune of a whip with nine-knotted cords. Those captives who refused to eat had their mouths pried open with an iron vice, the food forced down their throats.

After a full moon at sea, two English vessels attacked the ship. As the Portuguese and the English battled on the main deck, Fatimata and her people listened from the hold, speculating about their own fate. When the fighting ended, the Englishmen came below and seized thirty of the Banaans. They'd dragged Fatimata, screaming—her arms reaching for her mother—onto the *White Lion*, and brought her and the rest of the Banaans to Point Comfort.

Fatimata relayed this monotonously, hugging her knees to her chest. My rage grew as she spoke of what she'd endured, but so did my admiration. For the Banaans' physical strength. For their mental fortitude. For their spiritual resolve to overcome.

Soon thereafter, the English had brought the Banaans to Jamestown.

"Everything was different. Trees. Animals. Nothing felt like home. They made us stand on a wooden block, and the pale men bartered livestock or crops for us. The highest bidder dragged the person away. When it was my turn, a man in dusty clothes said something to me I didn't understand. His face was not unkind, and he didn't beat me like some men did others. He and his wife taught me how to till the land and milk cows. They worked beside me. I learned how to keep a pale man's house. I have been more fortunate than some."

The campfire crackled, its flames lashing out.

"The boredom is insufferable. Every day feels the same. But the wife taught me how to garden; it was my solace. I tried to spend as much time outdoors as I could. I miss the sounds of Banaan. The laughter, the music, our language. On trips to the store with the wife, I'd see Banaans, and we'd share glances of acknowledgment. Despite our circumstances, there's still determination on their faces. I'd heard there were African women here who looked different, but I hadn't thought it could be you. The farmer made me stay in the house until you left."

"Has it bothered you," Kayin asked, "being a servant?"

Fatimata shook her head. "Many of my people didn't survive at the hands of these men. I only prayed to Oshun that I'd be reunited with my family. To play games and laugh again. To cook with my mother. To listen to her long stories. My siblings and I used to complain, begging her to reach the end more swiftly. Especially if we hadn't eaten. I wish I could hear one of her tales now."

I hesitated. "And your mother?"

*Please do not let her be dead.*

Fatimata's lips quivered. "My nne, my nna, and my siblings remained on the Portuguese ship. I don't know where they are."

I pointed at Francisco de Silva, sitting with his back against a maple tree, asleep. "The captain said it was bound for New Spain."

"Where is New Spain?"

"Far away."

"And my family will be there?"

"Maybe. But they could have been sold along the way. And they might not be together."

Efe stared dagas at me.

"Then they could be anywhere," Fatimata said.

Efe slipped an arm around her waist.

From the satchel I'd brought with me from Kana, I pulled out the twig with goat-fur hair and millet grains for eyes. I handed it to Fatimata.

Her eyes filled with tears. "Kaminah. I never thought I'd see this doll again. Or you. It's as if I've awakened from a nightmare."

"That's not all I brought you."

I withdrew Yaa's headdress and held it out to her. Fatimata set the doll on the blanket and reached for her mother's crown, her hand trembling. She stared at the fish-glued branches and placed it against her heart, silently shedding tears. We waited while she wept.

At last, she said, "This headdress has been handed down in my family for generations. Thank you."

"You can thank me after you return it to Yaa."

"I've told you of my journey," said Fatimata. "Tell me about yours."

When we finished, Kayin asked her, "Are you excited to return to Banaan?"

Fatimata shook her head. "I can't leave. Not until I find my mother and the rest of my family."

Efe squeezed her hand. "It could take many seasons to locate them."

"Then I'll be here for many seasons."

## Chapter Nineteen

# ...and within

ONCE THE GROUP had dispersed, Efe and Fatimata lay on their sides talking face-to-face. Tears and laughter punctuated their whispers. I tried to stay awake to eavesdrop, but, having freed, fed, clothed, and housed the Aons and Zatopans and finding Fatimata, I fell asleep as soon as my head touched the rough blanket.

The following sunrise, Efe, Fatimata, and I, accompanied by Itoro and the twins, took off, heading north of Jamestown to conduct reconnaissance and explore this unknown land.

Fatimata couldn't guide us. She hadn't stepped beyond the town boundaries since she arrived in Virginia over a year ago. She kept telling me she wanted to find her family. I promised to show her—once I found a map—why that was impossible now.

But it wouldn't always be so.

The land was boundless and bountiful. We encountered strange animals: white-tailed deer, foxes, wild turkeys, and a bear. Efe's gaze darted everywhere, taking it all in. We did not see any giraffes, zebras, gorillas, hippopotamuses, elephants, lions, or chimpanzees. I missed the sounds of the hyenas and monkeys, the myriad of fresh fruits hanging from the trees.

We crossed a narrow stream and entered more woods. The air was crisp, the clouds low and full. I loved the balm of the forest. Even here, it was where I felt most at home.

"You know what I love about these trees?" said Efe.

"The better question," I said, "is what you don't like about them. You love all trees."

"More than people," added Kayin.

Efe stopped and patted the trunk of an oak tree. "They don't have any daga marks in them."

She laughed, but stopped when she noticed my stern expression. With a grin, she ran from me into a clearing; I ran after her and caught her. Breaking free, she tapped Fatimata on the arm. Kayin stared at Efe in bewilderment. Fatimata touched Kayin's arm and ran. Kayin paused, shrugged, and punched her sister beside her.

"Ow!" Kunto rubbed her shoulder before tackling Itoro.

We chased and tagged one another and laughed like little girls until we ended up sprawled on the cold ground, out of breath.

After a while, Fatimata stood, raised her arms, and spun around. "I've missed freedom. You can't understand what that's like until you've lost it."

I sat up. "We have some idea." I thought of Rotten Teeth slapping the manacles on my wrists in the Kanaian market. "You won't lose it again. Not as long as I'm alive."

"This I know," said Fatimata.

There was a hush, and a white dot fell to the ground,

followed by another. Everyone except Fatimata looked up at the sky. The dots weren't the white-yellowish-green color of bird droppings. We hadn't seen any birds in some time.

One of the flakes fell on my face. It didn't hurt. It was like a cold raindrop.

"That's snow," Fatimata said. "Cold water that's frozen."

Efe caught some and tried to examine them before they melted. Itoro's tongue poked out between her thick lips.

"What does it taste like?" Kunto asked.

"Water."

Kunto stuck her tongue out.

"Is it safe to drink?" Efe asked Fatimata.

"It comes from the goddesses. It must be safe."

A tingle crept up my neck: the same sensation I'd experienced on the long walk from Point Comfort to Jamestown. I signaled for everyone to stop moving, brought a finger to my lips, and stood, my hand on the pommel of my daga. The rest of them rose. I turned around in a circle.

Fatimata gasped and covered her mouth. "Oh!"

Itoro growled and stood by my side. Kayin's hands rested by her sides, ready to draw both swords.

Six women stood ten paces away. Their skin was not pale, but they didn't look like us, either. They wore deer-skin dresses. Their black hair was long and straight. They held long bows the same height as them.

"Indians," Fatimata breathed. "The pale men say they're dangerous and to avoid them. We should leave. This is their land."

"I want to stay and talk to them," Efe said.

"We don't know whether they're friend or foe," I said.

They didn't appear dangerous; their eyes were gentle. But

I couldn't be certain. I motioned to them we were leaving. We backed away slowly until we reached the trees.

"Back to camp," I ordered.

We turned and began running.

"This way, Kunto," I said.

Despite the uneven terrain, Fatimata pulled ahead of us, her skirt riffling behind her.

Kayin shook her head. "Who knew she ran like a cheetah?"

I recalled when Fatimata and I had raced in the obieze compound as children. Losing that race still didn't sit well with me. "I did."

∽

Back at camp, Kifunji was roasting turkeys over a fire and talking with Fatimata. Kayin, Kunto, Efe, Itoro, and I were still panting after our lengthy run from the forest. The fire snapped on the light wind. The aroma of meat and burning maple filled the air. The snow had stopped.

I took a sip of warm, herb-infused water and waited for a pause in their conversation. "Fatimata, tell us about the Indians."

Reluctantly, she turned from Kifunji. "It's so good to talk to someone again, instead of having make-believe conversations in my head." She sipped her water. "Jamestown used to be their land before the English took it."

"Why do the pale men think they're dangerous?" asked Efe.

"I'm not sure. They've caused us no harm, but they warred with the pale men for ten dry seasons until they negotiated a truce."

Silva, under the watchful eye of a warrior, brought more wood for the fire.

I finished my drink and placed the cup on the blanket. "Are there any relations between them now?"

"Yes. Trade." Fatimata waited for Silva to leave. "And otherwise."

"Otherwise?"

Her cheeks reddened. "The pale men lay with their women."

"Why do they trust the pale men enough to trade with them?" Efe asked.

Fatimata shook her head.

"You said the pale men call them Indians. What do they call themselves?"

"I don't know."

"We should ask them."

"I know someone who can help us."

∽

The following day, Efe, Fatimata, Kayin, Kunto, Itoro, and I set off in the company of a pale, yellowish-gray-haired woman.

When she first brought Bett into the camp, everyone looked at Fatimata as if she'd lost her senses. Our hands went to our weapons. Fatimata hurriedly explained that Bett was not like the others in Jamestown. She'd been kind to Fatimata when visiting the farmhouse. Thrice married, Bett had inherited her husbands' estates with each man's death, and had thus become wealthy. She lived on a plantation outside town and paid those who worked her land. And she possessed a passable knowledge of the language she called Algonquian.

I instructed a team of warriors to follow us in case we were walking into a trap. We trekked to the same clearing in the forest where we had encountered the Indian women the previous day. Kayin kept glancing at Bett while resting her hands on the pommels of her swords. A skilled warrior was relaxed prior to the tension of battle. Oblivious to Kayin's scrutiny, Bett straightened her sheep's wool waistcoat.

Our wait was brief.

A woman materialized from behind a tree trunk, clothed in a knee-length deerskin dress, leg coverings, and shoes that I would later learn were called moccasins. Beads held together her long black hair with a large white feather woven into it. She wore a necklace of hawk talons and a copper band around her bicep.

One by one, other women emerged from the trees.

I stepped forward. Bett and Fatimata joined me.

I held up my hand. "We come without ill will."

Fatimata translated my Kanaian words into English. Bett translated them into Algonquian.

Their leader stepped forward. "Who are you?"

Her nose was aquiline, and she possessed a lean build.

I waited for the translation.

"Princess Chibuike, heir to the throne of the Queendom of Kana and a lieutenant colonel in the Kanaian Army."

"Where is this Kana?"

"Across the ocean."

"You're far from home. Why are you here? To take our land and kill our people?"

"That's not our way. We have affairs to attend to."

"State them."

"The pale men stole our people, sold them, enslaved them, and brought them to your land. We've come to retrieve them."

She regarded me for a long moment and pointed at my daga. "*Pamisac.*"

"*Pamisac,*" I repeated.

"I'd like to show you something." She turned and walked on a trail, heading west.

I didn't move.

She stopped and looked back at me. "We've been watching you since you landed in our country."

I glanced at Kayin. "I told you we were being followed."

Kayin stared at their leader, ignoring me.

"If we wanted to harm you," the woman said, "we'd have done so. We don't attack unless we're provoked. We're not like them. Come, and your companions behind the trees can follow."

I jerked, startled. Kayin continued to stare at the leader. Efe nodded. The woman's eyes were unthreatening.

"We'll come with you," I said and made the drongo sound.

The Kanaian warriors came out of hiding. I joined the Indians' leader on the narrow path, with Bett and Fatimata following. Efe and the warriors fell in step with the rest of the Indians. I told Itoro that I would be all right and instructed her to join the others. She grunted her disapproval, but obeyed. Efe tried to engage the other Indians in conversation, but the language barrier was too wide. Knowing her, it wouldn't be for long.

The leader told me her name was Tahki now, and her tribe was called Powhatan. We walked west until we arrived at a village with long rectangular houses. On the village's eastern edge, the maple trees were less dense than in the woods near Jamestown. Many had been reduced to stumps.

Tahki followed my gaze. "They've taken our trees back to England. Their country must be treeless."

"That's horrible," said Efe.

"They think because we do not fence our land, we don't hold claim to it. Ten years ago, we experienced a terrible drought. Our people were dying of starvation. Instead of helping us, the English stole our corn at gunpoint and killed our women and children."

"The English way," Kayin said.

As Tahki showed us around, people stopped what they were doing and stared. It was still disconcerting to be gazed upon—not because I was royalty, but because my appearance was strange to these people.

Tahki laughed, the skin around her dark, intense eyes wrinkling. "They haven't seen many of you. But you must forgive them. They've learned the hard way to be fearful of strangers."

We passed a tobacco field, pens of hogs, turkeys, and cattle, and gardens filled with beans and squash. Tahki headed toward the largest dwelling in the village.

"This is my home," she said.

She led me, Bett, Fatimata, and Efe through the entrance, the rest of our parties remaining outside. Itoro stood by the door.

Supporting the bark- and marsh-reed walls were long sapling poles that met in the center of the ceiling, forming a conical shape. The roof was made of leaves and grass. Food baskets hung from the ceiling. Fishnets and a wooden fishing spear were attached to a wall. Animal hides covered the doors. There were no windows.

An older woman with a shaved head crouched next to a firepit in the middle of the room stirring corn in a clay pot. Smoke rose through a hole in the ceiling. I wondered how they kept out the snow and rain. She gestured for me to sit on the deer-fur carpet on the ground. Tahki must have told her she would invite us here.

"This is my mother. She built this house."

"It's lovely," said Fatimata.

Tahki gestured to the many men, women, and children sitting on the floor of the longhouse. They wore clothing and moccasins made from foxes. "My family."

When Bett finished translating, I scanned their proud, resolute faces and bowed my head. "I am honored to make their acquaintance."

Fatimata smiled at them until a shadow crossed her face. She was probably thinking of her own family.

"You told me your name is Tahki *now*," I said. "Did it change?"

"Our names change based on our accomplishments. I am the eldest daughter and received Tahki when I became the *weroansquas*. The leader of our village." A tight smile. "I'm still not used to it."

"What does it mean?"

"Cold."

I laughed. She didn't. "What does Chibuike mean?"

"My goddesses are my strength."

She caressed the stone point of an arrow she held in her hand. "Is it true?"

I found my strength in myself, my parents, and my destiny. My mother encouraged me to listen to the goddesses and to my ancestors. *Someone* was guiding me.

"Yes," I said. "How did you become a warrior?"

"In our community, girls and boys gifted in games of skill become warriors." Without braggadocio, she added, "I was the fastest child in the village."

"You should see her shoot an arrow," chimed in a man two dry seasons younger than my twenty-one. His eyes shone as if he were up to no good or solely privy to a joke. He was lying on his side, head propped up by his hand, on a mat next to the wall. He wore a deerskin garment that stopped at his knees with a finger-woven belt. Underneath, he wore leg coverings. His wiry arms and torso were bare, despite the chill in the room. His hair was short on one side and graced his shoulder on the other.

I remembered when the Jamestown man had attempted to attack Efe and been pierced by an arrow. "I think I have."

Tahki shot him a look. "My brother, Mingan," she explained to me.

Later, the Powhatans and Kanaians shared plates of roasted corn and tales about our respective lands. Our ways of life. I described the stripes of the zebras, the heights of the giraffes, the speed of the cheetahs, the dense forest, the warm waters of the River Ome, and the glorious sunsets. Tahki told us how beautiful their land had been prior to its desecration by the English.

"You could drink from the river without worrying about what was in it," Mingan added.

Efe glanced at him. "Maybe it'll be that way again."

Fatimata listened silently. How she had changed from the fidgety little girl on Queen's Day.

"Why are the pale men different?" I asked.

"*That* I cannot tell you," said Tahki.

"What if their way has nothing to do with us," Efe said, "but reflects their own character?"

"The *tassantass* act tough, but they're afraid of powerful women."

"I'll keep that in mind," I said.

As we watched the flames, Tahki's family spoke in hushed tones among themselves. My belly was full; the fire warmed me. Their home smelled of woodsmoke and game and comfort.

Tahki stirred the fire with a stick, a tattoo of an arrow on her forearm. "My anger grows every day the *tassantass* remain here. My people have suffered enough. We want them off our land."

"Perhaps we can help each other," I said.

# Chapter Twenty

# Until we prevail...

THAT NIGHT, THE Powhatans sheltered us from the cold in the longhouse. We'd sent a warrior back to the camp to let the rest of the party know that we were safe. Tahki, Kayin, and I—with the help of Fatimata and Bett as interpreters—stayed up late developing a strategy.

The following day, we moved back to the original campsite behind the hill on the east side of Jamestown. We didn't conceal our arrival. In fact, we were quite loud.

On the way home to her plantation, Bett mentioned to someone she passed in the street that she had seen many oddly dressed servants in the woods. The information must have reached the governor; the English approached our camp that night as the quarter moon rose in the cloudless sky. Some of them held sticks blazing with fire. We stood at the top of the hill, waiting.

The pale men didn't pause to consider why we were not wielding our weapons.

They raised their muskets, snarling.

"Surrender," one man said.

"You're coming with us," said another.

"No," I replied, "we're not."

Arrows soared through the air from behind us and pierced the bodies of the Englishmen on the front line. The Powhatans loosed another volley of arrows into the second line of men. My sister warriors and I stormed down the hill screaming, "Ike!" Moonlight glinted off our blades. Nsia moved like a dancer, though her dance partners fell, blood spewing from their necks and chests.

We dispatched the men at the bottom of the hill. Every one.

And we kept running. Fatimata caught up with us.

Tahki drew up next to me. Kayin was on my other side. She tilted her head and looked at the Powhatan warrior-leader.

Tahki gestured toward Nsia. "She could have been one of us." Tahki had said this in English. I looked at her in surprise. "I don't want them to know that we can speak their language."

After Fatimata translated, I said, "Don't get any ideas about Nsia. She's coming back to Kana with us."

Along the dirt road, we felled any pale man who came out of his house.

A small boy raised his musket at us.

"Don't shoot him!" Fatimata cried.

"That gun doesn't look real," said Efe.

"I'm certain it is," I replied. "They probably teach them how to shoot young."

"And hate," added Kayin.

She ran up to him and grabbed the musket, but did not kill him.

We didn't stop until we arrived at the governor's house.

The same woman from our homeland opened the door, scanned our faces, and stepped aside, letting us in without a word.

There was no one on the first floor, which consisted of a sitting room, a dining room, a kitchen, a council room, and a work chamber. The house smelled stale, oppressive. I raced up the stairs to the second level, Tahki and Kayin following closely.

Yeardley was standing in the narrow hallway, dressed only in a white linen undergarment. The five doors along the hall were closed.

"Angelo, what's that—?" His eyes bulged at the sight of us.

I pointed my daga at him. "All we want is our people. We don't want to war with you."

His dazed look faded. "You can't *war* with England."

"We want our land back." Tahki grabbed an arrow from the quiver on her back and drew back the arrow until the bowstring was taut. "It's time for you to leave."

Yeardley raised his hand. "Let's talk about this."

"We've talked enough—"

The governor whipped his other hand from behind his back. He aimed a gun at her.

"No!" Kayin shouted and dove at him as he fired.

The bullet entered the ceiling.

She cocked back her arm to punch Yeardley.

"Wait," Tahki said. "I have something else planned for him."

❧

At dawn the next morning, Tahki, her bow over her shoulder, dragged Yeardley, whose arms were bound with rope, out of his house. Warriors had guarded him throughout the night to prevent him from gathering the remaining pale men to retaliate against us.

The Powhatan leader brought him to a large patch of dirt in the town center that the English called the public square. Residents emerged from their homes, their pale faces aghast at the sight of the Powhatan and Kanaian warriors standing together. Guarded by a warrior, Silva stood to the side of the crowd. Itoro and a Powhatan warrior hoisted Yeardley—still in his nightshirt—onto a block of wood. A yellow streak of urine ran down Yeardley's leg. Sweat plastered his hair to his head.

A sizable crowd gathered. Tahki hopped on the block and grabbed Yeardley's arm.

"What are you doing with our governor?" a man shouted.

She yelled, "Does anyone wish to buy him?"

When she spoke, white fire came out of her mouth. I exhaled. I was breathing smoke, too.

"You can't sell him!" yelled another.

"Why not?" Tahki replied.

I kept silent. This moment was hers. Her people had also endured the pale man's violence. And this was her land. I couldn't imagine how it would feel if the English had settled in Kana.

"He's not yours to sell!" the same man yelled.

Kayin shook her head.

He cocked his gun and pointed it at Tahki. "Release him!"

She let go of the governor to grab and load her bow. Her arrow pierced the gunman's forehead.

As he collapsed to the ground, she scanned the crowd. "Anyone else?"

Yeardley mumbled.

"What?" she asked him. "Speak up!"

"Let them go." He shouted, "Let your servants go!"

Anguish settled upon the Jamestown residents' faces. The Kanaians and Powhatans wielded their weapons.

Yeardley stepped down from the auction block, landing awkwardly. Tahki didn't stop him from stumbling home. Pale men, women, and children cast looks of hatred at us and trudged back to their homes.

One by one, the former Banaan servants of Jamestown emerged from houses and left the fields to gather in the square. Fear and confusion blanketed some of their faces. Others beamed. Pale men called them back with promises of better working and living conditions, but the Banaans ignored them.

Yeardley left with his family that afternoon. Without a ship, I presumed he'd gone to one of the English settlements to the west along the James River, which Tahki told me was properly named the Powhatan River.

That evening, the Kanaians, Banaans, and Powhatans feasted in the square. Silva and Bett were the only pale people in attendance. I asked Bett why she had helped us. She raised an eyebrow. "Why wouldn't I?"

My lips were cracked from the wind. But the weather wouldn't detract us from enjoying this meal. We wore the pale men's cloaks and blankets, or the fox pelts the Powhatans had given us. The tables we'd taken from the houses and arranged in rows outside displayed plates of beef, corn, bread, salted yams, figs, and a vegetable I did not recognize.

I stared at the white mush on my plate. "What's this?"

"A potato," said Kifunji, seated midway down the table.

I poked at it with my wooden spoon. "It looks poisonous."

I scooped up a dollop and slipped it into my mouth. It was starchy and flavorless. I left the rest uneaten.

What brought me joy was the yams. As I took a spoonful, I recalled my beloved yam porridge, an ocean away.

"Not bad, Kifunji, but we'll need to show you how to plant a proper yam again."

Kayin chuckled. "What do you know about planting yams?"

*Nothing.* "More than you think."

"Eating and planting are not the same. You think you know everything."

"So do you."

Efe, seated to my left, lowered her spoon. "Do you two ever stop trying to best each other?"

Kayin and I glanced at each other and back at Efe. "No," we said.

I scanned the faces of the people sitting at the tables. "Look how happy they are!"

"We Banaans are resilient," Fatimata said. "We laugh to keep from crying. It's how we survived."

I stood and held up a cup of cider. "To the Banaans. To the Kanaians." I swung my arm toward Efe. "And to the Asantis. Together again."

Everyone raised their cups. "Together again."

After drinking the fruity libation, Kayin stood and held out her tankard. "To Kana! To home!"

"To Kana! To home!"

We drank again, and a woman at another table yelled, "To Banaan! To home!"

We repeated her words and drank some more.

Efe's lip quivered. She was the only one present from Asanti.

"To Asanti!" I said. "To home!"

Everyone echoed this. Tahki and her brother sat with us, the rest of their tribe intermingling with ours at other tables.

"And to the Powhatans!" I toasted. "Our friends and allies!"

I glimpsed a rare smile from Tahki as she bowed her head. She stood. "To the Kanaians! We are pleased to share this meal with you. You helped us reclaim our land. We'll never forget it."

Itoro no longer growled or tensed up at Tahki's presence. Kayin looked across the table and made eye contact with Tahki and gave her a respectful nod.

Night descended, and torches were lit. A few warriors clapped. Kanaians pushed aside several tables, sloughed off their cassocks and blankets, and danced. Banaans joined them. My gaze fell on Azeze, sitting at another table. He smiled at me. A return smile crept onto my face before I quickly looked away.

One woman danced alone, her arms swinging above her head. She had admitted us into Yeardley's home. He'd called her Angelo. I never learned her real name.

Fatimata's face was alight. "It's been too long since I've seen real dancing."

"You can dance whenever you'd like." Efe grabbed Fatimata's hand and mine. "Like now!"

I allowed myself to be dragged to the center of the dancers and soon lost myself in the rhythm of the clapping. I hadn't danced since the last Queen's Day, a dry season ago. I moved without restraint. It was a welcome release after leaving my home and my parents and journeying across land and ocean. I could not remember the last time I was this happy. This joyous.

Kayin, Kunto, Itoro, and Nsia joined me. We crossed our arms at the wrists and beat the wrists against our chests. The warriors took over the dance area. We turned, raising one arm, then the other, then turned to the other side and did the same. We faced forward, bent over, and crossed our arms again, then brought them to our hearts, shifting from leg to leg. We danced as one.

The warrior dance.

Everyone danced and drank for hours, while in the night sky, the stars of Gleti, the Moon Goddess, smiled down upon us.

∽

Most of the English left Jamestown for other settlements. They packed their belongings and departed during the night.

Tahki would permit us to stay until we found all of our people. The town reclaimed its original name, Tsenacommacah, which meant "densely inhabited land."

We moved into the deserted homes. Efe, Kifunji, Kayin, Kunto, Itoro, and I took the former governor's two-level brick house. We brought Silva with us, and a warrior to guard him. He was still part of my long-term plans, though I'd had little time to think of them. The rest of the warriors occupied the abandoned houses.

We set up security around the town's perimeter. Some Powhatans moved to Tsenacommacah to ensure the English who still lived there behaved. The area in the center of town became the Kanaian warriors' training ground. The remaining visitors from England observed us from their upstairs windows as we performed mock battles around the buildings, farms, and forests, defending against various attack scenarios.

After I was comfortable with our defenses, it was time to retrieve the rest of the Banaans. My homeland constantly invaded my thoughts, as did my mother. How was she faring? How was the queendom doing? What was Udo up to? Bamidele, the Aon king? I missed the food. And the weather. Would I ever see a palm tree again? I hid my anxiousness to return to Kana from everyone.

One day, the warriors, Efe, Fatimata, and I stood before a line of horses near the Powhatan village. The air reeked of the many piles of manure clumped on the grass. Mingan fed hay into a horse's mouth and wiped his hand on his deerskin bottoms. His sister sat bareback on her white mare, apart from us, watching.

Mingan looked at me, the long hair on one side shimmering in the cold morning sunlight. "Tahki said you wanted to learn how to ride a horse."

Fatimata translated.

I nodded. Tahki had told me it was a necessity if we wished to conclude our mission sooner. The settlements were too far away to travel on foot.

The coats of the horses shone.

"You tend to them well," I said.

"We didn't ride them before the white man came." He patted the neck of a black horse. "These were gifts from them."

"Inadequate compensation for taking our land," Tahki said.

Itoro could not stop staring at the horses.

Kayin poked her in the ribs. "You look like you're in love."

"Aba!" The lieutenant grabbed her side. "She's pretty."

I turned to Mingan. "What do we do first?"

A bale of hay bundled together with two long strings rested on the ground next to a black horse. Mingan stood on the bale. Setting his foot in the stirrup, he held the reins as he swung his leg over and sat in the saddle, his hair flipping over his shoulder.

"That doesn't seem hard," I said. "Do it again. Slowly."

He complied. "It's your turn."

I stepped onto the bale and inhaled the animal's scent, which was not unpleasant.

"Will you always bring hay with you?" called Kayin.

"I won't need it for long."

Imitating Mingan, I jumped and swung my leg over. My momentum carried me to the other side of the horse. I released the reins and landed hard on the earth. Pain stabbed my hip and shoulder. The mare whinnied.

Everyone whooped except for Tahki. Kayin laughed the loudest of all. Tahki smiled.

Mingan reached down to help me up. His raven eyes twinkled. "You're funny."

"I don't try to be," I said.

Ignoring his hand, I leaped up, brushing the dirt and grass off my clothes, hiding how much my hip hurt. I caught a whiff of Mingan. He smelled like dust and the horses he cared for.

Kayin stepped forward. "Do you want me to show you how it's done, Lieutenant Colonel Chi?"

I pushed her away. "Move. I'm trying again."

I swung too far the second time, but righted myself, fingerbreadth by fingerbreadth. After several practices, I mounted without the hay. It was Efe's turn next. She struggled to stay balanced on the bale until Mingan stood on it with her, lifted her by the waist, and placed her in the saddle. Efe smiled shyly at him. He lingered on the bale until he was sure she wouldn't fall off.

After the others practiced mounting, Mingan showed us how to guide the horses and for the rest of the afternoon, we trotted through the woods outside the village. We ventured to the grassy banks of the Powhatan River. The wind blew cool off the water's surface. Kayin rode ahead of me on a chestnut mare. With her back straight and head held high, she still looked like a warrior, despite the cassock and breeches she'd taken from the governor's house. Kayin's mare possessed the same swagger as her rider.

Kayin must have sensed my gaze upon her, because she turned to me. "Want to race?"

I'd made enough of a fool of myself for one day. "Yes, but not today. It will be dark soon."

"Atulu."

For once, I ignored her provocation.

After returning the horses and thanking Mingan for the lessons, we trekked back to Tsenacommacah. Kayin fell in step beside me, slapping me on the same shoulder that had hit the ground when I'd fallen. I winced.

"You walk like you're still riding that horse," she said.

"I feel like I'm still riding it."

As I walked stiffly to the house, I prayed to the goddesses that Kifunji would have a warm bath waiting for me.

# Chapter Twenty-One

# ...or die

"LIEUTENANT COLONEL...WAKE UP."

I was lying on my back on a soft, feather-filled mattress in the former governor's bedroom. I opened one eye to see Itoro in her linen undergarment hovering over me. She slept on a blanket in the hallway outside my door, though I'd assigned her the room next to mine.

Over a handbreadth of snow had fallen to the ground that afternoon, weighing down the boughs of the pine trees. The cold had shocked me when the snow seeped under my cloak collar. My teeth had chattered, and I could not make them stop. I missed the heat of Kana.

"What is it, Itoro?"

"A guard says a Powhatan is headed this way. He's alone."

My head was still hazy with sleep. "He?"

Tahki had been with us earlier, and I thought perhaps she had returned. I raised my head. It was dark outside my window. I ran through the possibilities of why a man from their village would be visiting alone. None of them was good.

I threw off the blanket and the woolly rug that kept me warm and slipped on a pair of loose-fitting, ankle-length breeches I'd found in Yeardley's wardrobe. In the mirror over the dresser, I smoothed down my unruly hair, which hadn't been this long since I was a child. It had grown four finger-breadths. It was too cold to require warriors to shave their heads.

I ran a brush through my hair and left the room.

Efe was awake in the hallway biting her lip, Mrs. Yeardley's robe cinched tight around her waist over her night shift. Fatimata was with her. They shared a bedroom down the hall from mine. Kayin and Kunto must still have been asleep. They'd remained in the kitchen drinking ale when I retired.

I strode past Efe and hurried downstairs, she and Itoro following me.

I opened the door and stepped outside.

A figure appeared in the fog, walking slowly toward us.

It was Mingan.

I rushed to him, Itoro beside me. His vacant eyes stared at an unseen object. Bare-chested, he wore only deerskin bottoms. A scorched odor emanated from his body. We each took an arm and guided him to the house.

Standing in the foyer, Efe's hand flew to her chest.

"Kifunji, bring him a blanket and prepare us a warm drink."

"Yes, Princess Chi."

"Come." I guided him toward the sitting room. "Let's sit."

I lowered him into a wooden chair near the enormous fireplace. I sat in the other one. The fire Kifunji had built earlier to ward off the chill still smoldered. She brought a brown horsehair blanket and coaxed Mingan to lean forward so she could wrap it around him. She gently pushed him back against the chair and left. He and I were in the same chairs where his sister and I sat earlier that night, talking. Efe and Fatimata moved to a settle.

Itoro stayed inside the room by the foyer.

"What happened?" I asked.

He opened his mouth and closed it.

After a few moments, Kifunji returned with cider and withdrew. I wrapped my hands around the mug for warmth, breathing in the rising steam. I sipped. I hadn't grown accustomed to its bitter taste, and at times I yearned for a millet beer, of all things.

Kifunji brought logs to restart the fire.

Mingan took a tentative sip, placed the mug on the small metal table next to his chair, and pulled the covering tighter.

"Our village…was attacked this evening."

"Attacked!" I said.

"I was out in the woods, hunting deer, when I spotted the fire."

My cup rattled as I set it on the table beside me. "Fire…"

Despite the tears wetting his cheeks, his eyes flared. "It was men from Henricus. I recognized one of the traders."

Tahki had told me about this village. When I'd inquired what it was called, she'd spat out, "They call it 'Henricus.' It's still Tsenacommacah."

"They weren't happy you ceased trading with them," I said to Mingan.

The Powhatans transported deerskin clothing, shoes, and pottery in canoes made of cypress trees to trade with English settlements along the Powhatan River. Tahki had returned from Henricus this evening, having told the villagers that the Powhatans would no longer trade with them. I'd asked whether that would cause hardship for her people. "Their being here is a hardship for my people. We'll miss the luxuries they bring from England. But we've lived without their goods for millennia. We can live without them now."

"Or because we helped free your people," said Mingan.

My breath caught. Would the Powhatans blame us for their troubles and seek retribution?

Efe wrung her hands. "What will you do?"

Mingan's lip curled. "Nothing."

The covering slipped off his shoulder. Efe adjusted it for him and returned to the settle.

"Nothing?" I asked. "Why don't you counterattack?" I leaned over and touched his hand, waiting until he looked into my eyes. "We'll help you. My army is at your disposal. After everything you have done for us, it's the least we can do." I paused, wondering why he, and not his sister, was here. "Where's Tahki?"

His lips quivered.

I removed my hand, my chest tightening. "Where is Tahki?"

He whispered, "She's gone beyond the mountains, and traveled to where the sun sets into the most pleasant fields and pastures."

"No!" said Efe.

A heaviness settled on me.

Mingan continued as if he were reciting a lesson. "The white men killed her, my mother and my father, my grandparents, my aunts and uncles, my cousins, and my sisters and brothers. And burned down all the houses in the village and the residents within them. *We* cannot fight back, because I'm the only one left."

❧

Later that morning, Efe, Itoro, Kayin, Kunto, Nsia, and I armed ourselves, and retrieved the horses the Powhatans had loaned us from the communal stables off the public square. Akaba, the first Banaan we'd saved, cared for them. We mounted our horses and left Tsenacommacah.

Mingan wasn't with us. When we departed, he was still sitting where I'd left him, unable to move. Or sleep. Fatimata also stayed behind. She didn't want the reminder of what had happened to her own family.

Dew frosted the leaves of the oak trees that lined the forest trail. Clouds streaked across the blue sky. I rode the same black mare who I'd fallen off of on our first day of lessons. Her name was Enyi; Tahki had given her to me as a present. Enyi galloped along the dirt road without guidance from me. The clop-clopping of the horses' hooves on the dirt lulled me away from thinking about what we'd find in Mingan's village.

When we arrived, the air reeked of smoke and death. A man's body was splayed next to a long stack of charred bark, marsh reeds, and maple wood. We dismounted and went over to him. Puckered skin surrounded the blood-congealed hole in his forehead, the result of a bullet from a blunderbuss. A woman lay beside him, the back of her head missing. Her hair and brains spread over the dewy earth. Underneath her was a smaller figure. The back of the child's head was missing, too.

"My goddesses!" I said.

Itoro swore. Efe backed away.

We remounted our horses and rode on, taking in the carnage. Efe looked dazed, and I wondered if she was thinking of Asanti. Itoro used the butt of her musket to beat back a fox who was sniffing a corpse's chest wound.

I hopped off Enyi and surveyed the remnants of Mingan's house. It had been burned to the ground. I recalled meeting his mother as she cooked over fire. She'd welcomed me into their home without hesitation. A weight of distress pressed on my chest at the undeserved suffering this kind family had endured.

A white feather lay atop the blackened wreckage, unmarred save for a drop of red. It was the one Tahki had worn in her hair. I picked it up and caressed it.

She and I had spent a great deal of time together since we'd met. I respected her intelligence, her courage, and her passion for her people and their future…and that she loved her land. She'd admired the same qualities in me. She'd taken pleasure in repeating my words in her language, and I'd echoed hers, enjoying how they rolled off my tongue. We'd grown comfortable enough with one another that we didn't need to fill the silences.

A tear trickled down my cheek as I envisioned her strong, confident face.

Efe dismounted and put her arm around me. "She was a brave woman. A kindred spirit. The Powhatans should be proud she took their land back."

"She was a great warrior," Nsia said quietly.

I looked up in surprise. She rarely spoke other than when spoken to. Itoro, Kunto, and even Kayin nodded solemnly.

I put the feather in the pocket of my breeches and shielded my eyes from the sun. The warriors were still on their horses. "You know what we must do."

"We're always burying people," Kunto said.

"It's better than being buried," Kayin said.

Efe shook her head in disgust before gazing at Tahki's former home. "Poor Mingan. I don't understand how their refusal to trade caused this amount of rage in the pale men."

Kayin hopped off her horse. "They don't need a reason for their rage."

I remembered when Tahki had said that the pale men were afraid of strong women. She had underestimated them.

"This was a message to other Powhatan tribes," I said. The fox paced underneath a nearby tree. I still wasn't used to this eerie quiet, though we'd encountered it in Banaan and Asanti. "Kunto, return to Tsenacommacah and bring back help. And tools."

That night, after a long day of searching for and burying the remains of the Powhatan villagers, Mingan and I once again sat in front of the hearth drinking ale. Fatimata and Efe joined us.

Mingan slumped in his chair. He stared into the fire with dull eyes.

After a while, he talked about his sister. Their childhoods. How he used to tag along with her when she fished and hunted.

I sipped my drink. "She was proud of you."

"I doubt that. I'm not a warrior like her."

"I'm sure she didn't expect you to be."

He paused. "I've never excelled at anything."

"That's not true. You're an excellent teacher. I haven't fallen off Enyi since that first day."

That elicited a small smile. "I'm grateful for your kindness." He waved. "For everything."

We watched the flames flicker in the hearth. The room was warm and cozy, unlike the front room in the private residence of the Thema Obieze, with its austere furniture. Although it was our living space, my mother discussed queendom business there. She couldn't help it. Kana was her life. But I also worked most of my waking hours.

Mingan twirled the quill of the white feather I'd given him. "What are you thinking about?"

"Kana." I glanced at the sturdy wooden beams that held up the ceiling. "You haven't talked about your plans. Will you try to rebuild your village?"

"Not sure when I'll be ready to return there." His eyes watered. I ached for him. "The memories would break me."

"I know the feeling," said Efe.

I sipped my drink. "Where will you go?"

"Maybe to another Powhatan village."

"You'd no longer receive tribute."

"They paid it to my sister, not to me."

"You could..."

"What?"

"Stay in Tsenacommacah. With us."

# Chapter Twenty-Two

# Arise, warriors of Kana!

BEFORE SUNRISE, KIFUNJI filled the basin in my bedroom with rainwater she'd collected in a barrel and heated over fire. A folded cloth and tallow-and-lye soap lay on the edge of the basin. Here, unlike in the obieze, I bathed myself. The warm water soothed my skin.

Aside from Kifunji and Itoro, no one stirred as I left the house, including Mingan, who was finally sleeping. And eating. Kifunji and Efe had kept after him to do so, and he'd succumbed. He hadn't made any plans about where he would ultimately live, but we had become close since his family perished. As with his sister, I'd fallen into the habit of staying up late into the night talking to him, Efe and Fatimata often joining us. Sometimes, Efe and Mingan continued talking after Fatimata and I had retired. They had both suffered from unimaginable loss and seemed to find comfort in sharing their grief.

Itoro followed me as I strolled down the main street,

which was empty except for the boys cleaning it of horse droppings. The stench of dung was pervasive throughout the town. Puddles pooled in the dirt, the yellowed grass wet from the previous night's rain. A high, three-sided wall formed by strong black locust trees enclosed and protected the town of Tsenacommacah.

We'd moved the training ground from the center to the east side of town, allowing the warriors to drill on different surfaces: dirt, grass, water, and woods. The woods were no longer known by their appropriated name, Sherwood Forest. Mingan had renamed them the Tsenacommacah Forest.

The door to Azeze's blacksmithing workshop was open. He'd commandeered it from the former Jamestown blacksmith, who had fled to another settlement. I hadn't had the heart to say that he'd best enjoy it, given he'd become the blacksmith's apprentice once again when we returned to Kana.

Azeze banged away on his anvil. The fire in the workshop was regularly lit. I slowed down and cut across the street to have a word with him. Tsenacommacah's only blacksmith had to pace himself. As I drew closer, I heard voices from within.

I hesitated at the door. Azeze and Efe were hunched over an object on the large anvil at the center of the shop. Azeze held whatever was consuming their attention between steel tongs.

I stepped through the entrance and cleared my throat. "What's going on?"

They started and turned to face me.

Azeze straightened and composed himself. "Good morning, Adaeze."

Efe rose slowly.

"You haven't answered my question."

No one said anything for a moment. Azeze looked hesitantly at Efe.

"What?" I demanded.

The room was sweltering from the forge alongside a wall. Efe stepped up to me. "Azeze is creating something for me."

"He should be preparing our weapons for battle."

I picked up an oblong iron object with a lion etched on the front and two handles attached to its back. My arm slid through the first handle, and I clutched the soft leather of the second.

"It's a shield," Efe said.

I shot her a look. "As the only warrior present, you'd think I would know that."

She grimaced. "Of course you do."

Azeze ran his arm across his forehead. Beads of sweat glistened on his face and on his bare chest and sinewy arms. "Efe designed it."

I placed the shield back on the table and crossed the room, which smelled of earth and fire. The object they'd been scrutinizing on the anvil was a spear. With a shaft made of fine oak bark, the iron-steel tip had been sharpened to a point I dared not touch.

"Why did this man make you a spear?" I asked. "You no longer fight."

From behind us, Azeze said, "This man has a name."

Efe's skirt rustled as she joined me at the table. "He made it at my request, but it isn't for me."

A flush of delight washed over me. My gaze returned to the weapon. I didn't use spears, but I would use this one.

"I'll treasure it always."

Efe shifted and glanced at Azeze, who stared at the floor.

My smile faded. I flipped the spear over. Carved into the wooden handle in italic lettering were the Kanaian words for Mingan's name:

*Gray Wolf.*

⨒

Efe and I stood on the riverbank watching the water trickle past.

Large stones separated the grass from the Powhatan River's edge. A frog croaked. Itoro stood at a discreet distance: far enough not to overhear our conversation, but close enough to reach me if needed. Aside from when I did my bodily business, she never let me out of her sight. When she slept, Nsia watched over me.

After I'd left Azeze's workshop, Efe had followed me to the river.

"Why would you have a spear made for Mingan?" I asked.

"I thought it would make him feel better. I'm not sure he'll even want it."

"Is there an untoward relationship between you?"

"No. But why would it be untoward? He's a man. I'm a woman."

I crouched, picked up a smooth pebble, and threw it side-long. It skipped across the water's surface six times.

"How did you do that?" Efe exclaimed.

"I don't know."

Some things came naturally to me, though my mother said my abilities came from my ancestors and the goddesses.

"So, there is something between you."

She shrugged. "He understands me."

"We'll be leaving soon. What will you do then?"

She looked at the water. "We don't talk about the future."

The water's scent was clean. With the English gone, maybe the Powhatans could drink from this river again. Before they perished, they had shown us the most favorable places to fish for sturgeon or catch oysters, and the areas of the freshwater marshes from which we could pick an edible plant named *tuckahoe*. The Powhatans would immerse themselves in the river every day, no matter how cold, to wash and wake up.

I grabbed another gray pebble, examined it, and cast it. "Doesn't it bother you he's...not one of us?"

"Why should it? He's strong, brave, and has a kind heart. As you well know. He's your friend, too."

I was trying to get used to the idea of a relationship between Efe and Mingan, and I was relieved she wasn't drawn to Azeze.

"There you are!" We turned. Fatimata walked our way. "I looked out the window and saw you both hurrying to the river and wondered what was wrong."

When she reached us, she eyed the water and stepped back. Fatimata had gained much-needed weight since her freedom.

"You still haven't learned how to swim?" I asked her, dumbfounded.

She shook her head.

"We must remedy that," I said.

"What were you talking about?"

"Nothing."

"Mingan," Efe responded at the same time.

Fatimata smiled at her. "He's handsome."

Efe smiled demurely. "Chibuike, you never told me how you saved Fatimata from drowning."

"Are you trying to change the subject?"

"No. I want to know."

Fatimata told her the story.

She concluded, "Chi pulled me to the bank"—she imitated my childhood royal voice—"'so I wouldn't *foul the entire river.*'" Fatimata giggled. "You were precocious. You strutted around like you were already the queen."

I lifted my hands. "Well…"

We shared a chuckle.

"Despite that, I saw your kindness and hoped we would be friends. I couldn't wait to see your reaction upon seeing me that first Queen's Day."

"Me, too!" said Efe. "She didn't know my mother was the leader of Asanti."

"That day was full of surprises," I said.

We spent the rest of the afternoon on the riverbank. The three of us hadn't been alone since we were youngsters. We chatted about everything and nothing.

Someday, people would tell stories about Efe, Fatimata, and me. How we brought home all the people that were taken from our continent.

❧

Astride his chestnut horse, Mingan wore a deerskin wrap around his waist. He was shirtless. Well-defined muscles rippled his back, chest, and arms. The long, raven hair on the right side of his head was anointed with walnut oil and bound with leather. He'd painted the bottom half of his face black. An arrow like Tahki's was newly tattooed on his arm. He'd been riding bareback, as she used to. Tahki had believed that without a saddle, she and her mare became one. Mingan looked like his sister, the warrior, although he was a reluctant one.

Efe had already proven to me that everyone can become a fighter.

It was the day after Fatimata, Efe, and I had spent the afternoon by the river. The Kanaian warriors sat on horses behind Mingan. I patted Enyi's smooth coat while I waited for the signal. Silva, Fatimata, and Efe were not with us. Efe no longer took part in military maneuvers, preferring to cloister herself in her bedroom thinking. "My mind is of greater value to the mission than my might," she liked to tell me. I left a warrior behind to guard Silva.

The previous night, I'd knelt on the floor in my room and prayed to Age-Fon, the Hunter Goddess, for strength and guidance; to protect the Kanaian and Powhatan warriors and make sure we all returned home whole; for success in battle; that the righteous would prevail. After the prayer, a calmness had come over me.

Mingan had sent word to other Powhatan clans, asking them to join in this fight. They'd agreed, and they now hid in position surrounding Henricus, a town twenty miles northwest of Tsenacommacah. I admired their loyalty. We didn't form military alliances with the nearby provinces; Kanaians fought alone. Maybe this should change, I thought, to defeat Bamidele.

Kayin sat tall on her chestnut horse. "There's someone who looks like us."

An adolescent boy held a tin pail, heading for a cow that grazed on the grass near a cross-wood fence. The homes here possessed chimneys atop pitched roofs.

Kunto pointed. "And another one." The girl was younger than the boy, carrying an armful of clothing to the river. "Why don't they run away?"

Neither youngster was chained or supervised.

I gave Enyi one last pat and straightened. "They don't know they have a place to run to."

Mingan whistled and screamed a war cry with anguish and rage. My blood surged as he sped forward. A pale man stumbled out of his dwelling, still half asleep, buttoning his trousers. Mingan speared him in the chest. The man shrieked and fell.

Kunto raced ahead. The Powhatans shot forward from their hiding places. Using their monohawks and tomahawks, they struck down men—many carrying muskets—running out of their homes.

Mingan speared anyone in his vicinity. As soon as he killed one man, he pulled out his spear and aimed it at someone else. I hoped none of our warriors would get too close to him. If the men didn't come outside, the Powhatans and Kanaians rushed inside and killed them. Although I did not dismount from my horse, pale men's blood coated my daga.

When the battle was over, the townsmen were dead or dying, their groans and whimpers fading one by one. Bodies lay on the street, in yards, and hanging out of windows. Hovering amid them was the stench of death.

The screaming women and children remained unharmed, cloistered in their houses. We might have been condemning them to a life of starvation without their men, but as I saw it, these were women—resourceful. I convinced Mingan not to burn down their houses as the Henricusans had done to the Powhatans' homes.

Finally, a hush settled—as it always did after battle—like the calm at the end of a harmattan.

Kayin went from house to house to retrieve the servants. Of various ages, none of them cried at the sight of their deceased former enslavers. One looked at the corpses as if they were horse manure on the street. A woman kicked a supine pale man in the head. Others looked away from the bodies.

They stared at us warriors, still holding our weapons and straddling our horses in our bloody tunics. I spoke to them in Kanaian and told them they were free again. I welcomed them to come back with us to Tsenacommacah until we took them home.

A barefoot girl with plaited hair stepped forward hesitantly, stopping a few paces from Enyi.

"Who are you?" she asked.

"I am Princess Chibuike of the Queendom of Kana. What's your name?"

"They call me Mary." She reached out. Enyi lowered her head, and the girl patted her muzzle.

"What's your given name?"

"Ebele." She lifted her chin, her serious, brown-eyed gaze meeting mine. "I want to go with you."

"Where's Kunto?" Kayin asked.

## Chapter Twenty-Three

# Because valor is our virtue

KAYIN TOOK OFF running. Itoro and I dismounted and ran after her.

Down the road, in front of a wood-framed house, she lowered herself beside a figure. My legs were sluggish, and my mouth was dry. Itoro looked stricken. I slowed but forced myself to keep walking. Kayin batted flies away and laid her hand on her sister's chest, over her heart. Into the stillness came a keening.

By the time we reached her, I was having trouble taking in air. Not Kunto! *Please, goddesses, may my eyes deceive me!* Kayin punched her sister in the chest, as Kunto had done to her after she'd almost drowned in the Powhatan River at Point Comfort. She punched her again. And again. Her sister's blood soaked her tunic.

I grabbed Kayin's shoulders. "She's joined our ancestors."

"No!"

The corpse of a pale man with a bullet wound in the chest lay nearby, his musket next to him. Kunto's gun rested beside her. The coppery smell of blood hung over both of them.

Kayin broke free from my grasp—her hazel eyes wild—ran across the grass, climbed the three steps to the porch of the house, and burst through the door. I ran after her. Itoro squatted next to Kunto, cursing.

A scream resounded.

When I entered the home, a stout woman cowered in a corner next to the hearth. The ashen faces of a boy and girl peeked around either side of her petticoat. The woman was blubbering, mucus dripping from her nose onto her blue linen apron. She looked up at Kayin, who was pointing her sword at the woman's eye.

I took a tentative step toward my sister warrior and raised my hand. "Kayin, what are you doing?"

"They should suffer."

"And they will. Every day. If they live. If they don't, they'll feel nothing." I held my hand out to her. "Come with me."

She glanced at me, her eyes flashing, the sword's blade unwavering. "I'm not done here."

I took another step. And another. She didn't move. I reached out, placed my hand on top of hers, and lowered the weapon.

I put my arm around her. "We're not savages."

The woman's eyes darted from Kayin to me.

I steered Kayin to the door. Before we reached it, she spun out of my arm and rushed toward the woman.

"Kayin!" I yelled. "This is not the way!"

"Ike!"

Her chilling scream planted my feet to the floor, like the massive roots of a mahogany tree in the Kanaian Forest. Kayin ran forward, her sword aimed at the woman's neck.

I closed my eyes, praying to Age-Fon for Kayin's spirit.

My prayer was answered with a thud—not the pulpy sound of steel entering flesh.

I opened my eyes. The sword's tip was stuck in the wooden wall above the woman's head. Kayin's hands were empty, her chest heaving.

Though the woman couldn't understand her, Kayin said, "Remember my mercy."

⏖

Kayin picked up Kunto's body and carried her through the streets of Henricus to her horse. She laid her sister gently across its saddle, mounted her own horse, and guided them both back to Tsenacommacah.

After the Battle of Henricus, the town's former slaves gathered in Tsenacommacah's public square, reuniting with their families from Banaan. Ebele ran to a pregnant woman, shouting, "Nne!" Another woman screamed as she embraced a young woman who resembled her. They drifted to the ground, holding each other.

When Kayin, Itoro, and I arrived, Efe and Fatimata hugged us despite the blood that still soiled our tunics. I stood with the warriors, observing the joyful reunions while overwhelmed by Kunto's death.

Mingan headed to the house where we were staying, and Efe watched him go.

The following morning, we gathered on the bank of the

Powhatan River, underneath a maple tree with budding leaves hinting at the arrival of spring. The low clouds heralded rain. After Yetunde said a prayer, I spoke at great length about Kunto. I held myself together, though inside I was numb with grief. I was younger than Kunto, but she'd been like a little sister to me.

Efe looked wan. She held Kayin, who wept unashamedly. Tears clung to Itoro's eyelashes but did not fall.

I placed a handful of walnuts on the blanket wrapped around Kunto, since the land did not produce kola nuts. In Kana, Kunto had gotten on my nerves chomping on them all the time. I smiled faintly, recalling the day she said she'd sleep when she joined her ancestors.

I cried. For Kunto. For all that we'd lost. For how tired I felt at that moment. Efe released Kayin and rushed over to me. She hugged me. I relaxed into her embrace and kept crying.

Kayin picked up her sister and walked out into the river. She held her for so long, I didn't think she would ever let her go. Until she did.

Afterward, Kayin, Kifunji, Fatimata, and I returned to the house. After Kayin dried herself off, we gathered without appetites in the dining room, eating food prepared by others. I wouldn't let Kifunji cook that day. She sat with the rest of us as we sipped ale and told stories about Kunto. During one of the tales, Kayin slipped out of the room.

She didn't return. I excused myself and went upstairs to the bedroom she'd shared with her sister. It was empty. The beds were made. Metal holders fastened to one wall displayed Kayin's two swords, crossed at their center. Kunto's musket and cartridge belt hung beside them.

A sniffle came from the closet.

I opened the door and found Kayin sitting hunched over on the pine floor, holding a tuft of hair. Tears stained her face.

"Kunto's?" I asked.

She nodded.

I sat on the floor in front of her, outside the closet.

The rain, which had started when Kunto's memorial service ended, beat against the shutters. Although it was late afternoon, it was dark outside. These torrential storms reminded me of Kana, but in Tsenacommacah, they lasted a few hours or a day, not an entire season.

"It's hard to breathe," she said. "How do I breathe without her?"

"You will grieve, but one day the pain won't be as great."

"I'm older. I was supposed to protect her. She saved me, but I couldn't save her." Kayin paused. "She never wanted to be a great warrior like I did. Hated the killing part. She did it because she wanted to be with me. I shouldn't have been so selfish." Her face contorted. "Why did the goddesses take her?"

It was difficult to hear her over the pinging rain. "That I cannot answer. But she didn't die in vain. She died for freedom."

"How can she be free if I am not?"

"But she is. She's with our goddesses."

"That's not a satisfactory answer."

"It's the only one I can give." I reached out and placed my hand on her shoulder. "You're not alone. You have me. Efe. Fatimata. Itoro."

"A part of me has died. You don't have a twin. You'll never understand."

I withdrew my hand. I'd always wanted a sibling. But being a twin meant something more. They were different people, and yet one.

"You're right. But everyone has lost someone."

She looked straight at me, the whites of her eyes tinted pink. "Except you."

An image of the empty bedchambers in the obieze's private residence came to me. "I lost four sisters I'll never know."

She cast her eyes downward. "I didn't know."

"You're not the only one hurting. Kunto was our sister, too."

"It's not the same."

"I know. But it still hurts."

"I wish I could take her place, give her a chance to carve out her own life. She was forever in my shadow."

"A long shadow, certainly. But she was a person in her own right. I will miss her."

Kayin sniffled. "I didn't have a chance to say goodbye." She looked at Kunto's tuft of hair, still in her hand. "I want to kill all the pale men."

I tried not to wince. "We killed a lot of them. Avenge her loss by remembering your purpose. Your work in our realm isn't finished."

She looked back at me. "Seeing the girl's face we saved— Ebele—felt good."

"Yes, it did." I took her hands in mine. "Let's pray."

Cross-legged on her bedroom floor, we prayed to Gbadu, the Goddess of Destiny, for Kunto, who'd joined our ancestors back in our homeland. Silently, I prayed for her twin sister, who remained.

After four sunrises of mourning for Kunto and the others who'd perished during the Battle of Henricus, we deployed troops to settlements along the Powhatan River to free the enslaved and bring them back to Tsenacommacah. Over the following full moon, after hearing about the town, others throughout the Colony of Virginia escaped enslavement and came, as well.

So far, none of their enslavers attempted to recapture them. Either word of our fighting prowess had reached their ears or they were biding their time. Many of the warriors were chafing to return home. As was I.

I prepared for the journey back to Kana.

✍

My eyes popped open.

Lying in bed, I stared at the wood-beamed ceiling, waiting to hear, again, the noise that had awakened me. Bang! Bang! Bang!

Someone was pounding on the front door.

Weak sunlight and a cool breeze came in through the open windows. It was too early for visitors. The second round of knocks was more insistent. I threw off the blanket, rushed to open the shutters, and peered out the window. I scanned the nearby buildings. No smoke. No fire.

Itoro was in the hall wearing the tunic she had slept in. She no longer bedded in the hallway outside my room, but in the small bedroom next to mine. She was a light sleeper. The noise had brought her to the hall as quickly as if she still slept there.

Efe and Fatimata emerged from their rooms in their night shifts, their faces creased with worry.

"Who could it be?" asked Fatimata.

"We shall find out," I said.

The door to Kayin's room opened behind me, but I didn't wait for her.

It was Nsia who had knocked on the door. She stood next to Kifunji in the foyer. They both looked up at me as I descended. Mingan wandered in from the sitting room, his torso and feet bare.

"What is it?" I asked.

Nsia's long lock was tucked behind her ear. She saluted. "Come with me."

"Tell me."

"Trust me, Lieutenant Colonel Chi. It would be better if you witnessed this with your own eyes."

I passed my hand over my face. I disliked riddles. And surprises. "Where are we going?"

"To the river."

Fatimata and Efe had joined us.

"Stay here," I said.

"No," they both said.

I didn't have time to argue. "Very well. Lead us, Nsia."

We walked past houses lining both sides of the road.

Kayin caught up to us, still in her linen shirt. "What's this about?"

She'd been in low spirits since her sister's death. I was pleased she joined us. As soon as she was ready, we would be returning to Kana.

"It's a mystery." I cut a glance at Nsia, who walked a few paces ahead.

Nsia didn't turn. "You'll see soon enough."

A butterfly with orange and black wings flitted among the fragrant wildflowers, following Kayin. Beyond the last house, we left the dirt and traversed the moist grass, slick beneath my bare feet.

I ducked under a low-hanging maple branch. Dew dotted a spiderweb that stretched from a branch to the trunk. Large stones lined the river's shore. A vulture circled overhead.

None of us said a word as we stared out over the water. The sight would have been beautiful had it not been so terrifying. Fatimata trembled. Kayin's jaw was slack.

At least sixty ships with great white masts crowded the river. From the top of each ship, flapping in the wind, rose an English flag.

## Chapter Twenty-Four

# Live to fight another day

THE FLEET OF ships had anchored fifty spear lengths away, unable to come closer in the river's shallows. We did not move or speak. A brown rabbit hopped nearby, oblivious to our predicament.

*Goddesses, help me.*

"Nsia," I said, trying to keep my voice steady, "rouse the rest of the warriors and tell them to meet us here."

"Yes, Lieutenant Colonel."

A brown and black owl with a white face and a spear-length wingspan let out a loud cry. She swooped down, grabbed the rabbit midhop with powerful talons, and flew off. The rabbit had also been oblivious to her predicament.

I headed back to town.

"Where are you going?" Kayin asked.

Over my shoulder, I said, "To get dressed. I can't fight the king in my bedclothes. Neither can you."

Itoro moved to join us.

I stopped. "No. You stay."

"But I must protect you."

I gestured toward the ships. "My enemy is without, not within. I'll return shortly."

By the time Kayin and I had dressed and returned, the warriors lined the shores, their muskets aimed at the vessels. Itoro had told them to wait for me unless fired upon. After a while, they lowered their weapons, but did not relax their attention.

Itoro looked at the river. "What are they waiting for?"

"I'm not sure," I said.

By nightfall, the English still hadn't attacked or communicated with us.

We slept on the riverbank that night. Fatimata, Kifunji, and Mukki prepared food and gathered water and blankets for us. The springtime night air was pleasant. Warriors took turns on watch, but it was difficult to sleep with a flotilla of ships pointing their cannons at us.

At daybreak, Nsia pointed at the water. "Lieutenant Colonel Chi."

From the nearest ship, a rowboat descended into the river with six men inside, one of them standing. He was holding a pole. Attached to it was a white flag.

"What does that mean?" I asked.

"It's a sign of peace," said Efe.

"How do you know that?"

"Books."

"Hold fire!" I yelled to the warriors. "But be ready!" To Efe, "In case you're mistaken."

The rowboat docked against the low pier. Three men in red uniforms walked toward us, the other three remaining in the boat. I didn't move, although my hand rested on my daga's pommel. Efe stood behind me. Kayin and Itoro were on either side of me. Itoro's breathing was audible. Fatimata arrived and stood next to Efe.

A man stepped forward. He was older than I and had a craggy complexion and blond hair. He smelled of the sea and the sweat of men who'd spent too much time together in an enclosed space. He examined my face. "Princess Chibuike of Kana?" I nodded. "My name is Anselm Chauncy, the Earl of Sussex. I represent King James of Great Britain."

Fatimata translated.

"He's not with you?"

Chauncy chuckled. "No."

*Atulu.* "Isn't he the king of England?"

"Scotland. But our king is ambitious."

"Great Britain. England. Scotland. I don't understand your politics."

"Sometimes, neither do I. Regardless, he sent me to inform you that you're trespassing."

Efe pressed forward, squeezing between me and Itoro. "This is not your land." She pointed at Mingan. "It belongs to him."

Chauncy didn't bother to look at Mingan. "The king issued a charter for this land to the Virginia Company."

"He has no jurisdiction here," I said. "And your government has no authority."

He glanced at the Kanaian warriors. Some were standing. Others sat astride horses. Armed with muskets, dagas, swords, or spears, they stared at the pale men, their faces expressionless. Chauncy calculated the odds. "You'll vacate this land and return our property at once."

"The buildings?" Efe asked.

"Yes…and the servants."

I shook my head. "That we won't do."

"Then prepare for war."

"We will. I don't care how many ships your king sends."

I whistled the sound of the drongo. Every Kanaian warrior thumped her weapon on the ground. I whistled again. They thumped their weapons twice this time.

But I was bluffing. I did not like our odds.

He sighed. "As you wish."

He headed back to the rowboat.

"Wait!" Efe called after him.

Chauncy hesitated. Everyone looked at her.

"Is it possible to resolve this without fighting?" she asked.

"We shouldn't negotiate," Kayin said. "We should fight."

"Ah!" he said. "You propose to settle this like gentlemen." We glared at him. "And ladies." He glanced at the vessels in the river. "Our king is…distracted. And he abhors war. I will relay your message."

"Tell him to take all of his people back to England," Itoro said.

Chauncy gave her a sharp look.

"Itoro…," I said. A token rebuke.

The men returned to the boat and rowed back to the ship.

"This is a waste of time," Kayin said.

A self-satisfied smile spread across Efe's face. "My mother was right. There's no need to fight if you find the right words."

❦

My grandmother appeared in my dreams.

A warrior queen, Nne Nne Thema had continued to lead battles after her reign began. Kana had been a village when she was born, but she'd transformed it into a town and expanded the queendom to its current borders. She'd commissioned the obieze's construction but didn't live long enough to see it completed.

In my dream, the two of us were walking through the compound. She kept saying to me, *You were chosen. You were chosen.*

A deafening boom woke me. Gunfire, but louder.

The light from the ascending sun shone through the window. I was in bed. Most of the Kanaians were still on the northern riverbank, but my officers had urged me to return to the house to rest.

After donning my tunic, I grabbed my daga and ran out into the hallway. Itoro was there, dressed and ready. Efe was rubbing her eyes.

"You should stay," I said to her.

"I can't. This is my fight, too."

"But there are no Asantis here."

"It's still my fight. We all have to stand up to their villainy, or it will never cease. This is my fault! I must go."

No time to argue with her. "Stay out of the way."

We hurried down the street toward the river. Plumes of smoke rose from the house closest to the river.

*Aba! Aba! Aba!*

"Anyone inside?" I yelled as I passed.

"No!" answered a warrior standing in front of it.

Another boom.

Birds startled from the trees. The cannon ball landed on several warriors. They dropped on the riverbank, their screams painful to my ears. Arms, legs, and heads detached from bodies. The all-to-familiar stench of gunpowder and blood and death surrounded us. Efe, standing behind a copse of trees, wrung her hands.

"Fight back!" I screamed.

I rushed into the warriors' midst, commanding them to engage. The ships' cannons continued to fire, the air smoky and acrid. More of my sister warriors fell. I whispered another prayer. *Goddesses, what shall I do?*

After a moment, I received an answer. From my belly. I scanned the water. We couldn't compete with cannons. Our best option was to…"Retreat!"

Except for Kayin, all the warriors stopped and looked at me as if I were mad.

"We refuse to surrender…" said Itoro.

"…and will never retreat," finished Nsia.

But we must this time. Or we'd all perish in this foreign land.

I rushed over to Kayin, who was still firing, and tried to grab the musket from her. She wouldn't let go. She flashed her hazel eyes at me.

"Fighting to your death won't bring Kunto back," I said.

"Valor is our virtue," she replied.

"So is the wisdom to know when we must change our ways. You must live to fight another day."

Kayin relaxed her gaze.

The warriors' faces and bodies were encrusted with blood and dirt and sweat. A lump formed in my throat. I shouted, "We, the elite warriors of Kana, are proud, brave, and fierce! But to triumph, we must not die today! As long as we live, Kana will stand!" Ignoring the cannon fire, I strode over to

Mingan, who'd been fighting with us, and grabbed his bare, slick arms. "We need the help of your people."

Lines creased his forehead. "Everyone in my village has perished."

"The other Powhatan villages. How large is your tribe?"

"At least thirty clans."

"How many people is that?"

"Around seventeen thousand."

"Send riders. And tell them to bring back everyone."

"But they'll expect tribute."

"Tell them your land—your future—is at stake!"

❧

After we retreated from the riverbank, the English ceased firing. Their options were to wait until we returned or to leave their ships and come to us. My scouts reported that the pale men hadn't lowered their rowboats into the water. Disappointed, I'd hoped to face the treacherous Chauncy again. I didn't need Kayin or Itoro to kill him. I reserved that opportunity for myself.

We carried the injured warriors to the house Mukambu lived in. The physician used the trestle table in the dining room to treat them. The herbs and instruments she needed rested on the sideboard.

By the afternoon, women and men warriors of nearby Powhatan tribes arrived in Tsenacommacah. The next day, more Powhatans arrived. The third day, we returned to the north riverbank, which was shrouded in mist. The scent of brine, algae, and wet earth filled my nostrils. The shore was teeming with Kanaians and Powhatans; there was no empty space to be found.

I stopped by Yetunde's house and asked her to pray over me. At sunrise, I stood before the warriors, my Nne Nne Thema with me for guidance and strength. I raised my daga. "Arise, warriors of Kana! These men wish to enslave you and your families. Or kill you. We must prevail to protect our way of life, and the lives of our children and our children's children, through eternity. If we shall perish, let the queen dance and sing our names forevermore!"

The Kanaians screamed the war cry.

Mingan shouted in Algonquian that the English coveted their land, but that the Powhatans would keep it or die. The clans roared back their assent.

Our adversaries didn't fire their cannons. Instead, fifty rowboats descended into the river.

"Patience!" I yelled.

A bird flapped its wings overhead.

As the English drew near, the men in the boats raised their muskets and fired. The Kanaian warriors fired in return. Gun smoke, mixing with the mist, made visibility difficult, but both sides continued to shoot. The Powhatans let loose with a shower of arrows, hitting the pale men in their faces, torsos, or legs. The men slumped over and fell backward in the rowboats or forward into the river.

Several of the boats reached the riverbank.

I yelled "Ike!" and rushed forward, Kayin, Itoro, and the warriors following me. I leaped into a boat. My daga struck any soft body part it found. Recklessly. Gloriously. A man tried to pummel me with his musket. I evaded the weapon and slashed his throat, back-kicking another man who advanced from my rear.

Ignoring the rising stench of blood, I fought with a fire

within me. My daga knew where to go to avenge Dayo, Yaa, Abeni, Tahki, Tahki's family, Kunto, the warriors who'd perished, Kana, Banaan, Asanti, Aon, Zatopa, Alkebulan, and all the people who looked like us we couldn't save. Or would save. This battle was for them.

Kayin fought without the glazed look that had settled on her face after her sister died; her calm and confidence had returned.

We dispatched the remaining men in the rowboats.

A shower of Powhatan arrows, their tips ablaze, sailed from the shore and arced toward the ships in the middle of the river. When they landed, the screams of the Englishmen on board reached us. Ships caught fire. One exploded. I presumed the flames had engulfed the gunpowder stored on the boat. A cannonball fired and dropped into the sea. The vessels retreated out of the arrows' range.

A hail of flaming arrows was loosed from the opposite riverbank. Besieged, more ships caught fire. Masts and sails crashed onto decks with loud thwacks. Blackened holes gaped in the hulls. Men howled and jumped into the water.

The Englishmen steered the few remaining ships southeast, heading for the Chesapeake Bay. We let them go. Someone had to relay this day's events to their absent king.

After the last ship departed, Kanaian and Powhatan warriors hugged.

Mingan stood nearby, his eyes shining, his face soiled with sweat and dirt. "That was for Tahki."

His chest convulsed, and he let out a sob. I wrapped my arms around him. My heart was still thumping, my body shaking. So many dead. Wounded. I clutched my daga so I wouldn't drop it.

He rested his chin on my shoulder. "I watched you fight. You reminded me of my sister."

He smelled of musk and blood. I held him tighter until we both stopped shaking. Efe watched us.

I parted from him. "Together, we are invincible."

He grinned. "Together, we are invincible."

I turned to the rest of the warriors. "Together, we are invincible!"

The Kanaian and Powhatan warriors echoed my cry.

"Together, we are invincible!"

My skin tingled as I repeated this a few times, and they responded.

A fallen warrior lay on the ground, her legs missing. Blood saturated the grass beneath her. The single lock of hair—no longer indigo, but a natural brown—was plastered to her forehead with sweat.

My heart sank. I rushed over and crouched next to her. I choked back a sob. "Oh, Nsia."

"It's…all right, Lieutenant Colonel Chi."

I touched her shoulder. My vision blurred. I could hardly see her pained expression. "I'm glad I found you in Doba."

She grunted. "We found each other."

"Thank you for your service to the queen. To me."

"I'm a warrior." She coughed. She still clutched her sword, the blade coated with blood. I bent closer to her mouth to hear. "This is…the only way my life could end. Let the queen dance and sing my name."

She stopped breathing.

"Forevermore," I said, lowering her eyelids.

I bowed my head and said a prayer to Goddess Age-Fon, the Hunter Goddess, for Nsia. Contrary to what I'd told

Tahki, Nsia would not be returning to Kana with us. But I'd tell stories for the rest of my life about the best swordswoman in the history of the queendom.

## Chapter Twenty-Five

# And as long as we live...

BIRDS CALLED TO one another. Yellow, white, and red flowers bloomed, their perfume impregnating the air anew. Bees buzzed as they landed on flower after flower. White fluff blew off small stems growing from the ground.

We ushered Nsia and the other Kanaian warriors who'd perished during the Battle for Tsenacommacah into the river and out to the sea, so they could join Kunto and the other fallen warrior and find their way back to Kana. The Powhatans took their dead home with them to their villages.

A few days later, Chauncy returned carrying his useless white flag. Two men accompanied him. They were all unarmed. He, Mingan, Efe, and I negotiated a treaty. The signing took place in the council room of the former governor's house.

The terms were as follows: the English were required to leave Virginia and either go back to England or settle in another colony. England relinquished the land back to the Powhatans, who, along with the Kanaians, agreed not to attack any settlements in the other colonies. In return, the settlements would not attack Tsenacommacah or any Powhatan village in the King's name. This agreement didn't extend to the rest of the British colonies.

It wasn't an ideal resolution. Settlements could attack Tsenacommacah, anyway, but Efe convinced me and Mingan that it was the best we could do. Mingan was satisfied, so I agreed.

I asked Chauncy to leave the map he'd brought with him. He shrugged. "I have others."

After he departed, Kayin, Efe, Mingan, and I remained seated at the table. Itoro stood by the door.

"Will they keep their word?" I asked.

"No," said Kayin.

"It's the English," Mingan said. "Who knows? But they heard the truth in your words."

"Chibuike can convince a zebra it needs new stripes," Efe said.

I'd argued with the king's representative that this was a battle they couldn't win. The Powhatans wouldn't allow the English to take their land, and we would help them protect it.

"Your guidance helped," I said to Efe.

She grinned.

"There's another issue we need to discuss," Mingan said.

I tensed. He wanted us to leave.

"From now on, Point Comfort will be called Kinnakeet. And it's yours. For helping us. Use it as your base. Where your people can find solace and refuge. To prevent slavery on our land in perpetuity."

Efe beamed with gratitude—and, if I wasn't mistaken, pride.

"That's…" I collected my thoughts. "Generous. And I'm appreciative. But we'll pay you."

"Your friendship has been payment enough."

Mingan and I didn't shake hands or sign a piece of parchment. Our word was our bond.

"I have news to share, too," I said. "We're going home."

Everyone in the room looked stunned.

"I can't leave," Fatimata said, "until I find my family."

"Me neither," said Efe.

I unrolled the map Chauncy had left and pointed. "This is our land."

The Alkebulan continent was covered in forests with a few castles on the coast and zebras and giraffes inland. But there were no city-states, provinces, villages, or towns. As if Kana, Banaan, and Asanti didn't exist. I dragged my finger across what the pale man called the Atlantic Ocean to the Powhatan's land. "This is where we are." I moved my finger south, down to Hispaniola. "Your families could be here." I moved my finger west to New Spain. "Or there." I drew a circle around all the surrounding land. "Or anywhere in between."

Fatimata's and Efe's looks were blank.

I was homesick and wanted to return to Kana. To bite into a celestial yam cake. To see my father and Ndidi. To hug my mother.

But a mission was a mission.

I sighed. I'd ceded my first argument. "I guess we're going to New Spain."

But there was something I needed to do first.

The day was glorious.

A flock of white-throated sparrows chirped. An osprey dove into the water, caught a fish, and flew off with it. The smell of brine and algae enveloped us.

I reached out. Fatimata took my hand.

"I'm afraid," she said.

"Have I ever let you down?"

She shook her head and allowed me to lead her into the Powhatan River until the chilly water reached our waists.

"Lean forward until you're lying on your stomach."

She hesitated.

I placed my hand on her belly. "I'll hold you up."

She complied.

I held her until she was floating.

"Now kick," I said.

❧

Next to the kitchen was a small room where Angelo had slept when the governor and his family occupied the dwelling. Now she stayed in a house with several warriors.

I nodded at the warrior guarding the painted white wooden door, pushed it open, and entered. The room was more like a closet and reeked of body odor. It contained only the mattress on the floor where Francisco de Silva lay. Kayin and Efe remained outside the doorway.

We allowed Silva out for walks and meals. He still drank but in moderation, and I once caught him praying when I passed his room. I hadn't interacted with him much for a few full moons.

He sat up. "Have you come to kill me?" he asked in Portuguese.

His voice was calm, his face serene. He didn't look afraid.

"Why would you think that?"

He shrugged. "You don't need me."

I squatted beside the pallet. "What should I do with you? You've done some despicable things in your life."

"Who hasn't?"

"Many people haven't treated humans like animals and transported them to be sold."

Silva glanced down at his shirt, absent of rum stains. We'd provided him with one of Yeardley's. "I don't believe in slavery. It was a job that paid well. But…it doesn't sit right with me anymore. I've watched you…and your people. You're not uncivilized."

"Why should I trust you?"

"You shouldn't," Kayin piped up from behind me.

After a long silence, he said, "All of my ancestors were Jews."

"Jews?" I asked.

"Yes, they were observant Jews, but forced to convert to Christianity or face persecution or death. They continued to practice their religion in secret and strictly followed the rules for what they could and could not eat. They honored the Sabbath. Although they lived in fear, they never abandoned who they were." He paused. "I, too, am a Jew. A *converso*. Pretending to be Catholic. I've never told anyone. Telling you puts my life at risk."

I didn't know what all of this meant, but I had some sense of what he was revealing to me. He hadn't tried to escape or caused any trouble since we landed here.

"I'll let you live. But I require something of you."

"What?"

"Take us to New Spain."

He blinked. "Excuse me?"

"We're going to search for the rest of our people."

To my surprise, his response came immediately. "I'll help you."

"He's betrayed us once," Kayin said.

Silva looked over my shoulder at her. He didn't know our language, but he said, "I don't want this on my conscience. I'll make it right."

Kayin leaned against the door frame. "Pale men do not keep their word."

Without turning, I asked in Kanaian, "Efe, do you believe him?"

"Yes."

Silva reached out his hand, perpendicular to the pine floor. I hesitated, but was ready if he tried to wrestle me to the mattress. He wouldn't dare with Kayin present if he wanted to live. I clasped his hand. He squeezed.

"This means we agree," he said.

I returned the squeeze.

At the door, I turned. "You know what will happen if you betray me again."

His smile was nervous. "I have an idea."

"Wherever you go, we will find you."

❧

Kayin and Efe followed me to the dining room, where Fatimata and Itoro waited. Fatimata's hair was still wet from her swimming lesson. The aroma of the chicken and rice supper Kifunji was preparing wafted from the adjoining kitchen.

"I'm hungry," Kayin said.

An echo of Kunto. My stomach rumbled. But business first. "He agreed."

Fatimata yelped with joy and clapped. After suffering so much sorrow, it was nice to see her happy. I prayed we would find her family soon.

I leaned over the table to gaze at the map I'd brought from the council room. "Let's plan."

Kifunji poured drinks, and we discussed our course of action and the date of departure until dinner was ready. We enjoyed the savory meal. I was mopping up the remains on my plate with a thick slice of bread when a warrior appeared at the dining-room door next to Itoro. "Lieutenant Colonel?"

"Yes?"

"A man has arrived with news."

Those seated around the table glanced at one another. Often, news wasn't good.

"Bring him in."

She ushered in an emaciated boy. Upon closer inspection, I realized he was my age or older. His coiled hair showed bald patches in spots, and his upper arm had been branded. His stench invaded the room.

"You're Banaan! Praise Oshun!" Fatimata exclaimed.

His eyes widened. He bowed. "I escaped…from New Spain…with others…and heard of this place. Where servants are free. It took us two full moons to get here."

He stared with longing at our empty plates and cups. A pang of shame shot through me. We were eating our fill, and he hadn't eaten at all.

"Kifunji," I said, "bring him some food and water."

Fatimata stood, her wooden chair toppling backward onto the pine floor. She rushed to him. Her hand trembled as she touched his shoulder. "Do you know what happened to my mother, Yaa?"

He shrunk back. "I...I was captured on the same day, my ruler, as you and your mother."

"My mother is the ruler, not I. Go on."

"Fatimata," I said, "let him eat, then he'll talk."

Kayin righted Fatimata's chair. Kifunji set a spoon, a trencher of chicken and rice, and a cup on the table and guided the man to a chair. Fatimata watched him as he gulped the water and attacked his meal.

When he finished eating, she said, "Tell me what happened to my family."

"After you and the others were stolen from the ship, your mother was distraught—we all were. She kept screaming your name."

"Where is she?"

"We were near Santo Domingo when—"

"Did she get off there or was she taken to New Spain? Tell me!"

"Neither."

Fatimata frowned. "Somewhere else?"

He hesitated. "Before we arrived at the port, your mother, your father, your sisters, and your brothers all held hands and climbed onto the railing. And they..."

"What?"

"...jumped."

"Jumped?"

"Into the water."

Efe rose slowly and moved toward Fatimata. A cold sensation crept into my chest.

Fatimata furrowed her eyebrows. "But some of them don't know how to swim!"

"They didn't try. They're with our ancestors, my ruler."

## Chapter Twenty-Six

# Kana will stand

THE FATE OF Fatimata's family cast a pall over us. That they had chosen death over enslavement was devastating. But it reinforced for me that our cause was just.

After Fatimata had screamed and fainted, Itoro had carried her to the room she shared with Efe. Fatimata hadn't left it since. She wouldn't accept any visitors, except Kifunji, who brought her meals, and only because I threatened to break the door down if she didn't eat. All talk of going to New Spain ceased. Even Efe was no longer inclined to go.

One day, I headed to the river to stretch my legs. I passed the cypress trees on the dirt road. As I came closer, I inhaled the freshwater scent. The grass was lush. A gentle breeze fluttered my tunic and offset the warmth of the sun on my skin. Black, white-throated birds with beaks that were half black and half red nested in an oak tree. I stopped moving as I was about to cross the tree line. Mingan and Efe stood by the stones talking, Mingan's bare back to me. A stray hair loosened from Efe's braid, and he tucked it behind her ear. She smiled at something he said.

I backed away before they could spot me.

After a week of mourning, Fatimata joined me, Kayin, and Efe for the evening meal at the oval cedar table in the kitchen. Her cheeks were sunken. My heart panged. Itoro hovered near the door. A flame flickered from a candle resting in a copper holder at the center of the table. The hearth warmed the room. Pork roasted on the grill iron.

Kifunji was at the cherry sideboard, slicing apples onto two plates covered with flattened breadcrumbs. She was a diligent worker, regularly arising before me. I presumed the sound of my footsteps in my bedroom signaled that her day was beginning. The aroma of fresh crisp apples, spices, and risen bread pervaded the room. My mouth watered. Kifunji retrieved cups from the press cupboard and poured cider into them from a metal pitcher.

"I'm ready to return to Banaan," Fatimata said.

"I want to go home, too," said Efe.

I sipped my drink. "We'll all go home."

Kayin raised an eyebrow. "Everyone?"

"Except for a contingent to guard Kinnakeet against attack and keep it a safe place for our people to escape to."

"But we'll need reinforcements."

"The Powhatans will help," Efe said.

I set my cup down on the table. "You speak for them now?"

She blushed. "Mingan told the rest of his tribe that Kinnakeet is a place of freedom and they must help protect it."

Kifunji turned from the sideboard. "I'm ready to go back."

"I promised to take you home," I said.

"No. To Kana. To serve you."

I could find a place for her, although taking care of us here was a much smaller endeavor than managing the obieze's kitchen. "I would welcome that."

Efe cleared her throat. "I also have news." Her eyes shined. "I'm to be wed."

"To whom?" Kayin asked, bewildered.

Fatimata smiled faintly. She knew as well as I did.

"Mingan asked me to be his wife."

⋰

Efe placed her hand in Mingan's.

His smile was as broad as the Powhatan River, and one of the few I'd seen on his face since the pale men had destroyed his village and murdered his family.

Efe wore a white pano she'd made herself out of cloth. With her braids piled high on her head, cochineal on her cheeks, and red berry juice on her lips, she resembled her mother, Dayo. How would the Asanti ruler have felt today? Was this the man she would have chosen for her daughter? But it would please her to see how happy Efe was.

The previous day, heavy black clouds had rolled in. Wind gusts had rattled everything that wasn't tied down. Rain had lashed against the shutters so hard I'd feared the water would break through them. Seated around the kitchen table, we'd flinched at every thunderclap. The ceremony might have to be moved indoors.

But the goddesses smiled down on Efe. Today, the sky was clear. Although it was hot, the heat didn't bother me. It was when I felt most comfortable in this faraway country.

Fatimata arrived late to the ceremony, her hair damp. I asked her where she'd been.

"Swimming. With some of my landswomen."

Mingan wore deerskin leg coverings, a fox skin on his arms, a chain of linked copper around his neck, and moccasins. He sported a painted black stripe on each cheek. The hair on the left side of his head had grown out, so it was all of equal length, and tied back into the shape of a pony's tail. Tahki's white feather, which I'd salvaged from his family home, was fastened to it with a leather string.

In front of the priestess's daughter, the couple looked at each other with reverence, in solidarity. They had lost their entire families and immediate tribes. They were more than husband and wife. They were like friends who had known each other in another life. They came out of their trance and turned, smiling, to face us, as an unsaddled white stallion tethered to a nearby tree whinnied. Tahki's horse.

After the ceremony, we feasted at long tables set up in the public square. Men and women cooked for days. Smells of foods from Kana, Banaan, and Asanti permeated the air, along with the aroma of a Powhatan stew made with roasted meats, shellfish, and wild berries. Mingan supervised its preparation. It simmered in large kettles throughout the day. Kifunji also prepared a potato porridge, for which I'd developed a taste.

I sat at the head of a table, wearing a sleeveless white tunic. A few chairs away from me, Kayin drank and talked loudly about the best way to teach a warrior the art of sword fighting.

"By watching Nsia."

I didn't realize I'd said it aloud until Kayin stopped speaking and stared at me. She hesitated, then raised her cup. "By watching Nsia."

Bett, the pale woman who'd helped us, sat next to Fatimata, who talked to Mukki on her opposite side. Beside me, Mingan and Efe conversed in low voices, temple to temple.

I set my heavy spoon on the linen tablecloth, rose, and approached a young Banaan man standing by a pungent barrel of apple cider. He dipped a tankard into the cask, filled it to the brim, and handed it to me. I took a long swallow. And another, and another. I finished, reached past him, and dunked the cup to refill it. He stepped away.

I sensed a sudden presence next to me.

"The ceremony was a nice blend of traditions, wasn't it?"

I turned. Azeze held his own tankard. I wiped the excess cider from my lips with the back of my hand. For once, he didn't smell like hard work. "Yes."

People danced in an area cleared of tables to an instrument made of wood and string played by a warrior. Itoro sang, accompanied by the song of blue jays and mockingbirds.

I took another long pull of my drink—how was my cup already empty?—and dipped my tankard in the barrel a third time.

Azeze glanced at the dancers. "Would you like to—?"

Dancing with him would not do. I was a princess; he was a blacksmith...a blacksmith's *apprentice*. "I must return to my seat at the table."

"Of course, Adaeze."

&

The next day, we packed our things. Efe beamed as we moved about the house. Fatimata grinned.

I couldn't take it any longer. "What's so amusing?"

"Efe," Fatimata said, drawing the name out.

"What about her?"

"Mingan put a hex on her."

"From his ancestors?"

"That's not the kind of hex I'm talking about." Fatimata shared a knowing glance with Efe. She had moved in with Itoro into the bedroom between mine and Efe and Mingan's. "The walls are thin."

Efe was radiant.

"Oh!" My cheeks grew hot. "That kind of hex."

We laughed.

I'd been so inebriated after the wedding festivities I'd stumbled to the house and fallen asleep in my bed fully clothed. Itoro must have escorted me, because I vaguely recalled her saying that Kifunji could clean up the chamber pot I'd knocked over in my room. I hadn't heard the newlywed couple's lovemaking, or anything else.

It was the first time I'd been uninhibited. My head still pounded like a warrior's drum from the cider.

When I left Fatimata and Efe, they were still giggling. At the top of the stairs, the closest bedroom door opened, and Mingan stepped out. His face reddened. "I overslept."

"I am glad you found happiness." I meant it. "What are your plans now that we're leaving?"

He looked at me, puzzled. "My home is wherever Efe is. I'm coming with you."

# Part III

# Chapter Twenty-Seven

# We would gladly die...

WE LEFT THE cool corridor beneath the Kanaian Forest canopy, the pleasant hum of oversized insects and the aromas of plants fading behind us as we headed toward the farms on the outskirts of town.

My tunic stuck to my body from the day's heat. A sheen of sweat covered my arms. At a row of stakes, I rubbed the green leaf of a yam plant. My spirits soared, accompanied by a familiar stirring of hunger in my stomach.

We entered the town, where residents lined Kana's primary thoroughfare. When we'd arrived at the empty castle on the coast, I sent our fastest warriors ahead to inform the queen of our return. The news must have leaked. I teared up at all the smiling faces. People wore their finest attire, from the merchants in their silky panos to the farmers in their second-hand wraps. Everyone was yelling, the noise assailing me like the force of a harmattan wind. As we drew closer, I could make out the words.

"Princess Chibuike! Princess Chibuike! Princess Chibuike!"

Kayin and Itoro walked on one side of me, Efe and Mingan on the other. Efe and her husband would live in Kana until the people of Asanti returned. The rest of the Kanaian warriors were behind us, along with Mukambu, Yetunde, Azeze, Mukki, and Kifunji. The Aons, the Zatopans, and the Banaans, including Fatimata, had left our caravan when we'd arrived at their villages.

Having been focused on rescuing the rest of the Banaans and protecting Tsenacommacah, I hadn't returned to Kinnakeet since we accosted the second Portuguese ship over four full moons ago, though I'd frequently sent a warrior to check on the settlement. When we arrived at the fort to begin our journey home, the Zatopans, the Aons, and the Kanaian villagers were still there, having occupied the buildings and built temporary lives. The animals and gardens provided food, and everyone was healthier than when we'd left.

The Kanaian warriors left behind to transform Kinnakeet into an operational base had seen us off. We waved at them, but didn't linger at the ship's stern to look back at the land we would never visit again. Instead, we moved to the bow. A flock of sparrows rose as one and guided us east. The *Isabella Maria* eased out of the Powhatan River and into the Chesapeake Bay.

When we reached the Atlantic Ocean, the Banaans and Kanaians gathered starboard.

Fatimata held up two apples. "In homage to my family and others who would rather die than be enslaved, I give you this gift." She kissed each fruit, held them up again, and thrown the apples into the ocean. "May this feed you until you find eternal rest with our ancestors."

The Banaans sobbed, as did many of the Kanaians. I remembered Yaa's caring face, her kindness.

People dealt differently with what we lived through. Some wanted to talk about it; some avoided it. Others were irritable. Many cried out in their sleep.

Silva navigated the ship expertly—including battling two violent storms. After having lived on the *Isabella Maria* for over six full moons, the Portuguese crew were more than helpful. They went about their tasks as if they were to receive payment. They, too, were anxious to return home. I would never know the consequences of letting them live. Would they kidnap others in the future? After leaving us at the castle, Silva was to take them back to Portugal. He was to return and take a contingent of Kanaian fighters to Hispaniola and New Spain to search for the Asantis and the remaining Banaans. Some of my sister warriors thought I was foolish to believe he would return.

If he didn't, we would make do; many warriors had gained sailing experience while crossing the ocean, and we now possessed a vessel of our own. A group of Portuguese sailors and Kanaian warriors brought back the ship from which we'd retrieved the Zatopans. It was docked at the castle.

It had taken four sunrises to trudge through the rivers, jungles, and plains. I sobbed as we waded through the shallows of the River Ome, the warm, familiar water rising to my waist and caressing my skin. After having crossed, we bathed and donned the clean tunics brought to us by the warriors who had remained at the Thema Obieze.

As we walked down the main thoroughfare, children danced in front of their parents. People lining the street reached out and tried to touch us. Breaking with tradition, I approached them and shook the rough hands of the miners and farmers, the smooth ones of the market traders. One woman wouldn't let go and kept saying, "Thank you! Thank you!" Her daughter's eyes were shining. She was taller, but I still recognized her as the one who'd tried to sell me fruit the day of our capture in the market.

"You're welcome." To the girl, I said, "I'll be by for a baobab soon."

She grinned.

The smells of Kana—smoked meat, fresh fruits, sweat, heat, life, joy—enveloped me. I was home.

We passed the last stall in the market, then several homes, and crossed the wooden bridge that spanned the ditch surrounding the obieze. I stopped and traced a rampant lion etched into the wall with my fingertips. I took a deep, satisfying breath. Everything I'd done, *we'd* done—all the triumphs, the mistakes, and, yes, the losses—had been worth it.

Two fanti in scarlet tunics stood sentry at the main entrance. They saluted me, saying, with uncharacteristic smiles, "Lieutenant Colonel," and they opened the iron gate.

Inside the compound, I teared up as I beheld the Thema Obieze, the sunbaked-clay walls, and the scarlet and white Kanaian flag lying inert on the roof. *Thank you, Gbadu, Goddess of Destiny, for bringing me home.*

Warriors in full dress, the sun beaming off their bald heads on this cloudless day, lined up on either side of the gate from the Grand Square to the obieze. The clay warmed my bare feet. The warriors snapped their arms in salute one by one as I walked past them. At attention, they didn't make a sound, but I glimpsed smiles on many of their faces. I wanted to hug them, but duty required otherwise. I smiled in return and kept walking.

At the entrance to the obieze, the queen stood tall in her purple pano, her hands clasped in front of her, her oval face breaking into an adoring smile. Behind her, Ndidi beamed with love and pride. General Udo's lips were pursed.

I picked up my pace, then ran, not caring that I was breaking with decorum. I hugged my mother fiercely, inhaling her lavender scent. Sobs racked my body, and I held on as if I'd drown if I let go.

"I've prayed for this day," she said. "Welcome home, my nwa."

&

That night, Kifunji filled the basin with water warmed by the hearth. I sat in the tub and brought the karite soap to my nose, deeply inhaling its scent. Afterward, in the private dining room, my mother, father, Efe, Mingan, and I shared a meal of yam stew, okra, and duck.

Efe and I told them about our journey and Tsenacommacah and the Powhatans. Mingan remained silent as we spoke of his sister, Tahki, and the rest of their family. He was more animated when we described our collaboration with the Powhatans in battle. We discussed the four seasons, and how it stayed cold for three full moons during the season the English called winter.

My mother cried when I told her the fate of Fatimata's family.

After everyone had finished eating and left the room, Adebola dismissed the attendants.

"Are you all right, my nwa?"

I lifted my head from my hand. "Why do you ask?"

"You have been through an ordeal. It weighs on me to hear it; I can't imagine living through it. Are you having bad dreams? Like when you were a child?"

I no longer had the dream filled with clicking noises. "No. I'm fine." I hesitated. "I have a question for you."

The question had burned within me since the day Udo showed up at the castle.

"What is it?"

"Why didn't you trust me to carry out the plan?"

She arched an eyebrow. "Every day you were gone, I wondered where you were. What you were doing."

"That's not telling me why."

"When you were a little girl, you would sneak out of the compound. You thought you'd fooled me." She smiled. "Long before you saw the pale man in the forest, my best fanti followed you. You were never alone. To answer your question, it was not a matter of distrust. You are my only child, and I sent her to look after you. I'd lost four children—four daughters. I would not lose you, too. I didn't understand why the goddesses asked me to sacrifice my only daughter. But I let you go. I love my queendom, and I love my daughter." A gentle touch of my cheek. "Don't fault me for that." She withdrew her hand. "But it seems I believed in you more than you believed in yourself."

I lowered my gaze.

She continued, "When a messenger reported that you'd been taken to the plain south of Banaan, I sent Ndidi out to calm our people. Rumors abounded the Portuguese would return for everyone else." She chuckled. "But I also needed Ndidi's help within."

I looked at her. "Why?"

"Your father wasn't speaking to me. He believed I'd placed you in jeopardy. I'd told him the plan when we were hiding in the barracks. He wanted to rescue you."

I smiled. "How did you respond?"

"I didn't have to. One look at the warriors stopped him. But Sola escaped from the obieze. Foolish." My mother shook her head. "The castle was the pivotal moment. When I received word we'd defeated them, I was relieved, but it didn't last long. Udo was heading back to Kana. You were not. I've spent the last eight full moons worrying. I had no way of tracking your whereabouts. I prayed in the temple every day and focused on my work."

Only one person could consume her attention. "Bamidele."

She nodded. "I learned he had shipped some of his residents. It was fortunate it was to the same place, so you could save them. Otherwise, I don't know where the Aons would be."

I recalled the Kanaians' hands I'd touched upon our return. Some were soft and others calloused. Did they work the land by choice?

"I have another question."

"Yes, my nwa?"

My mouth felt dry. "Some people in Kana are more prosperous than others. Shouldn't we try—"

She rose. "You're tired from your long trip. You need to rest. We'll discuss that at another time."

❦

The following morning, I picked up my daga from its rightful place on the hippopotamus tusk stand atop my dresser, sheathed it, and retrieved Efe from the bedchamber she shared with Mingan next door. We hurried downstairs and entered the Council Room for the weekly meeting.

I strode to my customary position behind my mother's golden chair.

"No, nwa," my mother said. "You've earned your place at the table."

My heart skipped a beat.

She gestured for me to sit at the opposite end of the mahogany table, and for Efe to sit next to me. Ndidi sat on one side of my mother, Udo on the other. One seat was empty. Adebola hadn't replaced Sola.

"You've impressed me," the general said to me. She turned to the queen. "You were right. Lieutenant Colonel Chi was the perfect choice for leading the mission."

My mother didn't acknowledge her comment. She was always right. She was the queen. "Chibuike, tell everyone what you've been through."

I recounted the tale I'd told my parents the previous evening.

My mother's most trusted attendant, Salamatu, brought cups of water. As I drank it, I considered how I wanted to communicate to the council the challenge ahead—one I hadn't shared with Kayin, Fatimata, or Efe, although Efe would have come to the same conclusion.

"But the mission has not ended," Adebola said.

The open shutters provided little relief from the heat, which I didn't mind.

"No, Nne. The problem is greater than the Portuguese. The English. The Dutch. Like ours, the Powhatans' lands are vast. The pale men think they can…take it. When they do, they'll need workers, since they aren't inclined to till it themselves."

"What can be done?"

I explained Mingan had given us Fort Kinnakeet to use as a base, a place where Alkebulans escaping slavery could seek refuge, and that we'd left a contingent of warriors there but would need to send reinforcements. I spoke of Silva's vow to return and extend the search for the Banaans and Asantis to Hispaniola and New Spain.

Udo's brow furrowed. "Can we trust this pale man?"

I still wasn't certain. "We shall see. The worst that can happen is that he doesn't return, and we have to navigate the ship docked at the coast ourselves."

"No. The worst that can happen is that he returns with more sailors and tries to recapture our people."

I recalled the secret Silva had confided in me. "I don't believe he'll do that."

"If he returns, we'll send our best fighters with him to New Spain to ensure his cooperation."

Efe sipped her water. Her copper bracelets tinkled as she set her cup on the table. "I'm sure any of your warriors can accomplish the task."

She hadn't learned that contradicting Udo was a dangerous proposition. Her belief in reason outweighed any inclination to self-preservation.

"How long will it take for us to retrieve everyone?" my mother asked.

This was the question I'd been dreading. The rolled-up map Chauncy had given me rested on my dresser upstairs. I envisioned the size of the area from Hispaniola to New Spain to English North America.

"How long?" Adebola pressed.

"It could take a generation," I said.

The morning sun cast a shadow on one side of my mother's face. "A generation."

"I'm not sure we can find everyone who's been kidnapped and bring them back, but what we can do is—"

"Prevent more people from being taken," she finished my sentence.

I nodded. I thought of the Powhatan clans. "Foreign Minister Ndidi, you must travel to as many city-states in the western region as you can and urge their leaders to band together to fight the Europeans. Discourage the selling of their people, so Europeans will have nothing to buy."

Ndidi tapped her finger on the table. "The riches to be gained in the future outweigh the guns and currency they would receive in the present."

"Yes."

"It sounds dangerous." Udo looked at Ndidi. "With respect, you're an elder."

Ndidi's eyes narrowed.

"Bamidele will not appreciate your visit," said Adebola.

I worried about Ndidi's safety, but she was the only one who had diplomatic relationships with the leaders of these city-states.

"We'll send a team of warriors to protect her," I said.

"I'll do it," said Ndidi.

## Chapter Twenty-Eight

# ...for Queen Adebola

THE FOLLOWING EVENING, the warriors who'd gone on the mission sat in the first three rows of the Thema Obieze's Audience Court. I was wearing a crisp, scarlet-trimmed white officer's tunic, with my amulet—a scarlet lion—sewn over my heart, my accomplishments pinned to a scarlet sash, a gold chain around my neck, and my daga sheathed in the brass scabbard on my hip.

The queendom's dignitaries and most prominent citizens sat in rows that extended all the way to the entrance. Azeze, wearing a plain tunic, sat two rows behind me. He'd bowed his head as I'd passed him. We had spoken on the ship's return voyage, but I hadn't seen him since we'd arrived in Kana. I wondered how he had been faring since he'd resumed his duties as the blacksmith's apprentice.

An attendant clinked a spoon against a chalice. I faced forward. The conversations in the audience ceased.

Seated in her golden chair on the dais, my mother was

wearing her golden crown rather than a dark blue gele to match her pano.

A fanti stepped forward, her voice carrying to all corners of the room. "Queen Adebola of the Queendom of Kana will speak."

The guard stepped back.

"We are gathered here today," my mother began, "to honor Kanaian warriors and residents who—without regard to their own safety—retrieved our people and brought them home." She scanned the room. "Thank you for your service to our queendom. Stories regaling your bravery will be told for generations." She looked at Udo. "General?"

Udo grabbed her cane and stepped forward. Next to her, an attendant held a cushion upon which lay gold medals. "Colonel Chibuike."

I stood, allowing a small smile at the unexpected promotion, climbed the stairs, and stopped before her. Udo pinned the medal on my sash, maneuvering as well with one arm as others did with two. She patted my shoulder and whispered, "When the day comes, I look forward to serving you as faithfully as I have Adebola."

I stepped back and saluted. "Thank you, General."

Perhaps Udo was beginning to see me as her equal.

My mother beamed at me. My chest swelled.

Kayin's name was called next. Udo gave her two medals, one of them for Kunto. Kayin cried, something she would never have done before her sister's death. After having conferred promotions and handed out medals to the rest of the warriors, Azeze, and Mukki, the general returned to her seat.

My mother joined the attendant and held up a medal. "Efe." Efe's jaw dropped. She hugged Adebola tearfully.

Mingan clapped enthusiastically. He wouldn't be idle in Kana. Despite her perception of men as inferior, Udo had agreed that Efe's husband could serve the queendom by teaching recruits the skills he'd learned from Tahki: how to shoot bows and arrows, throw spears, and track people without a sound.

He didn't move when my mother called his name. "Mingan," she said again. His jaw tightened, and he glanced at Efe as she returned to her seat. "Please come forward."

He rose and plodded up the stairs.

The queen held up the remaining medal. "This can't replace all you've lost, but it represents our gratitude for your hospitality and your help in bringing our people home. Welcome to our family. You're an honorary Kanaian for life." She smiled at him. "In this one and the next."

As I re-assimilated to daily life in the obieze, I noticed my mother's increased reliance on Udo. The defense minister had thrived in Sola's absence. The queen included her in every meeting regarding queendom business and sought her opinion on nonmilitary issues. I wanted her to rely on my counsel.

One evening, sitting alone with my mother in the front room of the private residence, I asked her about it.

She set her chalice of palm wine on the table between us. "You take me for a fool."

Her tone conveyed that she didn't wish to discuss the matter any further, and that it would be in my interest not to push her. I went from savoring the wine's sweet, milky flavor to forcing the liquid down my throat.

A few sunrises later, I left the officers' room and went

upstairs looking for my mother. I wanted to tell her I'd completed the itinerary for Ndidi's journey to the provinces and chosen the team of warriors who would accompany her.

The fanti stationed in the Great Hall directed me to the Audience Court. What was my mother doing there? There were no external events scheduled for that day.

A fanti opened the door for me. I stepped into the room and stopped. Adebola was talking to a young man. Behind them stood a woman and a man my mother's age.

I turned to leave.

"Chibuike!" my mother's voice echoed. "Come."

I walked down the wide aisle that cut between the rows of chairs remaining from the medal ceremony.

Up close, the man appeared to be about twenty-two, not far from me in age. He was shorter than I, but had a solid build and a regal bearing. He wore a smart green tunic and leather sandals. The four of them watched me approach.

"I'd like you to meet Okeke," my mother said.

The young man bowed low. His curly hair was cut short. His eyes sparkled. "It has been my misfortune to have seen you only from afar, Adaeze. Up close, you're as beautiful as your mother."

And like her, I was inured to flattery. "Hello." I waited for Adebola to disclose his identity.

A smile played at her lips, which should have alarmed me. "This is your betrothed."

"Betrothed?"

"Your future husband."

"My—" I recalled her telling me about him the day we found out the Banaans had disappeared. "But we're not permitted to marry."

Without a husband or offspring, warriors' sole fealty was to the queen.

"And these are his parents."

Okeke's father was the same height as Okeke, with the same stocky build. His mother was tall and muscular.

"It's an honor, Adaeze," his mother said.

"We'll leave you two alone to become acquainted," said my mother.

A stone dropped in my belly. Betrothed?

Okeke's parents followed Adebola. The queen's sandals flapped against the clay floor until silenced by the closing of the doors.

Okeke looked up at the high ceiling. "Quite the place."

I shifted my gaze from the arched window and the clear blue sky. "You've not been here?"

"My mother has. Not I."

Okeke told me his mother had been a warrior and served with Queen Adebola. Like my father, Okeke's father was the son of a warrior. Okeke had a wide nose and full lips. He was handsome, of which he seemed to be aware. We talked about the weather and the upcoming rainy season.

Okeke's gaze fell upon the golden throne and back at me. "I am counting the days until we're wed." He bowed. "Until I see you again."

A fanti escorted him from the room. I didn't watch him leave, but I stared at the throne on which I dared not sit.

Afterward, my mother informed me she wanted me to get to know him. We would be married in eight dry seasons, or upon her death, whichever came first.

～

"Your move," I said.

Ndidi and I were in her work chamber, down the hall from the queen's. Stacks of scrolls and parchments crowded her desk and shelves.

In a corner of the room, between two matching chairs, was a small ikoro table atop which, nowadays, sat a chessboard. Using the game I'd found in Silva's cabin on the *Isabella Maria* as a guide, Azeze had carved the polished pieces out of mahogany into the faces of a bishop (a likeness of the old priestess), a knight (a likeness of me), a pawn (Itoro, scar and all), a rook (Kayin), a king (my father), and a queen (my mother). Unlike Silva's version, the queen was the game's most important piece.

As when we'd played wari when I was a child, Ndidi won at chess most of the time. But not always.

She moved her knight. "That Efe is a bright young woman. I enjoy my conversations with her."

"I'm sure the two of you have a lot to discuss."

"She is someone you'll want to keep in your life."

I'd come to the same conclusion long ago.

Efe and Mingan had settled into a life in Kana. While he worked with the army, she spent hours reading historical texts borrowed from Adebola and Ndidi, and she'd learned that Bamidele wasn't the first Alkebulan king to profit from the slave trade. She understood better the threat he posed, but she had not given up on finding the Asantis. She and Mingan often went back to her village to prepare it for their eventual return; I sent fanti along to protect them.

"How have your travels been?" I asked Ndidi.

"Productive." The lines at the corners of her wise eyes

crinkled with merriment. "Although…men who aren't from Kana don't like a woman telling them what to do."

"When will you be visiting Bamidele?"

Her smile faded. "I leave tomorrow. I saved him for last. He'll be difficult to persuade. He continues to profit the most from the enslavement of others."

I moved my bishop. "What's he like?"

Ndidi swooped her queen across the board, bumped my bishop, and placed the piece on its side on the table. I cursed inwardly.

"He's suspicious and won't welcome my visit. He spends most of his time—when he's not with one of his wives—sitting on a golden stool where he receives wisdom from his gods."

I considered my next move. "We need to seize the castle on the coast." I moved my queen. "To prevent ships from landing. But Udo believes our army is stretched too thin."

"Then we need a larger army." Ndidi aligned her rook with my queen. She grinned. "As do you. Checkmate."

∽

That night, I lit a candle on the small iron desk, which sat under a window overlooking the darkened Grand Square. The shutters were open, but there was no breeze to temper the warmth of the room.

I dipped a quill into the small pot and brushed off the excess ink on its rim. The ink emitted a pungent, comforting scent. I still recorded my thoughts every night—a habit I'd formed on the first ocean crossing—keeping an account of everything that happened to me and my people. A living history, regardless of whether anyone would ever read it. I took a sip of wine, swirling the taste of milk and home on my tongue as I smiled, thinking of how proud Ndidi would be if she saw me writing the words she'd taught me. I didn't tell her about this nightly exercise, but I would when she returned from her trip to Aon.

After recording the day's events, I rose from the chair and extinguished the candle's flame. These sounds were a cue for Kifunji to enter the room and prepare me for bed.

There was a rap on the door.

"Come in, Kifunji.

Kayin entered, followed by Kifunji and Itoro. Her face was tight, shadowed by the light from the palm oil candles on the bedchamber's walls.

She was still wearing her officer's tunic.

"What is it?" I asked.

"You should sit."

I didn't move. "Tell me."

"On the way home from Aon, the warriors protecting Minister Ndidi were ambushed."

I started. "Ambushed!"

"Five of them were…killed."

"Killed?" I shook my head. "*Our* warriors?"

"One of them escaped and made it back. She said it was Bamidele's men."

"My goddesses!"

Kayin hesitated. "And the minister…"

My heart clenched. I grabbed her muscular arms. "Did they take her? Where is she?"

"Chi…" Kayin's hazel eyes softened. "They killed her."

I released her. Reaching backward, I groped for the top of the chair. I found it and sat. My vision clouded. I struggled to take in air. Kayin was talking, but I couldn't grasp her words.

Ndidi had been a contemporary of my Nne Nne Thema, a counselor to my nne, and a mentor to me. A maker of queens. Ndidi…gone?

Alone in my bedchamber, I alternated for days between crying and slamming my fists into my bedding. Efe remained in the bedchamber next door; she and Ndidi had grown close since we'd returned. My mother grieved, as well.

One morning, after Kifunji had bathed me, I dressed and went out to the front room of the private residence. My mother sat in a chair, holding a chalice of baobab juice.

I sat in the other chair. Kifunji brought me a cup of the same drink.

"You should eat something," my mother said.

I raised the cup but didn't drink. "It's hard. I feel guilty about Ndidi. The four warriors who were killed. Their deaths are on my soul."

"Blaming yourself will not help matters. As leaders, we must make difficult choices."

"I want to kill Bamidele myself."

I now knew how Kayin had felt when the pale man had killed her sister.

My mother's face was gaunt. "And get yourself killed? Nothing productive ever comes with haste."

"We should attack him."

"And we will. At the right time." She set her cup on the table. "Ndidi wouldn't want your anger to consume you, nor would she want you to grieve for long. She was proud of you and the work you are doing for our people and our country. But your work isn't done. Honor her memory by seeing it through." She paused. "You know what she once said to me?"

I shook my head, the tears falling anew.

My mother wiped them from my cheek. "'Chi is your daughter by birth, but mine by choice.'"

# Chapter Twenty-Nine

# The queen of queens

I DIDN'T UNDERSTAND how Bamidele's men had succeeded in killing Ndidi. Our least-skilled warriors could handle the best of the king's men with ease. Bamidele's men didn't fight with technique or grace, but with brutish force. Most of them were slaves and did his bidding against their will.

When I'd discussed it with Kayin, I'd said, "It was as if—"

"—they knew Ndidi was coming," she'd finished.

Queen Adebola and I had wanted to retaliate by declaring war on Aon. General Udo and Efe had argued for diplomacy first. Neither my mother nor I thought it would work, but we'd agreed to give it a chance, unwilling to risk the lives of any more warriors.

I'd been adamant that I be the one to talk to Bamidele. I owed it to Ndidi.

The contingent of warriors who'd accompanied me to Aon remained at the edge of the grasslands, far from the protective wall of Bamidele's castle and beyond reach of musket balls and arrows, waiting to be summoned if we were detained. I hoped we wouldn't need them.

Efe, Itoro, and Kayin strode beside me as we headed to the colossal gate.

Kayin held a white cloth over her head that she'd taken from the obieze. "This idea of yours is foolhardy."

"You are the goddess of understatement," I said.

A guard held up his hand. His eyes widened. He knew who I was. "State your business."

"Princess and Colonel Chibuike," Kayin said, "Lieutenant Colonel Kayin, Captain Itoro, and the Asanti ruler, Efe, to see the king."

"Tell him we've come in peace," I said.

Kayin waved the white cloth.

He held out his hand for my daga. Kayin removed both swords and gave them to him. Itoro grudgingly forfeited her hatchet. The second guard looked Efe up and down. She did the same to him. He moved to search her body, but Kayin said, "She's unarmed."

He hesitated. "This way." He spun and walked through the gate.

We followed.

Aon's compound was much busier than ours. Individuals dressed in silk tunics and panos crisscrossed the grounds with purpose. I paused several times, afraid of running into one of them, but they intuitively avoided us. A vivid memory came to me of when I was a child running in the Kanaian market and dodging pedestrians. Many Aons were dressed in wraps that only covered their private areas. A few of the slaves stared at us.

We passed courtyards with an array of vines cascading

down their stone walls. The scents from the abundant flowers along the clay brick walkways were celestial and oppressive. Mahogany logs held up a golden gong.

The white castle was wide and rectangular, with arches and a watchtower. With the sun no longer overhead, the building was in silhouette. The doors were made of gold, like everything we passed in the foyer: banisters, picture frames, a side table, a chandelier. The guard led us down a wide hallway with many portraits of King Bamidele lining the walls.

The king was standing in the center of the room, his hands clasped behind his broad back. He was several handbreadths shorter than I and wore an ankle-length kaftan of red, green, and black. Three women in bright wraps surrounded him. In some provinces, the greater the number of wives and children, the greater a man's wealth. In Kana, Asanti, and Banaan, husbands were permitted one wife. Bamidele had over a hundred. *How did he find time to rule?*

"Princess Chibuike. This is a surprise! Welcome to Aon. I hope King Kwasi and Queen Adebola are well."

He had big teeth like an elephant.

I didn't smile. "You know why I'm here."

He closed his mouth and waved. His wives hastened out of the room. Bamidele gestured at chairs made from dark wood. He clapped. A servant brought palm wine. I thanked the woman and set my cup on the table next to the chair. I wanted to keep a clear head…and I recalled the rumor that Bamidele's brother had died of poisoning. None of the other three women in my party drank either, although Kayin sniffed her cup before setting it down.

Bamidele sipped his wine and scrutinized me, Efe, and Kayin. "No pleasantries first?"

We glared at him.

He looked at Itoro and stopped drinking. "Itoro?"

Her eyes narrowed to slits.

"I'd recognize that scar anywhere."

Itoro didn't respond.

To me, he said, "Tell me. So there's no misunderstanding."

"You killed Ndidi."

He gulped his wine. "Ah! I heard about her tragic accident."

"It wasn't an accident."

"It had nothing to do with me."

"It was one of your gangs."

"Aon has many residents. I can't control them all."

Arguing with him wouldn't bring Ndidi back. "I'm here to deliver her message."

"Which is?"

"Cease kidnapping residents of neighboring city-states. Stop selling them and your people to the Europeans. Abolish slavery in Aon. And join Kana in making a stronger Alkebulan."

He barked out a laugh and leaned back in his chair. "Is that all? But why?"

I examined the opulent furnishings: the chandelier, multiple settles and chairs, and the golden stool in the corner. The room smelled like him: heavy floral scents and sweat.

From outside, the gong sounded three times.

I raised my hands. "Is all this worth losing our best men and women to the Europeans? Have you considered posterity? How can our countries stay strong without them?"

His jovial expression disappeared. "My responsibility is to the people of Aon. No one else."

"To you, you mean," said Efe. "How do you live like this, while others live in hovels, or worse?" We had passed them on the way here. Small, wretched houses—no larger than the maintenance shed on the obieze compound—that housed entire families. "How do you sleep? Do you not have honor?"

"Honor does not pay," he said.

"This is a waste of time," said Kayin.

"I agree," Efe said.

Kayin was right. He would not change his mind. We stood.

I pointed at him. "I will have vengeance for Ndidi's death and will not rest until I bring back our people. Including yours."

He raised his cup to me. "I wish you good fortune." He took another sip. "But the winds of progress blow in one direction."

As we headed to the door, Bamidele said, "I've missed you, Itoro."

Itoro faced him. "You're lucky I don't kill you."

The Aon king laughed.

She stepped toward him. He glanced at her taloned nails and stopped laughing.

Kayin grabbed her arm. "He's not worth it."

⋘

Before we left the Aon compound, we stopped at the gate to retrieve our weapons. I grabbed my daga and inspected the blade to ensure it hadn't been tampered with.

On the trek back to Kana, I asked Itoro, "How did you get that scar?"

She held the hatchet over her shoulder as she walked. "Before Bamidele was king, I was his slave. He was a despicable man. Held slaves in the same esteem as animals. Although he once hugged a lost goat, so maybe not even that much. He stole me from my mother's shack. He'd have killed her—and me—if she'd tried to stop him. He brought me to his house and stared at me with lust as I carried out my tasks.

"One day, I was tending the garden when his first and second wives left for the market. He sent for me. I was nervous when I entered his home, afraid he'd force himself on me. I was thirteen." Itoro's voice trailed off. "He held my face and told me I was beautiful, which was true." A shy smile. "I was the prettiest girl in Aon.

"My mother had been forced to lie with many men, so I never knew my father. It might have been him. The future king. I never wanted to live like her.

"He tried to pull me into an embrace, but I fought him off. After a few more attempts, he grabbed a knife off a table and slashed my face. He said, 'Now, you can never leave me, because no one else will have you.' I promised myself I would never endure pain from others. Only inflict it.

"He never tried to force himself on me again. To him, I was a sculpture. Owned and admired, but not to be touched. But he'd taunt me. Tell me I was ugly, or he no longer wanted me. People flinched when I passed them in the market. They remembered my beauty and knew he could do the same to them. I'm not sure what would have happened to me if not for General Udo. I owe her my life."

She told us how Udo, while in Aon on a diplomatic mission with Ndidi, had been impressed with Itoro's physique and believed she'd make an excellent warrior. The general had purchased her with cowrie shells brought from the obieze treasury and promised Itoro freedom on the condition she join the Kanaian warriors.

"I'll never be a slave again," Itoro said.

We were south of Doba. I stopped in the middle of the plain. "That's why you resisted my plan to be captured by the Portuguese."

She nodded.

"Thank you for telling us your story."

"And Bamidele was wrong." Efe touched Itoro's face. "You're still beautiful, my friend."

On the way back from Aon, we stopped in Banaan to check on Fatimata. Her house—along with the houses of the twenty other villagers who'd returned—had been restored. Fisherwomen and men had found their boats or built new ones. Conversation and laughter permeated the air, as did the smell of cooked fish.

Fatimata still slept in her old bed despite being the ruler. She couldn't sleep in her parents' bed or remove her siblings'.

After our quick visit, we headed for the River Ome and home. We crossed paths with Mukki, the Kanaian trader, who was carrying a bucket of water in the opposite direction.

"All's well?" I asked him.

His face twitched. "Yes, your Adaeze."

"Where are you headed?"

"To Banaan. I'm helping them rebuild."

Efe smiled at his generosity.

I frowned. The village looked rebuilt to me.

❧

Queen Adebola scanned the faces in the Council Room. Her chin was held high, her light brown eyes resolute. "Diplomacy did not work. We must prepare for war."

Udo stared at my mother. "Declare war on Aon? We haven't been at war in a generation."

Efe sat across from her. "We've been at war since the pale men started taking our people."

The general turned to her. "Surely, *you* disagree with this course of action."

"Although I believe in reason more than anyone—besides Ndidi—I've learned that approach doesn't work with everyone. Slavery is abhorrent. We must stop it."

"We must retaliate," I said. "He killed our top diplomatic official." And my friend. My mentor. "He needs to understand there are consequences for his actions."

General Udo raised her hand a few fingerbreadths off the table. "I'd counsel caution. Aon has grown to be a formidable force. They've received a substantial amount of weaponry from the Portuguese."

"You've said others aren't warrior people like Kanaians," Efe countered.

Udo ignored her. "If we lose this war, our country will be weakened. We won't recover."

"This isn't like you, Udo," said Adebola.

"I've learned from your lessons." The general leaned forward, her pitted face earnest. "Aon isn't the enemy. It's the pale man."

My mother regarded her. "Although I'm leaning toward war, I'll take your counsel into consideration."

*What's this? Udo might convince the queen to change her mind?*

Later, in the private dining room, I told my parents that King Bamidele had asked about their health. My mother asked me to repeat it. I didn't mention how he'd insulted her by asking after my father first. Usually an engaging host and conversationalist, this evening Adebola only spoke when addressed. The attendants brought out plates of pork, honey, and maize. The food smelled delicious. I was a child again, wanting my mother to finish the prayer with haste.

After we raised our heads, an attendant filled the queen's chalice with a generous pour of palm wine.

My mother studied the goblet and looked at the server. "Taste it."

The servant glanced around. They weren't permitted to drink libations while on duty. She hesitated before taking a sip. "Thank you, Your Amara."

She moved back to the service table to be ready in case any of us asked for additional servings of food, or the queen demanded more wine. Mingan and I were drinking millet beer. Efe, water.

Mingan glanced at his wife, who shrugged.

Adebola laughed. "I'm becoming as suspicious as Bamidele. Let us feast."

She reached for the chalice and brought it to her mouth.

A cough.

And another.

The servant who'd sipped the wine from my mother's cup was coughing and holding her stomach. She collapsed onto the clay floor.

My mother set the chalice down and rose, staring at the fallen woman.

"Fetch Mukambu!" I yelled to Salamatu.

"Yes, Adaeze!"

While she fled the room, I crouched by the young woman. White foam surrounded her lips, reminding me of Abeni's death aboard the *Isabella Maria*. I put my hand over her mouth. No breath escaped.

My mother's face was stricken.

"She's dead, Nne," I said.

## Chapter Thirty

# And, if we shall perish,...

SOMEONE HAD TRIED to kill the queen.

Everyone in the obieze compound—except for the immediate family—was under suspicion. Udo questioned every attendant and warrior in her office. As the sole interrogator, she could prevent collusion between the questioner and the one being interviewed and piece together stories from different people. I offered to help with the questioning, but she didn't believe I could be unbiased. She was right.

The general worked from early morning to late at night. She'd never married or had children. She had often remarked that she was married to the army, and the warriors were her offspring. While she conducted the investigation, Kayin trained the warriors in her stead in case Adebola declared war. I paced in the private residence. I recalled how Bamidele had asked after my parents' health. Had he tried to poison the Kanaian queen?

"Bring her in," my mother said.

Two fanti opened the Audience Court doors, and another pair entered with Ola, my attendant since childhood, walking between them. They proceeded down the long aisle and stopped in front of the queen, who sat stately upon her golden throne. Udo stood to my mother's left; I stood to my mother's right.

Tears and dirt stained my attendant's face. The fanti had kept Ola under watch on the lowest floor of the obieze since the previous day, after Udo had found a small bag of seeds among her belongings in the room she shared with Salamatu. Mukambu had confirmed that the seeds were poisonous. They'd been ground and mixed into the wine that had killed my mother's attendant.

My mother's head was held high. "Do you have anything to say before I pronounce your fate?"

"Your Amara, I did not do this! I would never wish you harm." She looked at me, her eyes pleading. "Please! I did not do what I'm accused of."

I tried to remain stoic. I'd always liked this woman, who'd patiently listened to my bath time jabbering and kept my childhood confidences. I couldn't imagine Ola harming anyone, much less trying to kill my mother. She seemed to be telling the truth. But we had proof. That was the part I would never forget or forgive.

"Given your long service to me and to my daughter," Queen Adebola said, "I am granting you leniency. You will not be executed."

Udo started. She bent over and whispered fiercely to my mother. "She tried to murder you. Execution is the only punishment."

"I agree with you, Nne," I said.

My mother's gaze was still fixed on Ola. "I did not ask for your counsel." Udo and I straightened. "Ola, I permanently banish you and your family from the queendom. We will confiscate your property and belongings. You will leave with nothing."

"But Your Amara—"

"I have spoken."

My attendant whimpered, then wailed as the fanti dragged her up the aisle. I tensed and did not relax until the doors closed and silence returned to the room.

Ola and her family would have difficulty finding a new place to live once the news of her crime spread throughout the region. Most likely, they would starve. Whatever their fate, the shame of her deed would stain her family for generations.

⋯

Four sunrises later, I strolled down the hall of the private residence and stopped. The sound of retching came from Efe and Mingan's bedchamber. I knocked on the door and waited. Silence. I opened it. The bed was unmade. Efe's inventions, in various stages of completion, were scattered across every flat surface, including the floor. I crouched, picked up a rectangular copper box, and examined the circles and numbers on top of it.

A gagging sound came from behind the screen shielding the privy. Holding the strange box, I rushed over to the screen. Mingan was still in the Kanaian Forest on an overnight training session, instructing new recruits on how to track human prey. He wasn't a great warrior, but he'd turned out to be an amazing teacher.

The acrid smell of vomit made me want to do the same. I peered around the screen. Efe was sitting on the floor hugging the canister.

She looked up at me, miserable. A white substance trailed down her chin. "I see you found my counting box."

"Are you all right?" It was a stupid question.

To my surprise, she proffered a tired smile. "I'm more than all right."

"Are you sure? With respect, I've seen you look better."

"I think I'm with child."

She bent her head over the bowl and threw up again.

A new child in the obieze! There hadn't been one in the building since…me.

The compound was aflutter with the announcement of Efe's pregnancy. Azeze built a small mahogany bedstead with high-slatted sides. He also created a wooden daga. "What would a baby do with this?" Efe asked him. He laughed. "She might need it." Mingan wanted her to be a warrior like her aunt. Despite Efe's feelings about fighting, she didn't give it back.

Adebola instructed Efe not to overexert herself. My mother tired herself out, doting on her. Did she wish I were with child instead? She seemed to have forgotten Bamidele. Her sole focus was Efe and the baby.

When the child's arrival neared, Fatimata came up to Kana.

I had asked whether she was concerned about traveling with Bamidele's gangs still about. "I will not be afraid in my homeland," she'd said. Regardless, Mukki and a few men from Banaan had escorted her to the compound gates.

Fatimata sat on the bed with Efe, holding her hand and

wiping the sweat from her brow with a soft cloth. Mingan held Efe's other hand. She yelped when he held it too tight. I paced near the foot of the bedstead behind Mukambu, who was bent over between Efe's legs, instructing her gently on what to do. Efe panted and cursed like Itoro. None of us was immune to her wrath.

A cry pierced the air. I stopped and hovered near the physician, looking at the object she held in her hands. It had eyes and limbs, but blood, fluid, and a thick white substance covered it.

And she was beautiful.

Mingan's head touched Efe's. He gave her a contented smile. Hers was one of exhaustion, although she examined the baby like it was one of her inventions. Fatimata cried. Joy surged through me. I clapped Mukambu on the back.

"Princess Chibuike." Salamatu stood in the doorway. "Mukambu. The king has summoned you."

I tried to maintain my smile so as not to upset Efe. My father had never summoned me. The healer and I followed the attendant to my parents' suite of rooms.

My mother was in bed, her eyes closed, coughing. My father sat beside her.

I'd never seen my mother ill. "What's wrong with her?"

His long face was pallid. "I don't know."

I sat on the edge of the bed and clasped my mother's hand. "What's wrong, Nne?"

She opened her eyes. Her lips moved, but no words came out.

Pain stabbed my stomach and flared to my chest. "I can't hear you."

Her eyes filled with tears, and she shook her head.

"What's happening?" I asked Mukambu.

The healer gently pushed me aside to examine her. I still held my mother's hand. She coughed again. Mukambu lifted Adebola's dressing gown, placed her ear to my mother's chest, and frowned. She felt my mother's stomach, chest, and neck. Her frown deepened.

"What is it?" I asked.

She said nothing.

"What is it?" I yelled.

The physician stood and looked at my father, then me. "Whether it's old age or illness, I fear we are too late."

"Too late for what?" my father asked quietly.

Mukambu stepped aside. My mother's cough grew weaker. Sweat poured down her wan face. Her other hand inched toward my father's. He held it. I climbed into the bed and held her other hand. Her eyes searched my face.

A sob burst out of me. "I love you, Nne."

*Please help her, Goddess Nana Buluku. Goddess Gbadu. Save her! Save me!*

I continued to pray as my mother stared at me, long after the light had faded from her eyes.

⁓

I didn't know how I'd ended up in my bed. The last thing I remembered was resting the back of my palm against my mother's mouth for a last kiss. Then screaming. Later, I found out that Itoro had picked me up off the floor and carried me to my bedchamber.

When I woke, my room was dark and silent. I jumped out

of bed and ran into the hallway, past Itoro, who struggled to stand. She'd been sleeping outside my door.

I prayed to the goddesses it had been a nightmare.

My mother was lying on the bed. My father sat slumped in a chair beside it, awake. No matter how she had spoken to him, ignored him, he'd never wavered. Although their marriage had been arranged, he'd grown to love his wife. She'd wanted a big family. After the death of each child, he'd loved her more, while she'd drawn further away.

But she had reached for him last night. Maybe she was turning back.

He looked up at me with a languid face when I entered. "Little One."

For the first time, my childhood nickname failed to elicit a smile from me. I stood over my mother. She appeared to be at peace. Asleep. As she used to pray, the line between life and death was blurred.

I cried out and fell on top of her. She was cold. Her arms did not encircle me. I didn't care who heard or saw me. Or whether I would ever stop crying.

How many tears could a body hold?

After my crying ceased, the attendants arrived to wash my mother for the last time. I pushed one of them aside, more roughly than I'd intended, and grabbed the cloth from her. I waited for them to remove her jewelry. She wasn't wearing her favorite earrings, the ones divided into four quadrants with a lion, the obieze, her, and me inside. I'd look for them later. They would accompany her into the afterlife.

I dipped the cloth into the bowl of lavender water and bathed my mother's forehead, nose, chin, breasts, stomach, arms, hands, legs, feet, and toes. My tears fell, mixing with the water on her skin.

The attendants held her while I washed her beautiful brown hair with karite soap.

I arranged her hands in prayer over her chest before gently wrapping her in a white shroud. I kissed her forehead and covered her head.

Mukambu couldn't determine the cause of death. She didn't believe it was foul play; she suspected the malady many Kanaians contracted when the seasons changed from dry to wet, although the wet season had yet to arrive.

I searched for my mother's earrings underneath the pillow, under the bed. In the dresser drawers. The wardrobe. I checked her work chamber and the Council Room, but couldn't find them.

Udo came out of her work chamber as I was leaving.

She walked down the hallway toward me.

"What do you need?" The general's face was ashen. She was grieving, too.

"I was looking for my mother's earrings. She'd want to be entombed wearing them."

"They'll turn up." She put her heavy hand on my shoulder. "But we must bury her soon, so she can join our ancestors. And you have a queendom to run."

I jolted. Engulfed in thoughts of my mother, I'd forgotten my country. My personal tragedy had blinded me to my duty.

"If...you need more time," she continued, "I would be happy to continue overseeing Kana's affairs until you're ready."

"Thank you, General, for all you've done for Kana...my mother...but I'm ready."

She narrowed her eyes. "Are you sure?"

"I've been preparing for it my entire life. If you'll excuse me. I must get back to her."

My father and I remained at Adebola's side for the rest of the day. We spoke little. He napped on and off in the chair next to the bed, his head cradled in his hand.

That night, we enjoyed an elaborate feast in the Dining Hall. Seated at the table on top of the dais, I picked at the yams on my plate. The food smelled delicious, but I wasn't hungry. Next to me, my father left his food undisturbed. People living within the compound and prominent Kanaian residents packed the tables, eating and drinking, celebrating my mother's life.

Efe didn't attend. She was still recovering from the birth of her child. I'd visited her bedchamber earlier that afternoon, while she was feeding the baby.

"Queen Adebola took me in after my family disappeared," Efe had said. "Took Mingan in. She treated us like family. I will always appreciate that. I've lost a second mother." She gazed at Baby Tahki. "And my child has the misfortune of not knowing either of our mothers."

I smiled with difficulty. "Oh, she will. Because we'll tell stories about them—"

"Forevermore," we said together.


After the feast, there was music and dancing in the Audience Court, where the queen's body lay. I didn't seek answers through dance or song. In a chair beside Adebola, my hand rested on her soft shroud, and I prayed.

The following day was dark, the clouds low and bloated with rain. Select Kanaian warriors carried the queen's body in a hammock, followed by me, my father, General Udo, and the rest of the warriors. Residents lined the streets in their finest white tunics and panos, chanting words that honored our ancestors. People cried. Some tore out their hair.

When we returned to the Audience Court, the old priest-ess stood over my mother's body and spoke of her greatness. She assured us that the queen had crossed over to the next realm in peace. Efe and Fatimata held my hands throughout the service. I was numb, but I didn't cry. A future queen could not cry before her subjects. But inside, I felt empty. My heart hurt, as though Itoro had split it in two with her hatchet. Fatimata squeezed my hand and reminded me to breathe. Afterward, Kayin hugged me briefly.

A drum boomed as we followed the warriors who carried Queen Adebola to the tombs beneath the obieze, where she would join my nne nne, her ancestors, and my sisters.

✍

After leaving the tombs, I stole away to my bedchamber and crawled into bed. A suffocating sorrow weighed upon me like the heavy wool blanket I'd needed in Tsenacommacah. I lay immobile, shedding silent tears. Instead of the clay strokes on the ceiling, I saw my mother. How was it possible that I would never see her again in this life?

There was a knock on the door, then it opened. I wiped my face. Without lifting my head from the pillow, I shifted my eyes to see who it was. Efe leaned in, her face tight. Behind her, Kayin and Fatimata looked at me with similar expressions.

They entered the room. Itoro remained by the door.

"I didn't tell you to come in," I said.

"Try to stop us," said Efe.

Kayin smiled sadly. "You're not the queen yet."

They stood by the bed looking down at me, dark crescents beneath their eyes.

My gaze returned to the ceiling. "At least have a seat. It feels like you're standing over *my* deathbed."

"You need to eat," Fatimata said.

"And sleep," said Kayin.

Efe touched my arm. "Mukambu can give you something to help with that."

I scowled. "I'll be fine. Fatimata, what are you still doing here?"

She took my hand into her soft one. "I stayed in case you needed me."

"How is Baby Tahki, Efe?"

I'd spent no time with the child since she'd been born.

"A wonder."

I looked at Fatimata's round, earnest face and Efe's slender, intelligent, and compassionate one. Kayin's clenched jaw; she was ready to fight. Her handsome, youthful face had hardened from her losses. With my eyes closed, I knew their scents: Fatimata's basal leaves and flowers, Efe's berries, and Kayin's warrior sweat. Despite my grief, admiration filled my heart. All my life, I'd wondered what it would be like to have siblings. But Fatimata, Efe, Itoro, Kunto, and Kayin had been there for me—my friends, my sisters—all along. Although my father was the sole person left who shared my blood, these women were closer to me than anyone.

"Thank you for being here." I paused, debating whether to share what I'd been thinking, my bravado to the general notwithstanding. "I...I'm not sure I'm ready."

"For what?" asked Efe.

"To rise?" asked Kayin.

"To reign," I replied.

❦

The next evening, Fatimata and I sat alone in the private residence's front room, drinking palm wine from golden chalices. Efe and Mingan had retired to their bedchamber. Kayin and Itoro were in the barracks. I'd ordered Itoro to take the night off; she had a long couple of days before her. Another warrior stood outside the door. It should have been Nsia.

"Mukki asked me to marry him."

I raised an eyebrow. "The market trader?"

"It's not the right time, but I agreed."

"You don't want to marry a Banaan?"

"When I met him at the feast in Tsenacommacah, I knew he was a special man. We've spent a lot of time together since. He's comforted me when I needed it."

The private residence was quiet. Baby Tahki must have been asleep.

"Ah! Now I understand how he was helping you 'rebuild.'"

She gave me a shy smile.

"Do you know he cooked for all of us on the voyage over?" I asked.

"It doesn't surprise me, although he isn't much of a cook."

"I know this firsthand."

Fatimata laughed. It felt good to hear it.

The wine's sweet scent rose to my nostrils. I took a sip. "And he'll move to Banaan?"

She nodded.

"How will he remain a prosperous trader?"

"He'll have to be prosperous at something else. Like creating our family." Her smile grew beatific.

I averted my eyes. "What's it like? To love a man?"

"As if your heart will burst from your chest, and you can't take another breath without him."

"I've never felt that."

"You've never expressed yourself in this way."

My cup was half full. "It must be the wine."

"You will find love." Fatimata squeezed my hand. "When you're ready to receive it."

I squeezed back. "You're welcome to marry here."

∽

Two fanti opened the Audience Court doors as I approached. They saluted as I glided by them on the sunbaked-clay floor. I wore a white silk tunic with a golden belt. I'd never worn a pano and wasn't about to begin doing so. Even though I was fully clothed, I felt naked; my daga rested on its stand in my bedchamber.

People filled the cavernous space. From the walls, palm oil candles in brass holders brightened the room. A large Kanaian flag was displayed behind my mother's golden chair. Three musicians played instruments in a corner, my gait keeping pace with their beat. I passed the merchants and traders, some of whom I did not know. Sitting next to the blacksmith, Azeze smiled at me. My lips twitched, but I didn't return the smile. It would be improper to smile at him and no one else. And whatever feelings I had for him, contemplating them wouldn't benefit anyone. I was betrothed to another.

My father trailed behind me, looking handsome in a

splendid royal blue tunic. The corners of his mouth were downturned. He was still grieving, as was I. Following him was the surviving minister, General Udo, keeping pace with us despite her cane. My first order of business as queen would be to name a foreign minister and a commerce minister to the council.

The warriors filled the rows at the front of the room. Efe sat in the first row with Mingan, who was bouncing their baby on his lap. Next to Efe was a beaming Fatimata, with Mukki by her other side. They were married; otherwise, he'd have been sitting with the other traders. The day prior, the old priestess had united them in our temple. It didn't matter to Fatimata that we prayed to different goddesses. Oshun was with her, wherever she was.

Fatimata and Mukki's eyes were locked in a tender, word-less exchange. Would Okeke and I look at each other the same way?

At the end of the row, Itoro sat nearest to me in case I needed her. Beside her sat Kayin, who winked at me.

I tried to take it all in…that this was happening to me. I wished my mother were present to witness this moment, though that would have been impossible in any case.

I stopped at the bottom of the stairs leading up to the dais. The old priestess stood alone by the throne, holding my mother's crown. The conversations in the room quieted as she motioned for me to ascend. I exhaled, climbed the stairs, and joined her. She smelled like incense.

"Oh, Goddess Gbadu, the Goddess of Destiny," she intoned, her voice carrying to the last row. "Before you stands your humble servant, your child. I call on you and on our ancestors to give her the strength to make righteous decisions in guiding this country through lack and prosperity, war and peace, tragedy and joy."

She dipped her forefinger into a small bowl of palm oil and rubbed it firmly across my forehead. "You are anointed."

Facing the audience, I scanned the warriors, servants, attendants, merchants, traders, officials, friends, my father. The people of Kana.

My people.

From behind me, the priestess placed the crown upon my head. Its weight was both physical and symbolic.

"Residents of the Queendom of Kana," she said. "I present to you Queen Chibuike."

Everyone in the audience stood and bowed their heads.

I thanked the priestess and took my seat on the throne. I rested my hands on its smooth, curved arm supports where my mother's hands had rested. Udo led the procession of warriors. One by one, they saluted me and pledged their sole fealty to me.

# Chapter Thirty-One

# Let the queen dance...

A PROCESSION FOLLOWED the ceremony. Down Kana's principal thoroughfare, several warriors danced. Others behind them threw their muskets in the air and caught them in step. The rest of the army marched in columns behind me.

Residents lined the streets as they had during Queen Adebola's funeral procession. But today, there were only tears of joy. Women, men, girls, and boys shouted my name. Rain poured from the gray sky, but it didn't stop us from marching or dancing. Kifunji moved toward me with an umbrella, but I waved her off. Kanaians weren't afraid of a little rainfall. I waved to the crowd and smiled bittersweetly. I'd looked forward to this day all my life, but had never considered its cost.

Afterward, I returned to the obieze, where people were no longer speaking in subdued tones as they had after Adebola's death.

Udo met me in the Great Hall. "Your mother would have been proud."

I teared up and nodded.

I went straight to my mother's—*my*—work chamber. Sitting in the golden chair, I ran my hand over the smooth surface of my giant ebony desk. Scrolls and documents unaddressed by Udo while I'd been in mourning sat atop it. Salamatu stood by the service table, ready to assist me.

The work didn't intimidate me. After many seasons of standing behind the queen, I'd learned the business of running the queendom: how to trade and negotiate for goods and services, calculate the levy earned on market revenue, engage in diplomacy, navigate the ministers' political machinations, and accept tributes from the grateful leaders of nearby city-states.

I dispatched most of the documents on the desk until the quill pen ran out of ink.

Salamatu gestured. "It's in the center drawer, Your Amara."

*Your Grace.*

I opened the drawer and reached for the ink jar. Next to it was a cream-colored parchment, rolled and sealed with the scarlet royal emblem. On it was written, "For Queen Chibuike."

My mother's bold penmanship was a caress to my grieving eyes. I hoped Salamatu could not see my hand shaking as I pulled out the document.

She limped over to the desk and lit a candle. She still wore her hair in tight braids, but now they hung past her shoulder.

I broke the seal, brought the parchment to my nose, and sniffed the faint scent of lavender. I swallowed hard.

*My dearest Chibuike,*

*If you are reading this, I am no longer with you. I am with our ancestors. Don't be sad, my nwa. Be joyous the goddesses graced us with being mother and daughter in this life. I have loved you since the moment the healer told me I was with child. And I have always been proud of you.*

*It is time for you to marry Okeke. Remove that scowl from your face.*

I laughed, catching tears in my mouth.

*I expect plenty of children. Do not stop bearing them until you have at least two girls. Our lineage must thrive.*

That was why my mother had worn a veil of sadness and anger. If I died, there would be no legitimate heir to the crown. My mother had also been an only child.

*It's your time. I have confidence you will rule with strength, with grace, and with the same resolute hand by which I ruled, and my mother, before me. Absorb the strength of our ancestors and govern this country so it will survive for more than one thousand seasons. Do not make decisions with haste. Consider everything.*

*And no matter where you go, I am with you.*

*Until we meet in the next life, all my love,*

*Your Nne.*

I wept at my desk. Wisely, Salamatu did not console me.

After a long while, I looked out the window. The rain had slowed to a trickle. An indigo bird landed on the window's ledge, its coat the color of one of my mother's panos. The bird sang. This was her incarnation…or her messenger.

I would uphold her legacy no matter what.

I wiped my tears. "Summon the Great Council." Salamatu hesitated, her expression revealing bemusement as to why I hadn't asked for Udo, given that she was the sole remaining member. "Tell Efe and Kayin to join us."

∽

In the Council room, Udo glanced across the mahogany table at Efe and Kayin, then at me, as if for an explanation of their presence. Kayin sat dressed in her officer's tunic in Sola's former chair, scanning the room. She'd never been in it.

After Salamatu closed the door, the muffled voices and footsteps of officials, attendants, and visitors came from the hallway.

I cleared my throat. "My first act as queen is to appoint Efe as my foreign minister."

Udo leaned forward. "With all due respect, she's not Kanaian."

"Neither are you."

She blinked.

"But I...," Efe started. Since Baby Tahki arrived, Efe invariably looked tired. When I asked for her, Salamatu often found her in the garden, reading, with the child on her lap. Efe had little time to explore.

"Your term will end when we find your people. I need you to visit the provinces that are against slavery and form alliances, as we did with the Powhatans. Finish what Ndidi started. Kayin, you'll be my minister of commerce."

"I know nothing about markets."

"I'll teach you."

More capable people in the compound could serve in these roles, but I trusted Efe and Kayin. I wasn't sure how long Efe would live in Kana, but I needed her guidance for as long as she stayed.

"Any further dissent?" I asked.

The three women shook their heads.

I ordered Salamatu to bring cups of plantain juice. "Next

order of business: Udo, post a contingent of warriors at the castle on the coast."

"What for?"

"To prevent ships from docking there and taking Bamidele's slaves across the ocean."

"But our army would be stretched too thin."

I sipped the sweet juice. "I anticipated you would say that, which leads me to my third order. We will teach all Kanaians to fight when they attain the age of sixteen, regardless of ability and gender, effective at once."

Udo's thick eyebrows drew together. "Women are better fighters under pressure."

I knew better. Azeze and the Powhatan men had fought well during our mission to find the Banaans and Asantis.

"We cannot protect the queendom with half the population. This is everyone's concern. Fourth—"

"You've been busy," said Kayin.

"No one in Kana should be forced into the same occupation as their parents." To Efe, I said, "This is where you come in."

She smiled. "You're allowing the residents to choose their vocations."

"And no one in Kana will know hunger. If residents cannot grow or buy sufficient food to eat, we will provide it for them."

"This is a lot of change at once," Udo said. "In deference to your mother's legacy—"

I stood. "I have spoken."

∽

The meals shared with my father, Mingan, and Efe were no longer quiet affairs. The mourning period was over, and Baby

Tahki made her presence known. She brought life to the obieze with her tears, laughter, squeals, and incessant demands. A glance at their child wrought a pang in my abdomen. I missed her aunt, her namesake. I wondered if this child would also grow up to be a great warrior.

Over the coming weeks, the obieze buzzed like the insects in the forest with preparations for the upcoming marriage ceremony. Attendants crisscrossed the compound and the halls bringing flowers from the royal gardens into the Audience Court; transporting cartloads of food to the kitchen; and showing Efe colorful fabrics to choose from to design panos for the occasion.

Amid all this activity, I stayed sequestered in my work chamber, the door closed to distractions. With only Salamatu to keep me company, I read briefings from the ministers on food stores or warrior movements or market revenue. Bamidele was still involved in the slave trade. After the ceremony, my attention would turn to him.

The only exception I'd made was to welcome Okeke's family—his mother, father, and sisters—into the private residence's front room to exchange gifts.

Outside my chamber's window, latticed clouds floated across the crescent moon. Stars abounded in the inky sky. I finished my work for the evening.

I needed air.

Grief was a curious thing. Anything could upend a good day, such as a woman wearing earrings reminiscent of my mother's favorite ones—which I'd never found—or a woman who tilted her head just so. I carried myself through such sightings with dignity until I could find a secluded place to cry. There were constant reminders of her—in the courtyard, in the Council Room, in my work chamber, and in the private residence, where she once belonged to only my father and me. I reread her letter a thousand times.

The fanti opened the obieze doors, and I stepped out into the cool night. A light wind brushed my face. I hadn't been outdoors in several sunrises. The rainy season had ended, but puddles still spotted the compound.

I passed the training ground but didn't stop for a throwing session. This surprised me and must have confused Itoro, too, because her footsteps had stopped behind me. They resumed as I continued walking. I stopped at the Obieze Temple; I hadn't crossed its threshold since I came with my mother over twenty-four full moons ago.

I climbed the step and entered, pausing to let my eyes adjust to the darkness. I passed the rows of benches, until I reached the statues of the goddesses—Nana Buluku, Gbadu, and Age-Fon. Behind me, Itoro scanned the room to ensure it was empty and then left to wait for me outside.

Before the Goddess of Destiny, I said a prayer for my mother and for myself. When I finished, I stared at Gbadu for a long while. My heartbeat slowed, and I received clarity of purpose. Peace. And strength.

I looked at Age-Fon, the Hunter Goddess, as if I were saying goodbye to the past, and left the temple to return to my bedchamber for my final night alone.

Tomorrow was my wedding day.

༄

The next morning, after the luxurious warm bath Kifunji had prepared for me, attendants fussed over dressing me in a purple silk tunic. They rubbed cochineal on my cheeks and berries on my lips. They scented me with lavender and set the crown upon my head.

There was a knock at the door.

My fanti blocked their entrance, but Efe and Fatimata popped their heads around her.

I waved them in. "It's all right, Itoro."

She remained in the corridor, closing the bedchamber door behind her.

Kayin wasn't with them. She'd been in a foul mood and had barely spoken to me. Or to anyone. I wasn't sure what was bothering her.

The attendants peeled away to stand by the wall as my two friends examined me from crown to feet, awestruck.

"What?" I asked.

"You look stunning!" said Efe.

Fatimata's eyes shone. "Beautiful!"

"You've never told me that," I said. "What did you think of my appearance before?"

Fatimata smiled. "You're more beautiful."

She and Efe continued to stare as if I were a fine sculpture in the Obieze Gallery.

Efe's expression softened. "But—" She glanced at the attendants standing by the wall.

I snapped my fingers. "Leave us."

They scurried out of the room.

Efe grasped my hand, her copper bracelets tinkling. "Are you sure?"

"About what?"

She hesitated. "Okeke. Queen Adebola is gone. Yes, it's time you marry, but you don't have to marry *him*."

My changed circumstances made no difference to my friends. They were still candid with me. I wouldn't have had it any other way.

"Do you feel as if your heart will burst from your chest, and you can't take another breath without him?" asked Fatimata.

"Or like the fire I felt the first time Mingan touched me?"

I glanced at my daga laying on the hippopotamus tusks. I didn't feel either of those things. "She chose Okeke for me. I must honor her wishes. Honor her. This has been a tradition in our family for generations."

"You're honorable. That's what I admire about you. But you are also a woman. You can choose what to do with your life. Create your own legacy."

I withdrew my hand from her clasp and touched her slender cheek, then Fatimata's soft one.

"It's her legacy, too."

꧁

Although I believed what I had said to Efe and Fatimata, I was miserable about marrying Okeke. He was pleasant enough. We'd spent some supervised time together walking around the obieze grounds, visiting the gallery, or sitting in the courtyard talking. Often, he'd presented me with fresh flowers: lilies, plumbagos, anthuriums. We'd never been alone, with Itoro or another fanti tarrying close by.

My mother had chosen Okeke because he was attractive and well-mannered, smart, and he carried himself like royalty. He came from a bloodline of warriors. And, most importantly, his parents had borne four daughters. He was not the passive type, like my father. In fact, I sensed the opposite; he looked forward to being the king more than to marrying me. He didn't realize his title conferred no official responsibilities except to keep me happy.

Prior to the ceremony, Udo walked over to where I waited in the hallway outside the Audience Court. The Obieze Temple wasn't large enough for the expected number of guests.

The general wore a rare smile on her pitted face. "You look pretty."

"Is that sarcasm?"

"No. I've known you your entire life, and for most of it you've been covered in mud and dirt, not face paint." We shared a laugh. Her eyes narrowed. "But why are you grim, today of all days?"

My attendants, Salamatu and Kifunji, were standing against the wall, out of earshot. Everyone else was inside being seated. My father was running late.

"I'm unsure if he is the man I should marry."

"But he's the one your mother selected for you."

"Yes."

"Then it doesn't matter what you want. We all have our destinies. Our duties."

"That's what she said."

"Adebola was wise."

"What if I'm not as wise as she?"

She clapped me on the shoulder. "That's the question, isn't it?"

I wasn't sure what she meant by that, or whether I wanted to know. After she disappeared into the Audience Court, the pressure from her hand remained. As did a familiar foreboding in my belly, which had never betrayed me.

My father, Kwasi, joined me adjusting his white tunic. "Late start this morning."

It was no use admonishing him. A zebra cannot change its stripes.

"You look beautiful, Little One." His eyes moistened. "Like your mother did on our day of marriage."

I teared up, as well. "Thank you, Nna."

"Are you ready? You've been through so much." He paused, a thought settling upon his face like the light of dawn upon a new day. "Does your heart belong to another man?"

I let out an exasperated sigh. "You, too?"

"Me, what?"

I wasn't about to tell him that Efe and Fatimata had also tried to talk me out of marrying Okeke.

"I saw how that other man smiled at you at the coronation. His heart belongs to you."

*And maybe mine to his.*

I couldn't think of Azeze now. "They're waiting for us."

He lifted my chin. "You've sacrificed enough. You should choose happiness."

I recalled the words of my mother's letter. "I'm marrying Okeke."

A drum beat as we marched toward my betrothed, who stood in front of the dais. He wore a sharp purple tunic with a matching hat and an oversize robe in the same shade as mine.

My father kissed my cheek and sat in the first row. I passed Okeke, climbed the steps, and faced the audience. There were no empty seats, and guests lined the back wall. Except for the warriors, everyone wore bright attire. Okeke's family stood with him, looking up at me. All of them—including Okeke—prostrated themselves on the sunbaked-clay floor to honor me. They did this four times before Okeke joined me on the platform.

The priestess held an iroko plate on top of which sat a kola nut. I sighed inwardly, wishing Kunto were present. After the priestess blessed the nut, I picked it up and cracked it open. The more pieces it broke into, the more prosperity my husband and I would receive. It separated into two pieces.

I turned. Fatimata covered her mouth. Efe shook her head. I worried about Kayin's reaction; the breaking of the kola nut would bring back hurtful memories of her sister. But she guffawed.

Okeke's eyes were sparkling.

*Do you feel as if your heart will burst from your chest, and you can't take another breath without him?*

When I announced that there would be no wedding, the mouths of some guests fell open. Others gasped. Okeke's mother swooned. Her husband held her up. Udo looked puzzled. Then she smiled. Okeke stared at me in disbelief.

"But I am to be king!"

The room fell silent.

"No," I said, "you are not."

Itoro rushed onto the dais.

Okeke's lip curled. "My betrothed and I are in conversation."

She glanced at me, and I tilted my head toward the door.

She grabbed his arm and pulled him down the steps, up the lengthy aisle, and out of the Audience Court, his dazed family following. After the door closed, the guests glanced at each other and spoke in whispers. My friends came up to me. Kayin said, "Good riddance." Efe was more diplomatic: "It wasn't meant to be." Fatimata hugged me. "Oshun speaks."

We proceeded to the Dining Hall to feast. My mouth watered from the mixed aromas of yams, jollof rice, spicy meats, cassava dumplings, plantains, and yam cakes. I ate heartily. We celebrated my continued freedom, Kayin leading most of the toasts. Whatever had been bothering her earlier no longer did so.

The noise level in the room rose the more the palm wine and millet beer flowed. At the table on the dais, I sat with my father, Efe, Mingan, Baby Tahki, Fatimata, Mukki, Kayin, and Itoro, who I'd insisted take the night off from guarding me. Kayin enjoyed herself most of all, as if she were the one who'd avoided marrying someone she didn't love. The guests talked and laughed as if this were, nonetheless, a wedding feast. Relief flowed through me; the burden of uniting with Okeke was a weight I no longer carried.

Azeze headed toward us between the long, crowded rectangular tables. He'd been sitting in the back of the Dining Hall with other tradesmen. Fatimata touched Efe's arm and giggled. Efe glanced at me, but I ignored her.

Azeze was wearing a simple black tunic that showed off his sinewy arms. He bowed to me. A smile creased his chiseled features.

"You look beautiful, Your Amara."

Udo wasn't the only one who'd mostly seen me dirty and sweaty.

"We could make room for you up here," offered Efe. I cut my eyes at her.

"My seat is acceptable," said Azeze. "Thank you." He bowed and retreated.

"I love the way he looks at you," Fatimata said. Indeed, something in my chest had stirred beneath his gaze.

"I remember how gentle he was with the Aons on the ship," Efe said. "He'd be a good match."

Kayin glanced at both of them in confusion.

Although I was grateful that my friends felt comfortable speaking to me truthfully, at times I wished they wouldn't.

A fanti rushed in. She scanned the room in search of someone. Having failed to find whomever she sought, she approached Kayin. She leaned in and spoke to her. Kayin, her expression grim, came up behind me. She whispered in my ear.

"Bamidele's army is on the outskirts of Kana."

# Chapter Thirty-Two

# ...and sing our names...

NO ONE IN the queendom had yet been born the last time it was attacked. I had mulled over attacking Aon but decided to wait until after my coronation and wedding. Bamidele must have anticipated this; he'd waited for the distraction of the wedding to act.

Our countries could not coexist.

Those of us who were tipsy from too much wine at the wedding feast sobered quickly. The villagers left the Dining Hall to return to their homes, while the warriors rushed to the barracks to retrieve their weapons and protective gear. I went to my bedchamber to retrieve mine. Messengers spread the news to residents throughout the Queendom of Kana to be prepared. Through my mother's foresight, everyone had received some defense training with household items. But Udo hadn't had time to implement my plan to train all residents who were sixteen and older to fight.

This battle would be left to the women.

As I was leaving the obieze's entrance, Kayin came up to me and said, "A word, Your Amara." She led me a few paces away. Warriors streamed out the grand doors.

"I owe you an apology," she said.

"For what?"

"I should have seen this coming. After only a moment with Bamidele, I didn't trust him."

"That makes two of us. There's no time for accusations." I patted her muscular shoulder. "Let's go."

On the training ground, Udo faced the warriors lined up in rows in front of her. I stood with the other officers beside the general.

"I will lead us into battle," I stated.

She didn't bother to lower her voice. "That's ludicrous. You're the queen. You cannot put yourself at risk."

"Are you questioning my wisdom?"

Udo hesitated. I glimpsed a tight smile, prior to her bowing her head. She was proud of me. "As you desire," she said.

The door of the obieze opened. Mingan emerged. Standing in the doorway, Efe held Baby Tahki in her arms. Mingan rushed over to me.

"I want to fight with you," he said.

"You have a child now, and you haven't been training. And it's not your war."

"You helped me fight mine. It would be my honor."

His dark eyes reminded me so much of his sister, Tahki's. "Very well."

Leading the warriors, I ran out of the compound and headed to the Kanaian Forest. We halted at the edge of town. Lights dotted the woods. At this time of night, they could only be human-made. Torches.

I was unsure of our odds. Udo shook her head. Kayin nodded.

I checked that the string underneath my chin secured the brass helmet, then shouted the war cry.

Armed with muskets, swords, dagas, and hatchets, we rushed at the men who had the audacity to attack the Queendom of Kana. I imagined Nsia running with us. Bamidele's army fired, but we kept running. From our side, arrows with poisoned tips soared across the sky toward their targets. Some of Bamidele's men fell, as did a few Kanaian warriors.

Gunfire smoke permeated the air, and it was difficult to see. I fired my musket, anyway, knowing the Aons were in front of me. I would reserve my daga for finishing someone. Beside me, Itoro was firing as quickly as she reloaded, using a mechanism developed by Efe and Azeze to reduce misfires and shorten the time it took to load bullets.

I cocked my gun and aimed at the chest of a man twenty paces away. His features were indiscernible in the darkness. My forefinger tightened on the trigger.

There was an explosion above my breast.

My chest was on fire.

A large red splotch spread across my white tunic. We officers shouldn't have worn our white tunics at night. Why hadn't Udo figured that out earlier? Why hadn't I? Dizzy, I released my musket. The shouting and shooting sounded far away. Blood filled my mouth, its taste metallic. The ground rose quickly, and my head landed hard.

*Nne Nne Thema. Nne. Help me.*

My reign was ending before it had barely begun.

❧

My eyes fluttered open, the cleft of Mukambu's chin coming into view.

The healer's serious expression relaxed. "Welcome back, Your Amara!"

"I'm still alive?" I croaked, my throat sore and scratchy.

"You gave us a fright."

I glanced at the sunbaked clay strokes on the ceiling. I was in my bedchamber, and not in Mukambu's evaluation room.

"How...how did I get here?"

"Kayin carried you."

"From the forest?"

"Without stopping. How are you feeling?"

"Like a horse ran over me." Enyi had been a good horse. I hoped her new owner was treating her well. "Why does my tongue hurt?"

"You bit it. I sewed the wound shut. You've been out for seven sunrises. I wasn't certain you'd live. I removed the bullet from your chest and used ogalu to treat the wound. You'll always have that scar as a reminder, I'm afraid."

"Was anyone else hurt?"

"Several warriors suffered injuries, but none of them died." Mukambu patted my good shoulder. "Visitors are waiting to see you, one of whom has been standing outside your door the entire time."

"Send her in."

The physician left the room and Itoro entered, the skin under her eyes puffy.

"Don't worry," I said. "I'll live."

She scanned the thin blanket covering my body. She didn't believe me.

I gestured. "Take a seat."

She sat in the chair by the bed.

I spent more time with Itoro, my head fanti, than anyone, though most of it was shared in silence. She absently traced the scar on her face with her finger.

"You look exhausted," I said. "You need to get some sleep."

"I've been so worried."

"Sometimes I forget you're not Kanaian. Your loyalty makes me want to be a better queen."

Her eyes widened.

I frowned. "I've expressed kind words to you before."

"I'm unaccustomed to it, Your Amara."

I grinned despite the pain. "Funny."

We talked a little more. I must have fallen asleep, because when I woke up, she was gone.

The shutters were open wide. Afternoon sunlight slanted through the windows.

Kifunji ceased straightening the room and poured a glass of water from the pitcher on the nightstand. She lifted my head tenderly and brought the cup to my lips. At first, it was hard to swallow, but my thirst for the cool liquid overcame the discomfort, and I guzzled it down. She rubbed a cloth drenched in karite soap all over my body and brushed my hair.

"Aba!" I said, as she struggled with a difficult entanglement.

She giggled. "I apologize, your Amara."

When she finished, I summoned Efe, Kayin, and Fatimata into my bedchamber. Fatimata and Mukki had remained in the compound upon my orders, since it hadn't been safe for them to return to Banaan.

"Are you all right?" Fatimata asked.

I nodded.

The whites of Kayin's eyes were shot through with red. "You look bad."

"And you seem sad. Were you afraid of not having anyone around to best?"

Her grin was tight-lipped. "Hardly."

"Thank you for carrying me. You're stronger than you look."

"I'm not that strong."

"Modesty doesn't suit you."

Efe took my hand. "Before you two continue, do you need anything?"

"The status of the war with Aon."

She shook her head, smiling. "I give up."

"We're holding Bamidele's army at bay," Kayin responded. "They haven't penetrated Kana proper, but I'm not sure how long we can hold out. The rules of war don't apply to them."

She told me that the Aons killed anyone in their path. They had slaughtered Kanaian residents living on the farms on the edge of town. They didn't bother capturing them—Kanaians wouldn't make great slaves.

"We need reinforcements," I said.

"Chibuike," Efe said, "someone else wants to see you." She released my hand, a gleam in her eye. Fatimata smiled. Kifunji opened the door.

Azeze entered, his face anguished. Kayin glared at him for interrupting. I didn't ask my friends to stay. They would anyhow. It would be improper for me to be alone with him anywhere, particularly in my bedchamber.

He bowed. "Your Amara. I...came to apologize."

"Whatever for?"

"Your weapon. I heard what happened. It's my fault it failed you."

I'd promoted Azeze to Kanaian blacksmith. His craftsmanship had surpassed that of the old blacksmith long ago. The former blacksmith would be provided for for life in return for his seasons of service.

"You did the best you could," said Fatimata.

"Since I designed it," Efe said, "the fault is mine."

"I don't blame either of you." I yawned. "It wasn't the weapon. It was me. I did not draw it fast enough."

He exhaled. "I'll let you rest. I will not let you down again."

Fatimata, Efe, and Kayin departed soon after he did.

That night, my ancestors did not join me in my dreams. I slept the sleep of the dead.

I woke to the aroma of yam porridge in a bowl on the nightstand Kifunji had prepared for me, and I savored every delicious morsel. When I finished eating, I struggled out of bed, used the privy, and allowed Kifunji to dress me.

The war raged for many sunrises. Despite General Udo's best efforts, we were losing. To save lives, should I order her to surrender?

I did not rejoin the battle. Although I was still recovering from my wounds, I was the queen now, and not just a warrior. I spent my days in the Council Room, Itoro, standing behind me, maps covering the large table. Officers stopped by to deliver updates.

I understood what Udo had tried to tell me. If I were killed in battle without an heir, no one could legitimately rule Kana. The queendom would be left…queenless.

One day, I left the obieze, crossed the Grand Square, and made my way to the temple. I knelt before Gbadu, the Goddess of Destiny. I prayed to her and Queens Thema and Adebola for help and guidance in saving our queendom.

The following day, they answered.

Male and female soldiers from the neighboring provinces of Podegon, Oso, and Zatopa—the same Zatopans we'd saved from the Portuguese ship at Fort Kinnakeet—arrived in Kana. We hadn't sought their help. The three armies fought with ours, turning potential defeat into victory. As the tide of the war changed, some of Bamidele's soldiers turned against him. The enslaved. The threatened. The tortured. They surrendered to us and sought refuge in Kana, most of them offering to join our army.

Bamidele and I met in Banaan, a village of peace, to declare a truce. He agreed to free the enslaved Aons and to stop kidnapping and selling individuals from neighboring tribes. In return, I agreed to leave him alone.

If Kana did not attack him, he'd have no more need for guns.

After seven full moons, I traveled to Banaan to visit Fatimata. Kayin and Itoro waited for me outside her house.

The Banaan ruler was in her mother's bed, propped up by straw-filled pillows, wearing a white night shift, her legs still tucked underneath a light blue covering. Her brothers' and sisters' beds were stacked along a wall. She was beaming. Her husband sat on the edge of the bed, talking to her. When he noticed me at the entrance to their house, he stood hurriedly and bowed.

"Your Amara, I was just leaving." He stole a glance at Fatimata and left the hut.

She was holding a bundle of cloth: the reason for my visit. I approached the bed. The baby stared at me, her brown eyes too big for her tiny head, and grinned.

"Oh!" I exclaimed.

Fatimata bounced the baby. "She likes you."

I removed my crown and set it on a nearby chair. I stood over Fatimata and grinned back at the infant. I cupped the back of the baby's head. Her scent was fresh. Innocent. Precious.

"She's beautiful. What's her name?"

"Kaminah Yaa Chibuike."

My eyes misted. "I'm honored."

"You saved my life. My people. And you're my friend."

I gently released the baby's soft head. "Wait! Kaminah. Wasn't that your doll's name?"

She nodded. "Now that I have a child of my own, I think a lot about those women whose children were stolen from them." She shook her head. "I'll never be separated from my children."

I understood what that statement implied. "I won't let you be."

"I'm glad you're healed. I was worried and would have visited…"

"I understand."

Fatimata bit her lip. "I have something to tell you."

The child gurgled.

"What?"

"Do you remember the day we met?"

"How could I forget?"

"I never told you why I was in the river."

The baby clamped on to my wriggling forefinger. "But you did. You said you were fishing and got pulled downstream by the current."

"That wasn't the entire truth."

"I didn't think so then. What is the truth?"

"I was chasing a fish. It was orange with black stripes."

"So you *were* fishing."

"No. I was trying to catch it with my hands. To be my pet. My friend. Her name was going to be Kaminah."

The baby still clutched my forefinger. I stared at Fatimata. "I almost drowned saving you because of a pet fish?"

She giggled.

After a moment, I joined her. My finger slipped from Kaminah's grasp. "Thank Gbadu!"

Fatimata appraised me. "You're good with children. You'll bear them someday."

"I'm without a husband."

"A situation easily rectified."

"How?"

"You can marry Azeze."

"But he's a commoner."

"As is Mukki, and I've never been happier." She reached out and held my cheek. "Azeze cares for you. He's a good man. And I see the way you look at him."

"You sound like Efe."

"You should listen to your friends. She asked me to talk some sense into you."

"I have a country to run."

"You're hardheaded."

Heat rose within me. "Who are you—"

"Men lead and marry. Why can't women?"

I exhaled. "That doesn't give you leave to insult me."

"It's not an insult, it's the truth." Her voice softened. "Don't wait. Life is not promised."

"But is he right for me? To be by my side as I rule Kana?"

"Only you can answer that. But you're the queen." She smiled. "You can do whatever you want."

Fatimata handed Kaminah to me. I held the baby away from me as if she were a delicate sculpture.

"She won't break," Fatimata said.

I brought Kaminah close to my chest and cradled her. She cooed. "What if…we don't enjoy the same relationship you have with Mukki? Or that Efe has with Mingan?"

"You won't."

"Why not?"

"Your relationship will be unique to the two of you."

"Kaminah, your mother doesn't fight, but she has a warrior's spirit. I'm sure you'll have one, too."

Kaminah smiled as if she understood. I kissed her crown and handed her back to her mother.

✦

Instead of returning to Kana, my retinue and I traveled to the castle—which I'd renamed Castle Adebola. A messenger had brought word that Captain Francisco de Silva had returned from Portugal.

Kayin was in an expansive mood throughout the trip. She was happy I had survived the Aon War. I suspected she was also glad that she, Itoro, and I were going on this adventure alone.

The coastal air was balmy, and the sun warmed my skin. The outside of the building was painted white. A plethora of flowers bloomed along the edifice's front. The first time I saw this building, I'd vowed never to enter it. Now it appeared welcoming.

Silva met me outside. Although his face was still weathered by the sea, he sported a trim beard, and his clean, wavy hair was cut to his shoulders. He was still a large man, but looked healthier. His eyes were clear. He grinned. Surprising myself, so did I.

He extended his hand. "It's good to see you."

I shook it. "You look good."

He exhaled. "My conscience isn't as heavy. Sailing is much easier without worrying your passengers will die in transit."

Kayin smirked. "Or kill you in your sleep."

Silva grimaced. "That, too."

"But you are a pale man who keeps his word."

"I had plenty of wrongs to right."

"And we would have hunted you down if you hadn't come back."

"There's that." Silva bowed to me. "Your Majesty, let me show you what your folks have done with the castle. They've been hospitable to me. Thank you."

Inside, the walls of the second-floor barracks had been painted. The warriors stationed there enjoyed new bedsteads, having replaced the ones the former Portuguese guards had slept in. The kitchen was immaculate, and the dungeon was also clean—and empty. The foul smell was gone. The castle was no longer a dark and dreary prison. It looked like a home.

After touring indoors, Silva led us outside, carrying a jug and a cup he'd picked up from the kitchen. As long as he wasn't sailing that day, I wasn't concerned about his drinking. We followed him down to the beach and to the rowboat floating in the water. Two warriors held it stationary by rope. After Kayin, Itoro, Silva, and I had settled into our seats, the warriors rowed toward the ships.

The ocean breeze stroked my face, its briny scent filling my nostrils. I was grateful not to see any sharks surfacing this time. Perhaps they'd eaten their fill.

"Silva, what happened when you returned to Portugal?" I asked.

"The shipping company released me after the crew told them what happened. I was lucky I wasn't arrested or hanged. I thought I'd be upset—I've never been dismissed from a job—but I was happy. As if an anchor no longer weighed me down. I found work fixing boats at the docks on the river near my family home. Though without a ship, I wasn't sure how I would fulfill my promise to you."

The sway of the boat settled me. "And yet you did."

"One day, while enjoying a drink in the tavern, a band of powerful men stopped in on their way to Lisbon. I overheard them saying that stealing humans and transporting them as cargo was a sin. Went against the Catholic faith. I introduced myself and told them about you Kanaians, and how I'd promised to help bring your people home, but I had no ship. Six months later, they bought one and patronized me to come here."

I smiled as we came closer to the ships. The word *Liberdade* was painted in black on the vessel's hull, below the Portuguese flag. And the name of the ship we'd captured in Kinnakeet had been changed to *Kana Royale*. A Kanaian flag flew high overhead.

"They're beautiful," I said.

"We have a big job to do," he said. "A lot of your people are out there."

The two ships, and their crew of Kanaian warriors, were bound for New Spain and Hispaniola to search for more Banaans and Asantis. Silva understood how long this mission would take, and he was willing to undertake it.

From the jug, he poured a dark liquid into a metal cup and handed it to me.

I sniffed it. It smelled like fruit. "Wine?"

He nodded. "Portuguese."

I hesitated. Someone had tried to poison my mother with tainted wine. "Why aren't you partaking?"

"You're not supposed to drink it. Hit it against the ship. It's for good luck."

Kayin shrugged. Another pale man's odd tradition. And a waste of wine. I stood, found my balance, and slammed the cup against the hull. The cup and its contents fell into the ocean. The liquid spilled on my hand. I shook it off.

"I'm not sure you needed to hit it *that* hard," Silva said, "but it means we're in business."

# Chapter Thirty-Three

# ...forevermore

UDO HAD TAKEN a bullet in the thigh during the Aon War. Mukambu had removed it, saving her from losing a second appendage. The general was still convalescing in her private room.

I was in my work chamber when Itoro announced Kayin wanted to see me.

Kayin entered, looking smart in a crisp, white military tunic.

"Anything to report?" I asked.

I'd placed her in charge of the army while the general was incapacitated and charged her with developing a plan in case Bamidele reneged on our agreement. She was thriving in this role.

"Still working on it. I wish I had a list of every person serving in the army."

"Udo should have one."

She turned to leave. "I'll look in her work chamber."

"Wait. I'll help you."

She cocked her head.

"My chamber feels confining," I continued. "I will never get used to working indoors all day."

"But how is it different from the adjustment your mother made from warrior to queen? And every queen prior to her?"

"Good point." I walked around my ebony desk and patted her shoulder. "But it also gives me an excuse to spend time with you."

She smiled. "And I thought you would change when you became queen."

"I hope I have changed." I returned the smile. "For the better. Please lead the way."

In Udo's work chamber, I said, "I'll search the desk. You take the table."

In the corner of the room was a small table piled high with parchments and scattered with wooden pieces the general used to simulate armies and battles.

In the middle drawer of Udo's desk, I found blank documents, ink, and a quill pen. A gold nugget rested in the corner. I picked it up and scrutinized it. I wondered where she'd gotten it from. I checked every drawer, but found nothing. Kayin sat at the table, deep in concentration, as she scanned the parchments.

The lowest drawer was locked. I searched for a key and couldn't find one. I wasn't wearing my daga.

"Kayin," I said, "I need your sword."

Dropping the parchment, she rose and brandished the weapon. She inserted the sharp tip into the lock until it clicked and the drawer popped open.

It was empty.

Kayin shrugged. Curious, I crouched and reached into the back, grazing a small wooden box. I withdrew it and opened it.

Inside were my mother's golden earrings. My hand shook as I picked one up.

"Aren't those—"

"My mother's."

We stared at the jewelry.

When I told Udo the earrings were missing, she had responded that they would turn up. It was as if someone had punched me in the chest. I struggled to breathe. I sniffed the earring. It smelled ripe, not like my mother's lavender fragrance.

I put it back in the box and closed it. "Take them to Mukambu. Tell her to analyze them for poison."

"You think Udo killed the queen? That's quite an accusation."

"Smell it."

Kayin complied.

"My mother did not die of an illness or old age."

That afternoon, the healer confirmed the earrings were laced with poisonous seeds from the ouabain plant. The poison had entered my mother's bloodstream through the holes in her earlobes.

After the healer delivered her report, she left my work chamber. Salamatu left with her. I leaned back in my chair, thinking. Kayin sat quietly in the chair across my desk.

"Remember the story she told us the night before the Portuguese captured us?"

"Of course," she replied.

"Do you remember the toast she made that night?"

"'Take back what is rightfully mine.' Why?"

"I don't think she was referring to our mission. She was talking about Kana. She gave token resistance to the plan of letting the Portuguese kidnap us. She suggested the best Kanaian warriors join me to remove them from the queendom. She let me take Nsia. She could dispose of my mother and claim the throne for herself. No one could stop her."

Kayin leaned forward. "Except we came back."

Another thought occurred to me. "Ndidi."

"What about her?"

I swallowed the lump in my throat. "It wasn't a coincidence the only person with diplomatic relationships was killed, along with our warriors, by an unskilled gang. The surviving warrior said it had been an ambush. Udo notified Bamidele that Ndidi was coming."

We were silent for a moment.

Kayin continued, "That story she told us. You don't know who the recruiting officer was, do you? The one who rejected Udo."

"I wondered, but never inquired."

"It was your mother."

I started. "How do you know this?"

"An officer told me when I first joined the army. She warned that given my propensity for insolence, I should be respectful in my interactions with the general. Or suffer Udo's wrath. Wise counsel, in retrospect. This officer didn't think Queen Adebola knew what she'd unleashed."

I lowered my head. "I should have protected my mother. She was so consumed with the enemy without that she didn't see the one within."

"What are you going to do?"

❦

Alone in my work chamber, I prayed to Gbadu before crossing the Great Hall to the eastern stairwell that led to Udo's private room in the ministers' wing. Kayin and Itoro fell in step behind me. My mind swirled with everything Udo had said in the past. Every action she'd taken. Every decision she'd made. I thought of Ola—Udo conveniently found the bag of poisonous seeds among Ola's belongings. I needed to find my former attendant and make amends.

When I reached Udo's bedchamber, I told my friends to wait in the corridor outside. I could contend with a lame warrior, even if she was a general.

Udo lay on the bed wearing a night shift, her thigh encased in a cloth. The room reeked of blood and odudu oyibo, the herb Mukambu applied to curb infection.

I stood out of Udo's reach. Although she was convalescing, I wasn't a fool. I recalled the war stories about her.

The general grinned. "It's about time you checked on me."

Inside, my blood burned like the forge in Azeze's smithy. My face shook with anger.

Her smile faded. "How do you know?"

"The earrings."

She sighed. "I should have destroyed them."

My tongue felt too large for my mouth. "Why?"

"I kept them as a small token of my victory. Adebola should have been more careful about what she wore. And whom she trusted."

"No. Why...did you kill my mother?"

"She didn't listen. I told her we'd be rich if we aligned ourselves with Bamidele. You might recall you interrupted that meeting."

It was after I'd seen a pale man for the first time, and I'd gone to my mother's work chamber. Udo had stared dagas at me as she'd walked toward me.

Her cane leaned against her bed. Its clicking sound across the sunbaked floor had plagued my dreams for years.

"I agreed long ago to help that imbecile. He paid me handsomely for it." The gold piece in her drawer. "Many people in Kana labor away their lives and still starve. At least, in service to the pale men, they would eat."

This was why the Aon woman asked whether I was like our general. She thought we were in the slave trade, too.

Udo shook her head. "Most of them wouldn't have been missed. But Adebola didn't listen."

"*Queen* Adebola."

"I told her the queendom could be richer. 'We're already wealthy,' she said." Udo imitated my mother's voice perfectly. "I responded, 'Wealthier. It's the future.' She said that would never be our future."

"You were willing to sacrifice Kana's greatest warriors."

"The Portuguese assured me you and the warriors wouldn't survive the ocean crossing." She adjusted the bed sheet. "And you! As a warrior, you were weak. If you'd been born under different circumstances, I wouldn't have selected you for our army. And you're not fit to rule."

"And you're not fit to lead. What good is wealth when your landspeople suffer?"

She waved this away. "You shouldn't be the heir to the throne because of happenstance."

"It's rightfully mine."

If she recognized her own words, she didn't show it.

The general's eyes glinted. "The crown should be bestowed

based on worth. I should have sold you and your mother into slavery."

Bile rose in my throat.

"My pathway to the throne would have been easier," she continued, "instead of waiting for her to die. For you to die."

In horror, I realized something else. "You wanted me to lead the battle against Aon so I would be killed."

She continued as if I hadn't spoken. "Adebola ruled with a soft hand. Kana grew weak, while Aon grew stronger."

I clenched my fist. "Do not say another word against my mother. You are not half the woman she is."

My mother had made few mistakes during her reign, but trusting Udo had been one of them.

The general's hard gaze did not waver. "I rose. Became Adebola's equal."

"No matter how high you rise, you will never be her equal. You are to be executed for treason."

"You're not going to kill me yourself?"

"That's not our way."

Udo was silent for a moment, contemplating her fate. Her arm shot out from under the sheet. A daga sliced through the air. I shifted, but not in time. The blade embedded itself in my throwing arm. Pain blazing, I yelped. Blood streamed through my fingers. She'd aimed for my heart. If I hadn't moved, I'd be dead. And the throne hers.

The general raised her thick eyebrows. "Did you think I was a fool? I'm armed with multiple weapons."

Kayin and Itoro rushed into the room. Itoro tore off the bottom of her tunic and tied the cloth above the wound on my arm. We left the knife in, as Mukambu always instructed us to do.

Kayin drew her swords and pointed them at the general. "Say the word, Your Amara."

"Lower your weapons." I clenched my teeth. My arm throbbed. "This is between the general and me."

Itoro and Kayin moved against the wall.

Udo pursed her lips. "I'm not worried about them. I see you, Itoro." Itoro tensed. "You've been a disappointment to me. I expected your loyalty. I should have left you a slave."

Itoro reached for her hatchet but stopped. "You're not worth it."

The cloth slowed the bleeding.

My next action was that of a warrior, not a queen.

I reached behind me and grabbed the pommel of my daga, nestled in a scabbard secured at my lower back. Ever since I'd ascended to the throne, I no longer carried my daga at my waist, which Udo knew. It would have alerted her if I'd done so today. But I wasn't foolish enough to meet the general under these circumstances unarmed. She would never surrender.

I flung the daga with my left hand, aiming for her throat. The pulpy sound of the blade entering flesh was loud in the silent room. The knife impaled her neck to the wooden headboard. Udo's mouth opened, like a fish marooned on the riverbank, and blood poured down her chin and onto her shift. Her eyes were wide, and no longer saw me. Her spirit departed from her body with nowhere to go.

She would not be joining our ancestors.

～

I lay in bed, still warm and relaxed from the herb bath Kifunji had drawn for me on Mukambu's recommendation. The healer had just left my bedchamber after wrapping my arm with a fresh cloth.

Salamatu had vanished. Killing my mother had been Udo's idea, but she couldn't have carried out the plan on her own. *I kept them as a small token of my victory. Adebola should have been more careful about what she wore. And whom she trusted.* The general hadn't dressed the queen. It was the attendant who was always with her who'd pierced her ears with poison—and planted the seeds among my favorite childhood attendant's belongings. Udo had probably threatened to send Salamatu back to Aon and into slavery if she didn't comply.

She would be executed as soon as we found her…if the general hadn't already killed her.

After the initial shock, the warriors were angry and felt betrayed by Udo's treachery. She'd been our leader. Recruited some of us. We'd entrusted our lives to her…And she had wanted to sell us like cattle. Itoro said repeatedly that she wanted to kill her; I kept reminding her that the general was already dead.

"She wasn't the general she should have been," Kayin said.

I called on Kayin to send warriors to search for Ola. They found her in Aon, where she and her family had been living in squalor. I issued a public apology to them in a crowded Audience Court; the people of Kana had never heard a royal admission of fault. In private, I asked her for forgiveness, and for her to move back into the obieze in exchange for higher compensation and her own room. I presented her family with a new, furnished home closer to the obieze, so that Ola could visit them frequently. She agreed to take care of Baby Tahki. One day, she would care for my children, if ever I had any.

With Udo's death and the ceasing of hostilities with Aon,

my life became routine; I spent time with my father and friends, dealt with the queendom's business affairs, and took daily trips to the temple.

∽

While returning from one such visit, I encountered Azeze leaving the obieze.

He'd flourished since I'd promoted him to the town's blacksmith. Because of the volume of business from the army and the villagers—we would never be surprised by an attack again—he had five apprentices working under him.

He was also the object of many unwed Kanaian women's affections.

"Your Amara." He carried a leather case. "I was meeting with General Kayin on the design of the new swords."

I'd promoted Kayin to Udo's vacant position. Leading the army suited her better than overseeing the markets. I'd appointed a successful market trader to oversee commerce.

"I'm sure they'll be magnificent."

"She told me you'd be out here. Coming from the temple?"

My conversations with Azeze usually regarded queendom business. This was a departure.

"Yes. Why?"

"Mind if I join you tomorrow?"

"Well, I don't think—" Why not? What was the harm in praying together? Efe and Fatimata kept urging me to give Azeze a chance. I also had to produce an heir. "If you wish."

He and I met every morning and prayed in the temple. We talked in the smaller courtyard. No one was permitted to throw dagas at the trees anymore. Saplings had been planted next to the ones I'd gouged. Wooden boards proliferated the training ground for knife-throwing practice.

I never invited Azeze to visit me inside the obieze, but I visited him in his workshop. The room smelled of fire and steel. Weapons, organized by function, were lined up in neat rows on tables abutting the walls. I admired the way he approached his craft, the precise movement of his hands. His arms were absent of the burn marks I'd noticed on the previous blacksmith.

One day, as he worked, I said, "Everything you do is exact."

He glanced at his hands. "My father was a farmer and lost the use of his hand. A hoe sliced through it. He made do, but he struggled. Since my livelihood depends on my hands, I've learned to be careful."

Over time, his social status lost importance, and there came a day when I couldn't imagine another one without him.

We married in a small ceremony in the Obieze Temple. My father, Kayin, Itoro, Fatimata, Mukki, Kaminah, Efe, Mingan, Baby Tahki, and Kifunji attended, as did Azeze's parents, five siblings, and fifteen nieces and nephews. Azeze and I exchanged words of promise; he wiped my tears as the priestess spoke.

That night, I sighed, elated, after Azeze and I made love. I finally understood what all the fuss was about.

⤠

The next morning, Azeze gazed into my eyes as we lay in bed, the scent of our lovemaking still hovering in the air. I thought of all the times I'd caught him staring at me. Now, it was I who couldn't stop staring at him.

"I love your ears," I said.

"The other children used to make fun of me. They called me 'Elephant Boy.'"

I climbed on top of him. Skin to skin. Our bodies fit. I leaned down, kissed, and nibbled one of his ears. "Their loss."

He traced the scar from the bullet wound above my breast. "Do you remember the first time we met?"

"You were the blacksmith's apprentice."

"Before that."

"How was that possible?" Too late to take back my rude question.

"My family lacked, yes. I worked on our farm as soon as I was old enough to walk until the blacksmith accepted me as an apprentice."

I rolled off him and covered my breasts with the bedsheet. "That doesn't explain how we met."

"When we were children—I was twelve, you were ten— you shared your agbalumo with me in the market."

I didn't recall meeting a boy, much less one outside the compound. "I don't remember."

"I told you I'd never eaten one." His eyes twinkled in the hazy air from the morning sun trickling through the shuttered windows. "I lied."

Ah! The boy who'd never eaten an agbalumo. "You asked me what it tasted like. Why would you lie?"

"For an excuse to talk to you. Otherwise, you wouldn't have spoken to me. You didn't see me during all those years you ran back and forth through the market like a panther.

When you handed the fruit to me, I knew at that moment I'd marry you."

*But you were a villager!* "But I was ten!"

"I still knew. That's why I made that daga for you."

He pointed at my beloved daga, the one my mother had given me when I'd joined the military. The one sitting in its rightful place on the hippopotamus's tusks.

"You didn't make it for me. The Kanaian blacksmith did."

He shook his head. "It was me. I was his apprentice, yes, but I begged him to allow me to create it for you. I convinced him that if I failed, at worst, he would need to recreate it himself. He countered that he'd release me, cease payment of my wages, and find another apprentice." Azeze smiled. "So there was pressure on me to make it perfect."

I marveled at the risk he'd taken. His parents would have relied on his earnings. "Why did you insist on making it?"

"I wanted you to touch something, every day, that I had touched." He eyed me. "Have you ever really looked at it?"

I thought of all the times I'd gazed at it over the years. "Of course."

"Yet you never noticed my initial on the handle."

I padded across the bedchamber over to the dresser. I examined the daga. His initial had been there all these years, below the lion.

Pressed against my palm.

# Epilogue

# A new song

*Queen's Day, 1660*

ADE SPUN HER daga on the back of her fist. It was my first daga. The same one my mother gave to me, and Thema to her.

"Aunty Kayin said I throw better than you did at my age."

I laughed. "She didn't know me then. Ready?"

Ade nodded and sheathed her daga. We walked through the obieze's grand doors. The fanti on each side saluted me. "Your Amara."

I nodded and kept walking, holding Ade's hand.

Outside, the rays of the midday sun shot through the gaps in the clouds, evidence our ancestors were present on this day. I wore a white silk tunic with scarlet edges. My golden crown rested on my long, silver hair.

My ten-dry-seasons-old granddaughter stood next to me in a matching tunic. On my other side were my younger daughter, Ime, and her family. Ime preferred the company of a book over a daga.

After suffering two miscarriages, I had believed I'd suffer the same fate as my mother, until I bore my older daughter, Chike. She died giving birth to Ade, despite Mukambu's best efforts to save her. My father's death a decade earlier hadn't pained me as much. A part of me had perished the day my daughter drew her last breath.

Mukambu could prescribe no cure for grief.

But Chike had left me with a precious gift: the precocious girl standing beside me. This child was as attached to my hip as my daga used to be. Ade had my eyes. My mother's eyes. I knew what she would look like when she grew up, because I still remembered my mother's face.

The dignitaries of the Queendom of Kana stood behind us. In the distance, the gates to the compound opened and a woman in an orange pano walked in, followed by a group of twenty people. I released Ade's hand and took a step forward. And another. I broke into a trot. I was violating the protocol of the introduction of the rulers. The woman, wearing a head-dress made of twigs, ran to me. She was no longer as fast as the wind.

We embraced.

"It's good to see you," Fatimata said.

Our visits were infrequent. I pulled back to gaze at her cherubic face. Her coiled white hair was short. Smile lines framed her eyes. Like many women in our region, she'd become more beautiful with age.

"And you, my sister."

A slender woman wearing a purple pano and a matching gele walked through the gates with slow, regal steps. Unlike her mother, she was on time. We ran—shuffled—to her. Fatimata arrived there first.

Small ridges lined Efe's face. My eyes moistened.

"Chibuike," she said, her cheeks damp with tears. "Fatimata."

We hugged.

"Aunty Efe! Aunty Fatimata!" Ade ran up to us, her shoulder-length hair flying, and grabbed them around the waist.

Although I was an only child, my children and grandchildren had several aunts.

I took Fatimata's and Efe's hands. "I have a surprise for you."

Inside, instead of going to the Council Room, I led them down the hall to the Obieze Gallery.

Next to the tapestry of my Nne Nne Thema were two blue silk cloths. I signaled to Kifunji to remove a cloth. Underneath was a statue of a younger version of me in a Kanaian warrior officer's tunic, brandishing my daga, and my sister rulers in panos, their heads held high.

"It's lovely!" Fatimata said.

Efe peered closer at the replica of herself. "The detail is exquisite."

After a long moment, Kifunji removed the second cloth to reveal a statue of Adebola, Yaa, and Dayo in their royal panos and headdresses, their arms around each other's waists.

Efe squealed. Fatimata wept, raising her hand to her mouth. My eyes misted, and I resisted touching my mother's likeness. Fatimata rested her head on my shoulder and slipped an arm around my waist, as did Efe.

We held each other as our mothers' likenesses did, swaying as we took in the image of those three intelligent, beautiful, and ferocious women. I recalled them talking and laughing and drinking palm wine at the feast on Queen's Day Eve all those years ago. Their destinies and ours had been certain then; the goddesses had their plans.

As we sat on the viewing platform in the Grand Square, the warriors of Kana, half of whom were men, paraded by, singing the warrior song.

Unlike when Adebola had ruled, I invited people from every strata of life into the compound for Queen's Day. Everyone took part in the feast, and the villagers could take any unconsumed food home with them.

Efe, Fatimata, and I sat in the shade of a conical tent, enjoying a chalice of sweet palm wine and watching our grandchildren play. An attendant fanned us with a large palm frond. Itoro stood several paces away. Near in age to me, she was not the best person to protect me. But she was the one I trusted the most.

Music played by warriors on handmade instruments filled the air. Fatimata and Efe caught me up on the goings on in their villages. Most living Banaans had been found and returned home. The same wasn't true for the Asantis. A small fraction of the original residents had been discovered. The rest were still missing. We had expanded our search to their descendants, but Efe had finally lost hope of locating them during her lifetime.

When some of her people had been recovered, she, Mingan, and their family moved back to Asanti. For a long time, I greatly missed her daily presence in the Thema Obieze.

Silva continued his missions for twenty dry seasons. When he retired from captaining, instead of returning to Portugal, he moved permanently to Alkebulan's west coast. He loved the generous and expressive people there, and that he could be a practicing Jew with no need to hide. Time convinced me my trust in him was well-placed. Kanaians captained voyages of the *Liberdade* and the *Kana Royale*, and of a new ship, the *Queen Adebola I*, bringing people home from New Spain and a place called Brazil.

Individuals from all over English North America and southern points found their way to Fort Kinnakeet, seeking passage home. Some stayed there or settled in Tsenacommacah with the Powhatan's permission.

Old King Bamidele of Aon and his sons had died mysteriously. Rumors abounded that, like Bamidele's eldest brother, they'd been poisoned. His eldest daughter still ruled the country. After her father's death, she formed a powerful alliance with me to protect our people from the pale men. Kayin and I would take the king and his sons' cause of death to our graves.

I'd learned something from Bamidele after all.

Victors write history. It might not happen in my lifetime, but we would be victorious in our mission of bringing our people home. My descendants, the Kanaian warriors, and all those who believed in freedom would see to it.

Azeze, my faithful husband for many years, was gone. His passing was another wound that would never heal. Mukki and Mingan had also died.

As if reading my mind, Fatimata raised her chalice for a toast. "To those we've loved!"

"'To those we've loved!'" echoed me and Efe.

We drank.

A familiar figure swaggered toward me in the white tunic of the Kanaian army. I lowered my chalice and placed it on the table next to me.

By the satisfied grin on her face, Kayin's mission of the last twelve sunrises had been a success. She still kept busy overseeing the army and partaking in her new hobby: growing yams in the Obieze Garden.

Kayin hugged Efe and Fatimata.

"I went to the coast to meet an incoming ship." Kayin pointed. "Look."

People poured through the open iron gate at the compound's entrance. They were young, old, and in-between. The musicians stopped playing. Efe rose slowly, dropping her chalice, which clattered when it hit the ground. White liquid seeped into the sunbaked clay.

These people looked like her.

My heart swelled at the sight of Asantis looking for their leader.

"My goddesses!" Efe cried. "They've come home!"

## The End

# ACKNOWLEDGMENTS

The genesis of this book sprung from a question my wife, Audi, asked after we watched *The Black Panther*. "The movie was exceptional, but did you notice the women did all the work protecting the king, and the men received the credit?" Afterward, I researched the making of the movie and learned it was loosely based on the women soldiers of Dahomey who protected their king. That led me to wonder about women warriors who protected their queen, thus the women warriors of the Queendom of Kana were born.

I've always loved alternative-history fiction and think about what would have happened if a certain person impactful in history had been born in a different era or country or missed their train on their way to an important event? And finally, what if slavery never happened or never took hold in the United States of America?

Like the characters in Kana, it takes a village to protect a queendom and to publish a book. I'd like to thank:

My editor, R., for understanding what I was trying to achieve with this novel and ensuring my vision came across on the page.

Breena Clark, David Anthony Durham, Elizabeth Hand, and JJ Amaworo Wilson all made this a better book in different ways. I would especially like to thank Liz and JJ for their unwavering support and faith in my writing and this novel.

In addition, Tobias Buckell, Robert Levy, Cara Hoffman, Ted Deppe, Elizabeth Searle, Theodora Goss, Susan Conley, and Debra Marquart, all provided words of wisdom I hope are reflected within.

Shout out to my SWAG writing group for their feedback and support: Shannon Bowring, Paulla Estes, Jillian Hanson, Nancy Hauswald, Aimee Kaiser, Sarah Marslender, Judy McAmis, Catherine Palmer, and Judy Sandler. Fierce writing warriors all.

Readers of drafts helped shape the final version: Dr. Joy Williamson-Lott, professor and dean of the Graduate School at the University of Washington, Sharon Pelletier, Dan McGinn, Shannon Bowring, Belicia, Becky Thompson, and all the USM workshop participants.

Emily Keller, a political science and public policy librarian at the University of Washington, for assisting me with the research for this novel and her enthusiasm for my work; Jamestown-Yorktown Foundation; and Megan MacGregor, instruction and outreach librarian at the University of Southern Maine. All of them pointed me in the right direction. Any mistakes are mine.

To Lorraine Rimson and Gwen Mathewson, for allowing me the quiet time to write a few chapters on your boat and all the support you've given to me. And Lo, for your editing suggestions related to Captain Francisco de Silva.

To Kellye Garrett for the pep talk when I needed it.

For their love and always showing up, my children, Jasmine, Travis, and Brandon.

And to my mother, Julia, for giving me the lifelong gift of reading, supporting me in all of my efforts, and ensuring I undertook all of my endeavors to the best of my abilities.

Every thank you starts and ends with Audi, who has been my partner throughout my writing journey. She is my Goddess Gleti, my muse, and my first reader. Without her, this novel would not exist.

# ABOUT THE AUTHOR

Julie L. Brown is the author of the alternative-history novel, *No One Will Save Us,* and the creator, under the pen name J. L. Brown, of the Jade Harrington series, political thrillers which include the novels, *Don't Speak*, *Rule of Law*, and *The Divide*, and the short story, *Few Are Chosen*.

Julie earned an MFA in Creative Writing from the Stonecoast program at the University of Southern Maine. She resides with her family in the Pacific Northwest, where she is working on her next novel.

You can find her on:

Website: www.julielbrown.com

Instagram: @julielbrownwrites

Threads: @julielbrownwrites